THE BEAUTIES AND HER BEAST

A.J. Hughes

Anicale Publishing—Madison, WI
Paperback ISBN: 978-0-9998967-4-7
eBook ISBN: 978-0-9998967-7-8
Library of Congress Control Number: 2025903902
Title: *The Beauties and Her Beast*
Author: A.J. Hughes
Digital distribution | 2025
Paperback | 2025

This is a work of fiction. The characters, names, incidents, places, and dialogue are products of the author's imagination, and are not to be construed as real.

This is a modernized work of fiction based on the original story idea from *Le Belle et la Bête* (*The Beauty and the Beast*) by Gabrielle-Suzanne Barbot de Villeneuve.

Published in the United States by New Book Authors Publishing

DEDICATION

To my mom, E. Hughes, for her support, editing *TB & HB*, and being my inspiration. If I hadn't had the honor of seeing your passion for writing first-hand growing up, I don't know where I would be or what I would be doing now.
   You are the one and only E. Hughes.

Your first fan,
A.J. Hughes

   p.s. I don't care about the readers you had before I was born nor could read, they don't count. Haha.

To my brother, Brandon, for your help discussing, and very passionately mind you, *TB & HB* with me. For helping me with any plot-holes, writer's block, and honestly, just the fun of our disagreements on events and opinions on the story.

To my stepdad, Byron, for his support and calling my brother and I nerds during our heated discussions. Haha.

To my siblings and family for their support.

To my Grandma Renee, love you always. Thank you for being an amazing grandma, always supporting me and my books, and being a part of my life. I couldn't wish for a better grandmother.

And to Aletha Williams, may you rest in peace.

OTHER BOOKS BY A.J. HUGHES

Book	ISBN
A Walk on the Other Side	978-0-9998967-9-2
A Day of Rain	978-1-7334454-2-9
A Life: Worth Living	978-0-9998967-0-9
Life as a Marshmallow	978-0-9998967-3-0
Everlasting, Us	978-0-9998967-1-6

Children's Books	
Everything Is Not Fine	979-8-9885907-4-3
I'm Not Afraid of the Dark	979-8-9885907-2-9
Spooky Night	979-8-9885907-6-7
Operation Christmas Revenge	979-8-9885907-7-4
Is Santa Real?	979-8-9885907-3-6

COMING SOON

Love and Flora Series: The Beauties and Her Beast
(Book Two)

Love and Flora Series: Through the Meadow: I Shall Find Thee

Everlasting, Despair
(The Everlasting Saga, Book Two)

The Kingdom of Encleadious
(Book One)

PROLOGUE

Once upon a time in a magical kingdom ruled a handsome young prince. He was famous for his early ascension to the throne at the age of seventeen.

Despite being ridiculed throughout the land for his refusal to marry, he was notorious for his ruthless and cutthroat leadership, stepping on many to achieve his goals.

By the age of 20, he conquered many nations expanding the Kingdom of Rosaceae with the power of a young sorceress by his side. He deceived the sorceress, with the promise of marriage, into helping him fight and win many wars.

After years of deceit, the prince announced his engagement to a nobleman's daughter. Hurt and disappointed, the sorceress confronted the prince asking why.

The prince looked down on her with disgust, reasoning that someone as ugly as her could not marry a prince as handsome as he.

Angered by his arrogance and conceit, the sorceress cast a nasty spell on the prince.

"Prove that this noble's daughter loves you. If you cannot attest that she truly loves you for the monster that you are by your 24th coronation, you will die an ugly beast." The sorceress struck the prince rendering him unconscious.

When the prince awoke, what awaited him in the mirror was a beast so hideous, even the heavens looked away.

CHAPTER ONE

Belle Holmes grabbed a suitcase from the SUV's trunk, her heart pounding against her chest. Belle's father, Freddy Holmes, continued to unload her luggage, as Belle turned and gazed at the magnificent castle that loomed before her. A soft glow emanated mystery and danger. Tears pooled in her eyes as her lips trembled. Tonight was the night she was sacrificed to beasts. She took a deep breath, steeling herself.

Freddy grabbed the last suitcase and placed a hand on her back. He whispered, "There's still time to turn back."

Belle shook her head, wiping the tears from her eyes. There was no way she could turn back. Not now. Not if it meant her father's death. Belle would do anything to save him.

"I promise I won't let them do anything," Freddy said, walking to the door. Freddy knocked, the sound echoing around them.

"Come in," a deep, daunting voice commanded.

Freddy slowly pushed the door ajar and walked in. Belle stared at the ground as she clung to her father's side. She had to in order to not faint.

"Welcome," the voice said. "Is this your daughter?"

"Y-yes," Freddy stuttered, he lowered his head to avert eye contact.

"And she consented to coming here?" he asked.

Freddy gave a slight nod, keeping his head down.

There was a brief moment of silence, drawing Belle into her thoughts. She reflected on how she came to be here....

***

Freddy drove down the highway. His snoring son slept in the passenger seat. The incessant cries from his twin daughters, Britney and Natasha were exhausting.

"Guys," he said, his voice raspy from hours of driving without a break. He wiped a frustrated hand down his face and said, "Calm down, what's done is done."

"Why should we have to suffer?" Britney complained. "It's not our fault you got fired for killing a patient!"

"Why did they have to take *my* stuff?" Natasha whined.

"Because it was my money that paid for it. Be grateful they let us keep the car. Now please, just… let me drive in peace."

Freddy turned the music up, drowning out their complaints. He felt a sense of comfort listening to his Lionel Richie CDs on road trips.

"You just—" Britney started to shout.

"Stop Brit," Belle said, her soft voice barely a whisper over the music.

"Nobody asked you." Britney rolled her eyes. "This is between the two of us and Dad."

"I'm standing up for *my* dad. You guys are acting like children."

"Says the child," Natasha sneered. "He uprooted our entire lives."

"Yeah," Britney said. "I left my boyfriend and my friends behind, all because he sucks as a surgeon."

"You didn't have to come with," Belle said. "You're both adults, still living off of daddy. Maybe you guys can get a job and stay in Newark."

"Shut up, Belle."

"Leave dad alone."

Britney opened her mouth in protest but Natasha grabbed her shoulder and shook her head. Britney rolled her eyes, sat forward in her seat, and put her earbuds in her ears. Natasha did the same.

Belle sighed in relief that the confrontation was finally over. She rested her head against the window, watching as the lights streaked by. She watched until she eventually closed her eyes and fell asleep.

***

Franklin (Freddy) Holmes was a general surgeon at a small hospital in Newark, New Jersey. He had performed thousands of surgeries over the years. He had a wife and five kids. His wife Angela was the most beautiful woman he had ever seen. They met when he was in college and married at twenty-five years old. He loved Angela dearly. When Freddy was in medical school, Angela took care of their growing family. Their eldest, Marcus, was now twenty-three, their second oldest child, Desiree, was twenty-two. She was a nursing student at UCLA. They had twin daughters, Britney and Natasha, who were eighteen, and their youngest daughter Isabelle, whom he called Belle for short, was only sixteen.

When Freddy's children were young, Angela was diagnosed with cancer. They did their best to keep the children happy. Aside from Desiree, Freddy's other children were spoiled and very dependent on him. Marcus was a wannabe rapper. Through missed opportunities and a failing music career, he continued to ask his father for more sound equipment, totaling over $200K. Freddy's twins were aspiring social media influencers. They had less than one thousand followers combined, but enjoyed using their daddy's money to flaunt new designer handbags on the internet. Belle was more down to earth and conscious of not spending her father's money, but she did have her share of wants, like her art supplies, anime merch, box sets, and trips to Japan. However, she admired Desiree's independence and wanted to follow in her footsteps. Belle planned to major in animation at UCLA when she graduated from high school. Freddy did his best to uphold everyone's wants and dreams.

When Belle turned eleven, Angela died. Freddy was distraught. He had done everything he could to save her, but in the end, cancer won. His heartbreak led him to drinking heavily and reporting to work with hangovers. When it was time to perform a surgery, although Freddy had sobered up in time, his negligence due to emotional and physical distress led to the death of a patient.

Freddy was sued for malpractice. The case lasted 4 years and resulted in a judgment of $10 million dollars and the revoking of his medical license. In order to pay the judgment, Freddy used Belle's college savings, sold their home, and all of their worldly possessions. He just barely managed to pay off the debt. With only a car left, he decided to move back to Meadow Lake, Wisconsin with his parents until he was able to stand on his own two feet again. Meadow Lake was a small town not on the map. It had a population of 400 and was the twins' worst nightmare.

They stopped for the night at a motel in Indiana. Freddy could only afford one room. They crammed inside. Belle and her sisters slept on the bed, Marcus on the armchair, and Freddy on the floor.

The next morning, Belle woke up at 5 a.m. Her siblings were still asleep. Belle searched around the room for her father and opened the front door. Freddy leaned on the banister staring at the passing cars. He looked lost in thought, not really looking at anything in particular.

"Are you all right?" Belle asked, standing next to him.

"Yes," he replied, snapping out of it. "Just thinking about life, I guess."

"Wanna talk about it?" she asked.

Freddy shook his head. "I don't know. I've already caused you and your siblings enough grief."

"It's all right, you can tell me." Belle smiled. "It can be between us."

Freddy smiled slightly and looked down at the parking lot, a tear rolling down his cheek. "I lost your mother, and now I've ruined everything we built all these years. Soon, I'm going to lose you and your siblings too."

Belle gave him a hug. "You aren't going to lose me. Mistakes happen. We lost all of our worldly possessions and my tuition, but at least we have each other. Besides, you really think they're going to move out and get jobs?"

Freddy laughed through pained cries. "You got me there. I just wish none of this ever happened."

"I know dad, me too," Belle said. She held his gaze. "But we can't change the past. We just have to make do with what we have."

"You're right," Freddy said. He smiled faintly. "If only your siblings were as thoughtful as you."

Belle and her father went back into the room. They woke the others up and continued on the road, stopping for breakfast on the way.

They reached Meadow Lake by the afternoon. When they arrived in the small town, Natasha and Britney cried even louder.

"What has our life become?" Natasha wailed.

"Hell," Britney replied.

"Oh, calm down," Freddy said. "It's exactly like it's always been when you visited grandma and grandpa."

"I hated it then too," Marcus mumbled.

Freddy glanced at him then said, "Shame, your baby sister is more mature about this than you all."

Natasha and Britney sneered at Belle and rolled their eyes. "She's so fake, we all know she hates it as much as us," they said in unison.

Britney continued, "Stop acting like a saint!"

"I'm not!" Belle said. "I actually loved visiting them. This place may not be as fun as the city, but it's still pretty."

"Shut up," Natasha barked, looking disgusted.

Grief struck Freddy right in the gut. These were the times when he wished Angela was here with the kids.

"Don't talk to your sister like that," Freddy said, looking in the rearview mirror. "And watch your mouth when we arrive. I don't want to hear any swear words or complaints about our living situation. Be grateful they're letting us stay here."

"Yes, dad," they grumbled in unison.

They drove to a partially forested area just outside of Meadow Lake. They turned onto the black concrete road and drove for another 10 minutes. Belle enjoyed the beautiful snowy scenery. She could see her grandparents' home in the distance. The dark brown exterior and the red-tiled roof contrasted against the snowy landscape. When they arrived at the home, Freddy's mother, Aletha, was sitting on the porch. When she saw them pull up, she squealed and walked to the car, arms wide open.

Freddy smiled as he left the car. He hugged her. "Hey ma."

"How are you feeling?" she asked.

"Could be better…"

"I'm sorry hun," she said, hugging him tighter. "Everything's going to be okay."

"I hope so," he replied.

Belle emerged from the car, shouting as she ran, "Grandma!"

"Oh Belle," Aletha exclaimed. She hugged Belle tightly. "Oh I missed you."

"I missed you too."

"Where is your brother? And the girls?" Aletha asked.

"They're still in the car," Belle replied.

Aletha released her and walked to the passenger side of the car. She waved at Marcus and motioned for him and the others to come out. They reluctantly got out of the car and gave half-hearted hugs. Once the greetings were over, they went into the house. It was truly, if not more, beautiful inside as it was outside. The blue floral wallpaper matched the navy-blue carpet. They had a blue and white striped couch, and dark wooden floors. Aletha showed them to their rooms. Belle was in her Aunt Flora's childhood room, Natasha, and Britney shared the guest room, Marcus and Freddy shared Freddy's childhood room. Everyone except for Belle and Freddy complained about the dust and how cramped the rooms were.

Belle asked where her grandfather, Luther was. Aletha told her, her grandpa was out fishing and wouldn't be back until evening.

Belle was disappointed about the wait, but she understood her grandfather's happiness came first.

***

Over the next few weeks, the Holmes children became more familiar with "simple living." They still missed their extravagant lives in New Jersey, but they were slowly coping with the changes. Everyone except for Belle, applied for jobs to afford their brand-named clothes. Natasha and Britney worked at a grocery store and Marcus worked at a hardware store. Since the school year had already started, Belle asked to start after winter break. Aletha backed her up and Belle was able to stay out of school for the next month and a half.

The idea seemed fun at first, except Belle didn't have much to do. She spent her days wandering around the woods drawing trees and animals.

The first two weeks in Meadow Lake, Freddy's family urged him to relax. He sat idly on the couch all day between helping his mother with housework. The following weeks he struggled to keep a job. It had been so long since he worked in retail. The self-entitled, rude, and disrespectful customers, being bossed around, and the busy crowds, were foreign to him. He wondered if he could ever hold a "regular" job.

Over time, he grew more accustomed to retail work, but was still unhappy with his situation. Living with his parents, not being able to take care of his kids without help, and not doing the job he loved.

Aletha and Luther came home with news for him. Luther's friend in Green Bay, WI, was looking for help at a new clinic he built. While he wasn't keen on Freddy's past, as a favor to Luther, he offered him a job as a receptionist. Freddy didn't mind. He was happy to be in the medical environment, even if it was just checking patients in. Freddy thanked his father and packed that night.

"We might be able to live in a bigger city," Freddy said, excitedly to his children. He called them into his room for a family meeting. "I have the greatest opportunity in Green Bay and I'm leaving tomorrow to scope it out. If all goes well, I could be making a nice salary again."

"Which means we wouldn't have to work?" Natasha asked, hopeful.

"Precisely," he said.

"Oh! While you're there, can you get us some souvenirs?" Britney asked.

"I can, what do you guys want? Nothing too expensive, I still gotta pay for gas and a hotel."

"Get me a Telfar bag!" Natasha shouted.

"I want Brother Vellies," Britney said, pushing Natasha out of the way.

"Get me some PerryCo shoes, white is good," Marcus chimed in.

"I don't know if I can get that, but I'll do my best," Freddy said. He looked at Belle and asked, "Don't you want anything?"

Belle shook her head. "No daddy, I only want your safe return."

Freddy smiled. Before he could say anything, Natasha said, "Will you shut up!"

Britney joined in. "Yeah, stop that phony crap. You're just saying that to make us look bad."

"How is that making you look bad?" Belle asked. "I just know dad is struggling, and he's already getting your expensive things. I'm not going to ask him for anymore."

"But—" Natasha started.

"Enough," Freddy snapped. "I told you no swearing in your grandparents' house…and stop being mean to Belle, got it."

Freddy turned to Belle and smiled. "Belle…let me at least get you something from Green Bay, okay?"

"But the price—"

"Don't worry about the price."

Belle looked worried for a moment, then finally said, "A rose."

"*A rose?*" Marcus scoffed. "Out of all the things you could get…"

"I love roses. I'm even fine with a small bouquet from a discount store. That way, Dad can afford your shoes and their bags."

"But a *rose?*" Marcus asked, again.

"A rose is fine—" Britney said in a syrupy sweet voice, "who are we to deny her wants and wishes. Right, Natasha?"

"Y-yeah. That way she doesn't have to worry about spending all of Dad's money," Natasha replied, shooting Britney an arch look.

"Are you sure that's all you want?" Freddy asked. "No sketchpad or pencils?"

"No, that's it." Belle smiled. "When you get the job, I'll ask for one."

Freddy smiled. He ended the family meeting and everyone went to bed. He was proud that two out of his five children were selfless. If only Desiree was with them, then Belle would have someone nice to talk to.

The next afternoon, he loaded his car, which there wasn't much to load except a briefcase and his winter coat. He loved driving in the evening, he felt serene. If traffic wasn't bad, he would reach Green Bay by 5 p.m. He said goodbye to his children and his worried mother, who warned him about a snowstorm. He didn't mind. A few inches of snow wasn't a problem for him. Unlike his mother, he believed most Wisconsinites knew how to drive in the snow. He turned his GPS on and set the location to Green Bay, and with his good ole companion Lionel Richie playing, he hit the road. As he drove away from the home, it began to snow.

Two hours later, Freddy was confused. He should have been in Green Bay by now. He pulled over and looked at the GPS.

Lacrosse? he groaned. The first part of the address was correct but he mistakenly entered Green Bay St. Green Bay, the city, was in the other direction.

"Come on, Freddy," he said. "Get it together."

He rerouted the GPS and did a U-turn. From his location, he wouldn't reach Green Bay for another three hours.

The snowstorm was picking up. The road was covered in snow and Freddy could barely see past what his headlights allowed. It had been a while since he last had to drive in a blizzard. He did not want to slow down, otherwise his trip would be longer. He looked at the dashboard and checked the gas, hoping he wouldn't run out before he made it to the next gas station.

He pressed the gas pedal slightly, increasing his speed. The car slipped and slid and he pressed the brakes, and lost control of the car, sliding off of the road.

Freddy opened his eyes. His airbag had deployed and his neck ached. He looked up from the airbag to the windshield. All he saw was snow.

How long have I been out? he thought. He opened his car door and snow fell from the roof of the car. He stepped outside. *Great!*

He had crashed into a ditch. There was no way to get out without a tow truck. He climbed back into his car and turned the engine off. He reached over and grabbed his phone from the floor on the passenger side. The battery was dead.

"You've got to be kidding me," Freddy groaned.

He climbed into the backseat and pulled the seat down. He reached inside the trunk and grabbed his emergency kit. Inside were hand-warmers, a blanket, and a flashlight. He wrapped himself in the blanket and stuffed his pants and shirt with the hand-warmers. He climbed out of the car and walked in the direction he was driving. He didn't know how far it was until he made it to a gas station. The last one, to his knowledge, that he stopped at was over 45 minutes away.

There had to be a gas station a few miles ahead. He walked for 10 minutes, surrounded by open road and blinding snow. His feet felt like blocks of ice. Freddy turned back around, he needed to warm up.

He leaned on the car door and put his feet up. He decided to rest for the night. He hoped the snow would stop and the roads would clear by morning. He turned his car on for a bit to warm up and turned it off again. He sighed and fell asleep.

The next morning, it was still snowing. Freddy was freezing and his car was buried even deeper. Even if someone passed by, they wouldn't be able to see his car. He needed to find help or he would be stuck in his car until he froze to death. He had already checked the path ahead, so this time he went back in the direction he came. Maybe there was a closer gas station that he missed. If there wasn't, he knew he could at least attempt to make it to the gas station he did see.

He walked for 30 minutes to no avail. He didn't see any gas stations or homes in the area. He was wet from the snow and recognized he was in the first stages of hypothermia. He was screwed. Unless by some miracle a car passed by, he was going to die.

Please, he thought. *Whoever is out there, please help me. I want to return to my kids. I don't want to die and leave them alone. Angela, if you're watching over me right now, please help me.*

Freddy felt hot. He started to take off his clothes. He dropped the blanket first, then his scarf, then his coat. He continued to walk as he dropped his suit jacket and unbuttoned his shirt. In a fevered delusion, Freddy crumpled in the snow.

A warm breeze caressed Freddy's cheek, conflicting with his still trembling body. He opened his eyes. He looked around him and sat up, blinking his eyes.

Where's all the snow? he thought. *I don't think we're in Wisconsin anymore.*

He sat on a cobbled road, besieged by vibrant green grass littered in red, yellow, and orange leaves on each side of the road. In the distance, beyond the cobbled road, he saw a castle with an impressive number of towers, some of them so high, they seemed to stretch into the clouds. The exterior was white with sky blue roofs. He stood and scanned the area for a not-so-important place. He walked for a bit and saw nothing but a long path that stretched into a roundabout.

He sighed. *I better go to that castle.*

As he walked, he thought about all the logical reasons for why he was there. The idea that made the most sense was that he was most likely dying of hypothermia right now and he was hallucinating.

He passed through the castle gates. He was in awe at the marvelous structure of the yard. Beautiful human-shaped topiaries were scattered alongside the path. Freddy glanced at the castle once more, sighed and climbed the steps leading to the large maroon doors.

Once inside, he looked around. The inside was different from what he imagined. It was still amazing and much like a royal castle, but small. The foyer walls were dark brown. The floorboards were wooden with a maroon carpet that stretched to wooden stairs. There was a large landing, before the stairs split into an imperial staircase. There were two rooms to both sides of the main hall. The tables, dressers, and furnishings were ornate and encased in gold. There was a small lounge area to the left of the door. Freddy walked in there first.

"Hello?" he shouted. "Anyone home?"

He glanced around the room. There was a couch, a small armchair, a coffee table, and a fireplace. How that would have been wonderful if the fireplace was lit. He turned around and entered the main hall again. He continued along the royal maroon-colored carpet and saw a table full of food in the dining hall.

He licked his lips and shouted, "If you don't mind, I'm going to take a bit of food. I haven't eaten in over a day now. I'm suffering from Hypothermia. Anything warm would greatly help."

He waited for a reply, but there was no answer. He hesitated before sitting down at the table and said grace. If he wasn't hallucinating, this was a huge blessing. Freddy went for the chicken noodle soup first, warming his chest as he imbibed the scorching hot liquid. His body broke out in goosebumps from the warmth. He took a sip of wine and washed it down with a glass of water. He stuck his fork into the pasta next, practically inhaling it. He continued to eat until he could no longer move. He took one last sip of wine and fell asleep.

When he woke, he was in the lounge on the armchair, bundled in a blanket and his clothes had been changed. He was dressed in Victorian-styled clothing. The fireplace had been lit and a warm cup of hot chocolate set on the end table with a bag full of food. Whoever the king was, he was a gracious and humble king. To let him eat his food, wear his royal clothing, and rest in his home. He was truly a kind person.

But Freddy couldn't escape the belief that he was currently dying on the side of the road. Was he in heaven? He hoped he wasn't and that he could return home to his children.

"I must get back," Freddy shouted. "Thank you for your hospitality."

He scurried to the lounge entrance when he noticed a beautiful watch on a dresser. He paused. *This could all be a hallucination and I'm probably dying. There isn't any harm if I take a few things back to my kids. I can at least die believing I did so.*

He stuffed the bag his generous host gave him with a golden watch for Marcus, a golden necklace with a blue sapphire for Natasha, and a golden ring with a large diamond for Britney. He looked around a bit more, grabbing spoils he thought wouldn't be a significant loss for the castle owner. When he thought he had enough gifts, he turned to leave. In the corner of his eye, he saw a beautiful doll neatly leaning on a sofa pillow adjacent to the chair he slept in. She wore a white dress with pastel pink lined around the hem of the dress and throughout the seams. Her hair was dark purple. The ends of her hair looped into very large curls. Her eyes were green, and she wore bright red lipstick. Mesmerized, he picked it up.

I know Desiree isn't here, he thought, *but I know she will love this.*

He searched the room one last time, but he couldn't find anything he thought would suit Belle. She wasn't a materialistic girl.

As he left, he shouted, "I hope you don't mind. Thank you again. I wish you the best. *It's all just a dream anyway.*"

When he opened the castle doors, the sky had darkened and looked as if it was soon to rain. The sudden weather change created an eerie atmosphere. Freddy's intuition told him it was time to get out of there. He rushed down the steps towards the gate. Something urged him to stay. Freddy laughed at himself. Thinking clearly about his situation, Freddy believed he had nothing to worry about. It was only the weather that scared him. If the king, or habitants of the castle, truly wanted to harm him, they would have done so already.

This was a once in a lifetime moment. If he was alive, he'd never have a story to tell his family. If he was dying, he worried that maybe once he left the gates, there was no turning back. He decided not to leave. Maybe explore a little, have a look around the extensive grounds. It should've been okay. The gates were open, meaning the owner allowed guests. He deviated right from the path. He walked along the trail. The topiaries were fascinating and realistic. He thought about how amazing their bush trimmer was to create such marvelous topiaries. Freddy's worries disappeared completely as he toured the castle grounds. It was so peaceful and quiet. In the distance, Freddy's eye fixated on an archway shrouded in roses. He made his way to the door and opened it.

There was a long trail with different colored roses lining the pathway. At the end, was a sharp turn to the left. Curious, Freddy crept past the entrance. He walked slowly down the path and peeked around the corner. There was a massive courtyard garden with grey bricks that spiraled near the center. Its elegant design making his mouth drop. He had never encountered such opulence before. Benches aligned the circumference of the courtyard. In the middle of the opening was a strange fountain with the statue of a man-like wolf wearing a royal mantle. It had large grizzly hands, the body of a wolf, and its lower-half was that of a lizard. Water spurted from the crown placed on its hip. Freddy whistled. He thought the king had…unique…taste in décor. Human-like bushes, and now a beastly statue? The statue brought an unnerving presence added to the gloomy sky and beautiful ambiance. Lightning streaked the sky and rain poured down in sheets. Freddy's intuition was now screaming at him to listen, but he couldn't leave just yet.

There were rose bushes larger than he had ever seen and rare colors he didn't think were possible, but he guessed that was one of the perks of being royalty. He counted, as he walked through the path, over 42 different colored rose bushes all bright, full, and blossoming along the courtyard, leading further into the garden. He searched the bushes for the nicest roses he could find for Belle's bouquet. He picked yellow, red, orange, blue, purple, black, and pink. He selected five multi-colored roses to place at the center. He smiled at his wonderful work. As he turned to leave the garden, he heard a shrill voice shout out to him.

"What the heck do you think you're doing?!" the voice screeched. It sounded like a young man.

Startled, Freddy searched for the source of the angry-sounding voice. In one swift landing, a beast appeared in front of him. His heart nearly stopped as he stared wide-eyed in fear of the monster that screamed at him. It was a chimera. The mix of a monkey, a lizard, and a wolf. It had the head, arms, and tail of a monkey, the humanlike torso of a wolf, and long lizard legs. The beast was atrocious and scary.

Freddy screamed. The beast stood in front of the entrance to the garden. Freddy ran the other direction, fleeing into the rose thicket. He had no idea where he was going, but he hoped his instincts would lead him out of the garden. He ran for a while, turning left and right along the rose trail. The rain blurred his vision. After running for what felt like miles, or enough to make the average couch potato's thighs burn, Freddy fell to his knees, splashing into a puddle.

"Who do you think you are?" it shouted, jumping over the wall of rose bushes. "My brother was hospitable despite you breaking into our castle. We provided you with food and a warm blanket by the fire and *this* is how you repay us? You're nothing more than an ungrateful thief!"

Freddy was immobile. Did the beast notice him take the items in the lounge? A chill traced down his spine. "Please, I'm sorry. I thought it would be okay to take some. I didn't think I was in a real place. Please forgive me! I—I'll put everything back."

"Shut up!" it screamed. "Do you think I'm dumb enough to fall for that? How can you put roses back on the stems?"

Freddy paused. Was this monster upset that he had taken a few roses? He couldn't imagine how this beast would react if it had found out he'd taken more than just a few roses. "I-I'm sorry! I don't think you're stupid! You're intelligent and almighty. Please forgive me for taking the flowers!"

"Never!" it yelled. "You're going to rot in jail!"

"Please no," Freddy cried. "I must return to my children!"

"Children?" the monkey chimera scoffed. "Do you think I care about your children? Perhaps you should have thought about them when you stole from us."

The beast grabbed Freddy by his collar. He screamed, "I'm sorry, please forgive me!"

"What is going on?" another voice asked. It also sounded like a young man but its voice was deeper and more refined than the chimera's.

"I caught this *thief* stealing your roses. I was about to throw him in jail!" the monkey chimera shouted.

Freddy turned and looked. His knees almost gave out. There were two of them. The second beast had the head and legs of a wolf, and the wings and human-like torso of a bird.

The bird chimera sighed heavily. "Esmé, you cannot imprison someone for taking a rose. Let him go."

"But Raoul!" Esmé exclaimed. "You worked hard on the garden and this ungrateful thief ruined it!"

"I need you to calm down and let him go," Raoul commanded. His voice was gentle but his tone was stern. "I have thousands of rose bushes. A few plucked roses do not take away the garden's beauty. Besides, I'm flattered that he wants to take them. What is the point of growing roses if no one can partake of its beauty?"

Esmé reluctantly freed him.

Raoul crouched to the kneeling Freddy and said, "I apologize for my brother's behavior. Please excuse him. You are free to go. Take more roses if you like."

"Oh thank you!" Freddy exclaimed, relieved.

Esmé tsked and looked away. Freddy stood to walk away. He took a few more roses from the path so as not to offend his generous, fearful host, clutched the bag on his shoulder, and started to walk the other way.

Esmé growled. He couldn't stand by while his brother's kindness was exploited. He snarled, "Fine! But he can't leave with our food!"

Esmé snatched the bag, and Freddy instinctively held onto it. They tugged back and forth until the strap ripped and the food, as well as the items Freddy had taken, flew out of the bag, scattering everywhere on the muddied trail. Esmé was even more furious. He snatched the doll.

"You're a liar *and* a thief!" he shouted. "How *dare* you steal my doll and my father's watch?! Raoul, imprisonment is not enough! He must be sentenced to death!"

Freddy's heart sank to his stomach. "Please, I'm sorry. I didn't know this place was real. Please spare me."

Esmé gripped him by the collar with immense strength and threw him in front of Raoul. Raoul's purple, humanlike eyes glowered disappointedly at the pitiful, disheveled old man pleading for his life.

Raoul sighed. "I can forgive you for taking my roses, but stealing from my castle is unacceptable."

Freddy cried louder as his last bit of hope shattered before his eyes. Raoul glared at the quivering old man. The bird chimera's kindhearted gaze was gone.

"Please," Freddy begged. "I have children waiting for me. I'm all they have left!"

Raoul's cold gaze softened.

Before he could respond, Esmé shouted, "Like we care! You aren't going to walk away from this!"

"Please! They recently lost their mother. It was my fault. I lost all of our wealth and possessions. I was desperate! If I could do something for my children to forgive me, I was willing to stoop to such lows. I did not steal any of these items to sell! They were all gifts for my children! The watch for my son, the doll for my second daughter, the necklace for my third daughter, the ring for my fourth daughter, and the bouquet for my youngest daughter. Please spare me!"

"Oh please—" Esmé sneered, rolling his eyes.

Raoul raised his hand for Esmé to stop talking. "What is your name?"

"F-Freddy," he stammered.

"Freddy, while taking flowers is not a big deal, for centuries theft has been a crime punishable by death."

Freddy cried, interrupting Raoul.

Raoul patted his back comfortingly.

"I have a proposition for you," Raoul continued. "I will spare your life *if* you give us one of your daughters. Do not worry, we will treat her with respect and care, but she *must* consent to coming here in your stead."

"You—you want me to give away one of my daughters?"

"Not so much as give, but for her to come willingly on your behalf to live out a minimum prison sentence. Though she will be a prisoner, she will be able to walk freely on castle grounds. Do you agree?"

"What happens if she says no?" Freddy asked.

"Then you must return here and face your punishment."

"And if you don't," Esmé interrupted. "I'll find and kill you myself!"

"What do you say, Freddy?" Raoul smiled, reassuringly. "You have nothing to worry about if one of your daughters agree. She will be treated like royalty…but also a prisoner…."

"And if I decline?" Freddy asked, looking Raoul in the eyes.

"Then I will let my brother do as he wishes with you, be it kill you outright, or torture you to death. It will be none of my concern."

"I'll torture him," Esmé said, a bloodthirsty look in his eyes.

"I—I accept," Freddy stuttered.

Raoul smiled brightly. "Great! You have a week to decide. I shall have a car send you home. Please take the things you were going to steal as a gift of agreement between us."

"Everything but the watch," Esmé corrected Raoul.

"And give those roses to your daughter on behalf of Esmé for how he treated you. He is not as terrifying a man as he may seem."

Freddy nodded. He collected the items and put them back into the broken bag. He grabbed the bouquet and walked down the path.

"Remember," Raoul shouted, "you have a week to decide if one of your daughters will come. A car will be waiting outside your home at the end of the week. Either show with your daughter or come alone."

He turned around as Raoul flew away and Esmé stared menacingly at him. Freddy hastened his pace. He couldn't remember the path he took. He peeked over his shoulder and saw that Esmé trailed behind him. He didn't have to ask. Esmé begrudgingly shouted the directions back to the garden entrance. When he arrived at the front gate, a black SUV waited with the door open.

"Is this for me?" he asked.

"Obviously," Esmé replied.

Freddy nodded once more then entered the SUV. The door closed behind him and he buckled his seatbelt as the car drove away.

Freddy slumped in his seat and thought, *What have I done? I'm such a fool! Please forgive me, Angela.*

He wanted to look out the window one last time to make sure everything that happened was real. The windows were tinted and he couldn't see outside. In fact, even the windshield was pitch black.

"E-excuse me," he said to the driver. "Do you know where you're going?"

No response.

Can they hear me? he thought.

He peeked over the seat to see that no one was operating the vehicle. The shock alone made Freddy pass out.

CHAPTER TWO

Freddy opened his eyes. The cold from the snow jarred him awake. He groaned. He struggled to lift his head as he looked up. He crawled to one knee and looked around him. He wasn't at the crash site prior to the mysterious castle. He was in the middle of a forest. In the distance, he saw his parents' red roof.

Home…? he thought. *But how? Was all of that a dream?*

Freddy stood. He shook his head and staggered his way to the house. His car was parked in the driveway. It looked almost new. There were no dents from slamming into the railing on the road. He walked to his car and examined inside. The clothes he wore, his cell phone, and the emergency kit were inside.

He turned to the house and went up the steps. He knocked on the door and Belle answered.

"Daddy!" she exclaimed. She hugged him tightly. She let go and shouted inside, "Guys! Dad's back!"

Aletha and Luther rushed to the front door, Natasha, Britney, and Marcus followed. They hugged him. They all began to chatter at once.

"Are you all right?" Aletha asked.

"Where have you been?" Luther chided.

"Were you lost?" Marcus asked.

"Did you get our bags?" Natasha whined.

"Why are you dressed like that?" Britney sneered.

"Let dad get in the door first," Belle admonished.

"It's fine," he said. He walked past everyone and sat on the couch. "I—I don't know what really happened to me. One minute I was stranded on the side of the road, the next in some magical kingdom. In one day, my life is more chaotic than before—"

"Uh, dad," Marcus interrupted. "You weren't gone a day…."

"What do you mean?"

"You've been missing for a month," Aletha said. "Your car returned by itself a week ago. We've been searching like crazy for you."

"That can't be," Freddy said. He reached over to Britney who had already lost interest in the conversation. "Let me see your phone."

He looked at the date, it was December 14th. He really was gone a month. But how? It was only one day in that kingdom. His heart sank, this meant what happened in that magical kingdom was real.

Freddy cried, "I'm so sorry."

"For what?" Luther asked. "You don't have to apologize. We're just glad you're safe."

"That's not it." He sniffed. "It's a long story, but promise you'll believe me."

They all said a different form of, "I promise."

Freddy explained what happened from inputting the wrong address to the driverless car. The situation was too much for Aletha. She grew weak and Luther led her to their room.

Marcus shook his head. As he left the room, he mumbled, "The perks of being a man."

"So let me get this straight," Britney said. "You stole from a magical kingdom full of monsters and what got you caught was the bouquet for Belle. You expect me and Natasha to volunteer ourselves, when it was Belle's 'selflessness' that put you in this mess? Thanks but no thanks."

"Neither am I," Natasha jeered. "Belle, you should be the first person jumping up to go. It was your roses that put dad in this position. What happened to being the goody two shoes that defends dad?"

Belle was silent. She stared at the ground as tears pooled in her eyes. She cried, "It's all my fault!"

"Oh, Belle," Freddy said, drawing her into his arms. "It's not your fault. I should have never stolen from them. None of this would have happened."

"But if you didn't stop for my rose—" Belle cried harder.

"I won't have you go," Freddy said. He turned and glared at Natasha and Britney. "You should be ashamed of yourselves! Letting your baby sister go to a place full of monsters. What kind of sisters are you?!"

"Smart ones that don't take the fall for our idiotic father and annoying sister," Natasha said.

"Also, Belle's a beautiful girl. I doubt they'll harm a hair on that pretty little scalp of hers." Britney smacked her lips. "Maybe she'll wow the monsters with that virtue of hers."

Freddy sat up furious at his daughters' words. He was going to yell when Belle stopped him.

"Daddy, don't," Belle said, wiping her tears. "I'll go. Regardless of what you did, I'm just as at fault. They're right. They shouldn't have to pay for my mistake."

Freddy's heart was crushed. His youngest child was risking her life to save him. What kind of father was he? He could have easily given his life if it meant saving Belle, but he was too much of a coward to stop her. He would never forgive himself nor his two daughters for ruining Belle's life.

Belle told her father to give her siblings their gifts after he refused to. She wanted that to be her last gifts to them. She loved the bouquet. But every time she looked at the roses, she remembered that in a week, she would be whisked away to some kingdom of monsters. Who knew what they were going to do to her?

***

Belle spent the next three days packing. She made sure to grab her sketchpads and art supplies. She packed only a few items of clothing. She didn't know if they were going to force her to wear prisoner garb. Freddy tried to convince her to stay and let him go by himself, but she rejected his pleas.

"I already lost mom," she said. "What point is there in knowing I can save you, but I chose my freedom? I'll be happy knowing you're safe and my siblings don't have to lose another parent. Please don't feel bad."

Hearing Belle say those words, crushed him. Freddy dropped to his knees and sobbed. He cupped his hands. "My… my poor Isabelle… I'm so sorry…."

Belle knelt beside her father and hugged him. "You're an amazing dad. All you've ever done was make sure we were happy. Don't blame yourself. Maybe mom saved your life in the snowstorm daddy. I'll be okay."

"B-but I—" Freddy gasped for air. He cried so hard, his chest hurt. "I can never forgive myself for this."

"You have to." Belle smiled. "What do you need to be forgiven for? I want to go see this magical kingdom and that magnificent rose

19

garden. If not for you, I never would have seen such unique flowers. It'll be fun drawing that garden."

Freddy was so taken aback he had calmed down on just her weird choice of words. He looked at her large, innocent black eyes, unfazed by her situation. Belle wiped his tears and hugged him again.

"You're thoughtful beyond your years. If only your sisters were as kindhearted as you. Dang it, why couldn't they show even an ounce of sympathy?"

"They've been like this since we were children. I'm used to it. Please don't hold it against them. I know deep down they love me and they're sad about what's happening. They just refuse to show it."

"Isabelle," Freddy said, solemnly.

***

It felt like time had gone by fast. There were only two days left until Belle and Freddy left for the monster kingdom. Freddy tried to no end to convince Belle to stay and let him take the death penalty but she was as stubborn as him. She wasn't going to leave her father to die. The Holmes family agreed to spend the next 2 days together to give Belle one final happy memory.

It was the evening of the second to last night before Belle left. Everyone relaxed on the couch watching Belle's favorite movies. They had just finished letting Belle open her Christmas presents. They heard a knock at the front door. Who could it have been at that hour? Freddy was afraid it was those beasts coming early to collect Belle. He cautiously walked to the door. With trembling hands, he leaned against the door.

"Who is it?" he stuttered.

"It's me," the voice said.

Freddy opened the door. "Desiree!"

"Dad?!" she exclaimed, hugging him. "I thought you were missing!"

"I returned earlier this week. Sorry to make you worry."

"It's all right, dad." Desiree entered the home and said, "So no one thought to text me dad was okay? I literally drove up here in a panic."

"Forgot," Marcus said, eyes glued to his phone.

"Maybe if you hadn't rushed to get here," Natasha started.

"We could have told you in time," Britney smirked.

Desiree rolled her eyes.

"Sorry, Desiree," Belle said, sheepishly. "We've had a lot on our minds the past couple of days."

"What's wrong?" Desiree asked, worried.

"Well…" Freddy conveyed an even more dramatic retelling of what happened to Desiree.

"What the hell is wrong with you people?!" Desiree screamed.

"Watch your mouth in front of your grandparents!" Freddy snapped.

"Grandma, grandpa, please leave the room," Desiree said, through gritted teeth. "I can't hold back right now…"

They both nodded and left. Both of them agreed that what was happening was stupid and selfish. They weren't going to stop Desiree from expressing what they felt as well. Desiree urged her father to leave too.

Desire waited until she heard their doors shut before continuing, "What is wrong with y'all? How could you let our *baby sister* march off to her death? What kind of siblings are you?"

"It doesn't matter if we're siblings," Britney said. "At the end of the day, it was her asking for flowers that got dad in this situation."

"If I'm not mistaken, dad is a grown ass man who can make his own decisions. He chose to steal. And as a matter of fact, he stole those things for *you*." Desiree pointed at each of her siblings. "Dad would have gotten off if it weren't for the expensive things *you* begged for. So it's your fault it escalated this far, not Isabelle's."

"I have nothing to do with this," Marcus said, standing up. "I can't change anything, nor can I volunteer to go. If I could, I might have done so, so don't you put this on me."

Marcus stormed out of the room. Desiree shook her head. He wasn't even worth responding to.

"Regardless, I'm not going, and they only want one sister," Britney said. "And we only go in a pair, so tough luck."

"If you're such a great sister, why don't you go?" Natasha asked, smugly.

"I am," Desiree said, with resolve.

"No," Belle exclaimed. "I already agreed to go! Whether or not dad stole, it was my gift that got him caught. I'm going."

"No, you're not," Desiree said. "I'll go."

"You aren't even part of this," Belle complained. "This is between me, dad, and the others, *not you*."

"I'm a part of it now," Desiree said.

"We lost mom, I don't want to lose you or dad."

"And I don't want to lose you. You're sixteen. Your life hasn't even started yet! You should *not* be the one to go."

"I'm going and that's final. I don't want you, dad or anyone to be harmed for what I caused. Just let me do this, please."

"Isabelle…you don't always have to make sacrifices."

"I want to. Besides, the monsters already know that I'm going, so nothing can be done."

"Really?" Desiree asked, skeptical.

"Yeah," Belle said. She stood ten toes down, her head slightly lifted to show Desiree she was serious.

"…When do you leave?" Desiree asked.

"Day after tomorrow."

Desiree didn't say anything. She took her bags, stormed out of the house, and drove away.

"Good job lying to her. Didn't think you had it in you, little miss saint." Britney laughed.

"She'll be *just fine*," Natasha said, wrapping an arm around Belle's shoulders. "Just give her some time. She'll be *happy* you went instead of her."

"Yeah, you're doing the right thing, Belle," Britney said. "You'll be known as the saint who saved her family."

Natasha snickered. "Yeah, yeah, sis. A hero…"

"Maybe those beasts aren't as bad as dad says." Britney smirked. "You know how he overreacts. They could be regular humans that dad imagined as monsters. He said he had hypothermia."

"M-maybe…" Belle said. "I just hope Desiree doesn't stay mad."

"She won't," Natasha said. "She doesn't even like you. It's all for show."

"I—That's not true…."

"Whatever you say, Belle. Goodnight." Britney sneered, walking past Belle.

Natasha followed after Britney. She patted Belle on the back as she left. "Just know she didn't put up *that* much of a fight to take your place."

Belle sighed and sat on the couch. *So much for a happy family night.*

Her roses caused more problems than she imagined. Now Desiree was mad at her. And if the twins were right, the person she admired most hated her. Belle didn't care what happened to herself anymore. She loved her siblings regardless of how they felt about her, especially Desiree. Belle just wished deep down that the twins were wrong.

Belle spent the next day locked in her room. She regretted lying to

Desiree. However, it was the only way to save her life. Desiree was the kind of older sister that would do anything to protect Belle.

***

Belle wasn't popular in school. She was an anime nerd and was treated like trash. She was bullied every day in middle school. It also didn't help that the twins were the main instigators of the bullying incidents. When Desiree caught wind of what happened, she skipped school and went down to Belle's middle school. She stormed the halls looking for the group of girls that tormented Belle daily. When Desiree found them in the middle of bullying her, she pushed one of the preteens against the locker and threatened to beat their asses. And every day they bothered Belle, the worse their beatings would get.

The teachers were alerted and the cops were called. Thanks to Freddy's influence and nice little donations to the school, Desiree was let go with a warning. When she got home, she fought the twins for not standing up for her. Afterwards, her bullies apologized, explaining that the twins were spreading rumors that Belle was gossiping about them.

Desiree had lectured Belle when they got home. After she'd heard everything and how Belle was easily giving the twins information to use against her, Desiree wanted to instill in Belle that she should never share her thoughts with her enemies. Belle was taking everything the bullies did to her to the twins and the twins in turn would repeat it to Belle's bullies.

Logically, one would think, as Belle did, that they could share their thoughts with family. Anyone that was expected to protect them. But that wasn't always the case.

Desiree said, "Stop sharing your business with them. I don't want to ever hear you tell them what hurts you. That's like shouting to your classmates in front of the principal that you found a way to cheat. You're causing more problems for yourself. Instead of broadcasting to the world what hurts you, only tell those you *can* trust."

Desiree told Belle that this applied to every facet of their lives. Even just sharing her thoughts on social media was a bad idea. That level of vulnerability could easily fall into the wrong hands. Issues should've been shared through word of mouth, not online where everyone could see it and create strong arguments against it.

***

Belle laughed, remembering what had happened. Desiree was such a menace when she was in high school. She was a pacifist and wouldn't even hurt a fly. Everyone around them knew this. But when it came to the safety of her siblings, they weren't taking that risk. Desiree was kind, she just had a mouth on her. If anyone was caught doing something wrong, she would confront them. No one wanted to deal with a nag session from Desiree. Around her, everyone acted like saints.

Belle's eyes welled with tears. If the twins were telling the truth, that Desiree that she knew would never stick up for her again. Belle thought about what she could have done to make Desiree hate her? Was it because Belle got her the wrong gift on her birthday? Was it when she'd forgotten to text her back yesterday?

Belle couldn't hold back her tears. She covered her face with her pillow and cried.

***

Freddy woke up in the early hours of the morning. He felt sick to his stomach. Today was the day his poor sweet Belle was sent to her death. He crawled out of bed, sluggishly walked down the stairs and into the kitchen. He made himself coffee. He leaned with his back against the counter. He held the mug in his hands but he stared at the floor, not taking a sip. Yet another piece of his heart was being ripped out. How much could he endure?

"Daddy?" Belle asked. "Why are you awake?"

"I can ask the same of you," Freddy said. He set his mug down and leaned on the counter as Belle stood next to him.

"Just…thinking about what's going to happen," Belle said. "…Since it's my last day, can I have some coffee?"

Freddy smiled. "Of course."

He grabbed another mug and poured her a cup.

"Thanks," she said, taking a sip. She frowned. "It's bitter…"

"I like my coffee black. Add some cream and sugar."

Belle gave her dad the side eye as she went into the fridge.

"You know," Freddy sighed, taking the cream and sugar from Belle and fixing her cup, "this is your last chance to back out. I don't mind dying to protect you and your sisters."

24

"I want to go." Belle smiled. "If I can do something for you, then I will. Our siblings need you more than they need me."

"Belle," Freddy cried. He hugged her. "You're the sweetest daughter a father could ask for. Promise me, you will try to survive, just until I can find a way to save you. Okay?"

"Okay." Belle furrowed her eyebrows. "Dad?"

"What is it?"

"Can you tell Desiree that I'm sorry I disappointed her."

"You didn't disappoint her. She loves you. She's only upset that she can't do anything to save you."

"You think so?" Belle asked. "'Cause she didn't say goodbye."

"Sometimes it's harder to say goodbye than it is to walk away. Forgive her."

"I'm not angry, really. I was hoping she didn't hate me. I guess, maybe I was overthinking things."

"I promise she loves you dearly."

Belle and Freddy talked for hours in the kitchen while they cooked all of her favorite foods. Waffles with strawberries and strawberry jam. Pancakes with blueberries, butter and maple syrup. Blueberry muffins, scrambled eggs with Colby cheese, cookies, and cakes.

Freddy made multiple lunchboxes for each dessert, and whatever leftover foods Belle didn't finish. He didn't know what kind of monster food they would serve Belle. At least she could have her favorite snacks to nibble on in secret. He placed the lunchboxes in insulated food bags.

By the time they finished, it was 11 a.m. They didn't know what time the vehicle would show. Every time they heard a noise outside, they flinched.

Freddy paced the living room. Gosh the anticipation of their arrival drove him mad. He wanted to rip out his hair.

"Relax dad," Natasha said. "Acting like this isn't going to change anything."

Freddy stopped and glared at her before continuing to pace. He was angry at their lack of sympathy towards their sister. What kind of siblings didn't care about their own little sister? Where did he go wrong in raising them? Maybe he shouldn't have spoiled them as much as he did. Perhaps they would have grown up like Desiree. But as much as he didn't want to admit it, maybe that didn't have anything to do with it. Belle was just as spoiled if not more, and she was the kindest of his children. No parent wanted to admit their child had a horrible personality, but there was no denying it. He vowed from that moment on, he would not coddle them anymore.

Belle came down the stairs with her luggage. She decided on only bringing two of her least favorite suitcases. Some of her clothes and her art supplies. What was the point of over-packing if it was going to be thrown in the trash after her execution? She put her bags in front of the door and walked next to her father who stood by the window.

They stared intently at the only road that led to her grandparents' home. The black car, contrasting the white snow, slowly appeared from between the trees. Freddy's heart raced. It was time. Belle's siblings approached the window and their mouths dropped.

"Daaang!" Britney said. "You're riding in that?"

"How rich are they?" Natasha asked.

"Regret not going?" Marcus smirked.

"Not in the slightest," they said in unison.

"These monsters just wanna give their meal an organic delivery," Britney said. They both laughed.

"You ready?" Freddy asked, as the SUV stopped in front of the door.

Belle nodded and they headed for the door. The left passenger door opened as they approached the SUV. Natasha rushed to the other window to see if anyone was inside, surprised that the door could open on its own.

Freddy carried her bags and put them in the trunk. He sighed and glanced at Belle. She was stiff as a board. She stared into the open car. Freddy placed a hand on her back.

"You don't have to do this," he said. "I know you're afraid. And that's okay. I'll go alone."

"No," Belle said, shaking her head, her eyes swelling with tears.

She turned to the house and waved. Everyone, including the twins, waved back. All scared to approach the SUV just in case it took them too. Belle inhaled and climbed into the car. Freddy followed after her. Once inside, she peeked over the driver's seat. There really wasn't a driver. She wondered how they were able to do it. After she buckled her seatbelt, the car started moving. It looped around and headed back the direction it came from. It drove slowly down the snowy path and onto the main road. Belle and Freddy looked at each other and hugged.

"It's going to be all right," Freddy said. "I'll make sure of it."

Desiree waited on the side street across from the road that led to her grandparents' home. She had been there since 8 a.m. After leaving her grandparents' house, Desiree checked into a nearby motel. She spent two nights planning what she was going to do to stop Belle. When it seemed like there wasn't an option that would stop Belle or the SUV, Desiree came up with another plan. She prepared the night before Belle's departure. She'd bought a notebook, pencils, blankets, a flashlight, and two days' worth of food. She didn't think it would take long to get Belle out of there. When she had breakfast and was fully awake, she arrived first thing in the morning.

At 11 a.m., she saw an SUV pull onto their road. It was like the one her father described. She sat up and turned on her ignition. "Showtime."

When the car emerged from the road, Desiree put her car in drive and pulled onto the main road three cars' distance away. She wasn't sure how in the world it would get to the magical monster kingdom her dad claimed it came from, but she was going to do whatever she could to go with it.

They drove for over an hour and a half on the highway. They took a turn down a road Desiree was unfamiliar with. In the distance, she saw what looked like fireworks popping and crackling on the ground. She squinted as a large portal opened, revealing a beautiful road and a castle in the background. It was night, leaving a mysterious and terrifying glow to the castle's grandeur. She didn't have time to marvel at the spectacle in front of her. Desiree floored the gas as the end of the SUV reached the portal. Making it by a mere second, Desiree slipped in behind them before it dissipated.

She turned off her headlights and hit the brakes, slowing down to not rear-end the SUV and raise awareness she was there. The road was pitch black, the only light source on the road was from the sky and the SUV's headlights. Desiree had to rely on the SUV to drive.

The SUV drove down a cobbled road for 10 minutes before going up a hill and turning onto a roundabout. In the middle of the roundabout was a large stretch of trees. A little ways down, the SUV turned into the castle's driveway. Desiree pulled over on the side of the cobblestoned road, just past the roundabout and watched as the SUV drove into the castle gates.

CHAPTER THREE

L ong slender tawny fingers gently wrapped around a green necktie, straightening it as best he could into the proper tie.

"Quit fussing," Raoul chided, tucking Esmé's tie under his suit jacket. Raoul wore a purple suit jacket, with epaulettes and his medals over his right breast. On the left was a large T logo wrapped in a rose. He tied his long white hair that was past his shoulders into a low ponytail.

"This is stupid," Esmé whined, attaching his medals to his suit jacket. "What's the point of looking presentable if we're going to turn into beasts when they arrive?"

"That's why I told you to change now so you don't ruin this outfit."

"Yeah, but we won't be able to stay human once she's here. I just want to enjoy it while it lasts."

Raoul ruffled Esmé's short black hair and handed him his cufflinks. "We won't be around her all the time. You have to give her space. If you ever need a break from looking like a beast, you can go into a room. Now change."

Esmé frowned. He breathed in and out, closed his eyes and winced as his body turned into its beast form. His bones cracked as his body puffed up. He grew black fur, his face expanded, his eyes widened, and he sprouted a tail.

The young men were cursed. The curse turned them into beasts. The transformation was painful as bones cracked and extended. Raoul and Esmé weren't directly cursed by a sorcerer. Their father had angered a sorceress. Despite it being his curse, he'd unknowingly passed the spell down to his sons. Raoul and Esmé were unfortunately born as beasts. Thanks to their father's "resourcefulness" after failing to break his own curse, a sorcerer, unable to break it altogether, altered the curse so that he only changed into a beast in front of others. They did not turn into beasts around other beasts and sorcerers. When a person was within eyesight, the young men would transform immediately.

Raoul smiled. "Good, you're just as tiny like this as you are a man."

"Hey!"

"I'm only teasing. Be on your best behavior. We want to impress her. No crude language and no speaking about violence."

Esmé tsked. "I thought she has to love us for ourselves, personality and all."

"She does," Raoul said, nodding. "However, you're not as hot-headed as you like to appear."

Raoul puffed into his beast form, scaring both of them. They smiled awkwardly. Raoul unbuttoned the top buttons on his blouse and said, "I guess they're here. Remember, suave, not grumpy."

Esmé walked to the door, it was already somewhat ajar, and opened it wider, just enough to peek through. He watched as they unloaded the trunk oblivious to his presence. He looked at Belle and blushed. She was beautiful and looked to be around his age. He gazed at her long black curly afro, to her large black eyes, and pink lip gloss, to the blue dress under her dusty rose coat, and white boots. He stepped back and stood next to Raoul. He fidgeted with his tail looking down.

Raoul chuckled. He had never seen Esmé so shy. She must have been a sight for sore eyes to make someone as grouchy as Esmé silent.

"Don't worry," they heard Freddy say. "I promise I won't let them do anything."

Raoul and Esmé glanced at each other with confused looks. Freddy knocked on the door.

Raoul shouted, "Come in."

The door slowly creaked open and Belle and Freddy cautiously walked in. Belle stared at the ground as she clung to her father's side.

"Welcome," Raoul said. "Is this your daughter?"

"Y-yes," Freddy stuttered, he lowered his head to avert eye contact.

"And she consented to coming here?" he asked.

Freddy gave a slight nod, keeping his head down.

Raoul smiled. "I apologize that we must meet under such extreme circumstances. You must be very kind to take your father's place. I'm Raoul Bellerose and this is my younger brother Esmé."

Belle gazed up at the towering figure before her and trembled with fear. She clung to Freddy's arm, drawing him close. Her voice quivered as she said, "I-it's a p-pleasure. My name is Isabelle."

"What a lovely name, right Esmé?"

Esmé nodded. He was also anxious, but not in the same way as Belle of course.

"Well Mr. Holmes," Raoul said, turning towards him. "You've completed your end of the deal. Your charges are dropped. We'll give you time to say goodbye and our car will see you off."

"W-wait," Freddy said. "I have one request!"

"What is it?" Raoul asked.

"Please don't harm her," Freddy pleaded. "She's a wonderful girl. She had an amazing life ahead of her. I beg you not to kill her."

"Kill her?!" Esmé shouted.

"Esmé," Raoul said, sternly. "Calm down."

"No!" Esmé yelled. "I won't let him treat us like this! We clearly said nothing bad would happen to her! Why would you think we would hurt her?! Because we look like monsters?! That's stupid and you know it! No wonder she's scared. You lied to her!"

"Esmé!" Raoul shouted. "Enough."

"We're not monsters!" Esmé cried. Even his brother who never raised his voice was angry with him. Esmé gritted his teeth and ran up the stairs and around the corner.

Belle and Freddy looked stunned. Partially out of fear, and partially wondering what the heck just happened.

"I apologize for that unsightly display," Raoul said, clearing his throat and approaching them. "He's still young and doesn't know how to handle his emotions. Please forgive him."

They both nodded.

"Mr. Holmes," Raoul continued. "I know you were afraid the last time we met, so I assume you did not hear me correctly. We have no plans on executing Miss Isabelle. That was only a punishment for you. We only offered she take your place as a prisoner. I promised she would live a comfortable life…as much as I can provide. I do not condone violence, however there are laws here that must be upheld, whether I agree or not. Please do not think we are such vile beasts."

"I-I'm so sorry," Freddy apologized. "I must have misheard…. I didn't mean to offend you, however you must understand that we come from a different…realm, I guess you would say. We aren't used to seeing creatures like you."

"I do understand," Raoul said. "However it doesn't make it any less offensive."

"I'm sorry," Belle said. "I didn't mean to hurt your feelings, especially your brother's."

"I accept your apology, Miss Isabelle." Raoul smiled. "We're used to it. While you're here, I hope you're willing to get to know us... beyond the way we look."

Belle nodded. She wasn't entirely sure that was a promise she could keep. While Raoul seemed like a nice, coolheaded bird…thing…she wasn't all too sure about his brother. With such lack of control with his emotions, who's to say he wouldn't lash out at her physically? She had to be there, but it didn't mean she needed to converse with them. Only when necessary, would she do so. She didn't want to hurt their feelings but they did have to understand this was something new to her and she was there as a prisoner. She appreciated their hospitality, but she would rather them treat her as such than give her a false sense of security.

"Please," Raoul said. "Let me show you to your room. You can say goodbye, Mr. Holmes, but you must leave right away."

"Thank you," Freddy said.

They walked up the stairs and to the left, the opposite direction Esmé went. They continued down the hall and turned the corner. Raoul opened a door on the right of the hallway and entered.

The room was extravagant. It was larger than her bedroom in Newark. Almost everything in the room was white, the walls, floor, the couches and tables, her dressers and vanity mirror, and the curtains. Her bed was white with pastel pink covers and pillows, the rug underneath the coffee table was also pastel pink. The room was situated with a large table and two chairs by the door, the dresser and vanity mirror behind the table, to the right of the room, was the couch, love seat, and coffee table in front of a fireplace, and her bed to the right corner of the room. A large window was on the left side of the couches.

"Wow," Belle said in awe. "This is gorgeous."

Raoul smiled. "I'm glad you like it. If you'll excuse me."

He stepped out of the room, then peeked back inside. "Mr. Holmes, do you know how to get back to the front doors?"

"Uh…" Freddy said. "I'm sorry, I don't…."

"That's okay." Raoul smiled again. "I'll wait at the end of the hall to assist you."

They thanked Raoul and he left.

The moment he closed the door, he turned back into his human form.

He walked into Esmé's room. Esmé lay on his stomach with his head resting on his arms.

"Are you okay?" Raoul asked.

"I'm sorry," Esmé said. "I blew it."

"You didn't ruin anything," Raoul said. He walked to his bed and sat beside him.

Esmé sat up. "I just don't see why they treated us like that!"

Raoul sighed. "Sometimes, people can be blinded by looks. To them, we're nothing more than beasts."

"I just don't understand why," Esmé said.

"It's not something to understand," Raoul said. He patted Esmé on the back. "Considering we're one of the unfortunate ones to be different from others, it's not something we will ever be able to understand. We just have to do our best to prove we aren't monsters."

Raoul watched Esmé pout, but nod anyways. He chuckled. "Besides what would be the point of this curse if no one was vain?"

Esmé smiled faintly. "I guess you're right. I should apologize to them, huh?"

"Only for lashing out," Raoul said. "You have every right to be hurt by their actions, and no one can tell you how to feel. You only have to say sorry for yelling."

"Okay."

"Come on. I promised Mr. Holmes I would help him make it back to the front door."

"How stupid is he?" Esmé asked. "It's literally a straight shot from her room."

"He's older. He might not be able to retain that knowledge. Be patient with him."

"Thankfully we won't have to deal with him anymore," Esmé grumbled, as they left his room.

"Who knows." Raoul shrugged. "If everything goes as planned, you'll see him again for the wedding."

"Ugh," Esmé said. "Please no."

Raoul laughed. As they reached the hall by Belle's room, Freddy was just turning the corner and they shifted back. Raoul smiled. "Just in time."

He nudged Esmé and Esmé said, "I…would like to apologize for my outburst…. From last time and today."

Freddy was taken aback but he smiled awkwardly. "I should be the one to apologize. I shouldn't have judged you two. I can't lie and say I'm not scared, but I believe that you aren't vicious young men. Do forgive me?"

"Uh…" Esmé looked at Raoul. Raoul nodded and Esmé continued, "You're…forgiven. I promise I won't be so mean to Isabelle."

"Thank you," Freddy said. "Please take good care of my daughter."

They walked to the door and Freddy scurried into the SUV.

***

Desiree exited her vehicle and walked towards the gate. She watched from outside the castle grounds as Belle and Freddy unloaded her bags from the trunk. When they went inside, she waited a bit to make sure the coast was clear, then ducked and walked stealthily to the bottom of the castle steps, checking the SUV to see if the driver was there. She heard yelling as she slipped into the bushes.

What the heck? she thought.

Desiree peeked into the window above her to see the monkey boy thing screaming at them. She couldn't make out what he was saying but it angered her. Who did he think he was shouting at her father and little sister like that? She needed to get Belle out of there and fast!

She watched as the birdman led her family members up the stairs and to the left. She had to remember that. She ran back to her car and took out the note she wrote to her father while they were arriving at the doors. She ran back inside the castle gates and opened the SUV. She stuck the letter into the pouch behind the driver's seat.

She was going to sneak into the castle when she heard her father's as well as the beasts' voices coming closer. She ducked back into the bushes and watched her father get into the car.

I'm sorry dad, she thought.

***

When Freddy entered the SUV, he cupped his hands and cried.

He was heartbroken that Belle was alone with two beasts. While he had softened a little towards them from Esmé's heartfelt outburst to his apology, they still were men, and he couldn't help but worry about her safety and mental health.

He wiped his tears and noticed a white envelope behind the driver's seat. He pulled it out. Written on the envelope was *To Dad.* He assumed Belle had left him this note. He smiled and took out the letter.

33

In the letter read:

Dear Dad,

I know you're going to disagree with what I'm about to say, but do know I won't let them harm Isabelle. You'll probably see my car on the side of the road....

Freddy's stomach sank. He recollected everyone that was inside the home. He looked out the window, just before entering the portal. He saw through the tented windows the silhouette of the silver station wagon he had helped Desiree buy. He quickly turned back in his seat. His hands trembled as he continued to read.

I'm not sure about this magical kingdom but I swear I will escape with Isabelle. I'm letting you know so you don't worry about me. If you can do me a favor and notify UCLA that I won't be back next semester, I'd appreciate it. I'll see you soon with Isabelle.

Love Desiree.

Freddy grew weak and leaned back in his seat. He wasn't expecting to lose two of his daughters. He truly hoped Desiree could save Belle. And if she couldn't, he at least knew Belle wasn't alone anymore. Desiree was a fierce older sister, and she wouldn't let any harm come to Belle.

***

Belle sat on the couch in her room, resting her hand on her arm. She was already bored. She had inspiration to draw her room, but lost all creativity after the conversation with her father. She thought back on it.

Raoul had just left the room. Belle and Freddy looked at each other and sighed simultaneously. They laughed.

"I guess we're both happy to be out of their presence," Freddy said. "Are you sure, you still want to go through with this?"

"Of course," Belle said. "Look at this room. I don't mind staying in here forever."

"You don't plan on leaving?"

"No," Belle said, a little offense in her tone. "I don't know how they are. I know they said they weren't violent, but that explosion of rage from the monkey boy makes me second guess them."

"Oh Isabelle," Freddy said. He motioned for her to join him on the couch. "I know this place is scary, and looking at them isn't pleasant either, but from what I gathered, they are good beings. They may look different from us—"

"And scary," Belle interrupted.

"And scary," Freddy repeated. "But we can't always judge a book by its cover."

"But daddy," Belle protested. "You told me they were vicious beasts!"

"I did, and I was wrong," Freddy said. "If they were, they would have murdered both of us or killed me and did whatever they wanted with you. And they didn't, did they? What opened my eyes was Esmé's outburst. It made me realize where they were coming from. Think of how we're treated in our world simply for the color of our skin. We're no different from bad people in our world treating them that way. And you know as well as I do, how much it hurts to be treated the way we are. They didn't choose to be born that way. His method for expressing himself wasn't right, but you have to understand where he's coming from."

"I do understand," Belle said. "But you don't prove you're not a scary thing by threatening to kill someone and imprisoning another."

"That's the rules of this kingdom. Don't forget how much I stole from them. The value was not only significant monetarily, but also sentimental. I can't call him a ferocious beast when I did commit a crime. And I guess their way of saving me from execution was replacing you as a prisoner. They promised to treat you well and not like one. A bloodthirsty creature wouldn't do that."

Freddy continued, "I'm not telling you to like them nor am I telling you to trust them. But you need to have an open mind to understand them. That's how your mother and I raised you. They do look scary, and I don't expect you to get used to the way they look any time soon. But at least try to hide that fear around them, and discern from their personalities if they're good or not. Esmé seems a bit emotional, but Raoul gives me hope all of this is nothing more than a misunderstanding."

"I… guess…I'll try to get to know the real them and not what's on the outside."

"That's my girl. I better go. I wish I could stay here with you and make sure you're okay."

"Me too," Belle said. "But it is what it is. I'll stay in my room until I gain my bearings, then I'll converse with them."

Freddy hugged Belle tightly. "I love you. You're the best daughter a father could ever have."

"I love you too."

Freddy stood up and took a deep breath.

Belle stood and nudged him. "I'm the one who should be nervous dad. Don't forget to tell Desiree I'm sorry and that I hope she can forgive me for how I spoke to her. I don't want her to hate me."

"Belle." Freddy turned to her, and clasped her shoulders. "I already told you. Desiree will never hate you."

"I know, but just make sure for me."

"Okay, I promise." Freddy hugged her once more, then left the room.

Belle could hear Raoul greeting him.

Belle snapped out of her thoughts when a loud knock sounded on her door. She answered, "Yes?"

Raoul said, "It's Esmé and I. May we come in?"

Belle stood up. Reality sunk in that she was alone with beasts. Her body trembled and it was difficult to speak. There was no way she could *not* judge them by their cover. Her life was in their hands and could be gone at the snap of a finger.

Esmé asked, "Is she sleep?"

"I'm not sure," Raoul responded. He knocked on the door again.

Get it together, Belle, she thought, lightly smacking her face. She took a deep breath. As she exhaled, she said, "Come in."

Raoul opened the door. "Sorry to bother you."

She really couldn't listen to Freddy's lecture. She nodded, unable to find her voice.

Esmé walked close to the couch, and Belle instinctively moved away from him.

Esmé kept his eyes lowered, staring at the leg of the couch. He mumbled, "I…would like to apologize for yelling earlier. I should have handled my emotions better and I didn't. I'm sorry."

Think! Belle willed herself to speak. She forced a smile and shook her head. "No, don't apologize. It's our fault for treating you like that. My father should've paid attention to you guys. Sorry for jumping to conclusions."

"Uh…" Esmé looked back at Raoul.

Sensing his plea for help, Raoul smiled and said, "I do hope you like it here. There are many wonderful things to see. Esmé can show you around in the morning. You're free to walk around the castle grounds. Nothing is off-limits so long as you stay within the gate."

"I can never leave?" Belle asked.

"No," Raoul said, chuckling awkwardly. "You still have to serve the punishment for your father's theft, but you're welcome to enjoy everything accessible to you."

Belle nodded. "When is my sentence up?"

"Well," Raoul said. "How about in 6 years?"

Belle nodded. *Seriously*

"If you will excuse me," Raoul said. "I must prepare dinner."

Raoul turned to leave when he noticed Esmé following him. "Please, do not end your conversation because of me. Stay Esmé, Miss Isabelle will need help finding the dining hall."

"If it's all right, I don't plan on joining you for dinner…"

"You shouldn't skip meals," Raoul said.

"I know, but I'm very tired," Belle said, feigning a yawn. "It was morning when I left my world. I've been traveling for hours. I also ate before I got here. I would like to rest."

Raoul looked disapprovingly at Belle.

Before he could speak, Esmé interrupted. "Let her rest. She doesn't have to join us if she doesn't want to. Come on."

Esmé didn't wait for Raoul and walked out of the room.

"Miss Isabelle," Raoul started. He was going to say something, before stopping. He smiled. "If, for some reason, the bathroom in your room does not work, there is restroom down the hall to the right. Have a good night. Our rooms are on the east wing. Please do not hesitate to ask for help, if needed."

"OK. Good night."

When the door closed, Belle exhaled and dropped to the floor. Tears fells from her eyes as she tried to catch her breath. *How am I going to last 6 years?*

***

Raoul caught up to Esmé. "I'm proud of you for taking the initiative. However, this wasn't the time to do it."

37

"It's obvious she doesn't want to eat with us; I'm not going to force her. Just makes us look desperate…."

"It is a desperate situation," Raoul said. "You're right. You made a good call. Our goal should be to get her to warm up to you."

"Why me?" Esmé asked.

Raoul glanced at him. "I thought we were in agreement that you would court her."

Esmé shook his head. "I said your curse has to take priority, remember?"

"She looks to be around your age. I am *not* courting a child."

"But what other choice do you have?"

"The choice of keeping my morals and an age-appropriate marriage." Raoul pushed the kitchen door open. "Maybe my ethics will lead a woman to me."

***

When Desiree felt it was safe to leave the bushes, she made her way back to her car. She grabbed her notebook and a pencil and began to jot down her thoughts. She needed to find some way to enter the castle without being seen. They didn't seem to have that much security considering Freddy stole and she easily entered the castle grounds on foot. So were the guards inside? It was night. Did they allow them to sleep?

Three pages of poorly drawn diagrams later, Desiree opened a bag, took out a sandwich, and a bottle of soda. She didn't think to bring enough rations to survive more than a few days. Judging by the situation, they may have to lay low in their kingdom.

Desiree didn't think this would be an easy mission, but she realized she'd underestimated the situation and should've prepared better. How would they even lay low when they were different from the monsters in this world? They'd stick out like sore thumbs. All the beasts would have to do was issue a warning for "weird" creatures. Would it have been better to hide on castle grounds? They didn't seem to be that intelligent and humans were much smarter than animals. Freddy said the garden stretched for miles, maybe they could hide in there? Then again, they wouldn't have enough food to survive, especially if they lost their way. She began to scratch out the sentence when she thought about what would be in the garden. Did beasts eat their veggies?

Only one way to find out, she thought. She grabbed the flashlight, her notebook, pencil, and opened her car door. She needed to scope the area out and maybe make a map. She walked past the roundabout, writing every memorable landmark. She walked down the hill, writing down to make a left. She knew from there it would be a long drive, so she returned to the castle.

She peered around the castle gates, checking to see if any guards had returned. With the coast clear, remembering what Freddy told her, she took a left and followed the path he said led to the garden. She wrote down her surroundings and any security details. Man was she grateful for spy movies. She reached the door and made a crude drawing of it in her notebook. She could not risk bumping into anyone as she entered the garden, so Desiree looked around for an opening. She walked along the wall of the garden until she saw a gap between the bushes and squeezed her way between them, until she made her way to the maze.

Here goes nothing, she thought.

***

It was midnight and Belle couldn't sleep. She sat on the couch wondering if they would sneak in while she slept. Would it have been smart to use this time to learn her way around the castle? If they lied and really planned on killing her, knowing any hiding spots would be beneficial. She took a deep breath and left her room. Instead of going to the stairs, Belle turned right. The castle was dark, candle light barely lit the halls. Belle guessed that was a good way to save energy, but a fire hazard no less.

The castle was quiet. Maybe the beasts *were* sleeping and not planning a sneak attack. It seemed like the hall led to the east wing, so she turned around, making a mental note to not turn right in an emergency. She went down the stairs and turned right again. There was a long hallway with a few doors ahead of her before becoming a dead-end. The left of the first floor was also cut off. Despite its appearance from outside, the castle was smaller than she thought. Were the upper floors through one of the doors? Or was it simply an aesthetic? Maybe that could be her goal while she was here. Find a route to the upper floors. She opened a door by the entrance, followed the hall and found the dining room. The room was pitch black. On the other side, light shined through the cracks of a door. She walked along the wall to not bump into anything.

39

She opened the door and heard a loud, "Ouch!"

She gasped. "I'm so sorry."

Raoul, shocked by the sudden transformation, uncovered his mouth. He set his glass of water down on the counter and said, "Please do not apologize. I just…stubbed my toe."

"I—I'm sorry, this time for intruding," Belle said, attempting to scurry away.

"Do not leave on my behalf," he said. "Are you hungry? I can make you something to eat."

"No, I'm fine. I was just exploring the castle."

"Well, can I get you a glass of water?"

Belle hesitated. She was dehydrated. She was so preoccupied with her situation to notice she hadn't had anything to drink in hours. She nodded. "Yes, please."

Raoul took a glass from a cabinet and a pitcher of water from the refrigerator. Belle watched him intently as he poured, confirming he didn't poison it. He handed her the glass.

"Thank you."

"You are welcome," he said.

They sat in silence, drinking their water. Raoul could tell she was terrified. What could he talk to her about? He couldn't remember the last time he spoke to a stranger. He had to walk on eggshells, but how long would they have to do that? He thought back to his social etiquette classes.

"Miss Isabelle, if you do not mind me asking, how old are you?" A bit impolite, but he needed to break the ice somehow.

"Sixteen."

"You're a year younger than Esmé," he replied.

She nodded. They were again in silence. Belle was close to finishing her water.

Raoul broke the silence again, asking, "Do you have any hobbies?"

"Yes. I'm an artist," she said. "You?"

"Gardening."

"Right…" Belle moved to the sink to wash her glass.

"I can clean it," Raoul offered. "Please sit it in the sink."

"Okay." Belle moved swiftly towards the door. "Goodnight."

"Miss Isabelle," Raoul blurted, "I do require that you share meals with us. Outside of that, you can do as you wish."

"If it's all right, I would rather eat alone."

Raoul sighed. "This may sound a bit untoward; however, I wish you would trust us a little more."

"I…think it's a little early for that," she stammered. "I've only been here a few hours."

He nodded. "I would prefer that you don't spend the next six years watching over your shoulder. Esmé and I are good people. We started off on the wrong foot and Esmé can lash out sometimes, but we would never harm you."

"How can I know for sure that you won't?"

"I would like to think your good health the last few hours could attest to that. In the last ten minutes we have stood here, have I done anything to harm you?"

Belle shook her head. "Doesn't mean you won't later, though."

"I apologize. I do not see the logic in waiting to harm you when you have nowhere to run. Neither Esmé nor I are sadistic."

Belle couldn't really argue against it. He had a point. They hadn't done anything to her…yet. Despite this, she refused to be so easily swayed. She'd only spoken to Raoul. In both her and Freddy's experiences, it was Esmé who proved to be the violent, ill-tempered one. Raoul may have come across as good-natured, Esmé was the one she had to worry about. Who knew if one mistake or offense would make him lash out? Would Raoul defend him or her?

Raoul waited for Belle to respond, when she didn't, he continued. "We will respect your space. All I ask is that you join us for meals. We do not have to speak outside of these times. Have a good night, Miss Isabelle. I will see you at breakfast."

"Give me a day to myself," Belle finally spoke. "I'll join you for dinner. Just let me have some time to decompress."

"I do not approve of skipping meals," he frowned. After a moment of thought, he sighed. "I will allow it if you keep your word to join us thereafter."

"I will." As she left, she said, "Goodnight."

Once the door closed, Raoul returned to his human form. He sighed and began washing their glasses. *This is going to prove more difficult than I thought.*

***

As the sunlight peeked over the rose bushes, Desiree used her map to find her way back to the gap in the bushes. She planned to wait and see how many people would appear, but it was too risky. She returned to her car, still unable to find a soul. Although Desiree wanted to stay awake, she knew she would prove useless if she was sleep deprived. She grabbed her blanket from the backseat and leaned back in hers.

She figured out enough to help Belle escape, tonight. The rose maze would be a last resort. She couldn't find any vegetables or fruits in the maze. They would starve to death hiding in there. They would have to hope the portal worked both ways.

***

Esmé and Raoul finished breakfast. He explained his agreement with Belle to Esmé. Urging him to leave her be for the time being. Neither one of them was content with letting her starve all day. Esmé volunteered to give her her breakfast. He promised Raoul he wouldn't linger.

Esmé knocked on her door. "Isabelle? Are you awake?"

No answer.

"If you are, I'll set your breakfast in front of your door."

Still no response. They were up pretty late. Maybe she was still asleep?

"I hope you have a good morning," he said, walking away from her door.

Belle sat on her floor eating cookies. After she returned to her room, she ate the rest of her breakfast. All that she had left to survive off of were desserts. She couldn't sleep. Maybe it was a time zone thing. Would jet lag apply to traveling through worlds? She'd heard Esmé, but didn't want to converse with him. Raoul agreed to give her the day to herself. Why was he bothering her? There was no way she could eat their food. What did beasts eat anyways?

At noon, Esmé showed up with lunch. He sighed when he saw that her breakfast had remained untouched. He knocked on her door, "Isabelle, I have your lunch."

Belle wanted to ignore him. A second time would be obvious she was. She didn't care about hurting his feelings, per say, she had to care about him lashing out. "I'm not hungry."

"I know it can be hard to eat sometimes, but you should. Raoul always told me, even if you aren't feeling well, you should always do your body a favor and feed it."

"I appreciate your concern," Belle replied, "I'm just not hungry."

"…Well…I'll sit your food in front of the door in case you are later."
Belle didn't respond.

Esmé took the hint and left. Even though her behavior was frustrating, he had to keep his emotions in check. Last thing he wanted to do was prove her right.

Belle spent the afternoon drawing her bedroom. It really was a beautiful place. They had decorated her room with such care. Her bed was soft. There were extra blankets in the wardrobe. There were dresses in there that were not her style but cute nonetheless. She wasn't sure if every bedroom had it, but she was given a room with its own personal bathroom. Which came in clutch with her never wanting to leave her room. It was stocked with bath and face towels. There was enough soap in the medicine cabinet to last her a few months. She had hot water. Aside from needing food, she could have easily stayed in her room for months.

She thought that she would listen to her father's advice after all. While they were terrifying to look at, they might have been good guys. They were relentless about getting her to eat. And they sort of respected her wanting to be alone. Maybe it was time that she looked past their appearance. How she treated them reminded her of the twins. She didn't want to be like them. Mean and judgmental.

Belle was nodding off when she heard a light tapping on the door. Her stomach sank but she sat up. "Yes?"

***

Desiree watched the beasts move around the castle grounds. She was only able to get 2 hours of sleep. The paranoia of someone seeing her car made it difficult to sleep. It was dusk and the monkey beast walked back into the castle. Desiree hurried to the window next to the door. She watched the beast turn in the direction they had led Belle and Freddy the night before. She waited a bit before entering the castle. She didn't know where the bird chimera was. She hadn't seen it since the morning. The door closed with a loud thud. Desiree grimaced, mentally kicking herself for not closing it slowly. She crouched as she ran up the stairs. She peeked around the corner. The coast was clear. Did they have any guards? It was strange that a castle wouldn't have some form of security. There weren't any servants either. Were these beasts pretending to be royalty? It wouldn't have surprised her. Monsters were deceptive like that. For all she knew, they could've manipulated Freddy to steal.

43

"Esmé?" Raoul asked, emerging from the dining hall. "Is that you?"

Desiree looked around the hall for a place she could hide. There were knight displays sparsely placed through the hall. She ran behind one as Raoul's footsteps could be heard approaching the stairs.

Raoul walked towards the stairs. He puffed back into his beast form when he reached the landing. He stared at his wings in confusion.

Is it proximity now, too? he thought. *Is she nearby?*

"Miss Isabelle?" he said out loud. He continued down the hall to her bedroom.

"Fine then!" Esmé shouted, opening the door.

He slammed the door shut and turned into his human form. When he approached Raoul, he puffed back into his beast form. He stopped and checked himself out. He also looked confused and gazed at Raoul. Raoul looked at him. He sighed and walked a few feet towards him, stopping in front of the knight Desiree was behind. She examined him through the crack between the knight's arm and torso.

She was amazed. While she was appalled by their appearance, the Greek mythology nerd in her took over.

"What happened?" Raoul asked. "Didn't I tell you to leave her alone until dinner?"

"She's rude," Esmé said. "I did my best to be polite and she was disrespectful to me."

"What did she do?"

"I asked her to marry me," Esmé said, "and she said no! Wh—"

Before he could finish, Raoul face palmed and said, "Why would you do that?"

"Because that's the whole point of this, right?" Esmé said. "I thought the best way to make progress with her would be to let her know my intentions. Wouldn't she be less afraid if I told her I wanted to marry her?"

"No, the point is for you to get to know her first. Not get married," Raoul said, flicking his forehead. "Go apologize."

"Not happening," Esmé said. "Besides, you should pursue her."

"Keep your voice down," Raoul said, he motioned for Esmé to follow him. "Not a chance. I'm not going to court a child."

"Who knows when another woman will show up?" Esmé said as they walked down the stairs.

"That's why I'm focusing on you. Even if she was close to my age, I wouldn't leave you at risk."

"But you'll—!"

"Hush," Raoul said. "We don't need her overhearing anything she shouldn't. We'll discuss this in the kitchen."

Desiree waited until she could no longer hear their footsteps.

Marriage? she mentally scoffed. *Not on my watch.*

She made her way to Belle's room. Esmé left the door slightly open, so it was easy to tell which door was hers.

Desiree slowly entered the room. Belle sat on the couch facing away from her. She closed the door and Belle turned around. Her eyes widened when she saw Desiree.

"What are you doing here?!" she exclaimed. She ran to Desiree and hugged her.

"Shh," Desiree said, returning her hug. "I'm here to get you out!"

"Are you insane?" Belle said. "What if they catch you?!"

"They won't. Look, I need you to listen to whatever they say. Don't anger them. Tonight, when they're asleep, we'll sneak out."

"How are we going to get out?" Belle asked.

"I drove. I'm sure there's some way to activate that portal."

"I hope so… Who knows how they'll react if we fail."

"I won't let them do anything to you."

"I'm glad you're here, I…I thought you hated me." Belle cupped her face and cried.

"Why would you think that?" Desiree asked. She took Belle's hands away from her face, and leaned over to look her in the eyes. "I could never hate you, Isabelle."

"But…but the twins…"

"You actually believed them?" Desiree rolled her eyes. "They are the last people you should listen to. How many times do I have to tell you to stop sharing things with them? You're only giving them material to mess with you."

"I know. But…you were really mad and they heard everything and told me that was why you hated me."

"Mad because you wouldn't let me go in your place, not because I hated you." Desiree sighed. She led Belle to the couch and hugged her again.

After hugging for a while, Belle asked, "Where are you going to stay until tonight?"

"Here." Desiree smirked. "What, you don't want me in your room?"

"Of course that's not it. You know I don't mind hanging out with you. It's just…they come and go."

"I know."

"What are you going to do if they show up?"

"Plenty of places to hide. Beneath the tables, under your bed, the bathroom. Stall so they don't see me. And tell them not to come into your room past 9 p.m."

"Okay."

Desiree spent the hour talking about how she followed them to the kingdom to her playing spy all day. Belle panicked over Esmé wanting to marry her. She couldn't even imagine spending 6 years with them, let alone a lifetime with someone so angry. It was like she took a step forward to trust them, and he made her take 5 steps back. He was a brute. What if he forced her to marry him?

They laughed about Desiree's lousy attempts at spying when they heard a knock on the door. Desiree hid under the coffee table.

Belle stepped behind the couch so whoever it was didn't get close. "Come in."

Esmé opened the door, avoiding eye contact with her. "It's time for dinner."

"Is it all right if I eat in here?" she asked.

"No!" Esmé yelled. "Erm… I mean, no. Raoul said you had an agreement and have to join us…"

"I remember," Belle said. "I'll be down in a second."

Esmé nodded. He stopped at the door and turned around. "I want to apologize for how I behaved earlier. I shouldn't have reacted that way."

"I forgive you," Belle said. She smiled, her eyes glazing over, hoping he would leave.

"Well…" Esmé said, awkwardly leaving the room. "I'll see you downstairs."

Belle watched as he closed the door then went around the couch to Desiree.

"I can't eat with them," Belle complained. "What are they going to serve?"

"Bird pellets and bananas." Desiree laughed. She teased, "Enjoy it, father always said to eat every bite."

Belle laughed. "Ugh. I'm going to bring you food to eat."

"I'm good."

She sighed and left the room.

Desiree stayed under the table. She didn't know if the chimeras would burst into her room randomly, and the last thing she needed was to be caught.

Belle walked cautiously down the hall. She remembered the way to the dining hall. Maybe she could pretend she was lost to prolong her unappetizing meal. When she turned the corner to the main hall leading to the stairs, Esmé waited at the end.

"You didn't have to wait," Belle said.

"Yeah, but I didn't want you to get lost…" he mumbled. Esmé motioned for her to follow him.

"Thank you…" she mentally sighed. *So much for that idea.*

They walked around the corner by the foyer. Belle's eyes lit up at the beauty of the dining room. She didn't get to see how beautiful it was last night. It had a dark mahogany floor and walls, a long wenge table, with a thin burgundy table runner that only covered the middle length of the table. There were sixteen gold lined chairs with red padding. The plates were set on the far side of the table.

Raoul stood. He bowed slightly. "Good evening, Miss Isabelle. Glad you agreed to join us."

As if I had a choice, Belle thought.

Raoul continued, "For tonight's dinner I made a turkey, bread rolls, barley rice, mixed vegetables, filet mignon, lobster ravioli, and roasted potatoes. For dessert cherry soufflés and chocolate mousses."

Belle examined the food. "Wow you made this by yourself?"

"Oh no, with Esmé's help."

"I didn't do as much as you…" Esmé said.

"Please do not let his humble attitude fool you. He is a remarkable chef."

"Can we please sit to eat?" Esmé asked.

Belle pulled out a seat on the far side of the table.

Before she sat, Raoul said, "Uh, Miss Isabelle, there's only three of us, please sit closer to the food."

Esmé pulled out the seat next to his and said, "You can…sit here."

Esmé did his best to hold back his emotions. He just couldn't understand why she was so afraid of them. Here they were being as hospitable as possible and she still treated them like monsters. "If you want me to move, I can…"

"It's fine," Belle said, sitting down as he pushed her chair in. "Sorry, I'm used to sitting in the farthest chair. I have a big family…."

Esmé rolled his eyes. *What utter nonsense.*

"Really?" Raoul asked. "It must be wonderful to have such a large family. How many siblings do you have?"

"Oh, well, three older sisters and a brother. As of right now, we…they're, staying with my grandparents."

"That doesn't account for ten other chairs…" Esmé mumbled.

"Esmé," Raoul said, giving him a stern look. "So your mother and father, grandparents and your siblings. That certainly is a lot."

"My mother passed away," Belle said.

"I am sorry," Raoul said.

Esmé glanced up to his side at Belle. He didn't know what to say, but some of her pain was similar to his.

"It's okay," Belle said.

Hoping to lighten the mood, Raoul smiled and said, "Miss Isabelle, please try the food."

Belle nodded and looked down at her plates. The plates were already filled with one of everything on their respective plates. It was against many rules for Esmé and Raoul to serve anyone and Raoul would be damned if he had his guest and Esmé's potential wife serve the food. He preemptively, while setting down the dishes, filled each plate. He had searched the rule book and laws prior to make sure it was allowed. As Belle wasn't aware of the circumstances, but assuredly by that point noticed, there were no servants attending them. She was curious as to why, but figured she could wait until later to inquire about it.

She was nervous, whether they were beasts or not, they still exuded a fancy air and surely table etiquette was of the utmost importance. She reached to the farthest depths of her memories for useless facts. She was thankful to her younger self. Out of boredom, she watched table etiquette videos online. She just needed to remember each step. She reached for the bread roll, her hand quivering as she picked it up and ripped a piece of it off. She grabbed her butter knife, spread it onto the piece, and placed it in her mouth. She chewed slowly. The bread was light and fluffy, almost melting in her mouth.

When she swallowed, she covered her mouth and said, "Wow, it's delicious."

Raoul smiled. "I am glad you like it."

"May I ask who made them?" she asked.

"Rao—"

Raoul interrupted Esmé and said, "Esmé did. He is quite the up-and-coming chef."

"You did an outstanding job," Belle said, turning to Esmé.

Esmé with his head down, mumbled, "Thank you…"

Esmé shot Raoul a look. As if Raoul could read his mind, Esmé thought, *Why the heck are you lying?!*

Knowing his little brother all too well, the corners of Raoul's mouth curved into a slight frown as he tried to hold back his laughter.

"Well, we should not let the food get cold," Raoul said, clearing his throat. "Shall we?"

Belle and Esmé nodded in unison and dug in.

During dessert, Belle fell in love with the cherry soufflé. She gushed with admiration over the dish Esmé "made." Raoul offered to have Esmé make them every dinner if she wanted. She gladly accepted the offer. She was disappointed Rao… Esmé only made enough for the three of them.

Esmé, with his heart beating the inside of his chest, slid over his ramekin. Mumbling again, he said, "Here you can take mine."

"No, you don't have to give me yours," she politely declined, despite her heart and stomach saying otherwise.

"It's fine. I don't really like soufflés…" he said, still avoiding eye contact. "If you want, we can just trade. My soufflé for your mousse."

The deal was hard for her. She wanted to try out the chocolate delight that lay beautifully in a sherry glass with a raspberry on top. But she also loved the soufflé and did not want to reject Esmé's kind gesture.

"Deal," she said, handing him the mousse. Their fingers gently brushed each other in the exchange sending butterflies to their stomachs. They both looked awkwardly at their desserts.

While it was understandable to Esmé why it happened, Belle was dumbfounded. She did her best to brush it off as his fur tickling her hand and dove into her soufflé.

The overall dinner was rather pleasant. Nothing like the horrors she and Desiree imagined. Normal human food, they ate like gentlemen, on the rare occasion of Raoul scolding Esmé for using his hands, and their conversations were delightful.

After dinner, they moved to the lounge Freddy stole from and talked away. She learned many things about them, like their hobbies. She was informed about the recreational building behind the castle and Raoul's garden. All open for her to explore whenever.

Their castle seemed more and more fun as they spoke. It was a shame she had to escape with Desiree in a few hours. While the dinner had lowered her guard significantly, she still preferred not to serve a 6-year prison sentence, full of fun or not.

As the evening came to an end, Belle offered to clean the dining hall, but Raoul insisted on Esmé giving her a proper tour of the castle. Belle adamantly refused, she thought maybe the servants were going to clean up, and if her assistance was no longer needed downstairs, she wanted to return to Desiree as soon as possible.

She said her goodbyes and went back to her room. When she was far enough away, Raoul and Esmé returned to their human forms.

Raoul used that cue to say, "That turned out better than expected."

"I guess. She seemed less scared." Esmé started to clear the table and Raoul joined him.

"As they say, the best way to a man's heart…or woman in this case, is through her stomach."

"Do you actually believe that nonsense?"

"Did we not just witness it?"

"Well…she still didn't want to spend alone time with me."

"That takes time." Raoul balanced the plates on his right arm and patted Esmé with his left as they entered the kitchen. "She needs time to catch her bearings. Don't take it to heart. With how well you're doing, especially that dessert move, I'm sure she'll fall for you in no time."

"I hope so…I mean if you weren't so stubborn, you could easily win her over."

"Absolutely not. Again she's a child. Secondly, I can't court her knowing there may never be a chance like this again. I can move on, knowing at least you're safe."

Esmé pouted. He hated how considerate his brother was at times. He was running out of time, yet he cared more about what happened to his little brother. He was too stupidly kind for his own good.

***

Desiree lay under the table. Her back was killing her and the confined space raised her anxiety through the roof. She was grateful they supplied Belle with a bookshelf. She pulled a random book off the shelf after Belle left. It was a great way to occupy the time. The book was short, and by the time Belle entered the room, she was on the last page.

Desiree finished the last bit and leaned forward to see whose shoes were walking towards the bed. Belle dropped to her knees.

"You can come out now."

"You sure monkey boy didn't follow you?"

"He didn't. I told them I was going to sleep. They have decorum so I don't think they'll disrupt us."

"Looks like you've taken a liking to them."

"Not so much that, but I guess they're nice." Belle helped Desiree off the floor. She gasped and let go of her hand. "I forgot to grab you something to eat!"

"It's cool. I can wait until later tonight. There's food in my car."

"You still have to eat something now." Belle threw open one of her suitcases and grabbed a lunchbox. "We made them yesterday."

Desiree opened the lunchbox and pulled out a slice of cake, cutely decorated with different heart-shaped toppings. "Are you sure you want me to eat this?"

"Yeah. We're escaping anyways. Me and dad can make another one."

Desiree smiled. "Seeing as this has been percolating since yesterday, I doubt it was safe for you to eat anyways."

Desiree unfolded the pink mini fork in the lunchbox and ate. She finished the food and they sat on the bed. Belle gushed about the dinner, mainly the cherry soufflés. Desiree stated if the situation was different, and they were human, she would gladly love to try some. Belle was slightly conflicted about Desiree's slander. After having gotten to know them on a deeper level than their looks, she felt wrong speaking ill of them, mainly Raoul with his gentle nature.

She changed the subject every time Desiree said something mean about them. She didn't have the heart to correct her sister, especially not after jumping into a magical portal to save her. And after a while, Desiree caught on, and refrained from making snide comments about them. She wondered why her sister, the one who spoke horribly about them earlier, liked them, now. Was it a magical potion in the food? Had she been brainwashed? Desiree desperately needed to get her out of there. She prayed it wasn't a case of *Hansel and Gretel*.

Towards 10 p.m., they could still hear the beasts roaming around. Belle fought the urge to doze off, her head bobbing every second. Desiree persuaded Belle to take a nap and promised to wake her when the beasts were asleep. Belle took the offer without hesitation and was out within seconds.

Desiree laughed. She loved how sweet and innocent Belle was. She frowned. She couldn't let her little sister be corrupted or harmed. She questioned why they were still awake. Were they planning to attack when Belle closed her eyes?

Desiree clenched the blanket. *Not on my watch!*

Her grip loosened when she felt Belle shivering. She stood up and slid the blanket from beneath her and placed it on top of Belle. She moved under the covers and hugged Belle.

"I won't let anything happen to you," Desiree whispered, "even if it costs me my life."

CHAPTER FOUR

Esmé tapped on Belle's door. No answer. Was she still asleep? Esmé walked to the clock on the stairs. It was 7:45 a.m. Raoul insisted last night they both woke up at 7 to serve breakfast. Esmé hated having to cut his night short, and hated waking up early even more.

He grumbled as he walked back to her room. *What a waste of time.* If he had to wake up early, so did she. He knocked again.

***

Desiree stretched. She hadn't slept that well in so long. She heard Esmé knock on the door. *Crap!*

Just as she sat up, Esmé entered the room. His eyes widened as he made eye contact with her.

"What are you doing in here? Who are you?" he exclaimed. Esmé turned around and ran shouting, "Raoul!"

Desiree scrambled to her feet. She shook Belle. "Belle, wake up. We overslept!"

She yawned. "What?"

"Monkey boy saw me! We gotta get out of here!"

"What?!" Belle said, jumping out of bed. She looked at the clock, and her heart sank even further.

"Who knows what they'll do if they catch me!" Desiree searched frantically around the room. She grabbed her jacket and checked the pocket for her keys. "We have to go, now!"

Belle nodded as she put her boots on. She didn't bother grabbing her suitcases. It would only slow them down. Desiree ran towards the door but stopped abruptly. She heard their footsteps fast approaching.

"We gotta find another way," she said.

***

Esmé burst into the kitchen as Raoul took a skillet off the stove.

53

"Slow down," he chided.

"No time!" Esmé grabbed the skillet and put it back. He pulled at Raoul. "There's a woman in Belle's room!"

"Esmé, she's a young lady, a girl. Please stop trying to force her on me."

"That's not—" Esmé shook his head. "I mean there's a strange woman in there. She was sleeping *next* to Belle!"

Raoul's eyes widened. "What?"

Raoul couldn't believe what he was hearing. There was no way someone else could have gotten to their castle. And the SUV certainly wouldn't have moved if there were more people than expected inside. He had to see for himself what Esmé was talking about.

They ran down the hall as fast as they could. Halfway down the hall, they transformed into their beast forms. Unfazed, they continued until they reached Belle's room. The bed was empty. Their eyes shifted towards movement by the window.

"Please, it's too high!" Belle shouted. While her room was only the second floor, it was 40 feet high. "We can just go right!"

Belle tried to grab her jacket but Desiree swatted her arm. "We don't have time!"

"Hey!" Esmé screeched.

They both whipped their heads around. The startle caused Desiree to lose her footing and she slipped out the window headfirst.

Belle screamed and cupped her mouth. Tears filled her eyes. Raoul instinctively darted towards the window and jumped out. This was possibly the most grateful he felt for having wings. He dove faster than her and pulled her close.

"I got you," he said, trying to flap his left wing.

Desiree was too frightened to think rationally. She wrapped her arms tightly around him and shut her eyes.

Trying to fly with one wing proved more difficult than he imagined. His next approach was to grab something, anything. He turned his head to see what was beneath them. They were getting closer to the ground, but his eyes caught onto the roof of their veranda and he reached for it. He gripped it for a split second before pain shot through his arm and he lost his grip. He winced. There was nothing left he could do. He pulled Desiree's arms from around him, and held her close, shielding her head with both wings and crashed into a bush.

He gasped, the wind knocked out of him. Blood spurted from his mouth and he lost unconsciousness.

Desiree sat up, distress on her face. "Oh my gosh! I'm so sorry! I—"

"Raoul!" Esmé was about to jump out the window but thought about Belle. He turned to the door and shouted, "Come on!"

They ran as fast as Belle could out and around the castle. When they arrived, Raoul was regaining consciousness. Desiree carefully placed his head on her lap as she apologized profusely.

"Is he okay?" Esmé asked.

"I-it looks like it. But some of his bones are definitely broken," Desiree replied.

"Can't you do something?" Belle asked. She was on the right track. Desiree was in the nursing program. However…

"Yeah, but they don't teach you how to heal… you know… animals." Desiree whispered the last part of her sentence. "There's nothing I can do."

Hearing her speak so casually, made Esmé's blood boil. He tried repressing his rage, but it consumed him. "This is all your fault! What the heck were you thinking?!"

"Don't talk to my sister like that!" Belle said. "It was an accident."

"An accident?" he jeered. "Look at him! All because your 'sister' decided to jump out of a window."

"She didn't jump; she fell. And she wouldn't have fallen if you hadn't scared us!"

He scoffed, incredulously. "So you're saying it's my fault?"

"It's…no one's fault…" Raoul groaned, weakly.

"Raoul!" Esmé said, kneeling beside him.

Raoul tried his best to speak. The pain in his chest stabbed him every time he took a deep breath. "Esmé what did I…tell you abou… about yelling at women?"

"You're reprimanding me now of all times?" Esmé complained. "This fool almost killed you!"

"Esmé!" Raoul yelled. Pain struck and he coughed, blood coming out of his mouth again.

"Don't talk," Desiree interrupted. "He's right, it's my fault. I'm sorry. If there's anything I can do…."

Esmé brooded silently while Desiree continued to apologize. That's when an idea hit him. Esmé leaned forward and growled, his breath blowing across her face. "As second prince, I, Esmé Nicolas Bellerose of Rosaceae, hereby sentence… whoever you are… to death!"

"What?" they all screamed in unison. Desiree and Belle's stomachs dropped. What did Desiree get herself into?

Raoul groaned. "Esmé, you…"

Esmé raised his hand to silence Raoul. His nostrils flared. "Trespassing, breaking and entering, squatting, property damage, attempted murder."

"What? I…" Desiree stammered, trying to explain, but the words would not come out.

Esmé continued to tack on more charges, many he, himself, had never heard of. "You've gravely injured the crown prince. The charges against you, in this kingdom, are punishable by death."

"Death? I am so sorry," Desiree started. "I—is there anything I can do to stop this?"

Esmé inwardly smirked. Everything was going according to plan. He straightened himself, pulling down his suit jacket. "You must remain here until further notice. Got it?"

Desiree nodded. Her heart was thumping so loudly, she couldn't hear herself think. She kicked herself mentally. *How could I be so careless?*

Esmé ordered the young ladies to help carry Raoul to his chamber. He stated he could easily carry Raoul—a lie his told himself—but doing so would only hurt Raoul more. With Desiree's instructions, they made a makeshift stretcher out of a blanket and two long sticks. Each lifted a part of him, Desiree lifted his shoulders, Belle his legs and Esmé lifted him from his torso and thighs. They gently placed him on the "gurney" and Desiree and Esmé carried him to his bedchamber. They lowered him onto the bed, and slid the blanket from underneath him. Raoul's eyes were closed, seeming to have fallen asleep. Esmé took this chance to elaborate on Desiree's punishment without his well-mannered brother interfering. He studied Desiree, as she and Belle cleaned up the sticks and blanket. Although Esmé didn't like her, she was Raoul's last chance. What would be a good punishment? It had to be something that kept her there long enough.

"Listen," Esmé said, glowering at Desiree. He motioned for her and Belle to join him on the sofas. "I am in charge while my brother is incapacitated. This means I will decide what your sentence is and your punishment. You hear?"

Desiree nodded. It was over for her. She hoped she could survive long enough for Belle to escape.

"As I said earlier, your sentence is death. But," he said, pausing for emphasis, "I'll clear the charges on one condition."

"Anything—you ask…" Desiree paused, "your… majesty."

"Esmé is fine…." Esmé reciprocated the same uneasiness at 'your majesty.' "You must take up all castle duties. Cleaning, tending to my brother's garden and the rest of the castle ground's plants, and nursing my brother back to health. When he is healed, we'll continue our discussion on how long you'll stay here. Your actions will determine if you're lucky enough to sleep in a bed or rot in a dungeon. So no funny business or the deal's over!"

"I accept," Desiree said, her head down. The uneasiness of not knowing when her actions might cause her death made her nauseous.

"Esmé," Raoul called, faintly, "you're being too harsh."

"How?" Esmé asked, rushing to his side. "That was a fair deal."

"I can tend to my own garden. She can—" Raoul gasped. "Where are my manners? I am Raoul Bellerose and this is Esmé. May I have the pleasure of knowing your name?"

"I'm Desiree. And again, I'm so sorry you were injured," Desiree answered.

"Accidents happen," Raoul said.

"'Accidents happen,' only applies to things that *don't* almost kill people," Esmé grumbled.

Raoul glanced at him. "Regardless, thank you for your kindness."

"Kindness, she almost killed you," Esmé scoffed.

Not that I have a choice, Desiree thought. Out loud she said, "It's the least I can do. But…shouldn't we get a doctor?"

Esmé looked at her like she had said the dumbest thing in the world. "While you were breaking into our castle, did you see anyone walking around?"

"No…" Desiree responded cautiously.

"Exactly. So where the heck are we going to get a doctor?"

"Aren't you a prince? Order one here," Belle commanded.

"No need," Raoul said. "I will heal on my own."

"But…" Desiree started. *If you do that, I'll stay here longer….*

"It is just me and Esmé, and…now you two. That is why you must take care of the castle in my stead."

"If what Esmé required was 'too harsh,'" Desiree asked, "what does that entail?"

"Cooking and cleaning. Although my brother and I do not make messes, the castle needs to be dusted and swept regularly."

"Don't worry," Esmé said, proudly, "I can take care of the cooking."

"Please," Belle said. "Desiree isn't the best cook."

"No!" Raoul sprang forward, sitting up as far as possible, as if he had healed instantly. He groaned from the sudden movement, shrinking in, and spoke quickly, "No…y-you know the laws, you do not serve others. You are a prince…."

"Fine…" Esmé said, disappointed.

"But didn't you make food for me last night?" Belle asked.

"T-that was an exception…." Raoul panicked. He had to think of something. He was having flashbacks of the last time Esmé cooked.

Esmé was 14 years old at the time. He wanted to help Raoul at least once with chores. Raoul, thinking his brother was a prodigy in everything, agreed to let him cook that night. What he wasn't expecting, was what Esmé called chicken noodle soup. It was a green sludge, with partially-cooked chicken chunks, and stiff, poorly cut vegetables. The green color was due to Esmé pouring green dye in the soup because "it looked cooler." Raoul didn't have the heart to tell Esmé his food almost killed him, and possibly came to life. Since then, the only help Esmé was allowed was to chop vegetables and hand Raoul ingredients. Raoul also couldn't correct Belle. He had lied to her the night before about Esmé's wonderful cooking. For Esmé's sake, and breaking his curse, he needed to keep Esmé as far away from the kitchen as he could.

Raoul continued, "I did in fact…cook for the three of us. However, technically I was cooking for Esmé and I. I simply made large enough portions to give you."

Belle ahhed as if it made sense. "And because there's two of us, he can't do the same."

"Exactly." Raoul sighed in relief.

Desiree on the other hand, couldn't make sense of it. There were so many holes in his excuse she was confused on how the others could fall for it. But the last thing she needed to do was anger him, so she remained silent.

"Well…" she said. "If there's nothing you need from me now, maybe I should go."

"No, there is nothing else," Raoul said. "Esmé, please give her a key to a room near Miss Isabelle's."

"Why do I have to do it?" Esmé complained.

Raoul didn't respond. He stared at Esmé and he got the hint. Esmé grumbled as he led the young women out of Raoul's chamber.

Raoul leaned back on his pillow, stared at his hand and sighed. "So I have a chance…."

Esmé complained under his breath as he went into a room next to Raoul's. He searched around until he found a set of keys. He pulled one off the keyring and motioned for the two to follow him. He stopped not too far from Raoul's door and turned abruptly, startling the ladies. "Raoul may have said you only have to cook and clean, but I expect you to still help him, got it?"

"Yes…" Desiree answered.

Esmé hmphed and turned on his heels. They arrived at a door across from Belle's chamber. Esmé unlocked it and gave Desiree the key, and without another word, turned and walked away. He quickly returned to Raoul's bedchamber, only to discover that he was not alone.

When he entered, he saw a beautiful woman standing next to Raoul's bed. Her movements were graceful and elegant as she stepped forward to Esmé. She was 5'9. She had curly, black, waist-length hair. Her skin was of the deepest, most beautiful ebony. Her long pink dress matched her almond-shaped eyes, her pink irises twinkling as she smiled.

"What a pleasure it is to see you, Esmé," she said.

"Lady Orchida." Esmé bowed. "What brings you here?"

"Raoul." She clasped her hands together. Lady Vanda Orchida was a powerful sorceress from a neighboring kingdom. The previous king tasked herself with the eradication of the nasty spell placed on Raoul and Esmé. "I see things are off to a lovely start."

"Not funny." Esmé rolled his eyes.

"I think so," she responded, her sly smile never wavering. "Our hero, the first prince, jumping out of a window to save a young lady. Quite a remarkable and selfless act. Although…I planned to save her myself. She would have come out unscathed and so would his highness."

"Then how come you didn't save Raoul?" Esmé asked.

"He's not dead is he?"

"No…but—"

"Do you think he could survive a fall from 40 feet high, hitting his head on impact?"

"If I may be so frank," Raoul said. "Why did I not come out 'unscathed' as you planned for Miss Desiree?"

"I don't have to answer that one for you."

"No, I think I understand why," Raoul said. "But how am I going to interact with her if I am bedridden?"

"Simple." Lady Orchida snapped her finger and a wand appeared. She grabbed it and aimed at Raoul. A bright light twinkled from the wand and flowed around him. His wounds healed and the pain in his body subsided.

Raoul sat up rejuvenated and excited. He winced and gripped his left arm. "Why?"

"If you're healed, why would she stay?" She waved her wand again and a cast appeared on his arm.

"Except," Esmé joined in, "he has wings, so what's that gonna do when he transforms?"

"You underestimate me. I…*cast* a spell on his cast. When he transforms, it will shape with his wings. Don't worry, they won't notice that anything is amiss."

Raoul smiled. "Thank you, Lady Orchida. You are always looking out for us. I am eternally grateful to you."

Raoul glanced at Esmé.

"Yeah, ever so grateful…" Esmé mumbled.

"Do not be grateful or give thanks until the job is done. Now if you'll excuse me, there's something I must see to."

A portal opened and she disappeared.

***

Desiree watched as Esmé left the room. She waited until he was out of ear-shot and slammed the door. "We don't have much time."

"What do you mean?" Belle asked.

"We're still leaving, or… you will. With bird man injured, you can probably escape. If monkey boy tries to stop you, I'll block him."

"I'm not leaving without you."

"You're going to have to." Desiree dug through her pockets and pulled out her car keys.

"I can't drive."

"Yes, you can. You have a permit."

"You drive a manual. I can't do this!"

Desiree stuffed the keys in Belle's hand, clasping it tightly. "I need you to be brave. Don't worry about me. You'll figure it out. If you need a day, I'll distract them."

"No!" Belle screamed, snatching her hand away from Desiree and dropping the keys. "I won't leave you."

"Isabelle," Desiree said, cupping her face. "You have to. Who knows what they'll do if they catch us trying to escape again?"

"And you think it'll be any better if I'm missing? We both go or I stay."

60

"Why are you so stubborn?"

"I learned it from you. Are we going or not?"

Desiree sighed and peeked out the door. The hall was empty. She whispered, "Come on. Forget your things."

"Was planning to."

They rushed down the hall and out the front door. Desiree screamed, "Run faster! My car's this way!"

They picked up the pace and ran through the castle gates. Desiree's car was still there but covered in leaves. She didn't bother wiping her windshield. They jumped in the car and Desiree started the engine. She hit the gas going straight. She drove around the bend of the cobblestone road, her speed increasing as they turned. They cheered as the castle disappeared in the background, somewhat cautiously excited. They continued around the bend only to arrive back at the castle.

"What?" Desiree stopped the car and pulled out her notebook. "There should've been a hill after the roundabout. Did I mess up my notes?"

She drove slowly around the bend, glancing up from her notebook every so often. In the distance the castle appeared again.

"You've got to be kidding me!" Desiree yelled. "How is this even possible?"

"Didn't you say there was a portal?"

"Yes! It shot me out onto a straight road, then you go up a hill and you make it here to the roundabout!"

"Maybe go the other direction? What if you missed a turn?"

"Maybe I did." Desiree u-turned and drove slowly down the road looking for any hidden paths. Nothing. They looped their way around to the castle. Desiree put the station wagon in park. She cupped her face in her hands and sighed.

Belle said, remorseful, "I'm sorry I brought you into this."

"You didn't do anything. It's all dad's fault." Desiree turned off the engine and opened her door. "Better get back before they realize we're gone."

"Right." Belle nodded.

They made it back to their wing of the castle. Esmé was just leaving Desiree's door as they arrived.

"Where did you go?" he asked.

"Uh…" Belle looked at Desiree.

"To the rose garden…" Desiree said, placing her hands on Belle's shoulders. "Or, tried to go there."

"Well, you can't. It's almost 10. You have to prepare for lunch at noon." Esmé walked away. He shouted, "Let's go. I'll show you the rose garden *after* lunch."

Desiree rolled her eyes. Belle snickered as she started walking.

Esmé gave them a rundown of what their meals required. The vegetables were freshly picked from Raoul's garden, no leftover fruits and vegetables were allowed at the end of the day. They had to pick the exact amount they planned to use. They needed a balanced diet and proper portions. Again, no leftovers were allowed. They couldn't make multiple meals at once for the entire day. Raoul had a recipe book Esmé carried with him.

Desiree and Belle cooked while Esmé bossed them around. Of course, that was at Raoul's request. Meal prep proved more daunting than the young women anticipated. That was expected of royalty. It could also be expected that they would make the easiest dishes in the book. They made a pasta salad, garden salad, lemon rice, and soup.

Esmé commanded Desiree to bring Raoul his food. He helped her carry the cart up the stairs and returned to the dining hall to eat with Belle.

Desiree knocked on Raoul's door. "I have your lunch."

"Please enter," Raoul said, sitting up.

Desiree peeked inside as she opened the door. She wheeled the cart into his room and to his bed. "How are you feeling?"

"Much better, thank you for asking."

Desiree placed the tray on Raoul's lap. She remembered Esmé's order to spoon-feed Raoul, and she shivered. If Belle wasn't with her, she definitely would have defied him. "Are you able to eat by yourself?"

"Yes, please join the others for lunch."

"Are you sure? It looks like it'll be a struggle…."

Raoul looked down at his wings. Both arms were horribly wrapped in gauze and strewn in shoulder slings. *When did she?*

Out loud, Raoul said, "Uh…maybe I will. But please, you do not have to if you do not want to."

"It's fine, I *am* the cause of this…."

She stared at the poorly wrapped bandage. She pulled a chair to the side of his bed and grabbed Raoul's wings. "Hold still."

Desiree unwrapped the gauze around Raoul's wings and grabbed the bandages by his bedside table.

How do I even do this? she thought. Wrapping the wings of a small bird wasn't hard for Desiree. But a bird larger than a human, she didn't even know where to start. The only thing she could do was use what she'd learned so far in her nursing program. She picked up the sticks they used to carry him inside and broke them in halves. She pulled Raoul's wings together, causing him to wince, and set the sticks along his wings. Desiree folded his feathers as best she could and wrapped his wings together.

"Sorry, I only somewhat know how to help humans…. Just keep your ar—wings like this and they should heal better…."

"Thank you." He smiled.

Desiree put away the medical items and set the bowl of food on her lap. She lifted the spoon. Her trembling hands scooped up a spoonful of rice and raised it to his mouth.

Raoul was just as anxious as her. One, he had never been fed by anyone before, and two, he was self-conscious over his large mouth. He knew she was terrified of him and barring his fangs wouldn't help his situation. He could never tell Esmé his insecurities about his looks. As the older brother, he did his best to carry the burden for both of them.

He slowly opened his mouth, just enough for her to slip the food in. He looked away from her, hoping she would do the same.

Desiree stared at his fangs. *One bite is all it takes.*

His jaw was stiff, making it difficult to chew. It was sheer agony for them. Esmé and Lady Orchida's plan backfired tremendously leaving one embarrassed and his insecurities at an all-time high and traumatizing the other for life.

***

Esmé returned to the dining hall. Belle had just finished setting the table. He sat down in the chair across from hers and picked at his plate. They ate in silence. The air was unnerving, but neither knew what to say. Although Belle wasn't nearly as judgmental as her sister, the morning's events made her uncomfortable around them again, especially Esmé.

Esmé on the other hand knew Belle was terrified of him. It also didn't help that he sentenced her sister to death. Helping his brother possibly ruined his chances with her.

"Look," he said, staring at his plate. "I'm sorry for how I acted this morning. I shouldn't have given your sister the death penalty."

"Apologies can only go so far," Belle responded. "If you continue to do what you apologize for, it's nothing more than empty words."

"I understand that, but your sister nearly killed my brother. It's irrational to think I would be calm in that situation."

"And yelling is how you cope with it?"

"…Yeah…well, just because it's not happening to you, does not mean you get to invalidate how I feel."

"I'm not 'invalidating' your feelings! You can't just go around threatening to kill people at the slightest displeasure."

"So stealing valuable items, breaking into my castle, and injuring the soon to be king are all minor things to you? We have a kingdom to run, we have laws to uphold. And those are offenses punishable by death! I don't care if it's your sister or some old lady, laws are laws. I'm not some bloodthirsty monster!"

"I never said you were!"

"You act like it!" Esmé screamed. "You don't think my brother and I *know* how you guys feel about us? We do, and it's not right. You're here because of your father's crime. You volunteered to come. We didn't force you. Stop acting like some innocent little flower kidnapped by beasts. If you were going to hate us, you should have stayed home and let your father die!"

Belle's blood boiled. She stood up and stormed out of the dining hall. *How could he say something so cruel?*

Esmé slumped down in his chair and covered his face with his hands. *There goes my chance of breaking the curse.*

He wished Raoul weren't injured. He could have stopped him from arguing. If only he could communicate as well as him. He rested his chin on his fists and played with his food. It had been drilled into him by Raoul to finish his plate, but he just couldn't do it.

***

Desiree shivered as she walked down the hall. She carefully lowered the cart down the stairs. If it weren't for her barely eating the night before, she would have lost her appetite completely from fear.

It was fascinating to look into the mouth of a wolf. But also frightening to imagine he could've bit her arm off if his mood changed.

When she arrived at the dining hall, only Esmé sat at the table. "Where's Isabelle?"

"I don't know," Esmé mumbled, standing up and walking past her. "When you're done eating, clean up this mess and get started on dusting."

"Where are the cleaning supplies?"

"Figure it out yourself!" he snapped.

Desiree waited until he was far away before she tsked. She walked over to the food and saw Belle's plate was barely touched. She had a sinking feeling in her stomach. She ran to Belle's room and burst through the door. "Isabelle!"

Belle was curled up on her bed sniffling, her eyes red and puffy.

"What happened?" Desiree asked, rushing to the bed. She wrapped her arms around Belle.

"I had an argument with Esmé."

"You what?!" Desiree let go of Belle and grabbed her shoulders. "You know you're not supposed to anger them, especially not monkey boy. He could have killed you."

"I don't think he would do that…"

"Isabelle, he attacked dad and put me on death row. He is capable of anything. What did you argue about?"

Belle explained everything from the moment Desiree left to where she was then.

Desiree sighed. "I know it's frustrating staying here, and constantly hearing his want to kill someone, but this is where we're stuck until your sentence is over…. That's assuming they follow their word. I know I taught you to stand up for yourself, and if this situation were any different, I would praise you. You could have been seriously hurt angering him."

"Yeah but…"

"But nothing. Sometimes you just need to suppress your anger. It's not worth losing your life."

Hearing Desiree's judgmental words helped Belle understand what Esmé was talking about. They were treating them like monsters.

"Are you saying this because of how they look?" she asked.

"What?" Desiree responded, confusion on her face. "It has nothing to do with how they look. Beasts or not. The problem is that they've done nothing to prove they aren't violent."

"Like Raoul jumping out a window to save you?"

"That… was different…."

"How so? I mean, if he really wanted you dead, he would've watched. He's literally incapacitated because of you."

"Why are you defending them?"

"I just feel like we're too harsh on them. Yeah, it was basically forced on us, otherwise…death… but after dad and I spoke with Raoul, he explained that he wasn't going to harm me. He'd treat me like royalty, and we're free to roam the castle grounds. They aren't like monsters in movies. They're nice guys…well Raoul is…."

Esmé and Raoul explained to Belle they weren't going to hurt her; there was no excuse for her to be afraid of them. At least Desiree had some justification for her behavior. She hadn't spoken to them before Esmé threatened her. Belle wanted to leave as much as Desiree, but it didn't mean they could simply say whatever came to mind, no matter how mean it was.

"I have to see for myself if they're good or not. I can't take your word. You're sweet and trusting of everyone. I need time to figure that out. But…" Desiree sighed. "I'll…refrain from badmouthing them. Okay?"

Belle nodded.

It would take time for Desiree's opinion to change. She hoped she was wrong. There were little things that conflicted with her thoughts, but it was difficult thinking of them differently. But for Belle's sake, Desiree would try. Desiree excused herself to do her tasks.

Belle promised herself the next time she saw Esmé, she would apologize for treating them like monsters. He, nor Raoul, deserved to be treated the way they were, especially not because of how they looked.

***

Esmé walked through the roses in Raoul's garden. He brushed his hands delicately across the roses as he went by. He walked until he was standing in front of a large oak tree. When he was a child, he begged Raoul to plant a tree. Raoul could never say no to his little brother and reluctantly planted one.

Every day, Esmé waited beside the sprout for it to grow. By the time he was 12, the tree had grown 30 ft. Raoul's garden had the ability to grow plants at significant speeds. It was something Raoul was proud of.

Raoul unfortunately hated the sight of the oak tree. Esmé let it grow whichever direction it wanted to, and it looked unseemly. With the help of Lady Orchida, they built a treehouse for Esmé and brick walls to block the trunk of the oak from being seen in Raoul's garden.

Since the creation of the treehouse, Esmé spent his time there. It was like an escape from reality. No pressure from breaking a curse, he could see villages in the distance, and he could imagine he was a part of society.

Esmé reached the top, and entered his treehouse. He sat on the ledge facing a village and rested his head on his knees. He was definitely sure that his chances with Belle were over. He realized it was wrong to say her father should've died. Esmé and Raoul knew better than anyone else what it was like growing up without parents. And while Raoul did everything in his power to make Esmé happy, and keep his mind off their situation, Esmé still thought about it. He only smiled when Raoul did kind things for him to keep his brother's spirits up.

Belle had already lost her mother, losing her father would destroy her. He understood why she volunteered and thought it was commendable. She came believing she would die to save her father. Whether the real reason was lost in translation, she still had reasons to be scared. He regretted lashing out, but it just angered him how judgmental they were. They wouldn't even give them a chance. Was he that repulsive?

When he was sad, he would always go to Raoul for comfort. He couldn't this time. He knew his brother would be disappointed if he found out what happened. Esmé knew Raoul would take Belle's side, and he couldn't handle another scolding.

He had to fix whatever remained of their relationship. Just enough so the women wouldn't rat on him. He thought about how Raoul would go about fixing it. An image of Raoul bowing a full 90 degrees apologizing profusely flashed in Esmé's mind. He couldn't help but laugh and cringe at the thought.

Esmé didn't believe he was in the wrong, and he thought apologizing was beneath him. But ending the curse was at stake for him and Raoul.

He had to suck up his princehood and utter an apology. It didn't need to be as elaborate as Raoul would've done it, but something was better than nothing. Whether Belle accepted wasn't a concern. In his book, Raoul would be proud he tried.

***

Desiree grumbled as she cleaned the dining hall table. How was she supposed to clean if Esmé was too moody to tell her where the cleaning supplies were? She sighed. She didn't want to ask Raoul for help so she decided the best bet was to look for it herself.

She searched the kitchen and an adjoining room and found the cleaning supplies in a closet. As she dusted the kitchen, Desiree thought about how the path could disappear. It just wasn't possible.

There was no way she imagined her little espionage mission two days before. Her notes were proof that it wasn't just her imagination. Was there magic at play? Did the beasts have that much power they could make entire roads disappear?

She had to see for herself. She spotted a watering can in the supply closet earlier and thought of a good plan to leave the castle. She filled it with water and began watering the bushes that led to the castle gates. When she saw no one was around, she "stealthily" made her way out the gate.

She walked down the roundabout and sure enough she looped back to the castle. Instead of returning, she turned around and went to the foliage that had replaced the road down the hill. She pushed her way through the leaves. On the other side was the rose maze.

"How's this even possible?" she asked.

Desiree turned around and walked along the bushel, peeking every so often through the leaves and finding another part of the maze. She did this until she found her way back to the castle gate.

If they could replace roads with mazes, it certainly was possible for them to have brainwashed Belle. How were they going to survive there for years? The last thing Desiree wanted was for Belle to marry a beast. She shivered at the thought.

Were they going to brainwash her next? She needed to find out how they did it. Was it the food? She doubted it. Since they were now in charge of meals, it wasn't going to be a concern. And the beasts wouldn't give them control of their meals if that was the case.

As she made her way back to the castle, Desiree decided her goal would be to find the method they used to brainwash Belle…. And of course, avoid it herself.

CHAPTER FIVE

Belle x Esmé

Belle paced the halls around the stairs. She hoped to run into Esmé. She wondered if it was okay for her to apologize so soon. He was most likely still mad at her and she had no right to expect him to forgive her so easily.

As Freddy told her, she didn't have to be friends with them, but the least she could do was get along. 6 years in an isolated castle with "people" she hated would be sheer misery.

She waited for 30 minutes. She wanted to go to her room but she didn't want to miss seeing him. Desiree came up the stairs and shook her head.

"Standing there isn't going to make him appear," Desiree said.

"I know, it's just…I don't want to miss him."

"And your apology can't wait? It's only been a couple hours since your fight, you don't have to make up right away."

"You're only saying that because you don't want me near him," Belle mumbled.

"No. I'm only *saying* this because you meandering the halls for him looks sad. But your choice."

Belle stuck her tongue out. "At least I'm trying."

Desiree smiled. "While I may not agree with you 'commingling' with monkey boy, I'm proud of you for standing by your conviction."

"I'm making amends, not befriending him."

"Whatever you say," Desiree said, waving as she walked to her room. "By the way, all of the dishes have been cleaned, rooms dusted, and I've prepped for dinner. Let monkey boy know if you find him."

"Okay," Belle shouted.

She sighed and sat on the top step of the middle landing. Did it really look that pitiful of her standing in a hallway waiting for him? She thought it showed she cared more. That's what they did in anime.

Pointless timelapses of waiting to apologize or talk to someone. It wasn't like Esmé and Raoul had cell phones and she doubted there was any reception for hers.

Just when Belle was about to give up, Esmé walked in, his eyes lowered. Belle stood immediately. The movement in Esmé's peripheral made him look up and they made eye contact.

Esmé's first instinct was to avert eye contact and run away, but he stopped himself midflight.

"I'm sorry," they said in unison. Both were startled by the other's apology.

"What do you have to apologize for?" Esmé asked. "I was the one out of line."

"We both were." Belle walked down the stairs as she spoke. "You were unnecessarily angry; however I had some time to think about it, and your reaction was valid. I can't imagine how I would feel if someone treated me like a monster. It was wrong of us."

"…Then I'm sorry for my behavior up 'til now, and what I said in the dining hall. I never had the chance to grow up with parents, so I can't understand how it feels to lose one. But I would never wish on my worst enemy to be without them. I'm sorry I said your father should die."

"We both said and did some harsh things. Let's just squash it and start over." Belle extended her hand. "I'm Isabelle Holmes. Just call me Belle."

Esmé took her hand. "Esmé Nicolas Bellerose."

They smiled, but the air was still awkward. Neither one could fully get over what the other said, but they hoped through action, they would get along, Esmé secretly longing for more than a possible friendship.

"Did…you ever get to see the rose garden?" Esmé asked.

"What do you me—? Oh! No, the uh chance hasn't come up today."

"After dinner prep, I can show you."

"Desiree already finished preparations. But we can go tomorrow, if you're available."

Esmé nodded. "Then I'll see you and Desiree at 6 in the kitchen."

Esmé wanted to tell Raoul he had made up, but he thought it was weird to go in the same direction as Belle, especially after being rejected. He knew it was normal to let their apologies sink in, but it still hurt his ego a little. Esmé said goodbye and left through the dining room doors. When he entered the kitchen, he opened the window and jumped out.

Esmé walked around the castle until he reached Raoul's window. He grabbed onto the trellis beneath it and climbed. The trellis ended halfway and Esmé had to hold on to small grooves he'd punched into the wall from previous climbing attempts.

He peered over the ledge into Raoul's window. Raoul was in his beast form, staring at his teeth in the mirror. Esmé wondered why. He didn't have guests. Raoul spotted Esmé's green eyes through the mirror and transformed back into a human. Esmé slid the window open and crawled inside.

Raoul turned around and crossed his arms. "How many times must I tell you to not scale the castle?"

"I won't fall," Esmé said, sitting on Raoul's bed. "I have something more important to tell you."

"What?"

"First, promise you won't get mad."

"What did you do?"

"Promise…you won't get mad."

"Okay, I promise, what is it?"

"During lunch Belle and I had an argument…"

"You—!"

"You promised you wouldn't get angry!" Esmé interrupted.

"Esmé, you clearly aren't taking this seriously enough! You could ruin your chance of breaking your curse! How can I *not* be upset?"

"But I didn't, it actually made things better. Please, just listen."

"Fine, what happened next?"

"I apologized, and she apologized for how they treated us, now we have a date tomorrow."

"A what?" Raoul asked, astonished. To think his baby brother would woo a young lady before he could even converse normally with Desiree. It was embarrassing. But nonetheless, he was happy Esmé was a step closer. "As in, you both consensually agreed upon meeting at a certain time, with the intent to further your romantic relationship?"

"Well, no…" Esmé said, looking away. "I don't really know what to call it."

Raoul sighed. "Please don't rush things. I'm sure it's nothing significant, but it is a step in the right direction regardless."

"Are you proud of me?"

"What do you mean?"

"That I apologized and I didn't screw things up."

"Esmé, I'm always proud of you."

"But you've taken their side on everything."

"It's not that I'm choosing sides," Raoul sighed. "I'm trying to teach you to be a proper gentlemen and ruler."

"Why does it matter when I'm not gonna be one?"

"You don't know what the future will entail. If you do become king…I don't want you to become like father."

"I will *never* be like that tyrant!" Esmé grimaced.

Nicolas Alexander Bellerose, former king of Rosaceae, was a power-hungry ruler. He was ruthless, ill-tempered, and used his looks to get whatever he wanted. He selfishly brought Raoul into the world, later neglecting him, only to then, years after, father Esmé. He abandoned both of his sons, leaving them with the burden of fixing his past mistakes.

Raoul hugged Esmé. "Of course not. You're a thousand times better than him. I'm sorry for mentioning him. I just want you to treat others better. Just because we're royalty, does not mean we can walk all over our subjects."

Esmé nodded. "I know…."

"Remember to be a gentleman on your 'date,'" Raoul said, sitting beside Esmé. "Be a good listener, learn about her hobbies, and *watch your temper.*"

Raoul nudged him and continued, "Things are new to her. You have to be patient and understand that she's not going to open up immediately. She's in a new world, with 'creatures' she's never seen before, under the premise that she's a prisoner. Don't lose your temper if she says something insensitive. You have time. Don't rush the process."

"I'll try…"

When dinner time arrived, Esmé helped Belle and Desiree cook. He complained about having the same meal as lunch.

Desiree responded, "If you want something else, cook it yourself."

After finishing dinner, they set the table and this time, he didn't urge Desiree to spoon feed Raoul. She was grateful she didn't have to experience that nightmare again.

When Desiree left with the cart, Belle sat in the seat beside Esmé. He felt so nervous around Belle, maybe it was because they planned to meet the next day.

She smiled and said quietly, "We should pick a time to meet tomorrow."
Esmé's face burned as he replied, "A-any time works for me…."
"How about after breakfast?"

Esmé nodded. Before he could answer, they heard Desiree wheeling the cart down the stairs and Belle rushed back to her seat. While Desiree knew Belle's attempts at befriending Esmé, what Belle failed to tell her was that they were now hanging out together. Belle, of course, didn't want to hide her blossoming friendship with Esmé but she also didn't want to disappoint her disapproving sister. It was obvious, and Desiree certainly didn't conceal it, that she disliked them.

When Desiree turned into the dining hall, the air was so awkward. Esmé's bashfulness, Belle's secrecy, and Desiree's hatred for her and Belle's current situation, made for an interesting dinner. Afterwards, Belle and Desiree said goodnight to Esmé and retired to Belle's room.

"I don't know how much more of this I can take," Desiree complained, plopping on Belle's couch. "If I have to lug that cart up those stairs again, I'm going to go crazy."

"It's only fair you help him…" Belle mumbled. "He did injure himself trying to save your life."

"But it then goes around to Monkey boy. If he hadn't scared me…well, you know." Desiree shrugged. "Besides, Wolf boy wouldn't be injured if they hadn't taken you prisoner."

"Let's…just stop talking about them," Belle said, uncomfortably. "You promised you wouldn't say anything bad."

"You're right," Desiree replied. "I have to break that habit huh? Give me a few more days, and I'll be good."

Belle nodded. Belle could never stay mad at Desiree. She was her favorite sister, and even though they were completely wrong about Esmé and Raoul, Desiree still jumped through an unknown portal to save her.

Belle and Desiree tried to keep positive vibes in Belle's room, but they both knew it was better to separate for the night. Before Desiree left to her own room, she apologized once more to Belle, promising to be civil with Raoul and Esmé.

Belle fell back onto her bed. She couldn't wrap her head around why Desiree couldn't accept them. In her world, she was so accepting of others regardless of appearance. Yet, she couldn't even say one nice thing about Raoul and Esmé, despite Raoul saving her life. Desiree would always thank people, no matter how small their actions were. She wondered if maybe something in their world was changing Desiree's personality. Next to befriending Esmé, Belle made the decision to change Desiree's mind about Raoul and Esmé. She wasn't going to spend 6 years having to pick sides.

***

Esmé stared in the mirror, fixing his collar. He put on his second-best outfit. He didn't want to boast that he was royalty, but he also wanted to show that he was at the same time. He took off the medals Raoul handed to him indiscriminately. Every little achievement Esmé did, he was handed an important medal unrelated to what he actually accomplished. He was still dissatisfied with his clothes. It was too formal and didn't show the real him. He pulled off his epaulets and unbuttoned the top button on his blazer.

As he put in his huggie earrings, a knock sounded on his door. "Come in…. Wait!"

Esmé was worried if Desiree or Belle had knocked on the door. He scrambled to pick up the clothes on his floor and tossed them into his wardrobe. He sloppily made his bed and took a deep breath.

"Don't worry, it's just me," Raoul said, opening the door. When he entered, his eyes automatically fixated on Esmé's relaxed appearance. After their talk yesterday, Raoul was trying his best to not nag Esmé as much. He cleared his throat. "I don't think it's a good idea for you to wear those earrings before transforming…"

"Right…" Esmé said, removing them. "Why are you walking around?"

"My arm is broken, that doesn't mean I can't walk. Besides, I don't think I can handle Miss Desiree bringing my food to me. I don't think forcing her to nurse me back to health is going to make her love me."

"Does this mean you're joining us for breakfast?"

"Yes…" Raoul watched as Esmé plucked off and altered his clothes. After he took his blazer off entirely, Raoul spoke quickly, "If I may offer a suggestion. You should transform into your beast form. What might not look good in your human form, may look differently in your other. Besides…I told you before that your clothes might fit differently, so you should change before putting your clothing on. Last thing either one of us wants, is for your buttons to pop when we see them."

"I hate changing," Esmé grumbled. He winced as his body changed.

74

"If all goes well, it won't be much longer until you don't have to." Raoul smiled.

"I hope so…"

"If I can make one more suggestion…" Raoul said.

In the end, with…many…of Raoul's suggestions, Esmé settled with the original style of the suit, with the exception of the removed medals. Esmé understood that Raoul had his best interest at heart. He wouldn't let him go on a "date" horribly dressed. It was also because Raoul was a stickler for dress codes. He'd spent their childhood chasing Esmé around to put on his "princely attire." So it was natural to Esmé that Raoul would be quick to get him back in appropriate clothing.

Raoul and Esmé made it to the kitchen. Desiree and Belle were already inside preparing breakfast. When both men saw them, they became nervous. Raoul, so used to speaking for Esmé and himself, overcame his nerves and greeted them.

"Good morning," he said, slightly bowing.

"Morning." Desiree glanced at him before continuing to chop vegetables.

Raoul chuckled self-consciously.

"Good morning, Raoul." Belle smiled. "Excuse Desiree. She…isn't a morning person…."

"Of course. I took no offense," Raoul replied.

"Good morning, Esmé," Belle greeted.

"Oh, g-good morning…" Esmé said, averting eye contact.

Belle inconspicuously nudged Desiree.

She sighed. "You healed mighty fast…."

"Yes, for the most part. My arm is broken. But that is not a reason to stay bedridden."

"Sure isn't," Desiree mumbled.

"Does this mean you'll cook again?" Belle asked.

"I do not mind helping, but it really is against the rules for us to cook for…non-royalty," Raoul said. "Oh! But if it is too bothersome, I am sure I can bend the rules…somehow."

"It's fine," Desiree said. "It's what I was sentenced to do, right?"

"Yes, but please do not feel obligated to do so."

Silence filled the room. Desiree wanted nothing to do with them, Raoul struggled with keeping the conversation going, Esmé was nervous about their "date," and Belle wanted to side with Desiree, but was troubled by her rude demeanor.

After a few moments, Raoul collected his thoughts and said, "I do not know how you all have set a system, but I am happy to help wherever."

"No need, Isabelle and I have everything set for breakfast. There's nothing for you two to do."

"Well," Belle spoke quickly, "you could set the table…if you want."

"Yeah, let's just do that," Esmé grumbled, pulling Raoul to the cupboard. They grabbed everything needed in one go, and left.

Belle waited a minute to make sure they weren't coming back. When the coast was clear, she turned to Desiree and pouted. "I thought you said you were going to be civil!"

"Was I not? I spoke to them didn't I? What else can I do? There's nothing to talk about."

"Speaking in clipped tones isn't civil. You can at least try to have a good relationship with them."

"Isabelle, it's been three and a half days. You can't expect me to just open up to them like that."

"Why not? They're nice," Belle said. "You literally make friends with everyone you meet at home."

"Three days is not enough time, especially considering the circumstance we're in." Desiree continued to cook as she spoke, "You're the last person to talk about opening up to people. It takes weeks for you to speak to anyone new. So the question is, why are *you* so trusting of them?"

Desiree couldn't fathom that in three days, Belle's demeanor could change so abruptly. This wasn't the Belle she knew. Her suspicions of brainwashing were slowly being confirmed.

"They just seem different from the people in our world…."

"Because they are different."

"I mean personality wise," Belle said, smacking her lips. "Their energy feels different. Like, when I speak to them, it's genuine. I don't have to worry about what I say or if they're judging me. Despite everything that happened, I feel welcomed here.

"Raoul promised nothing bad would happen to us," Belle continued. "And nothing has—"

"Again, it's only been three days. You can't say, 'nothing bad has happened.' They could be waiting for the right moment for all we know."

"Yeah, but think about it. If they really wanted to, they could've done something day one. We're trapped in a different dimension with no way to escape. Why would they need to devise a plan to harm us?"

Desiree sighed, and moved away from Belle to wash pots. Belle, disappointed her words weren't getting through to Desiree, moved beside her.

"All I'm saying is, I feel like I belong. It doesn't matter how long we've been here. When you know, you know. And I'm willing to get to know them to make my years here comfortable." Belle waited for Desiree to respond. When she didn't, Belle took the pot from Desiree and continued, "I admire you. I loved that you were tolerant of others, I loved that you looked beyond appearance to determine if someone was good. You and dad taught me the importance of getting to know someone first. You've always protected me, and I will always have your back. If…you want me to stay away from them, just tell me, and I will…."

***

Raoul and Esmé hurriedly placed the dinnerware on the table. Raoul could tell Esmé was frustrated but neither one of them wanted to speak first. As they folded the napkins, Esmé couldn't hold back anymore.

"I think we need to let Desiree go home and find another woman."

"What are you talking about?" Raoul chuckled. He knew *exactly* what Esmé referred to.

"She lacks all of the traits Lady Orchida said were needed. She's not going to fall for you. There's not enough time to waste on her."

"You're right, we don't have time. Not one woman has shown up to this castle since father was here. What are the odds they will after her?" Raoul asked. "If not for Freddy, we wouldn't have this opportunity to begin with."

"But she won't even look at you!"

"Lower your voice," Raoul commanded. "They arrived almost four days ago, no one is going to open up that fast. Getting to know someone takes time."

"Time we don't have," Esmé mumbled. "If it takes so long, why am I hanging out with Belle later?"

"…It's different with children. Kids befriend each other quickly, and once you and Miss Isabelle find common interests, it will only deepen your bond. Adults on the other hand, we're apprehensive of others. We prefer to weed out any bad qualities before we get close to them. Kids are more trusting of others. I do not blame Miss Desiree for her skepticism."

"What are you going to do if her behavior doesn't change in a month?"

"We'll just have to wait and see." Raoul shrugged.

"So you're really going to gamble with your life over one woman?"

"I'd rather take the risk with courting her than to wait on a woman that may never come."

"You're always telling me to take things seriously, even the most mundane tasks," Esmé said, solemnly, tears in his eyes. "Yet, when it comes to your life, you act like it's a game."

"Esmé," Raoul sighed. "I am not playing games with my life. Please do not confuse my patience with negligence. For now, I think it's best that you focus on Miss Isabelle. I don't want to stress you any more than I already have."

"I can't not worry."

"Then how about this, focus on breaking your curse. You may check on me ever so often. If things are looking grim in two months, you can intervene. Deal?"

Esmé nodded and hugged Raoul.

As Raoul loosened his hug to speak, the kitchen doors opened and the brothers pushed away from each other. Esmé looked the other direction and quickly wiped his tears.

"Are we…interrupting something…?" Desiree asked.

"Not at all," Raoul replied, sitting down. "We were just… confirming that we set the table properly. It is better to view the table from this side of the room."

"Right…" Desiree nodded slowly. She wheeled the cart with food to the table. "We made ricotta hotcakes topped with bananas and raspberries, panettone french toast with bananas, bacon, and omurice."

"Wow, it looks delicious," Raoul said.

"What's 'omurice'?" Esmé asked.

"It's a Japanese dish," Belle explained. "It's fried rice wrapped in an omelet. It usually has ketchup on it, but you don't have any…or any condiments for that matter."

"Very interesting," Raoul said. "I'll have to look into 'ketchup.'"

"Why'd you make this?" Esmé asked. "Yesterday, you made the same thing, and said that's all you're making."

"Well…" Belle said, sheepishly.

Desiree waited for her to explain. When she realized Belle couldn't, Desiree intervened, "I did want to make something easier, but Belle insisted on something 'fancier.'"

"I thought it would be nice to eat something different… Sorry…" Belle mumbled.

Raoul tapped Esmé's foot with his.

"Uh, no, it's okay. I was just curious. Thank you for the meal…."

"Yes, thank you. Both today's and yesterday's meals are delicious."

Belle sat down across from Esmé and Desiree placed everyone's plates in front of them. When she sat down, they began eating. The only sound made was faint scraping from silver hitting ceramic.

The only person seemingly unfazed by the silence was Raoul. "This 'omurice' is amazing. This is from your world?"

Belle nodded. "A country called Japan."

"And 'ketchup' would make this even better?"

"Yep, it's one of the main ingredients."

"Fascinating. I am curious of the difference in taste." Raoul rubbed under his chin as he thought deeply. "I must acquire this 'condiment.'"

Something about his fascination with omurice and condiments was funny to Desiree and she let out a small laugh before quickly clearing her throat.

Slightly embarrassed, Raoul also cleared his throat. "Well, I shall look into the matter later. Miss Desiree, how was your morning? Did you sleep well in your room?"

Desiree snuck a glance at Belle and smiled. "Yes, it was wonderful. My bed here is 10x more comfortable than the ones at home. How is your arm?"

"Fine, thank you."

Belle and Esmé watched, stunned at their encounter. They looked at each other and smiled. For the remainder of breakfast, Desiree and Raoul held a natural conversation. Belle was proud of Desiree. It looked like her heart-to-heart talk helped Desiree see that they were good peop—animals.

When everyone finished, Desiree cleared the table. Belle whispered to Esmé that she would see him after she cleaned the dishes.

Raoul, overhearing, said, "Why don't you two enjoy your morning? Miss Desiree and I can clean the kitchen and dining area."

"Are you sure?" Belle asked.

"Yeah, totally," Desiree said, beaming with enthusiasm. "Have fun, I'll see you later."

"Okay!" Belle said.

Esmé waited for Belle to leave and gave Raoul a thumbs up. He thought it was strange for Desiree to change in only an hour, but he wasn't going to question it and jinx Raoul's luck.

Esmé exited the dining hall and searched for Belle in the foyer. When he found her, she was in the lounge Freddy had stolen from. She picked up a golden watch.

"I don't mean to bring it up," Esmé said, startling Belle. "But that's the watch your dad stole from us."

"This?" Belle asked. The look on her face was enough to figure out she thought it was hideous.

"Yeah…" Esmé let out. "It's not that nice-looking, but it was my father's so we have to keep it."

"I wonder who my dad would even give this to. No one would like it."

"He said someone, but I don't remember." Esmé shrugged. "Are you ready to go?"

"Yeah."

Esmé nodded and turned towards the door. As reality sank in, he became nervous. They were really hanging out alone. And it wasn't that he didn't acknowledge the other conversations they'd had, but he was more self-aware he'd have to speak to her without Raoul's help. He was rigid with awkwardness, but he forced his body to move.

They made it to Raoul's garden and Belle's face lit up. The garden was more beautiful than Freddy described. The sun shined brightly adding a vibrant ambience to the garden as Belle looked around. The roses were blooming with bursts of colors. Morning dew glistened on the leaves. Rose petals covered the stone path. It looked as if they were walking on a rainbow. The stone path branched off in different directions. Human-shaped topiaries were placed along the path and walls, each with a different gesture and position. As they walked further into the garden, the rose bush walls turned into grey bricks covered in vines and flowers.

"It's beautiful!" she exclaimed.

"Of course, Raoul's worked diligently on it since we were kids."

"Did you help?"

Esmé shook his head. "Gardening's boring."

"Oh…"

Esmé facepalmed wondering why he said that. It was obvious Belle was impressed with the garden. And from how Raoul told a little fib to help him at dinner, Esmé should've learned to pretend he liked gardening. But he just couldn't understand why he had to act a certain way to impress her. The stipulations for breaking the curse was that a woman must love them for who they are, not what she wanted him to be. So why did he need to fake that he liked things he didn't? Why did he have to be perfect at everything? He hoped feigning to be someone he wasn't, wouldn't affect his chances.

"What I mean is…it's not really my cup of tea…. It's Raoul's, so I don't want to impose on his hobbies. But I did help grow that," Esmé said, pointing to his oak tree.

"Wow!" Belle smiled. "Is that a tree house?"

Esmé nodded. "Yeah. I built it when I was a kid, with help of course."

"I've always wanted a tree house, but it's not really possible in the city."

"Well, did…you want to come up?"

"Really?"

"Yeah, and you're welcome to visit any time, even if I'm not here." Esmé led Belle to the trunk of the tree and around to the ladder. "Are you able to climb it?"

"I'm tougher than I look," Belle said, flexing her 'muscles.'

She grabbed onto the rungs of the ladder and started climbing. Esmé grabbed the rope to stabilize it.

"You coming?"

"I'll hold it until you're at the top. Just push the door."

"Okay, thanks."

Esmé waited, with his head down, until Belle shouted that she was inside the tree house. Esmé let go of the rope and took his time climbing the branches to the top. He had to mentally prepare himself to speak casually with her.

Belle walked slowly across the room, absorbing everything around her. Esmé's tree house was surprisingly neat and minimalist. Belle expected there to be nothing but the one window she saw from the ground. But inside was like an actual house, designed like a cabin. The shape of the tree house was round. It was large enough to fit 30 people inside. The furniture, aside from the couch, was made from oak. There was a square wooden table to the left of the door, with 4 chairs on each side. Following the curve of the wall, next to the table, were blue curtains. Next to that, was another window, with the blue couch facing towards it. That window was open and faced the castle. In the middle of the room was a large, round, red and white rug. And to the right of the door, was a play area. It had building blocks, Legos, a foam castle, rainbow foam playmat, a blue and red painted cubby, and a small table with two chairs. On the top of the table, was a pack of crayons, markers, and a stack of paper splashed with colors.

Belle walked to the table and picked up the stack. She glanced at each paper that had been scribbled with crayons. With every page turn, Belle noticed the drawings becoming clearer. The scribbles soon became poorly drawn illustrations of Esmé and another creature. Belle couldn't tell what it was. It couldn't have been Raoul, this beast had all white fur, and looked to be a normal animal, one with limbs that belonged to the same species. She couldn't help but giggle at the drawings. They were terrible, but also adorable.

Esmé took a deep breath before opening the door. When he entered, he caught Belle giggling at his drawings and his face grew hot. He ran over and snatched the stack from her. He scrambled to pick up the ones placed back on the table and apologized.

"I'm sorry, I forgot to clean up…" Esmé threw the drawings in a cubby drawer. "I…wasn't a good artist…."

Belle stifled her laugh and said, "It wasn't bad, really."

"You're laughing at them."

"I wasn't laughing at them, I just thought they were cute. Was the other person in the picture your friend?"

"What person?" Esmé asked, opening the drawer. He looked at the first paper and thought, *Is there no rock Lady Orchida left unturned?*

He had drawn another human, as well as himself as a human, yet Lady Orchida managed to turn even his illustrations into beasts.

"It was only me and Raoul here. I didn't have any friends as a kid…. Not, to sound like a loner or anything…. Just…wasn't allowed…."

"It doesn't sound lonely at all," Belle lied. "If you don't mind me asking, was there a reason why you couldn't have friends?"

"Being royalty has its perks. Like never wanting for anything materialistic, but the downside was that due to some *questionable* actions from my father, Raoul and I had to stay locked away in the castle. We weren't allowed around others."

"So because your dad did something bad, and you two had to pay for it? That's horrible."

"It is," Esmé said. "But it wasn't all that bad. I had Raoul, and he was like a friend to me. I also created the character in the drawings. He was my go-to when I couldn't tell Raoul my thoughts."

"Your imaginary friend."

"Is that what it's called? When you put it that way, it's kinda…"

Picking up on his embarrassment, Belle said, "Don't be embarrassed. It's normal, I had like 2 imaginary friends as a kid. A talking unicorn and a girl named Blue. They used to fight for my attention all the time."

"Is it really normal to have them?"

"Yeah, I don't think there's a kid in both of our worlds that hasn't had at least one. And in any case, you don't have to think about your imaginary friend anymore—"

"I haven't thought about him. You just reminded me about him. He's not around anymore…."

"Well, what I'm trying to say is, you don't have to be lonely anymore. I'll be your friend."

"Wait, really?"

"Of course."

Esmé smiled sweetly. He was happy to have made a friend. "Well, I guess I don't need these drawings anymore."

"Keep them, it'll be like a memory of when you didn't have any. And this…" Belle said, grabbing a sheet of paper and the crayons. She sat down at the table and drew a quick sketch similar to Esmé's, but better, with her and Esmé holding hands. "…will be our symbol of friendship."

"You're just trying to show off," Esmé mumbled.

"No, I'm not! I really meant to draw this so we could have a memory of our first day as friends."

Ignoring her explanation, Esmé asked, "Are you an artist?"

Belle nodded. "I am."

"How long?"

"Since I was 8. I only did it for fun, but when my mom developed cancer, it was the best way to cope with it. Eventually, it became something I love to do."

"What's cancer?"

"Basically, it's when the cells in your body start to grow and won't stop, then it makes you sicker until you die."

"And there's nothing to cure it?"

"I mean, it can be. You can go into remission or something. But they have to do a lot of treatments for you to survive."

"Is that how your mom died?"

Belle nodded. She looked away from Esmé and wiped her eyes.

"I'm sorry," Esmé said, aloud.

"Don't be," Belle said, turning back to him and smiling. "Death is a part of life, and at some point we all have to face it. I miss her, but I know she's watching me from Heaven."

Minutes of silence passed. Esmé didn't know how to change the subject, and he wasn't sure it was okay to do.

Belle eventually spoke up, "Do you want to learn how to draw?"

"I don't think I have the talent."

"No one does in the beginning. My drawings looked worse than yours." Belle moved over and patted the floor next to her. "It'll be quick."

Esmé scooched to the table and grabbed a sheet of paper. Belle's demeanor changed as she directed him on what to do. They spent 30 minutes going over shapes and Belle did her best to explain how shapes worked with art.

While Esmé still wasn't the best artist, he did improve slightly. Belle could at least tell what it was he tried to draw. Even though she knew it was going to be a challenge for Esmé, she suggested they draw Raoul's garden with crayons. Esmé knew he wouldn't do a good job, but he didn't want to bring the mood back down. They grabbed blank sheets of paper, leaned on the window sill facing Raoul's garden, and began drawing. Belle's was certainly more detailed than Esmé's, but he proved to himself, he could draw better than before.

As noon slowly approached, the sunlight shifted partially to where Belle could barely see her paper.

"Do you have any lamps?" she asked.

Esmé shook his head. "Sorry."

"Don't worry about it, we can use natural light." Belle stood before Esmé could process what she said. She pulled open the only curtains that Esmé had intentionally kept closed.

"Wai—!"

Belle squinted as she stared out the window at a village in the distance. Was her mind playing a trick on her? How would it even be possible with the castle's layout? Esmé swallowed and approached her.

"I didn't know there was a village close by," Belle said. "There's no paths leading there, so I thought we were in a secluded area."

"How did you know there's no paths?"

"Uh…" Belle chuckled nervously. If they were going to be friends, she knew she shouldn't hide things from him. "To be honest…Desiree and I tried to escape yesterday. After what happened to Raoul, we made a break for it. I'm sorry."

Esmé sighed wearily. "It's all right. After everything that happened, I don't blame you. Just know, there's magic involved so no matter how much you try, there's no way out."

"I didn't know you guys could do magic."

"We can't." Esmé shook his head. "We didn't choose to put it there."

"Who did?"

"I can't tell you."

"But, does that mean you and Raoul can't leave either?"

Esmé shook his head.

"And you're just okay with that?" Belle asked, concerned. "Why not find a way to break the spell?"

"I don't have a right to be upset about it. It was my fault it was placed to begin with." Esmé leaned against the window and folded his arms. "I feel guilty that Raoul has to suffer for what I did."

"What did you do?"

"I…" Esmé hesitated. He wanted to tell her but he didn't know if it was a good idea to. "I…can't."

"Why not?"

"I've already said too much. Raoul's gonna be mad at me as is. Besides, I don't want to ruin the mood with my sob story."

"You aren't going to ruin anything. You can trust me. I promise I won't tell Desiree and I won't let Raoul know that I know. We're friends now, I won't judge you." Belle placed her hand on Esmé's shoulder. "If you don't want to tell me, that's fine. But I think friends should be open with each other. I told you about my mom and Desiree and I trying to escape. If anything, I already brought the mood down. I doubt it could get any worse."

Esmé sighed. Of course, he couldn't tell her all the details of what happened, but a simple twist of a few reasons wouldn't reveal his curse.

~ ~ ~

It was the Rose Festival, a national holiday that celebrated the blossoming of roses. It was a week-long event that symbolized the first days of spring. On the road that led to the castle, was a small rose garden and every day that week, a set of blue rose bushes bloomed.

The streets during this time were covered in flowers. While the rose bushes by the castle had not bloomed, others around the kingdom usually did a week before. And the villagers decorated their homes with red, pink, yellow, and orange roses. At night, the streets illuminated bright pink, and music could be heard from the castle. It was the second to last night of the Rose Festival and as a customary thing, fireworks filled the skies in every part of the kingdom.

Esmé watched the village from the top of the castle gates. His eyes sparkled with excitement as fireworks exploded in the sky. The castle was at the top of a hill and that made the fireworks seem even closer.

"Let's go, Esmé," Raoul said, jumping from the gate. "It's time for bed."

"Aww, can we watch for 5 more minutes? Pweeeeaasssee?" Esmé asked. He could barely pronounce the words.

Raoul sighed. "Fine, but don't expect me to defend you if Mylan gets upset."

"I won't." Esmé patted the spot next to him. "Hurry, the next one's gonna happen!"

Raoul shook his head and flew up to the gate. Their eyes lit up when a blue firework shaped like a rose covered the sky. It was captivating. Towards the finale, the sky erupted in bright colors. Raoul was moved by the fireworks. Esmé looked elsewhere.

"Do you think we can go down there one day?" Esmé asked, staring at the village.

"Once we break the curse, we can."

"I hope it happens soon."

"Me too." Raoul smiled.

After 10 minutes, the fireworks show ended and Raoul carried Esmé on his back as he flew down. As they landed, Mylan's carriage pulled up in front of the castle. Both boys yelped and hid in the bushes.

"I saw you," Mylan said, exiting the carriage. Mylan was their father's chancellor. He was tall, he had black shoulder-length locs, and bags under his eyes. Since their father's disappearance, Mylan was appointed king until Raoul was old enough to rule. He was an aloof person but had a soft spot for Raoul and Esmé.

"We're sorry," Raoul said, sheepishly as he stepped away from the bushes.

"Don't be." Mylan smiled. "It is a special occasion."

Mylan crouched to their level and reached into his cape. He pulled out two masks, one a monkey and the other a wolf. Mylan laughed. "I thought this would be perfect for you two."

"What is it?" Esmé asked.

"Masks. Look, you do this." Raoul grabbed the wolf mask and put it over his face.

Esmé burst into laughter. "It looks just like you!"

Mylan handed Esmé his mask and said, "I know it's tough staying here. Just bear with it a little longer, okay?"

Raoul and Esmé nodded.

"If nothing comes up tomorrow," Mylan continued, as they walked to the castle, "let us have our own Rose celebration."

"Okay!" Esmé said.

"What's so important about the masks?" Raoul asked.

"Oh…nothing of importance. It's an old folk tale that no one pays much attention to. Now, please go to your rooms."

"Yes, sir," they said in unison.

Esmé jumped in his bed and grabbed his doll. He hugged it and lay down. "Mommy, we're gonna have a fun day tomorrow."

Esmé opened his eyes to Raoul's smiling face. He rubbed his eyes and sat up.

"Are you ready to celebrate Rose Festival?" Raoul asked.

Esmé nodded, still groggy.

"Madame Paquet laid your clothes out." Raoul pointed to Esmé's table.

"Why do I have to wear that?" Esmé pouted.

"'Cause we're princes, we have to." Raoul grabbed his clothes and tossed them neatly on the bed. "Do you know how to transform yet?"

Esmé shook his head.

"That's okay. It should still fit you when we see Mylan."

Esmé dressed and put on his mask. He met Raoul down the hall and they headed outside. Mylan waited for them, but he was in his formal clothing. He crouched when they approached.

"I'm sorry, a disaster has happened towards our southern border. I must leave immediately."

Esmé pouted.

Raoul said, "We understand."

Mylan pulled over a box of handheld fireworks. "Paquet will assist you while playing with these. Stay within her sight. I will return as soon as my duties are finished."

Raoul bowed. "Goodbye."

Esmé still pouted and Madame Paquet tried everything to cheer him up. Raoul approached with the box of fireworks and asked Madame Paquet to light some. When Esmé saw the sparks, his mood changed instantly and he had forgotten about his previous disappointment. They spent hours playing with the fireworks, playing hide and seek, and tag.

At noon, Madame Paquet called the boys over. She fed them lunch then ushered Raoul to his royal lessons.

"But it's the last day of the festival. Can I continue lessons tomorrow?"

"Absolutely not," Madame Paquet said. "It's my duty to ensure you are receiving the proper education. Please make your way to the study room."

"Yes, madame." Raoul sulked.

Madame Paquet smiled and turned to Esmé. "Your highness, you are more than welcome to join us."

"No." Esmé walked past her. "I'll play by myself."

"Yes, your highness. Please stay by the study room or return to your bedroom."

Esmé nodded.

Esmé stared at the wall in his room. He had played with every toy for the past hour, but it just wasn't enough. He wanted to have fun like he was promised. He pulled out his favorite book, *Les aventures de Larun.* While he wasn't the best reader and needed Raoul or Madame Paquet to read for him, he still liked looking at the pictures.

As he flipped through the pages he took notice of Larun, the main character's attire. Esmé smiled and ran to his closet. He put on black clothing, black gloves, a cloak, and his monkey mask. He was going to play as a thief. With this outfit on, it was hard to tell that underneath it was a little furry child.

Esmé ran around the castle taking things…and putting them back later…. He ran into the study room and both Raoul and Madame Paquet gasped.

"Esmé! What are you wearing?" she asked, panicked.

"I'm not Esmé, I'm Larun. Give me your jewels."

Raoul was flabbergasted then snickered. He handed Esmé his pen and a medal from his blazer.

"You must return to the attire I selected this morning!"

"It's okay, Madame Paquet. He can wear it for a while. It's the least we can do for breaking our promises of playing with him."

"But, your highness, Mylan would not allow this!"

"As long as he's changed by the time Mylan returns, we won't tell him," Raoul said. "I'll take all responsibility if Mylan does find out."

Madame Paquet sighed. "Fine. But Esmé, please return his highness' things and play in your room."

"Yes, madame." Esmé, with his head lowered, gave Raoul's things back, and turned to the door.

"We'll play thief when my lessons are over, I promise," Raoul said.

Esmé nodded and closed the door.

Esmé kicked the air and mumbled, "It's so boring here."

He went to the castle gates and climbed to the top. He stood on the top and looked down at the village. "Larun stared at his next target. The Rose Festival. He was the bestest thief in Ro…Rosasee and couldn't be stopped!"

Esmé carefully climbed down, jumped, and ran down the road to the village below.

When he reached the garden, his eyes lit up. There were so many people. He ran to the first person he saw and shouted, "Ha! Ha! Ha! I'm Larun, the bestest thief, give me all your jewels."

The woman laughed and gushed over Esmé. She reached into her tote and handed Esmé a pink rose. She said, "Oh no, Mr. Larun, I don't have jewels but I can give you this."

"Hmm, this will have to do. Thank you for cowapowating."

Esmé ran to every person he saw and asked for a rose. When he collected enough for a bouquet, he quickly ran back to the castle and put the flowers by the study room door. He ran back down to the garden, this time passing the gates into the village.

He saw a group of older kids playing, each wearing a different animal mask. He ran to them and they stopped.

Esmé shyly asked, "C-can I play with you?"

"Sure, we need a monkey anyways," one of the kids said. "We're playing beasts, do you know how to play?"

Esmé shook his head. The kid explained the rules of the game. One kid is the beast, and the other kids had to chase him around and "defeat" him. And the one who defeated him was the next beast, and so on, until everyone had a turn.

Esmé had to sit out the first game but once they were finished, he could join the next one.

At the castle, Raoul boredly scribbled on his paper. Madame Paquet noticed and said, "Your highness, you must pay attention."

"I'm sorry, Madame Paquet. I just cannot focus while everyone else in the kingdom has fun. If I must learn something, can it not be about the Rose Festival?"

"What is it you want to know?"

"The significance of the masks."

"Uh…well…" Madame Paquet averted her eyes.

"Please."

She hesitated then sighed. "It's an old folk tale. Over two centuries ago, it was said that past the Burgavalian border, ravenous beasts dwelled. However, they weren't originally beasts. They were terrible humans that invaded kingdoms, slaughtered everyone, even women and children. They left no one alive in their path."

"Like father."

"…Yes…." Madame Paquet cleared her throat. "One day, the beasts came upon a famished village. They were especially cruel to the villagers. They tortured them endlessly until they died. The beasts continued on their plight and made their way to the village witch's home. She gave them one warning, to leave and never come back. The beasts were incredibly confident to test the capabilities of the witch.

"They slayed her. In her dying breath, she cursed the beasts to suffer the same fate as her village, their appearance and mentality to reflect their true hearts. The beasts grew mad with every day of hunger, and rather than admit their wrongdoing and atone for their sins, the beasts began raiding villages to eat humans. The beasts only attacked humans, yet never their comrades. When word passed about this discovery, humans wore animal masks to avoid being attacked."

"But couldn't they see past that?"

Madame Paquet shook her head. "They were extremely stupid. A paper mask with hand drawn animals was enough to trick the beasts. With no more humans to eat, the beasts eventually starved themselves into extinction, at least that was the assumption humans came up with after their disappearance. As time moved on, less and less people wore the masks. Now, it's become a tradition to wear them during Rose Festival."

"Did you and Mylan hide this from us because you thought we would be offended?"

"You're very intelligent for your age." Madame Paquet chuckled. "Yes, that is why."

"That is not something that would hurt us. It wasn't our behavior that caused this curse."

"You are right, your highness."

It was getting dark and finally it was Esmé's turn to be the beast. He could barely keep up with the older kids. They intentionally lost so that Esmé could have a turn and they planned to go easy on him.

One of the kids grabbed the hem of his cloak and asked, "Isn't it easier to run without this? Here, I'll put it on the wall."

Esmé backed up quickly. "I can't!"

"Why not?"

"My…dad will get mad."

"Fine! But don't cry when you can't run fast and get caught!"

"I won't."

The kids turned around and began counting. Esmé ran and hid behind a fruit stall. The kids searched everywhere for him, when they finally found him, he let out a small "eep!" and ran. The kids laughed and chased him around. The kid from earlier caught up with him easily and yanked on his cloak.

Esmé tried to keep the cloak on but the kid pulled with so much force, he overpowered him. They stopped running and the kids circled Esmé.

"Why are your arms so hairy?" a kid asked.

"Look at his head!" Another pointed.

A man from one of the stalls was watching the kids when the older one pulled off Esmé's cloak. He stormed towards them and yanked off Esmé's mask. "He's a beast!"

"No! I'm not!" Esmé desperately searched around the growing crowd for a friendly face. He saw the woman from earlier, but the happy face she showed him was now one of disgust and fear.

He whimpered, "Help."

"Why are they back?" someone shouted.

"Where there's one, there's more!" another said. "We have to kill it!"

"No!" Esmé gasped.

He pushed past the group of children and ran. He didn't know his way around the village, and while playing with the children, he moved further and further away from the castle gates. And at every turn, he was met with fear or disgust. Villagers hurled insults at him, calling him a "monster," "beast," or "thing." More people joined the mob that chased after him until it seemed like the entire village was against him.

"I'm not a monster!" he shouted. He thought, *Someone help me! Please!*

Madame Paquet, still feeling bad for telling Raoul the origins of the masks, dismissed him earlier than she originally intended.

When he left the room, he spotted the bouquet of flowers and his stomach dropped. Either Mylan came home and caught Esmé dressed as a thief or Esmé went somewhere he shouldn't have. "Esmé!"

"What's wrong?" Madame Paquet asked.

"Look." Raoul showed her the roses. "I don't think Mylan is home yet."

"Your highness?!" Madame Paquet shouted. "Your highness, you search upstairs, and I will search here and around the castle."

Raoul nodded and ran. They searched everywhere and Esmé was nowhere to be found.

"I think he's in the village," Raoul said. "I have to find him!"

As Raoul ran to the gates, Mylan's carriage pulled up. He flagged him down and explained what happened. Mylan, as panicked as them, ordered Raoul to search from the sky and he would search from his carriage. Madame Paquet was to stay behind and continue searching the castle for him.

Raoul was frightened to fly. The highest he had flown was to the castle gates. There was no way he could fly in the sky. He sighed and ran back to the castle. He ran to the top of the castle tower and climbed out of the window.

"Be careful," Mylan shouted.

Raoul gave him a thumbs up and jumped. He struggled to stay in the air. As he plummeted towards the ground, Mylan ran underneath and stretched out his arms to catch him. Raoul managed to steady himself before reaching the ground.

"I got it!"

"Hurry! I will catch up to you soon!"

Esmé ran as hard as he could but his legs were giving in. He turned a corner and ended up at the dead-end of an alley. With his back against the wall, the villagers filled the alley.

The villagers picked up rocks. "We have to move quickly; it could call for more!"

"We're not going to let you beasts kill us!"

Tears streamed down Esmé's eyes. "Please, I'm not a monster!"

"Liar!"

The first villager threw a rock, only missing Esmé by an inch. Empowered by his throw, more villagers threw rocks. Esmé cowered, covered his head, and closed his eyes.

After a moment, he opened his eyes. He gasped as he stared at the figure in front of him that took the blows. "Raoul!"

"I told you! Only more are going to come. This thing is calling them!"

The villagers threw more rocks and Raoul endured the pain. Through gritted teeth he said, "Esmé, you gotta climb over the wall and run. The castle isn't far from here."

"I don't want to leave you!"

"You have to, it's only going to get worse."

"I can't," Esmé cried harder.

"You need to be brave. Don't worry about me."

Esmé's legs trembled. There was no way he could run away. Even if he was willing to leave Raoul behind, his legs wouldn't take him far. He hugged Raoul from behind and cried.

The villagers called them nasty names, they threw anything within reach, and shouted how much they wanted them dead.

The man who snatched Esmé's mask off, grabbed a shovel and stormed towards them. The man swung back to gain momentum, Raoul pushed Esmé backwards and crossed both wings above his head.

A loud, powerful voice rung through the madness. "Enough!"

The villagers stopped throwing objects and looked in the direction the voice came from. Mylan, looking disheveled, walked swiftly from his carriage. Something in his mannerism was different from what Raoul and Esmé had seen. It was a kind of power and intimidation that halted the villagers and temporarily erased their rage.

"What is going on here?!" he shouted.

"Your majesty! Beasts are invading!"

"The beasts are nothing but fairy tales," Mylan said. He quickly made eye contact with Raoul and continued, "These 'beasts from Burgavalia' were eradicated centuries ago, cease your anger…."

"Can you stand?" Raoul whispered.

Esmé nodded.

"Good. Climb on," Raoul said, kneeling.

Esmé did as told and Raoul flew over the wall without anyone noticing their departure. His wings hurt too much to fly farther, so he ran. Esmé tightened his arms around Raoul's neck and buried his face in his back.

When they made it past the first set of castle gates, Raoul moved off the path into a thicket of trees and sat down. They ran for a long time through the village and still had a mile to trek uphill to the castle.

Out of breath, Raoul asked, "Are…you okay?"

Esmé didn't respond. His face slowly contorted as he looked at Raoul's injuries. His head was covered in blood, and he couldn't open his right eye. Unable to hold it any longer, Esmé burst into tears and hugged Raoul. "I'm sorry!"

"Don't apologize," Raoul's voice quivered. Tears slowly streamed from his eyes and he reciprocated the hug. "It's not your fault."

"I just wanted to play," Esmé sobbed.

"I know."

"Why do they hate us?"

"People hate what they can't understand."

"Are we really monsters?"

"No…"

"Why did they treat us like one?"

"Esmé," Raoul said, moving Esmé away to look him in the eye. He sniveled. "*We* did nothing wrong. This is something that I can't explain, but we aren't monsters and we never will be. Anyone that hurts *us*, is the monster."

Raoul stumbled to his feet and continued, "Come on, we're almost home."

"I can walk," Esmé said, wiping away his tears.

Raoul opened an area of the thicket. His body transformed back into his beast form once he was in the open. Before, although he didn't like it, he didn't mind being a chimera. He knew someday it would all be over. But changing back that night, his heart hurt even more and he dreaded the moment anyone saw him. Raoul and Esmé walked slowly up the hill holding hands. They could hear galloping and wheels fast approaching from behind. Their stomachs lurched. Did the villagers really track them all the way to the castle? Raoul squeezed Esmé's hand and started running.

"Boys, wait!"

They looked back and saw Mylan hanging outside of his carriage.

He pulled beside them and opened the door. "Take it easy the rest of the way."

"I don't want to get your seats bloody," Raoul said. "I can walk."

"Get in," Mylan demanded.

When Raoul sat down, Mylan reached out and lifted his chin. He tsked and gritted his teeth. "I should charge everyone involved with assault to a member of the royal family!"

"No, it's all right. I'm fine…" Raoul gently moved Mylan's hand away from him. "Let's not make a bigger deal out of this."

"Why not?" Esmé grumbled. "They deserve to be pummished for what they did…."

Raoul stared at Esmé. "Uh, well, we don't want them to know we're royalty. The point of us staying hidden was for us to have a fresh start. Telling them we're related to royalty will only raise more questions."

"You're correct," Mylan said. "I'll have to figure out another way to deal with this."

When they arrived at the castle, Madam Paquet rushed to Esmé. "Your highness, please do not worry me like this again!"

"I won't," he mumbled. He brushed past her and went to his room.

He played with his doll's hair, not really thinking about anything. He heard a knock at the door. "I don't feel like twansfoaming."

"It's me," Raoul answered, opening before Esmé could respond. "Mylan is summoning the sorceress that's helping us. He wants her to check our wounds."

"I don't want to twansfoam."

Raoul sighed and closed the door.

A moment later, Raoul knocked again. "I'm coming in."

Raoul opened the door. Accompanied by him was a beautiful woman in an elegant dress. Esmé braced himself to change but when he didn't he gave her a confused look.

"A curse as weak as yours does not affect me." She smiled. "Come, let me see your wounds."

"I'm fine," Esmé said. "Raoul was hurt."

"I've already tended to his wounds." She gestured to Raoul.

His injuries really were healed. Raoul looked as if nothing had happened, in fact, he even looked healthier than before.

Reassured that Raoul was okay, Esmé got out of bed and approached Lady Orchida.

She crouched and asked, "Where does it hurt?"

"My legs."

She had Esmé turn around a few times, checked his head, and said, "My, it really is only your legs." Lady Orchida tapped her wand on his legs.

"Wow! It worked!" Esmé exclaimed.

"Of course, I am the most powerful being in the world."

"Even more than Raoul and Mylan?"

"Much more." She winked. She stood and continued, "It's late. Raoul please tuck Esmé in, and head to bed yourself."

"Yes, madame." Raoul bowed. He waited until the door closed and led Esmé to his bed.

"Will you sleep with me?" Esmé asked, lying down.

Raoul glanced at the door with a concerned look. He smiled and lay next to Esmé. "Sure."

"Was dad really a bad person?" Esmé asked.

Raoul's lips pursed. "He…did some very bad things…"

"Like what?"

"I'll…tell you when you're older…."

"How come we're being pummished for it?"

"It's not that we're being punished for his actions, more like we were born because of them."

Esmé grew teary-eyed. "Does that mean we're bad people?"

Raoul panicked. "Don't cry. I phrased that wrong. You're not a bad person. What I mean is… I'm sorry. I don't know how to answer that. Just know, we aren't bad people."

"Is that why we're monsters?"

"We're not monsters. Look at me," Raoul said, lifting Esmé's head. He stared into his eyes. "You and I are human, we aren't monsters. What you see in the mirror when you wake up is what you are, not what we are around others. Our beasts are a reminder of what we have to do to break father's curse on us. It doesn't reflect our hearts, and we should never let it. Okay?"

Esmé nodded and soon, he was fast asleep.

A bright light shined in Esmé's face and he woke up. Through squinted eyes, he watched Raoul's figure transform into a beast and closed the door.

"Raoul?"

He swayed out of bed and to the door. He could see only Raoul's tail as he followed him. He peeked around each corner to make sure Raoul didn't see him. Raoul turned a corner too quickly and Esmé lost him. He searched the halls until he found Raoul outside of the lounge area. He leaned against the wall as quietly as he could. Esmé walked slowly down the stairs and approached him.

He whispered, "What are you doing?"

Raoul raised his finger to his lip and Esmé covered his mouth. They listened quietly. In the lounge Mylan, Madame Paquet, Monsieur Paquet, and Lady Orchida discussed something Esmé couldn't understand.

"But what will they do?" Madame Paquet asked, alarmed. "Surely you don't mean—"

"I do," Lady Orchida said. "There are too many risks if they stay connected to the kingdom."

"But—!" Madame Paquet started.

Mylan sighed. "Paquet, we must listen to her advice. I do not like it no more than you do, but if it will help them, then we must do it. I say we leave tonight before things are complicated."

"Can I not stay with them? They are too young."

Lady Orchida shook her head. "They deserve time to not transform in their own home. And at any day now, a young lady may arrive."

"How can she arrive if the castle is sealed off?" Madame Paquet exclaimed.

Esmé gasped and covered his mouth.

"What did I tell you about eavesdropping?" Mylan reprimanded.

Raoul motioned for Esmé to remain quiet and walked into the room. "I apologize. I was worried."

"Regardless, you cannot listen to conversations you were not invited to." Mylan moved his locs out of his face in a frustrated way. "Return to your room immediately."

"Wait," Lady Orchida said. "I think it's fair he, and Esmé, listen to plans concerning their future."

At the sight of Esmé emerging from around the corner, Mylan seemed as if he was going to pull out his hair. "How can we trust them to look after themselves, when they can't even stay in bed?"

"I know you are concerned," Lady Orchida said. "But with the event that took place earlier, it is not wise to give them access to the rest of the kingdom. Besides, who's to say the village doesn't one day storm the castle looking for them? I know you all are worried about their livelihood, but we must ensure they have lives to worry about."

"If I'm not mistaken," Mylan said. "Did you not agree to erase the village's memories of what happened?"

"I did, however, what is the point of erasing their memories, if the possibility of Esmé returning is still high, or that a child not suited for breaking their curse makes their way to the castle? You cannot be sealed away with the castle, don't forget you are king."

"Then why can't I stay?" Madame Paquet asked. "I have no nobility status, no power. I'm nothing more than a nanny. I have seen both his highnesses grow since the day they were born. I don't think it's fair to remove me from their lives."

"Again, Madame Paquet, if a young lady were to arrive at the castle and see two humans living among two presumed beasts, do you think she could never discern that they too were human? It is too risky. If you cannot leave them, then the option I gave to the rest of the staff still stands."

Madame Paquet looked to her husband and he nodded.

He said, "We'll discuss it."

"Thank you for understanding."

"Is it my fault they have to leave?" Esmé asked.

"No," Raoul reassured him.

"Then why can't they stay?" Esmé cried.

Mylan looked away from him.

Madame Paquet cried and rushed to him. She hugged him. She wiped his tears. "We have to listen to Lady Orchida. Don't worry, the moment your curse is broken, I'll be back. Okay?"

"But I don't want to lose anyone. I'll be good. I won't play anymore; please don't leave me."

Seeing Esmé cry made the feelings Raoul had bottled up finally erupt. He covered his face and cried silently.

"Let's leave now," Mylan's voice croaked. Keeping his head up, he walked past Raoul and Esmé, tapping Madame Paquet on the shoulder as he went.

"Please don't leave!" Esmé begged, grabbing onto his pant leg.

"Esmé," Raoul said, solemnly. He shook his head.

Esmé let go of Mylan's leg and looked down. They followed the adults out of the castle. Monsieur Paquet climbed in the driver's seat and Madame Paquet into the carriage.

As Mylan entered the carriage, Raoul said, "Thanks for being here and for everything you've done for us."

Hidden in his voice was pure sadness. It was something most could not hear, but as Mylan had helped raise Raoul since he was an infant, he knew when Raoul was bottling his emotions in.

Mylan stepped out of the carriage. He dropped to his knees and hugged both Raoul and Esmé. "Be strong. When it seems as though everything is turning dark, remember that light will always find its way to you. If it takes 1 year or 10, you'll find your light."

As Raoul and Esmé watched them ride off, Lady Orchida appeared behind them. "It's time for bed."

She led them to Esmé's room. He was too distraught to sleep alone so Raoul offered to stay with him. Lady Orchida tucked them in.

"Sleep tight. When you wake in the morning, I will not be here. You two must learn to live on your own—"

"Can you stay with us?" Esmé asked.

"I wish I could, but I live too far away," she replied, softly. "I have a little one, smaller than you that needs someone to take care of her."

"But why can't she live here?" he asked.

"Well, there are a lot of reasons why she can't," she said. "The most important being that she, nor her siblings, can find out the truth behind your curse. Or you may never break it. And I'm sure you wouldn't want to have to walk around all the time as a beast, would you?"

Esmé shook his head.

"I do have one concern," Raoul said. "While I believe I'm capable of taking care of Esmé and myself, what are we to do when a situation does need an adult's guidance?"

"You raise a great question." Lady Orchida cupped her hands together and with tight fists pulled her hands apart revealing 3 rose necklaces. The first purple, the second green, and the last white. She handed one to both of them and placed the third around her neck. "If you ever need anything, tap the rose and tell me, and I will arrive as soon as I can. Does that sound fair, Raoul?"

He nodded.

By this point, it was around 2 a.m. and Esmé could barely keep his eyes open. Lady Orchida took the pendant from his hand, and replaced it with his doll. She said goodnight, and left through a portal.

A single tear rolled down Esmé's right cheek as he continued to stare at the village. "I caused everyone we loved to be forced out of our lives. Can you believe all of that happened because I wanted to play and make friends? I felt so guilty for the longest time and even now, sometimes when I look at Raoul, I feel bad. For a while, it was sad being alone with Raoul, but now, I don't mind as much. As long as I have him, I know I'll be okay."

Esmé heard tiny sniffling and turned to Belle. She cupped her face and sobbed uncontrollably.

"B-Belle! It's not that sad, really," he stuttered. He didn't know how to handle someone's emotions. He wiped his face vigorously. "I'm over it. See? It was so long ago, I'm fine…."

"But…who does that?"

"Huh?"

Belle dropped her hands from her face and, through teary eyes, looked Esmé in his eyes. "It wasn't your fault your dad did terrible things… So why did they blame it on you?!"

Belle wailed even louder. "It's wrong to treat you differently and like a monster because your dad was one. It's not fair!"

"That's just the way things are. If everything goes okay, in a few months when Raoul inherits the throne, we can undo everything my father did. It's okay, we're both fine!" Esmé panicked. "Belle…I-I didn't mean to make you cry. I'm sorry. Please stop crying."

Belle continued to sob. "I can't."

Esmé led Belle to the couch. Once she was settled, he sat on the floor with his knees to his chest. "Great, I made my first friend cry."

He turned away from Belle, his shoulders slumped. They sat silently for what felt like an eternity.

Esmé finally lifted his head. "I'll be right back."

He jumped out of the tree house and ran to the kitchen. When he entered, Raoul stood by the sink, staring at the ground.

"Are you okay?" Esmé asked.

"Huh?" Raoul snapped out of it.

"You okay?" Esmé repeated.

"Yes, of course. I am fine." Raoul's eyes looked glazed over as he spoke. He turned to toss his rag in the sink before glancing at the clock. "Ah! It's almost noon?!"

"Yeah, are you sure you're okay?"

"Of course, I already said I was fine. How was your 'date' with Belle? Why are your eyes swollen?"

"I'm okay. We're still hanging out. I just came to get her some water."

"Is *she* okay?"

"Sort of, we were talking about sad stuff and she started crying and hasn't stopped."

"Did you say something mean to her?"

"No, we were just talking about her mom and stuff and she got sad. We're actually friends now." Esmé grabbed a glass from the cupboard and filled it with water. "How did clean up go with Desiree?"

"Like how you'd expect it to go with her…" Raoul chuckled awkwardly. "But don't worry about me, please bring Miss Isabelle the water."

"Okay," Esmé said, concerned. He knew something was wrong, but he knew pressing Raoul to speak would only cause him to shut down more.

They parted ways and Esmé took one last glance at Raoul before returning to his garden.

Belle climbed down the last rung and took the glass from Esmé. Her eyes looked 10 times worse than Esmé's. "Thank you."

"Are you done hanging out?"

Belle nodded. "Crying made me really tired. I can't keep my eyes open."

"I understand, please get some rest." Esmé reached out to take the empty glass from Belle.

She handed it to him and walked away.

"Belle! I'm sorry for making you cry!"

"You didn't make me cry, and I'm glad you shared something so personal. I think that means we're on the path to becoming good friends. Please let Desiree or Raoul know I'm taking a nap, so I won't eat lunch."

"Okay, sweet dreams." Esmé waved.

Esmé returned the glass back to the kitchen and sighed. He hadn't planned on telling her something so deep. He could *never* tell Raoul what really happened. Esmé knew he'd get lectured for giving away something so important. Raoul wouldn't have cared if Esmé left out that they were being chased for being beasts and not who their father was, he didn't tell her the stipulations of the curse, or that they were cursed to begin with. But, Raoul was an overly cautious person, and worried since they were younger that Esmé would somehow spill his secrets.

Esmé shook his head. *No, I didn't do anything wrong. He won't know and I'm sure Lady Orchida won't snitch on me.*

Esmé walked to their side of the castle. Raoul was standing in the hall, staring blankly at the bedroom door.

Esmé thought, *Okay there is something up!*

He called out to Raoul and he looked up. Raoul smiled like usual and inquired about how Esmé's date went.

Esmé wanted nothing to do with the small talk. Esmé knew Raoul like the back of his hand. When Raoul was upset, he became absentminded. When he lied, he spoke formally to Esmé, and if he overly smiled, he was hiding something.

Esmé pushed Raoul into his room and closed the door.

CHAPTER SIX

Desiree x Raoul

Desiree, with her head buried in her pillows couldn't stop thinking about what happened after Esmé and Belle left.

Desiree smiled brightly as Belle left the dining room. The moment she disappeared from sight, her smile dropped. She rolled her eyes and grabbed the cart from the corner of the dining hall. She forcefully dropped items from the table onto the cart.

As she did so, Raoul waited patiently on the other side of the table. While he was used to speaking for himself and Esmé, something about speaking to a woman, alone, frightened him. Desiree finished loading the cart and wheeled it to the kitchen.

Raoul followed behind her. "I-is there something I can help with?"

"Nope, I got it." Desiree tossed the dishes in the sink and scrubbed the counters and island.

Raoul glimpsed around the kitchen. It seemed both Desiree and Belle were the type to clean after they finished eating. It looked like more than Desiree could clean alone. He walked by her and began picking up pots. He put the dirty pots in the sink and unused pots back in the cabinet where they belonged. He grabbed a plate from the sink with his right arm, set it on the counter, and wiped away. With his left arm broken, he was embarrassed by how much time it took to clean one plate.

Desiree did her best to ignore him, but every scrape, every clink, every woosh of water, made her angrier and angrier. Fed up, she slammed the towel on the counter. Her body trembled with rage, until she could no longer hold it in.

"I said, I can do it myself."

"But—"

"I really don't need your help. Please leave."

"I know you do not need my help, but if we work together, you will be able to enjoy your free time."

"'Free time?' What free time?" Desiree asked. "You mean staying in my room until you need me to do some menial task?

"Miss Desiree, that is not what I mean. There is no need for you to stay in your room. There is plenty to do and enjoy here—"

"Look, my idea of free time, is being home with my little sister. Not in some faraway kingdom where I don't belong."

"I apologize, but that is not an option as of now…" he said. "Miss Desiree, there is a recreational building behind the castle. You are free to move around and partake of the facilities."

"Is that how you're brainwashing Isabelle to like you? That recreational building? It's not going to work on me."

"Miss Desiree, that is not our intention…"

"Cut it with the formalities already; I don't believe you! You threatened my father. You imprisoned my sister. I don't believe you. You are nothing but monsters! The nice guy act might work on my naïve little sister, but it's not working on me. Like, how *sick* do you have to be to give us a false sense of security, if you're only going to kill us in the end? Just get it over with already!"

"Miss Desiree, I'm not '*faking*' anything. I truly want to help. We're not monsters. Yes, you both have to serve minimum sentences, but that doesn't mean we have to treat you as prisoners."

"Stop! You can't fool me! Your nice guy act really ticks me off. Constantly telling us we're going to die then in the same breath, say that we aren't treated like prisoners. Do what you wish. Just get it over with, you freak of nature!" Desiree stopped to catch her breath. She knew she messed up and had said too much, but there was no going back now. 'Calmly,' she said, "If you want to be a 'nice guy' then finish this by yourself."

Desiree stormed out of the kitchen, leaving Raoul an empty mess from her words.

***

Desiree groaned in frustration. "I'm so stupid. Why did I do that? He's gonna tell Isabelle. I just know it."

She had no control over her emotions and snapped. Desiree couldn't understand why she had done so. She was usually the kind of person to not let things upset her. But the moment she stepped into their world, she felt like she was becoming a different person.

"What's happening to me?" Desiree groaned, fussing with her hair. "It's probably their fault."

Desiree glanced at the clock and sighed. "Better go make lunch…."

Desiree got up and opened her door. Belle was just opening hers to enter.

"You ready for lunch?" Desiree asked.

Belle shook her head. "No. I'm taking a nap."

Belle turned to Desiree and Desiree gasped. She lifted Belle's face. "Oh my gosh, are you all right?"

"Yeah, I'm fine. I thought about mom."

"Oh Isabelle," Desiree said. "I miss her too."

"It's not fair," Belle said.

"I know, Belle. Life isn't fair, but we do the best we can. Mom's in a better place. As they say, 'death is where our life really begins and our life now is the punishment.'"

"Is that why people have to suffer because of someone else's actions?"

"What do you mean?"

"Like, let's say dad did something terrible, and everyone blamed us for it? Is that an example of life being a punishment?"

"Isabelle, you don't like it here, do you?"

"I would rather be at home. But under different circumstances, I really do like it here," Belle said. "There's so much I want to explore in the castle and kingdom. I still need to see the recreational building, but I told you earlier, I like it here."

So that isn't their method for brainwashing, Desiree thought. She sighed. "Isabelle, go get some rest. I'll leave leftovers in the fridge for you."

Belle nodded, and went to her room. Desiree made her way to the kitchen.

***

"What happened?" Esmé asked, folding his arms.

"I do not know what you mean…" Raoul responded.

"You know exactly what I'm talking about."

"I really do not."

"Why are you acting so glum?"

"Esmé, I don't want to talk about it."

"It was Desiree, right?"

Raoul rested his chin on his hand, and looked away.

"I knew it. Rather than shut down, just tell me what happened. I tell you *everything* that happens between Belle and I." Esmé stepped in front of Raoul and bent over to eye level. "Why can't you confide in me? Even just this once?"

"Esmé," Raoul sighed. "I can't tell you, because I don't want you to overreact."

"I won't, well, I'll try my best not to…. Of course, I'll be upset. Family sticks together. Just tell me what happened."

Raoul sighed. He recapped everything from when Esmé left to them meeting again in the kitchen.

Esmé threw his arms in the air. "*This* is why I said we're better off finding another woman! She's a terrible person! Who says that to someone?!"

"Esmé, it's not that big a deal. To normal humans, that's what we are."

"We are 'normal humans,'" Esmé said. "Belle doesn't think we're monsters, or 'freaks of nature,' whatever that means."

"You don't know what she thinks."

"I do, we talked about it earlier. She knows we're 'beasts' but she doesn't think we're monsters. There's a difference. I know you want to try with Desiree, but she's just not the one."

"We don't have time," Raoul mumbled.

"Lady Orchida can do anything. I'm sure she can find a woman."

"We will talk about it later." Raoul stood and walked to the door. "We have to prepare lunch."

Esmé was speechless. He always imagined his brother as this strong-willed guy that knew when to step up. Yet, he was letting a woman mistreat him in his own castle, on the land he was soon to rule.

Esmé spoke soundlessly until the words finally found their way to his mouth. "You're still going down there?"

"Yes," Raoul said, averting his eyes. "Miss Isabelle is waiting for you. We also have to uphold our end of the arrangement."

"Don't go down there! Don't worry about Belle."

"Your future is my main concern, Esmé," Raoul said. He faced the bedroom door and spoke to it, refusing to look at Esmé. "Don't ruin your chances with her because you're upset about me."

"I said not to worry about her because she's taking a nap! Just let Desiree sit down there alone. If that's what she wants, let her have it!"

"You know that goes against everything Mylan taught us."

“Then let me go!”

“Esmé, you can’t control your emotions. Just like you’re upset that she ‘hurt’ me, do you think Miss Isabelle would be okay with you yelling at Desiree? Is that not what caused your first argument in the first place?”

“Then let’s figure something out, but do not go down there.”

“Then how are we to inform her that no one’s coming to lunch?”

Esmé scanned Raoul’s room. His eyes locked on to Raoul’s desk and the pen and paper on top of it. “Write her a note, and I’ll bring it down.”

“I will write and deliver it myself. You’re too worked up to do anything. That’s our compromise. I won’t talk to her, and *you* do the same as Miss Isabelle, and take a nap.” Raoul walked over to his desk and began writing.

“I’m not taking anything. I’ll wait here until you come back,” Esmé said, lying in Raoul’s bed.

Raoul nodded, and sealed the note in an envelope. He opened the door.

“You better come right back, or I’ll really be angry!” Esmé shouted.

Raoul smiled, genuinely this time, and closed the door behind him. He took a deep breath. His body trembled as he walked down the hall. He moved swiftly down the stairs to avoid any chances of Desiree seeing him. Raoul could *never* tell Esmé, but he had given up completely on Desiree. He knew there was no hope of her liking him. No matter what he did, she still thought of them as nothing more than monsters.

He knew there was no time left to find another woman. It was only on sheer luck that they found Belle and Desiree. He would rather Esmé worry about him courting a difficult woman, than him trying desperately to find a woman and failing. That would be more discouraging than seeing Raoul waste away on one woman. It was also for Esmé and Belle’s sake that Desiree stayed. Raoul believed it was because Belle had someone she could trust on her side, that she could open up to Esmé so quickly. He also knew Desiree would fight tooth and nail to bring Belle home with her. Raoul’s heart would never change to anything malicious towards Desiree; he wasn’t that kind of person. But he knew for his heart’s, and self-esteem’s, sake, he would keep Desiree at a distance.

He opened the kitchen door and his heart dropped in his stomach.

Desiree stood at the counter island skinning red potatoes. She glanced up at him, and continued working on lunch.

He unconsciously crumpled his note. When he realized what he'd done, he thought it was better to tell her directly than passing on a note anyways. He was too anxious to speak. That's what caused her to lash out.

Before he could muster the courage to speak, Desiree mumbled, "I'm glad at least one person is here. Isabelle will not be joining us, so I guess it's you, Esmé, and I."

"Esmé's not joining either…" Raoul said, quietly. "I also ca—"

"So, it's just you and me? If that's the case, we better get started on lunch," Desiree said, unable to hear Raoul. She glanced up at him. "I could really use your help."

"A-are you sure, mi—" He cleared his throat. "Are you sure, Desiree?"

"Yes," she replied. "Also, you don't have to change the way you speak because of me."

"I don't want to do anything you don't like."

"I'm…sorry for what I said earlier. And I know it's not an excuse, but I don't know what came over me. I should've never said what I said. The way *I* acted was disgusting, not you guys. You're fine as you are. You're not a freak of nature."

Raoul smiled wearily. "Don't be, there's truth to what you said. We are monsters…"

"You're not monsters." Desiree sighed. "If anything, Isabelle and I are. We're in your world and *we* look completely different. Y'all should treat us like monsters."

"We'd never treat you as monsters." Raoul smiled, a little more comfortable around Desiree. Now, he didn't fully forgive her from her apology, but if she really meant it, what harm could come of it? "You two aren't the first humans we've seen."

"So humans have been here before? Where are they now?"

"Oh! I'm…" He didn't mean to slip up. He thought of a good explanation. "This was almost 20 years ago when my father was king. He used to allow a select few from your world to travel to ours. After he left, the portal was closed."

Desiree nodded slowly. She didn't know the context for anything he said, but it would explain why there was a random portal in the middle of a Wisconsin highway. She could tell Raoul didn't want to continue on the subject and she wanted to move on with lunch.

"Um, I know you don't like leftovers and food should be fresh, but I figured since Isabelle and Esmé aren't coming, we should leave their lunch in the fridge. If they wake up before dinner, I don't want them to starve."

"That's fine. I understand."

"I'm making one of Isabelle's favorite dishes my mother used to make to cheer her up. If Esmé's feeling unwell too, why not make him his favorite meal?"

Hearing Desiree care about Esmé's wellbeing made Raoul happy. He thought maybe what happened in the morning was just a fluke and that he pushed her to snap not listening to her plea to be alone. He partially opened his heart to the idea that maybe he still had a chance.

"I will make Esmé's. But we must also make sure lunch is well-balanced."

"Of course…"

Desiree made sliced potatoes, seasoned with garlic, salt, and basil, baked, and topped with cheese before baking again until the cheese was melted. Raoul made Esmé's favorite dessert, cherry soufflés. Esmé had a sweet tooth, and Raoul knew if he didn't enforce a well-balanced diet, Esmé would eat sweets for all 3 meals and in-between. To accommodate the dessert, Raoul picked a variety of vegetables from his garden. He made a vegetable medley, individual salads for Esmé and Belle, and one large bowl for him and Desiree to pick from. Desiree made a pasta salad with the leftover vegetables.

When lunch was complete, they put Belle's and Esmé's lunch in the fridge. While it didn't matter who got what, Raoul took the envelope for Desiree and ripped off two small rectangles. He pulled a pen out of his shirt pocket and wrote their names.

He crumpled the rest of the envelope and tossed it in the trash.

Desiree finished setting the table. She knew it was a long shot that Raoul would even want to eat with her. But she had to get on his good side. It was the only way to ensure he wouldn't tell Belle what she said.

Raoul exited the kitchen and his eyes went right to the table and Desiree standing behind her chair. He didn't know what to do. He was still hurt by what she said, but he also didn't want to offend her. He took his time approaching the table, deciding on what to do.

"I know it's unlikely that you'll agree to eat with me, but I figured we could restart over lunch?" Desiree asked. She looked Raoul in the eyes, then to the table.

"I would like that very much," Raoul said, "but I'm not hungry...."

"Oh..."

"I'm sorry," Raoul said. He felt Desiree was disappointed they couldn't make amends, of course that wasn't the reason, and quickly said, "I'm not hungry, but I can eat with you if you want."

"No, it's all right," she declined. "We all have our moments when we don't want to eat. You shouldn't force yourself. It'll only make you feel worse. I'll pack up lunch after I'm finished eating."

Raoul was surprised. This was the first time someone didn't force him to eat. Lady Orchida, Esmé, Mylan, and others throughout his childhood, constantly ignored his cry to skip a meal. Stating things like, "you can't starve yourself," "eating makes you feel better," "only children make a fuss over meals," and so on. It was shocking that the person who thought of him as a beast was the first to tell him he didn't have to.

"I can eat a little," he said. "What kind of example would I set for Esmé if I skipped meals?"

Raoul pulled his chair out and Desiree did the same. They began eating in silence. Every so often Raoul glanced at Desiree. He didn't like the silent atmosphere but he also couldn't trust her not to snap at him again. His emotions were conflicted. He knew he shouldn't get close to her. It would only hurt him in the end, yet he was also drawn to her. And each kind little gesture pulled him in.

"Hey," Desiree said.

"Y-yes?" Raoul replied, startled.

"You have a recreational building, right?"

"That's right. Are you interested in going?"

"Sorta. More like Isabelle wants to go but I think she doesn't know where it is."

"Really? I'm terribly sorry, I should've been more thorough in my directions."

"You already told her?"

"Yes."

"Then maybe she does know, I was assuming."

Raoul rested his hand on his chest and sighed. "Thank goodness."

"Were you really worried that you didn't tell her correctly?"

"Yes, I prefer not to be a bother to others and I like to make sure everything is convenient."

"Hmm." Desiree nodded. "I think that's silly."

"Huh?"

"Trying to make sure everything is easy for others. It's good to have that mentality, but it's also good to understand that that's not always going to be the case. You're going to inconvenience someone sooner or later, and that's okay. They're not going to die because it took them an extra 5 minutes to do something."

"I know, it's a habit I'm trying to break…."

"Don't completely change, it's good for a king to think about others. That's rare."

"I'm not a king yet," Raoul said, awkwardly. "Are kings in your world bad?"

"We don't have any royal families. Maybe like a few centuries ago, but not anymore. We have a select group of people, that we, the people choose to run our countries. Or I guess in this world, they would be considered kingdoms?"

"Fascinating. I'm sure a system like that helps spread responsibilities and not one man can hold all power."

"That's exactly why," Desiree said. "It's better for society to not leave one person to rule over everything."

Raoul planned to remember that. He knew something like that wouldn't work in his world, but it was something to consider. If everything progressed the way it did with his curse, Esmé would be left in charge. And Raoul knew Esmé wouldn't be able to handle the responsibility. Even just wearing formal clothing was too much of a hassle for him.

Raoul remembered their previous discussion before branching off into politics. "Desiree, did you want to visit the recreational building?"

"As of now, not really no. But I wouldn't mind knowing where it is."

"I know you said to not worry about inconveniencing others, but I would rather show you where to go. I don't want you to get lost. Esmé is asleep and I have duties to attend to, so you wouldn't have anyone to help you find your way back."

How far away is the building? As a matter of fact, how big is the castle ground to worry about me getting lost? Desiree thought. From the few angles she saw of the castle grounds, it didn't look that big. She assumed it was more of Raoul's worrying than anything else. "Sure, let's finish eating first."

"Of course," Raoul said.

As lunch progressed, Desiree and Raoul had interesting discussions. They spoke more about politics in their worlds. Raoul explained how he made the soufflés, and Desiree the potatoes, and the significance of them in her family. They talked about Esmé and Belle as children, Raoul leaving out any negative experiences they had. By the time lunch was over, Raoul's heart opened once again to Desiree. He thought about Desiree's behavior throughout their conversation, and decided it was nothing more than a fluke, an outburst she didn't mean. That the woman sitting in front of him was the real Desiree. The one that genuinely smiled, laughed at his jokes, and *really* listened to him. This was the real her.

He knew she would have reservations on loving a beast, but if things continued at the rate it was, maybe even she could lower her standards for someone like him. Raoul hadn't fallen in love with her. But he opened his heart to the idea of it happening.

Desiree's guard did drop a little over their conversation. She still couldn't trust him as far as she could spit, but he didn't seem like that bad of a person. But as lunch went on, that same irritability from the morning slowly crept its way back into her heart and mind. It was like the more they spoke, the angrier she got. All she could do was smile. It was something her mother taught her when she was a child. Whenever she felt upset, smiling would erase her sadness. Desiree knew that was nothing more than her mother trying to stop her from crying, but considering how she felt now, it was something she was willing to believe.

When lunch was finished, Desiree began clearing the table. Her mind had gone cloudy. She reminded herself not to snap at him for Belle's sake, but the urge to get angry pushed and pulled at her.

"Do you need help?" Raoul asked.

"I got it."

"Then I'll wait out here for you."

"Okay…."

Raoul waited for the door to close before sitting down and slumping in his chair. He thought, *What happened in the last 10 minutes for her mood to change so suddenly? Did I say something inappropriate? Are women really this hard to figure out?*

He remembered Monsieur Paquet. He was a man of few words, but when he did speak it was always a slick or funny comment. Monsieur

Paquet's famous words were, "Women are so difficult to please. You do one thing wrong and they have a fit!"

Of course, his word of advice to Raoul always came after he did something to upset Madame Paquet. Raoul usually sided with Madame, but after dealing so much with Desiree's mood swings… maybe he had a point?

Desiree aggressively scrubbed the dishes. There was nothing Raoul said to her that irritated her. But something happened that made her so angry. She tried her best to think back to when it might have happened but to no avail. In fact, their conversation was delightful. There was nothing for her to blame her anger on.

"Urgh!" she groaned. "Get it together."

After finishing the dishes, Desiree smacked her cheeks a few times. She needed to stay on Raoul's good side to ask him that little favor of hers. "For Isabelle."

When she opened the door, Raoul still sat in his seat. He twiddled his thumbs and tapped on the table.

"You're still here?" she asked.

Raoul gasped and stood immediately. "Yes, remember I said I would show you where the recreational building was?"

"Right… I completely forgot." Desiree forced a smile.

Raoul showed Desiree the way to the building. They left the castle, and walked to the back. The path led to a grassy field the size of a football field.

"Here we are," Raoul said.

"You're kidding, right?" Desiree was shocked and confused.

Surely Raoul was playing a trick on her, he had to have been. There was nothing in the field but poorly mowed grass and a tiny shed that matched the same colors as the castle. And to call it a recreational building when it only took up three feet of space was absurd.

Seeing Desiree's reaction made Raoul laugh.

"That's not funny!" Desiree said. "You can't expect us to know you guys don't have one."

"It's not that," Raoul said, unable to stop laughing. "There really is a recreational building. I just wanted to see your reaction to this. Please continue to follow me."

Desiree smiled. Her irritability subsided. Raoul rarely laughed, but when he did, it was contagious. Desiree followed Raoul, but as she walked a chill ran down her spine, and she broke out into a cold sweat. Soon, she was angry again.

What's wrong with me? she thought. She tried her best to not blame it on Raoul. Logic was telling her there was something wrong with her, but her emotions told her it was Raoul's doing.

Raoul calmed down when they reached the shed. "This is it."

"How long are you going to do the same joke?" Desiree asked.

"It's not a joke. We have all kinds of things to do in here."

Desiree didn't even respond. She glared at him until he got the message.

Raoul twisted the doorknob and opened the door. Inside was a long white hall with two doors on each side.

"Huh?" was all Desiree could say. She peered inside, then back and around the shed. "How?"

"Magic," Raoul said. He tapped the air next to the shed and a ripple wave revealed a tall grey building before disappearing again. "I thought the building ruined the aesthetics, so I asked a sorceress to hide it."

Raoul continued, his tone a little bitter, "The only thing ruining how the castle ground looks now is that unseemly grass. It cuts itself but it's uneven."

"Wow," she said. She pointed inside. "Can I?"

"By all means. You are free to enter whenever you wish."

Desiree entered, and walked to the first door. Raoul wanted to follow her, but he didn't know how much his heart could take of her mood swings.

"I must return to the castle," Raoul said. "Please enjoy yourself."

Desiree turned to Raoul and smiled as she twisted the doorknob. "Thanks. And thanks for having lunch with me."

"You're welcome."

Raoul turned to leave before Desiree called to him. "Raoul?"

He turned around, hopeful she would ask him to stay. "Yes?"

"Can you not tell Isabelle about what happened this morning?"

Raoul scoffed quietly at how foolish his thoughts were. "It's our little secret."

Desiree smiled and entered the first room. Raoul closed the shed door.

Desiree looked around. The room had a volleyball court. The only light in the room was from the 4 windows. Desiree wasn't much of a sports person. She continued on to the next room, basketball, then soccer, and badminton. The first level was all sports.

She spotted a stairwell to the right of the hall and made her way to the second floor. That floor was designed for arts and crafts, there were multiple art rooms, a knitting room, a crochet room, a room for resin, and even woodworking.

She climbed to the third floor, and by this point she was exhausted. Desiree preferred as little physical activity as possible. She complained, "Did they really not think to install an elevator?"

But then Desiree thought about it more carefully. Neither one of them needed an elevator. Raoul most likely flew and Esmé climbed the railings. Unlike the other two floors, the third had a door at the top of the stairs. Desiree opened the door to a large, empty room. It resembled a gymnasium, but fancier. Desiree continued to the fourth floor.

On the fourth, and last floor, was a planetarium. There were few seats and they were spread randomly through the room. In the middle of the room, surrounding the projector, were two large hammocks and one bed covered in pillows. 2 telescopes were placed on each wall in the room.

Desiree loved astronomy. It was her second choice to major in if she had decided not to go into nursing.

They can create this? Desiree thought, walking to the projector and turning it on. She was amazed by the planetarium, but it did raise questions about how dated everything else in their kingdom was, but the recreational building looked modern and from her world.

Desiree didn't quite know how to use the projector; she let whatever it was previously set to play and still enjoyed herself.

Raoul placed his ear to his door and listened. Silence. He hoped Esmé returned to his own room. He could only imagine how upset Esmé would be if he found out Raoul broke his promise. He opened his door slowly and peeked inside.

Esmé was still in his room. He had fallen asleep in Raoul's bed. Raoul crept into his room. He walked to his bookshelf and grabbed a random book. He slowly sat on his sofa and leaned back. He opened the book and sighed in relief.

"You lied," Esmé mumbled.

Raoul jumped, his heart practically rising to his throat. "What do you mean?"

Esmé sat up and stared at Raoul. He looked exhausted. "You promised to come right back."

"I'm sorry," Raoul caved. He thought about lying to him, but he knew that would only make matters worse. "I did intend to return after leaving the note, but Desiree was already cooking. She apologized for her behavior this morning and we had a delightful lunch."

Esmé didn't believe him, and it showed on his face.

"I mean it," Raoul insisted. He retold what happened over lunch and taking Desiree to the recreational building.

"She clearly had an ulterior motive," Esmé said. "There's no way she'd just change like that."

"I do not think so," Raoul lied. He lied even to himself. He felt foolish hoping Desiree would ask him to stay. He also wondered how he couldn't see through Desiree's intentions. "I think that was bothering her. As long as she knows what happened was wrong, I do not mind her using Isabelle as a way to apologize."

"That's nonsense and you know it," Esmé said. He preferred to speak respectfully to Raoul; however he knew Raoul was too nice to speak badly of others. No matter how they treated him. Esmé believed the hard truth and speaking brashly to him was the only way at this point. "What's wrong with you? Why are you so stuck on Desiree? She's mean, judgmental, and close-minded. She's everything Lady Orchida told us to avoid!"

"The condition for breaking the curse is for a woman we love to love us back," Raoul said. "Her personality doesn't matter."

"Do you really 'love' her after four days?" Esmé asked, appalled. "What about her is loveable?"

"No." Raoul shook his head. "I don't love her."

"Then why are you so hung up on choosing her?"

"I'm not. I just know there's no chance after she leaves. I've told you numerous times. It took 17 years for a woman to show up. I'm sure after getting to know Desiree, her opinion will change. There's still time."

Esmé's face reddened. "No, there isn't! 5 months is not enough! You need to take this seriously."

"I am. As I've told you before, as long as your curse is broken, I'm fine with whatever happens to me."

"'Whatever happens?' You *know* what happens!" Esmé cried. "Are you really just going to let yourself die?"

"Esmé," Raoul sighed. "That's not guaranteed to happen."

"It is if you continue with Desiree."

Raoul and Esmé's curse was more complex than just turning into beasts. If they did not find someone who truly loved them despite their appearance, they would die. They had until the day they turned twenty-four to find someone to love them. And Raoul was only five months away from his twenty-fourth birthday.

Raoul had accepted that he was going to die before the ladies arrived, but Esmé couldn't accept it. Raoul was his world. Raoul was the person that would take a bullet for Esmé, and Esmé would do the same. When Esmé was sick, Raoul was there for him. When he had bad dreams, Raoul let him sleep in his bed. When he wanted to play at unreasonable hours, Raoul let him. Whatever he wanted to do, Raoul obliged. He was the best brother to Esmé, and Esmé would do anything to save his life.

Esmé pulled his pendant out, and pressed the rose. "Lady Orchida, I need your help."

Raoul gasped, and frantically pressed his. "No, everything is fine! Please do not come on our behalf!"

Lady Orchida ignored Raoul's request and arrived in minutes. When she saw Esmé's tearstained face, she asked, "What's wrong."

"Lady Orchida," Raoul interrupted. "Everything is fine."

"Desiree isn't a good choice for Raoul," Esmé said, ignoring him. "She lacks all of the qualities you said were needed to fall in love."

"Why do you say that?" Lady Orchida asked.

"She's fine how she is," Raoul said.

"She's just not a good match," Esmé said.

"Lady Orchida, please do not bother with Esmé's concerns. Please don't worry about us."

"Please elaborate," Lady Orchida said to Esmé.

"Is anyone listening to me?" Raoul complained.

Lady Orchida gave Raoul a stern look, then zipped his lips shut. Raoul covered his mouth, his eyes reflecting sorrow. He bowed to apologize.

"Please tell me what's happening."

Esmé explained everything that Desiree had done the past four days, making sure to put emphasis on what she did after breakfast.

"That's very odd," Lady Orchida said. "I looked into Desiree's and Belle's background upon their arrival. Both meet the requirements."

"How?" Esmé asked, annoyed.

"As I said, they both meet the requirements and are perfect matches for you two. I also placed an additional spell when I sealed the castle. This was done so that no one with malicious intent could enter. And Desiree came in without any obstacles." Lady Orchida turned to Raoul and said, "Are you ready to comply?"

Raoul nodded and Lady Orchida unzipped his lips. "I apologize for my actions. It was wrong of me to interrupt your conversation. I was too emotional."

"There is nothing wrong with expressing your emotions," Lady Orchida said. "But know, I will not tolerate suppressing other's voices."

"I understand."

"What about her is good?" Esmé asked. "Maybe her 'good qualities' only work on those *she* deems human."

"I think not," Lady Orchida said. "To be sure, I must have a close examination of her."

"How?" Raoul asked.

"You can't just walk up to her," Esmé said.

Lady Orchida didn't respond. She mumbled an incantation under her breath and pulled a blue rose-shaped necklace from her palm. "You must give this necklace to her. It's coated in a spell that will allow me to study her heart."

"You're always one step ahead," Esmé said. "Except, the only problem with that necklace is that Desiree hates our guts. She's not going to accept it."

Lady Orchida scoffed and conjured another necklace with a pink rose and handed both to Esmé. "Then give Belle a necklace as well. Tell her they are gifts from you two. I'm sure you can figure out an excuse for giving them. Please do this by tonight, the longer you wait, the less time Raoul has."

With that, Lady Orchida disappeared. Originally, she had hoped Raoul and Esmé could handle courting the young ladies by themselves and she could let them have their privacy. But sadly, she would have to guide them in the right direction. She knew better than anyone, that Desiree and Belle were perfect matches for the princes. It was a matter of figuring out why Desiree was so averse to the two.

Raoul and Esmé sat in silence. Esmé was 100% sure Raoul was angry with him. They made a promise to leave Lady Orchida out of their courting process. She had done so much for them over the last decade and they wanted to do at least one thing by themselves. Yet there he was, snitching on Raoul's inability to let someone, he believed was toxic, go.

Raoul on the other hand was embarrassed and disappointed. It was already humiliating that Esmé saw he couldn't woo one woman. It was great to be admired by someone, especially his younger brother. Raoul wanted to always be the perfect brother that could do anything in Esmé's eyes. Yet there he was, off to the side while Esmé spoke of his failures to a woman that dedicated her life to helping them. How much more embarrassment could he take?

Raoul expected himself to die, even before meeting someone as difficult as Desiree. The only wish he had for his final moments was for Esmé to be proud to call him his brother. How could that happen when he was so meek?

"I'm sorry," Esmé said.

"For what?" Raoul replied.

"Telling Lady Orchida."

Raoul smiled. "Don't worry about it. You did the right thing."

"You're not mad?"

Raoul shook his head. "Let's just hope Lady Orchida figures out what's wrong."

Esmé nodded.

At last, his tiredness caught up to him. He tried to fight it off but his head bobbed and dipped. For the first time in a while, Raoul's real smile formed. He ushered Esmé to bed in his own room, promising to remind him to give the necklaces to Belle once they were both awake.

Raoul was finally alone with his thoughts. He hated how big of a deal his situation with Desiree had become. He didn't have the mental fortitude nor the attitude to make Desiree like him. He came to terms with his death years ago. He was content with dying so long as Esmé was okay. And Belle was a sweetheart. They had already overcome the first hurdle in such a short time. He knew when he was dead, Esmé would be all right. It was only his emotional state that Raoul had to prepare him for.

Raoul grabbed the book he left on the sofa and lay in bed. He wasn't really in the mood to read, and he was almost as exhausted as Esmé and Belle. He needed to stay awake. He didn't want to ruin his sleep schedule.

***

The projector turned off and the lights in the room turned on. A dim light flickered on. Desiree sat up and stretched. She didn't know what time it was, but it had gotten significantly darker. She returned to the castle and looked at the grandfather clock in the foyer and sighed. It was approaching 7 p.m. and she wasn't in the mood to cook dinner.

Desiree felt so relaxed, she wasn't up for any physical activities or her responsibilities at the castle. She dragged her feet across the foyer into the dining hall. The room was empty. In fact, as she thought about it, the castle was so quiet she could hear a pin drop. She wondered where everyone was.

Desiree pushed open the kitchen door. In the corner of the kitchen, Raoul quietly placed food onto plates. He hadn't noticed her. When Raoul expected to run into Desiree or Belle, he'd transform into his beast form prematurely to avoid the discomfort of the sudden change. And of course, transforming was his only indicator of when they were nearby.

She stared at him, contemplating whether to speak to him or not. She wasn't in the mood to talk nor to help cook, and since he hadn't realized she was there, she could've easily slipped out and went to her room. But, she also didn't feel right leaving such a heavy task for him to do alone.

Before she could decide, Raoul turned around to sit a plate on the cart. When he saw her, he jumped, almost dropping the plate and let out a soft, "Ah!"

Like any other person's reaction to scaring someone, Desiree burst into laughter.

Raoul's heart raced as he stumbled on his words, "M-miss Desiree…I didn't hear you. I apologize for not greeting you."

After calming down, Desiree said, "Don't worry about it. Sorry… for scaring you."

"That was my own fault.…"

"Did you cook dinner by yourself?" she asked.

"Yes, Esmé and Miss Isabelle are still asleep, and I wasn't sure where you were."

"I'm sorry, I lost track of time. You should've waited for me to cook."

"No, it's fine, really. I didn't want to miss our dinner schedule."

"Man, you're a real stickler for your schedule," Desiree mumbled. "But I think it would've been better to be late rather than you break a law and cook for 'commoners.'"

"Oh…uh…" Raoul chuckled, awkwardly. "Every uh, once in a while is fine. I can bend the rule with—"

"'Technicalities,'" she interrupted.

"Yes."

"The least I can do is help set up the table. I take it we'll be putting Isabelle's and Esmé's plates in the fridge?"

"Mine as well," he replied. "I'm not in the mood to eat."

"Ok." Desiree nodded.

Raoul helped Desiree sort their plates out. The refrigerator was fairly large and each shelf had their meals on it. Raoul hated seeing the leftovers from lunch, but Desiree made a valid point earlier about them waking up hungry. It only became irrelevant since neither one awoke before dinner….

After everything was put away and Desiree's dinner set on the table, Raoul apologized for not being able to eat with her, giving her the excuse he was too tired. Desiree understood, she inquired as to why he didn't take a nap earlier, but he stated he wanted to stay on schedule.

But the real reason he didn't eat was because he wasn't ready to speak to Desiree. He was actually starving, and planned to eat his dinner after he knew she was finished. He'd forgiven her for her actions earlier; he just couldn't risk himself being hurt again if he invaded her space too much. Until Lady Orchida found the reason for why she was so harsh to them, if there was one to begin with, and the situation was fixed, he preferred to avoid her at all possible. He apologized again in his head and returned to his room.

Desiree sat at the table; the dining hall was eerily quiet. She had already gotten used to eating with others, now, it was nothing but off-putting silence. She couldn't take it any longer, rushed to finish dinner and retired to her room.

CHAPTER SEVEN

Belle x Esmé

Belle stretched and yawned as she sat up in bed. Still in a stupor, she stared at nothing smacking her lips. She glanced out at the night sky, confused as to how long she'd slept. She finally had the energy to move and went to the bathroom. When she exited, her stomach growled and she mumbled, "Hopefully dinner's ready."

She made her way, as slow as possible, to the kitchen. When she opened the door, Esmé glanced up from the fridge. His fur was ruffled, and he looked more tired than she did.

"They left dinner and lunch in here," his voice croaked. He pulled out Belle's plates and handed them to her.

"Thank goodness," she sighed, setting the plates on the counter. "I'm starving."

She looked around the kitchen before realizing they didn't have a microwave. She sighed and pulled out a few pans. She handed one to Esmé and they placed their food in the oven. While they waited, they leaned against the counter island, both too tired to speak.

Esmé remembered the necklaces in his pocket and said, "This is for you and Desiree."

"They're beautiful," Belle gushed.

"The pink one is yours…" he mumbled, bashfully.

Belle smiled wistfully. She didn't say anything, she just stared at the necklace. After a moment of silence, she asked, "Is this a Christmas present?"

"What do you mean?" Esmé asked.

"Well, tomorrow would be Christmas in my world."

"What's that?" Esmé asked.

"You don't know what Christmas is?"

Esmé shook his head.

"It's a religious holiday, but my family doesn't celebrate it for that reason. So it's a day where…" Belle started. "I should start by saying it's a 2-day event sorta. There's Christmas Eve and Christmas Day. We spend a month or two prior decorating and preparing for it. And it's where family and friends come together to celebrate the holiday. We exchange gifts, put up a Christmas tree with lights and ornaments, we sing Christmas carols, and sometimes, we throw Christmas parties. It's even more fun when there's snow on the ground!"

"It sounds fun," Esmé said, smiling.

"It is…" Belle said, lowering her eyes and fidgeting with the chain of her necklace. "But, I don't think Desiree even remembers that it's Christmas."

"She's too busy hurting Raoul's feelings to notice," Esmé mumbled. He bit his lip regretting bringing up such a negative topic.

"What did you say?" she asked. "What did she do?"

"Nothing," Esmé said. "Sorry for saying anything."

"Esmé," Belle pleaded, "what did Desiree do?"

Esmé sighed and explained everything that happened to Raoul starting in the morning after they left to hang out.

"What!?" Belle exclaimed. "How could she say that?"

"Raoul promised Desiree he wouldn't tell you, and he made me promise I wouldn't tell you… please don't say anything about it to Desiree."

"That's not like her," Belle mumbled.

Why would she fake liking them? Belle thought, ignoring Esmé's request. After hearing what happened to Esmé and Raoul as children, she couldn't look the other way.

"It's okay," Esmé said. "Just make sure she gets that necklace. Raoul wants her to have it…but don't tell her it's from him. I know she won't wear it."

"Yeah, you're right…" Belle felt sick to her stomach. She was so upset she'd lost her appetite. The more she thought about it, the angrier she got. Desiree was her favorite sister. She wouldn't choose anyone over her. But there had to be a limit to what was acceptable and forgivable. And Desiree had passed that limit. Hurting others? What was she doing? This was *not* the sister she grew up with. Did she really change that much since going to California?

Belle didn't want to bring the mood down with Esmé, so she excused herself. She promised to give the necklace to her.

***

Belle thought about the situation between Raoul and Desiree as she walked down the hall to her room. She felt so betrayed. How could Desiree lie to her? Belle truly believed her conversation with Desiree in the morning had gotten through to her. Did she even care about how she felt? How much it would hurt if she found out?

Belle stopped in front of her door and lowered her head. Tears brimmed the corner of Belle's eyes as she thought about it. Clearly Desiree did. She knew how her actions would upset Belle otherwise she would've never asked Raoul to keep it a secret. Belle was hurt and confused as to why Desiree was behaving this way. She reached out to grab her doorknob before turning around to Desiree's. She wanted to ask her directly. If Belle kept quiet about what she knew, it would slowly eat away at her.

Unable to hold back her disappointment, Belle pushed the door open with immense force and shouted, "How could you?!"

The loud bang from the door hitting the wall startled Desiree awake. She, through bleary eyes, said to Belle, "What's wrong?"

"You speaking to Raoul the way you did is 'what's wrong.'"

The shock of Belle finding out jarred Desiree awake. Thinking clearly, she asked, "What are you talking about?"

"Don't play stupid!" Belle shouted. She tried desperately to hold back her tears. "I know what you did!"

Desiree grimaced, roughly moving her braids out of her face. "Why would he tell you? He promised me—"

"He didn't tell me! I overheard him and Esmé talking. So don't you *dare* lash out at him," Belle yelled. She lowered her voice and said, "They've been abused their whole lives. How could you treat Raoul like that?"

"Isabelle, I—"

"He literally *risked* his life saving *you*," Belle interrupted. "He can't even cook or eat without struggling because of *your* carelessness. Yet you can sit there and call him a monster?"

Belle continued, unable to hold back her tears, "You don't know what they've been through and how deep that word hurts them."

"I'm sorry," Desiree said, throwing the blankets off of her to get up and console Belle. "I don't know what happened. I didn't mean i—"

"I don't believe you," Belle said, moving away from Desiree. "You meant every word that you said. You hurt him so much Desiree."

Desiree was speechless. She wanted to calm Belle down, but didn't know how. Belle was such a gentle person. She had never heard her raise her voice before. Desiree understood she'd messed up immensely. Yet, she still hadn't pieced together why she did it. She wondered why she hated Raoul so much—she just did. If anything, Belle's anger made her dislike him even more. The only thing Desiree could do was to apologize to Belle.

"Ever since we got here, you've been acting different," Belle continued, breaking the silence. "The Desiree I grew up with would never act like this. You're my favorite sister, the person I look up to the most. You told me to treat everyone with kindness and respect— and now you're talking like this. I love you. But I hate it when you treat him like this. It has to stop."

Sixteen years of love between sisters fractured. Tears pricked the corners of Desiree's eyes. She didn't think her actions would ruin her relationship with Belle. But...why was she putting these animals before her own family? She'd tried her entire life to be an amazing sister...and Belle grew up to be a beautiful person, unlike her other sisters, Desiree felt she'd done something right.

"I'm sorry," she mustered to say. "If there's anything I can do to change your opinion of me—"

Belle gave the blue box Esmé had given her to Desiree and said, "Here! I want you to wear this every day, all day, even when you're asleep. You've been so fixated on painting a negative picture of Raoul that you didn't even realize that tomorrow was Christmas."

"Thank you," Desiree said, a little hopeful that Belle hadn't given up on her completely. "I will. Merry Chris—"

Desiree tried to hug her but Belle stepped back to avoid her.

"I'm still mad at you. Until you prove that you're my kind-hearted sister again, the one I always looked up to, I won't be talking to you."

Belle turned to leave. Before she walked away, she glanced back at Desiree and said, "If you were going to turn into the person you are now, it would've been better if you had never come here at all."

Dumbfounded, Desiree stared at Belle's back until she disappeared into her room. Her mind blank, she closed the door and lay back in bed. The shock of what happened made her unable to speak.

Belle fumed as she paced around her room. She felt bad for what she'd said to Desiree, but reminded herself every time she almost buckled and apologized, that Desiree had hurt someone and shouldn't be forgiven so easily. Belle was terrified that Desiree would become like the twins. It was a snowball effect. After their mom died, the twins began picking on Belle. From there, Britney and Natasha couldn't be controlled anymore and they began tormenting others. Belle would do anything necessary to prevent Desiree from becoming like them.

There was no way Belle could look at her for a while. It would upset her. She just prayed Desiree's attitude towards Esmé and Raoul changed quickly. She loved her sister and wanted to talk to her about everything she and Esmé talked about. And she hoped they could all genuinely have a peaceful mealtime together.

All of Belle's crying made her fall fast asleep again.

***

At 6 in the morning, Lady Orchida called Esmé to Raoul's room. Esmé forced himself to fall asleep after eating. He didn't want to be nagged by Raoul for staying awake all night. He grumbled his way to Raoul's room.

When he entered, Lady Orchida sat poised on Raoul's armchair drinking tea. He thought, *How is she fully awake?*

"Good morning, Esmé," Lady Orchida said, sipping her tea.

"Good morning, Esmé," Raoul parroted.

"Morning," he replied, uneasy. He sat next to Raoul on the other sofa. The air seemed tense and he wasn't ready for whatever Lady Orchida had to say.

"As you know," she said, breaking the silence, and startling both boys, "Belle and Desiree received the necklaces early this morning."

"Is that so?" Raoul inquired, his voice quivered.

Lady Orchida nodded. "Yes, and in doing so, has caused a rift between the young ladies."

"Why?" Esmé asked.

"I think you know exactly why it happened," Lady Orchida said, glancing at him. "Poor Belle couldn't stay silent about what Desiree had done to Raoul. But—"

"Esmé, did I not ask you to keep what happened a secret?" Raoul admonished him.

"It slipped out," he responded, defensively. "I asked her not to say anything!"

"You should have never said anything," Raoul said, covering his face with his hand. "Now, Desiree will believe I told her."

"But that's not *my* fault!"

Before Esmé could continue, Lady Orchida cleared her throat. Both young men sat up straight and turned their focus to her.

"I believe I was still speaking," she frowned.

"Sorry," Esmé said.

"Your highness, there is no need to be upset with Esmé. Please control your emotions. If you cannot keep your own secrets, how can you expect others to do so as well?" Lady Orchida chided, nodding to acknowledge Esmé's apology.

"I apologize for interrupting you. Esmé, I'm sorry for blaming you. Lady Orchida is right, it was my mistake for voicing my opinion on what happened. I shouldn't have told you to begin with."

"I can assure you both that Belle did not tell Desiree you told her, but that she overheard you. This is water under the bridge, there are more pressing issues to address." Lady Orchida retold the situation that unfolded between Belle and Desiree and Belle's stipulation for fixing things. "Belle helped more than she needed to. If Desiree follows Belle's demands, I can study her temperament clearly. It will be easier now. Raoul, I know this may be difficult for you, but you must interact more with Desiree so I can see how she behaves firsthand."

Raoul nodded.

"Can't you just use your magic to fix whatever is wrong with her?" Esmé asked.

"How can I do so without knowing what needs to be fixed?" Lady Orchida answered.

Esmé stayed quiet.

"Raoul," Lady Orchida continued, "no matter what Desiree says to you, it is not true. You are not a monster. You are human. You may not be the same as I or the young ladies; however, once this curse is broken, you two will be normal humans. You are kind and considerate. Desiree does not know your character. She is not right when she slanders you. Please remember that when approaching her."

Raoul smiled. "Thank you for your kind words, Lady Orchida."

"It is nearing your breakfast, please continue with your morning." Lady Orchida stood to leave.

"Wait," Esmé shouted, standing. "I…have a favor to ask…."

"What is it?" Lady Orchida asked.

"Well…Belle told me last night that today is Christmas in her world," Esmé said, bashfully. "She was upset that Desiree didn't remember and she couldn't spend it with her family. And, I may have made her feel worse after telling her about Desiree…."

Esmé fidgeted as he tried to spit out his request. He hated asking Lady Orchida for help. But, for Belle, Esmé was willing to be a burden one last time. He'd considered the idea carefully last night.

He took a deep breath and asked, "Can I throw a 'Christmas party'?"

"A what?" Raoul asked.

"It's a custom in their world. And we're already being selfish forcing them to stay here. I don't think it would hurt to accommodate their traditions."

Lady Orchida smiled. "It's been so long since I've attended a Christmas party."

"Wait, you've been to their world before?" Esmé interrupted.

"Plenty of times. I know their customs like the back of my hand."

Esmé's face brightened. "Then you can help us with the decorations!"

"Unfortunately, I cannot," Lady Orchida said. "I will be too busy handling Raoul's difficult courting partner."

"Please do not worry about me. I think helping Esmé is most important. Breaking his curse is my only objective," Raoul interjected.

"Esmé's relationship with Belle is going according to plan. What he wants is not a priority. It is not as important as your situation with Desiree."

"But…"

"It's fine," Esmé said, "I agree with Lady Orchida. You're worse off than me."

"Don't you want to have fun with Miss Isabelle?"

"Yeah, but having a brother that's alive seems like the better deal."

"I just…I want you to have fun with Miss Isabelle."

"I didn't say I wouldn't help him," Lady Orchida finally said.

"How? Aren't you focused on Desiree's thing?" Esmé asked.

"Yes, but that does not mean I can't lend you a hand." Lady Orchida walked out of Raoul's room, motioning for them to follow her.

They walked down a long corridor until they reached the back of the castle. Lady Orchida opened the window and pointed her wand out. A light flowed from the tip and onto the ground. Boxes of Christmas decorations and a faux tree appeared and crowded the walkway.

"It will be more sentimental if you bring them into the recreational building and decorate it yourself. You can even invite Belle to help," Lady Orchida said.

"I want it to be a surprise," Esmé said, shaking his head. "I…have one more favor…."

"What is it?" she asked.

"Can it snow for the next month or so?"

"Snow!?" Raoul exclaimed.

Esmé nodded.

Before he could respond, Lady Orchida said, "You will need to discuss it with Raoul."

"I want Belle to have the full experience of her world. She said Christmas is better with snow," Esmé said. "And, we've kept this half summer, half autumn setting for years. I've never gotten to see snow since we were kids."

"But, my garden…" Raoul smiled nervously. He considered his words before continuing. "My plants will die if it's cold. I would have to start all over again…."

Esmé looked dejected. "I understand. We don't have to do it. Sorry for asking."

Raoul sighed. He hated disappointing Esmé. He smiled wearily and said, "I'm okay with it snowing."

"Really?" Esmé shouted. His once frown blossomed into a bright smile.

Raoul was relieved, seeing him so happy again. "Let's make it snow."

"Are you sure you're okay with it?" Lady Orchida asked. "You worked hard on the garden."

"I like gardening. Starting over will be just as fun."

"Let's compromise," Lady Orchida suggested. "If I change the weather to winter for two months, I will only cover a mile of Raoul's garden. Everything after that will still remain as summer. He will not lose all of his hard work and Esmé can cheer up Belle. I will also wait until the day of the party to make it snow. Deal?"

"I don't mind." Esmé nodded. "But what if Belle notices it's not snowing further out when she's in my tree house?"

"Then I will cast a spell that covers your eyes. All of Raoul's garden and the village will look as if it's covered in snow when you two are high enough to see in the distance."

"Desiree too," Esmé said.

"Of course," Lady Orchida said. She turned to Raoul and asked, "Do you agree, Raoul?"

"Sure." Raoul smiled. Hearing Lady Orchida's plan put Raoul's mind slightly at ease. He'd still lose a mile of his plants. But that was better than losing acres of it.

Lady Orchida excused herself, reminding Raoul to converse with Desiree. After she left, Esmé and Raoul went to the ladies' side of the castle. Raoul knocked on Desiree's door and Esmé on Belle's. They both asked if they were coming down for breakfast.

Belle answered Esmé quickly, stating she didn't want to see Desiree. So she wasn't coming down to breakfast. Desiree also answered Raoul fairly quick. She apologized for not being able to follow through with her agreement, but she didn't want to go down. When Raoul relayed her answer, Belle overheard and decided to go down after all.

This continued for two weeks. Belle stuck to her word about not speaking to Desiree until her attitude changed. On the chances that they were attending meals at the same time, Belle would not acknowledge Desiree. She set up a seat on the other side of Esmé so Desiree sat alone. Eventually Raoul gave up his seat so they could stay uniform.

Belle hadn't seen much of Esmé either. He was so engrossed in decorating the recreational hall, he was there morning, noon and night. He'd rush off after eating before Belle could ask to hang out. Raoul disappeared after meals as well. She was bored out of her mind. She sat in her room staring at her bookshelf. She wasn't much of a reader. When she did read, it was manga, or graphic novels. And they didn't have much of a variety.

Belle remembered that she'd brought her art supplies. She'd been so focused on her new life, that she'd forgotten she packed a suitcase almost entirely with her art supplies. So, Belle spent her time drawing. Before coming to their world, Belle almost never missed a day of drawing. If she ever did miss a few days, it was because she was too sick to lift her head.

She took her sketchbooks, her canvases, and easel into Raoul's garden and drew the roses. She did this every day until she used all of her canvases, and filled 3 sketchbooks. On the 7th day, Belle searched her suitcases to see what else she'd packed. She dumped everything out of one of the suitcases and found 4 brightly wrapped Christmas presents. She was unaware that her family had more gifts planned for her. A large smile grew across her face as she lifted the first present. It was from her grandparents. Belle ripped open the giftwrap and a card fell out. In the card read,

Belle wished she could tell her family she was fine. She set the card down and opened the box. Inside was a beautiful egg-shaped pastel pink and blue music box. When she turned the key, the lid opened and a soft melody played. A tiny ballerina with a small afro in front of an even smaller town rose from the middle of the music box. The ballerina twirled around the town in circles until the music stopped and it disappeared. Belle loved the music box.

The next present was from Freddy. There was an envelope on top of his present. Inside, the letter read,

Belle cried. She wanted to tell Freddy she was adjusted to her new life and that she would never hate him for what he did. If it wasn't for him, she would've never become friends with Esmé. She would've never seen a garden as amazing as Raoul's. She never would've lived in a beautiful castle. In time, she hoped to explore more of their world. None of this would've ever been possible if Freddy had agreed to their original sentence.

Belle wiped her tears and opened his gift. Inside was a silver heart-shaped locket bracelet. It was engraved with her name and the words, "To Belle, a special locket for a special girl."

Belle smiled and grabbed the next present. It was from Marcus. There was a penguin Christmas card. Inside read,

Merry Christmas Belle. If you're gonna die there make sure you don't go down without a fight.

Marcus

Belle laughed. It was so like her brother to be so nonchalant about everything. She knew he cared about her. He was just an indifferent person. If he'd become mushy in his note to her, she'd really feel depressed.

His gift was simple. It was the 6th volume of a random graphic novel she hadn't heard of. She would still read it, despite not knowing what exactly was going on in the story. And for her, it was the thought that counted.

She grabbed the last present. It was from Natasha and Britney. Belle smiled. She'd never gotten a gift from them before. She thought maybe they did care about her after all. She grabbed the crumpled piece of notebook paper that was taped to the present. The note read,

Just an FYI, they're forcing us to buy you a gift. We still don't like you. It sickens us that we're being forced to give you a present. It's a waste of money. You're gonna die before you can even read this. I bet the monsters will think you taste gross. You're not special. Dad only wanted to save his own life. He didn't care who was picked, nor did those monsters. You'll die a nobody. I hope it was all worth it.

The letter didn't have a name, so Belle couldn't figure out which one of the twins wrote it. Belle laughed at how silly she was for believing her two miserly sisters had actually changed. Their note didn't hurt her feelings. She was used to their verbal abuse. It would've been unexpected if the twins had gotten her a present of their own volition.

Hell would freeze over before the twins were nice to Belle. Belle had already given up on Britney and Natasha. She'd had a similar heart-to-heart discussion like Desiree's, with them a year ago, only to be mocked and ridiculed. Their exact words to Belle were, "We don't want to be someone *you* look up to. The only thing you'll look up at in life is a big—" …a phrase not appropriate to say to one's younger sister. After that, Belle gave up on trying to help her sisters. They would never change and as long as they weren't hurting other people, Belle did not care how they treated her.

Belle smiled and shook her head remembering how silly that conversation was. She didn't think it was appropriate to open their gift. They expressed they didn't want her to have it. But, she was raised to accept gifts regardless. Belle planned to open the present but never use it.

She opened the present and frowned. It was one of the sketchbooks she'd wanted since forever. Sadly, the twins had drawn an obscene image on the front cover in black marker. Middle fingers, insults and other swear words, were drawn along the edges of the sketch. They would rather ruin it and waste their money, than to give her something nice.

Their behavior wasn't new to her, but she still felt uncomfortable seeing the drawings. She took out a sharpie and, using a drawing method she'd unwillingly learned from one of her art friends, changed the obscene image into a bunny. The middle fingers were turned into hands holding roses. She connected the letters of the words to create a spiral pattern along the edge. Belle had turned such an explicit drawing into a beautiful work of art.

She admired her work before putting the sketchbook back into her suitcase. She stood to tell Desiree what their family did, but she stopped herself at her door. She remembered she was giving her the silent treatment. She frowned and plopped on her bed. She missed Desiree. But she had to stand ten toes down on her decision; otherwise Desiree wouldn't change. And Belle couldn't trust that any recent interactions she'd seen between Desiree and Raoul were organic and genuine. It was apparently easy for Desiree to lie to Belle. Belle thought, *Fool me once, shame on you. Fool me twice, shame on me.*

She wasn't going to fall for the same lie again. Although, Belle understood she wouldn't be able to know if Desiree's behavior towards Raoul was sincere just by looking at them, she believed when the time was right, she'd know it.

Esmé grunted as he, with the help of Raoul, lifted the faux Christmas tree onto a round, white stand. Esmé said through labored breaths, "You don't have to help me, really."

"It's fine," Raoul replied, smiling. His arm had been killing him. But he saw how diligently Esmé worked to decorate the recreational building, and it inspired him to want to do something. "I'm benefitting from the party as well. I should do my part, right? That is, *if* Miss Desiree and I are invited."

"Of course, you're invited," Esmé said, almost offended that Raoul would even think for a second he wasn't. "I don't want you helping because of your arm."

"It's only one arm, the rest of my body works just fine. I'm not going to stay on bed rest because of it." Raoul lifted a large box of miscellaneous decorations above his shoulder with his right arm.

Esmé tsked, "Show off."

Raoul smirked. "What about Miss Desiree?"

Esmé flinched and fidgeted as he put the tree skirt on. "You know I don't like her…. Besides, Belle's not on good terms with her. The point of the party is to make Belle happy. If Desiree's there and Belle gets upset, then it defeats the whole purpose. Not to mention, she'd probably just ruin the mood."

"That is a possibility, but I think Miss Isabelle would prefer to have her sister at an event you said was for family. I don't want what happened between Miss Desiree and I to come between her relationship with you or Miss Isabelle."

"I'm never going to like her."

"You say that now, but at some point, if everything goes as planned, you and Miss Desiree will become in-laws. You don't want to hate your family, for Miss Isabelle's sake."

Esmé sighed. "Fine, she can come to the party! But if Desiree does anything to hurt your feelings before then, I'll rescind my invitation."

"That's a fair decision."

"Don't say anything about it until I tell Belle."

"My lips are sealed."

Esmé and Raoul continued to decorate the recreational building. Lady Orchida had given them more than enough decorations, so they decorated the other floors as well. The first and second floors were already cluttered with its respective items, so they only hung small decorations, like a few Christmas stockings, paper snowflakes that Esmé spent 3 days cutting, window stickers, and lights in the windows. They wrapped the railing in the stairwell with garland. The fourth floor couldn't have any lights because it would conflict with the projector. So they placed Christmas plushies on the chairs and in the corners of the room. The bedding was switched to Christmas themed blankets and more plushies were added on top. When the decorations were finally finished, Esmé and Raoul stood in awe.

The gymnasium had become a winter wonderland. A festive garland adorned in gold-colored ornaments and red bows lined the ceiling walls. Candles flickered from crystal sconces fixed to the wall, with matching candelabras on each table. Bright green wreaths decorated with giant red bows and pine cones hung on the windows. Warm white Christmas fairy lights strung from one side of the gymnasium to the other, gave the room a soft gentle glow. The Christmas tree set in the middle of the room.

Esmé sighed. Raoul noticed that the Christmas tree had not been decorated. He asked Esmé why.

"I want to decorate it with Belle the morning of the party. She told me one of the funnest parts of Christmas was decorating the tree."

Raoul thought it was extremely adorable how much effort Esmé put into making Belle happy. He was glad Esmé found something that he was passionate about.

Raoul broke down all of the boxes and packed them in the closet for sports equipment.

"You two did an excellent job." Lady Orchida applauded. She studied the layout and smiled. Esmé had really outdone himself. In two weeks he'd turned a gymnasium into a ballroom. His dedication was admirable. And for that, Lady Orchida truly believed he deserved to have snow to complete the ambiance.

"Thank you," Raoul said, bowing. "But Esmé deserves all of the credit. I only helped the last two days."

"Be it once or twice, you still did your part and should accept credit where it's due," Lady Orchida said.

The only problem now, was how Raoul would take the news of snow. She knew the princes better than anyone else. And she knew Raoul treasured his garden. The moment his plants died, he'd spiral into depression. She had to think of a good compromise. In the real world, Raoul would have to face disappointment. He wouldn't get the same special treatment he'd had in their little castle. Lady Orchida wouldn't be there forever, and there wouldn't be magic to fix their problems. So disappointment was something she'd also have to teach them. It also wasn't fair that it was Raoul's word over Esmé's. While Raoul did try to treat Esmé fairly, there were things he wouldn't budge on. He wasn't king just yet, so his word wasn't absolute. Lady Orchida didn't want them to grow up like their father. She made sure, whoever became the next ruler, wasn't as selfish and tyrannical as him.

In the end, Lady Orchida figured it was best to speak to them individually. She just had one question so neither of them would be blindsided. "When do you plan to throw the party?"

"If you think everything looks perfect, and if all goes well, I'd like to start it tomorrow evening."

"Then I will create snow tonight." Lady Orchida glanced at Raoul to see his reaction. Although he hid his displeasure easily on his face, she could look at his eyes and see he was upset. "I'd…like to speak to you both privately. It's getting late anyways."

"Yes, Lady Orchida," they said in unison.

***

Lady Orchida waited for them to finish prepping for bed and retired to their rooms. She stopped by Esmé's room first. While Lady Orchida didn't choose favorites, she adored Esmé, ill-temper and all. Seeing him so excited for tomorrow made her happy. The young men had gone through so much, and they acted like they were stepping on eggshells even around each other. Both giving up things they wanted to please the other. Lady Orchida had noticed a while ago that Esmé didn't have much of an influence on their castle's décor. Raoul's garden extended for miles; the front of the castle grounds had to look appropriate and "royal-like." The recreational building was for both of them, and neither had used it in recent years; and that was Lady Orchida's gift to them so they would find something meaningful to do. What did Esmé have besides his small tree house?

Lady Orchida didn't have much to say to Esmé. She only wanted to run a few things by him. Like what to wear. Esmé hated the medals on his clothing; however, she insisted for his ball, that he wore them. She requested his favorite color, and crafted winter gear. She made a green coat, scarf, gloves, hat, and boots. The material could conform to his body in either form. She also informed Esmé that she had one other gift.

"What is it?" Esmé asked.

Lady Orchida smiled and waved her wand. A mannequin appeared, and a beautiful high neck ball gown followed. The dress was pastel pink, with traces of iridescent blue, yellow, and purple in the tiered skirt. Next to the mannequin were pastel pink ballerina flats that matched the dress.

"That's for Belle, right?" he asked.

"Of course," Lady Orchida said.

"Are you sure it's okay to give that to her?" he asked. "We don't even know her favorite color."

"I know what she likes, don't worry about that. Your party looks more like a ball. This sort of thing is a girl's fantasy. Give her the dress, she'll love it."

"If you say so…thanks…." Esmé was doubtful of Lady Orchida's gift, but he put all trust in her. She was never wrong.

Raoul twiddled his thumbs as he waited for Lady Orchida to arrive. He was glum about the snow. At any moment, over a decade's worth of work in his garden would be destroyed. But what could he do? He thought about how much work he would have to do to get the garden to even half of its once beauty. He wondered if it would even be worth continuing. It seemed to him that Esmé's wants would always override his wants and needs. And of course, he didn't mind. With how things were going to break his curse, it seemed appropriate to slowly integrate more of Esmé's choices and establish him as the next ruler. It was just so disheartening to think about.

A knock on the door took Raoul out of his thoughts. He stood and said, "Come in."

Lady Orchida entered and sat on his sofa. She gestured for Raoul to sit beside her. "I know it's going to be hard for you to watch the snow fall. However, I do want you to know that I will not make it cold enough to destroy your plants."

"Please, don't dilute the experience for Esmé," Raoul interrupted. "I want him to have fun. Surely there's some fun in starting over?"

"Of course there is," Lady Orchida answered. "Back in my own kingdom, I had a large garden. Not as grand as yours. This was way before I had become as powerful as I am, so I couldn't use magic to sustain it like I can yours. I'd spend the entire year tending to the garden and by winter, it all withered away. I think the fun part about gardening was planting new seeds and nurturing them until maturity. It felt like a reward to harvest what I'd spent months caring for.

"Using magic to keep your garden alive the past decade has made you forget the joys of gardening. If you don't have much to do besides pick vegetables, I can see how hard it must be to lose that convenience. I believe this will be good for you in the long run. A king who understands what commoners must do to survive, is a king worth following."

"That's if I make it…" he mumbled.

"I have faith in you." Lady Orchida nudged him. "This can also be used as a bonding moment with Desiree."

"How so?"

"I'm sure she'll help if you ask Belle and Esmé to assist," Lady Orchida suggested. "Gardening is a joyous activity. You'll have fun together."

Raoul smiled. "Maybe you're right. Maybe this will be a valuable lesson. I'm sure I can find the joy in it."

"Good," Lady Orchida said. "Now, it will be chilly. I am making winter gear for you and Esmé. What color do you want yours to be?"

"I'm fine with anything."

Lady Orchida fashioned a purple and black coat, black boots, purple gloves and hat, and a striped black and purple scarf. She explained the same as what she told Esmé. That the winter gear would adjust to both forms. She also gifted him with a dress for Desiree. It was a light blue, off the shoulder ball gown. It had a similar design to Belle's outfit, but the tiered skirt was the same solid blue color as the top-half. There was one particular thing that caught Raoul's eye. On the neck of the mannequin was a pale blue choker with a sapphire blue rose on the side.

Raoul gave the rose a bewildered look, then asked, "Are you sure it's appropriate to give her that?"

"I don't see why not."

"But…the blue rose is a gesture of courtship…. It even resembles the royal necklace. Don't… you think it's too early to give it to her?"

"Not at all. For one, it's not the royal necklace, so there's no commitment. Two, just because the rose is blue, doesn't mean it has the same meaning as sapphire roses. And lastly, Desiree likes wearing chokers, so she will gladly accept it."

"But, it'll be awkward…"

"Only if you tell her the meaning of a blue rose." Lady Orchida opened a portal. "And in any case, whether she knows the purpose or not, it should be known that you are courting her. So let her choose to wear the choker. If she agrees, you can call that her answer. Please get some rest, Raoul. Good night."

"Goodnight," Raoul said, bowing. "Thank you for the visit."

Once Lady Orchida's portal closed, Raoul spotted in the corner of his eye something white gently falling past his window.

He walked to the window and smiled widely. *That quickly, huh?*

CHAPTER EIGHT

~Desiree x Raoul~

Desiree opened her eyes. The room was freezing. She pulled the covers over her head and snuggled in. *Why is it so freaking cold in here?*

She peeked from under the covers, her eyes sparkling. *It's snowing!*

It was like her inner child had been released. She sat up quickly and ran to the window. The castle ground was covered in a blanket of snow. It had already snowed 5 inches and was still going. Oh how she wished Belle was talking to her, they could go outside and make snow angels.

Remembering how much she upset Belle, made Desiree lose the excitement she felt when she saw the snow. She sighed and got dressed then searched around the fireplace in her room to see if there was some way to light it. With no luck, she wrapped herself in a blanket and went downstairs to prep for breakfast.

Elsewhere in the castle, 2 out of her 3 housemates were also waking up excited by the snow. Belle also struggled to light the fireplace, but she didn't care. She put on her warmest dress, tights, her boots, grabbed her coat, and rushed out of her room.

Esmé lit his fireplace and called for Lady Orchida to help heat the rest of the castle. She unfortunately declined. Lady Orchida said he would need to light the fireplaces and experience the cold weather and snow. She wanted him to be more independent. She gave him a pair of shovels then bid him fun and farewell. Esmé grumbled, dressing himself in the winter gear Lady Orchida had created the night before. After he bundled up, he ran out of his room. Esmé was the second person to reach the main stairs. He saw Desiree by the fireplace in the lounge next to the foyer and approached her.

"Why are you sitting here?" he asked.

Desiree looked at him and smiled. She couldn't help laughing at how bundled up he was. He was covered from head to toe, and all Desiree could see was a little monkey in winter clothing. Aside from his personality, Desiree thought he looked adorable.

"I don't know how to light the fireplace in my room," she said. "I'm sure Isabelle doesn't know how either."

"I'll help her." Reluctantly, he suggested, "Why don't you ask Raoul for help?"

"It's fine, I don't need his help." Desiree shook her head. *It would be awkward to ask him for help after the way I treated him.*

Somewhere during the conversation, Belle made her way downstairs where she overheard Esmé and Desiree talking. Belle sighed. She pulled Esmé aside and said, "We still have time before breakfast. Let's play in the snow!"

Desiree lowered her eyes and stared at the fireplace, then mumbled, "I didn't mean anything by that."

I guess that's another week of the silent treatment.

Belle wasn't the only one giving her the silent treatment. Esmé was always the first to leave, and Raoul wouldn't even look in her direction. At first, Desiree didn't mind all that much that the young beasts were ignoring her. She believed it was their fault her relationship with Belle fell apart. But, as the days went on, she was sad that everyone was avoiding her. She was bored and lonely. She was the opposite of Belle and loved reading novels, but the few books in her room were mind-numbingly boring. So she spent most of her time alone with her thoughts.

Desiree just couldn't acknowledge that it was her choice to say what she'd said to Raoul. She couldn't figure out why she lashed out the way she did. No matter how much she tried to find something to blame her behavior on, nothing came to mind. Raoul was only trying to be helpful and if she said it was because of that, it would only make her look worse. The more she thought about her situation with the others rationally, the more she, grudgingly, had to admit that it was none other than her actions that caused her current problems.

Most of her suspicions were also refuted. Belle, to Desiree's displeasure, was right. They'd been there for almost three weeks and nothing horrible happened to them. By now, if they really were the monsters Freddy had portrayed them to be, Belle and Desiree would've been killed and eaten. Reality was being shoved in her face, and she had to accept it. They weren't bad people… beasts…and she needed to stop treating them as such. Now, Desiree still had reason to worry. They did sentence her to death. Of course, she'd have issues with them. But three weeks had passed and it did seem like they were keeping their word. No hidden intentions or abuse of power. And most of the time she forgot she was even a "prisoner."

Desiree genuinely wanted to apologize to Raoul, but she knew they would think she was insincere. And if their opinion about her apology stopped her from apologizing, wouldn't that mean she wasn't really sorry? Desiree was so annoyed by all of this. She just wanted her sister to talk to her again.

After a few more minutes of wallowing in self-pity, Desiree left the lounge to prep for breakfast. She could see Belle and Esmé playing outside in the snow from the dining hall window. *At least you're having fun.*

Desiree entered the kitchen. Raoul wasn't there. He was usually the first person awake in the morning and had most of breakfast ready. She groaned. The vegetables for the day weren't picked and Raoul's garden was covered in snow. As much as she loved this wintery surprise, she did not want to go through his enormous garden and pick everything before they froze. Not to mention, since they'd only been there under three weeks, she spent most of that time locked in her room. Raoul always picked the vegetables in the morning before anyone was awake. She had no idea where to find his vegetable garden.

She was in a dilemma. If she asked the two playing outside, the air would be awkward and she wouldn't be able to handle the cold shoulder from Belle. She didn't want to ask Raoul, it was clear as day he was avoiding her. But if she didn't prep while everyone else was "busy," she'd end up criticized for her unhelpfulness. Somehow or another, she'd be accused of being spiteful. Out of all the crummy options, she chose to ask Raoul for help. It was unusual for him to sleep this long anyways.

Desiree climbed the stairs and peeked around the right corner. The last time she'd been to their side of the castle was when she—Raoul, broke his arm. Walking down the hall felt weird. She peeked around another corner and saw Raoul staring out the window. They stood there for what felt like minutes. Raoul was so focused, he didn't notice that he had transformed.

How long has he been standing there? she thought, standing on her toes, and trying to get a good look outside the window.

Desiree emerged from around the corner and walked to him, keeping her eyes on the window to spot whatever he looked at. As she approached, Raoul saw movement in the corner of his eye, and he slowly gazed at her. When he recognized who it was, he quickly walked away. Desiree had opened her mouth to speak but lowered her eyes. Her heart sank when he turned. It did not feel good to be snubbed, and it reminded her about how she'd mistreated him. She understood that he didn't want to speak to her, nor did she blame him for not wanting to. But just because she understood it, didn't make it less hurtful.

Why was she so upset by it? Wasn't it what she wanted? To be left alone, to keep Belle and herself away from the "dangerous" beasts? Now that she'd gotten her wish, it hurt her feelings? Desiree turned to leave; it was better to just search for the vegetable garden herself. They were going to blame her for any problems anyways, so why did it matter if she was late starting breakfast?

"Wait," Raoul said. He couldn't walk away; she'd already seen him. He was so obvious. As uncomfortable as things were, he did not want to be rude. He smiled wearily and said, "I'm sorry. Is…there something I can help you with, Miss Desiree?"

Normally, Desiree's pride would get the better of her and she'd continue to walk away. But, with how everyone was acting, if she ignored him, she would take three steps back out of Belle's good graces. She swallowed her pride, turned to face Raoul, and replied, "I was…going to ask where the vegetable garden was…."

Raoul's smile wavered, but came back stronger and wider than before. "Don't worry about the vegetables. They're most likely frozen by now. We'll just have to make do without vegetables for a while…."

"What do you mean?"

"The garden's going to die, and it'll be a long time before I can grow everything back."

"It's just snowing." Desiree was confused. Yeah, the plants were covered in snow, but she was sure most of it would survive the winter if properly covered. The vegetables freezing wasn't even a problem. "Why don't we just grab what we can for now?"

"They're frozen," Raoul said, as if Desiree had lost her marbles.

I forgot, he's Mr. No Leftovers. Clearly he wouldn't know about frozen vegetables if he rarely used his fridge, Desiree thought. She chuckled. "I'm sorry for laughing, but in my world, you can freeze vegetables to cook later. The vegetables outside are fine. We'll pick what's salvageable and use today, and the rest we'll blanch and freeze."

Raoul was shocked. Lady Orchida never mentioned that, and he obviously had no one to teach him such important tips. With a glimmer of hope in his eyes, he asked, "So it's not ruined?"

Desiree shook her head. "Put your coat on and let's go harvesting."

Raoul rushed back to his room and put his winter gear on. He met with Desiree by the stairs and they went outside. When they reached the vegetable garden, nothing was frozen. Raoul wondered if Lady Orchida had a hand in it. He made a mental note to thank her later. They picked just enough for breakfast.

"Where's Esmé and Miss Belle?" he asked. They walked cautiously through the snow to the castle.

"Somewhere playing outside."

"I hope we find them on the way," he said. "We're already behind on breakfast."

"Let them play," Desiree suggested. "Isabelle loves snow."

Raoul hated putting their responsibilities aside, but if this was another chance to boost Belle's affections for Esmé, he'd allow it.

"Then, I'll look for them later," he said.

Desiree and Raoul decided on making vegetable soup and a salad for breakfast. The soup was the perfect choice because the castle was cold and Belle and Esmé would be freezing once they got inside. Soup and salad for breakfast was also the perfect way to use the vegetables they couldn't freeze.

Raoul searched for Belle and Esmé while Desiree set the table. When they sat down, the awkward silence returned.

Shivering, Belle gave a curt, "thank you," as Desiree handed her a bowl of soup. Which of course hurt Desiree's feelings. But she just had to accept that it would take time for Belle to forgive her. After breakfast, Belle and Esmé were the first to leave.

Raoul was still focused on saving his plants while they washed the dishes. After contemplating starting a conversation, Raoul asked, "Is there a way to protect the plants from the snow?"

"Yeah." Desiree nodded. "I don't know much about it, but my mother and father used to garden a lot. When it randomly snowed, they would cover the plants."

Desiree stopped drying a bowl and set the rag on the counter. She continued, "If I remember correctly, you'll need burlap, or something like that…um…twine, mulch, and plastic cloches. I think that's it. You're supposed to do this before it snows, but it's better late than never, right? Do you have those things?"

"I do, please wait by the door while I grab them!" Raoul shouted, running out of the kitchen.

"Do you need help carrying it?" she asked.

However, Raoul was already gone.

Raoul closed his bedroom door. He grabbed his necklace to summon Lady Orchida but there was no need. She'd kept to her word about studying Desiree's temperament. She had been listening to their conversation and created everything Desiree said was needed and more. Lady Orchida put the materials in a cart to make it easier for Raoul to carry them down.

As he grabbed the handle, he wondered why Lady Orchida still had not healed his arm. It was such an inconvenience to have a broken arm, and a sling wrapped around a large wing. He looked silly. The sooner his arm healed, the faster he could feel useful again. Once he made it to the stairs, he saw Desiree waiting at the top. She worried Raoul would have a hard time carrying the items she requested, and she was right.

Desiree grabbed the handles, expecting Raoul to move to the side but he did not.

"Miss Desiree, I would prefer to wheel it to the garden myself," he said.

"There are a lot of things we all want to do, doesn't mean we can," she responded, nudging Raoul to the side. "If you want to help, you can grabbed the other end, and help me carry it down."

~Belle x Esmé~

Belle rolled the snow until it was large enough to make a snowman. She hadn't said a word since breakfast. She was still annoyed with Desiree. She wondered how long Desiree would continue to be rude to Raoul. She originally planned on speaking to Desiree today, but when she heard her snippily tell Esmé she didn't need Raoul's help, they were back to square one.

"Are you all right," Esmé asked.

"Yeah, why?"

"You've been spacing out for like 20 minutes. I asked if you could help me lift the snowball."

"Oh! Sure," Belle exclaimed, hurrying to help him.

As they lifted the snowball, Esmé asked, "Are you thinking about Desiree? Why don't you just talk to her?"

"Don't want to." She shook her head. "I can't ignore her actions anymore. Raoul is so nice. I hate that she's being so unfair."

She shuddered at the thought of Desiree turning into the twins.

"It's infuriating, trust me I know. But, knowing Raoul, he probably thinks it's his fault that your relationship with your sister is strained. He's not okay with this."

"At this point, it's not even about him." What she couldn't say was that she was terrified of Desiree becoming more like the twins. Belle went back to making the snowman's big round belly.

"Aren't you lonely without her?"

"I have you." Belle smiled.

"That's right, we're friends." Esmé beamed. Esmé contemplated for a second before approaching Belle. "I wasn't gonna tell you so early but…actually, I think it's better to show you."

"Show me what?"

"Just follow me."

Esmé led Belle to the recreational center. Belle was just as confused as Desiree was when she first saw it. An empty field covered in snow.

"You wanted to show me a bigger field to play in?"

"Huh? No," Esmé said, shaking his head. "This way."

Esmé took her to the small shed. On the door was a Christmas wreath. The sight of it instantly brightened Belle's mood. "That's cool. Is this another secret hideout of yours?"

Esmé ignored her and opened the door. "Yeah, you can say that."

Belle stepped inside. To her surprise, inside of the tiny building, there was a massive corridor before her.

"H-how is this even possible?" Belle said, her mouth agape.

"Magic. It was a gift from that sorceress I told you about. It was given to us because she wanted us to stay active and have hobbies."

"Why's it invisible?"

"I don't know. Something about it not matching the castle's aesthetic."

Esmé led Belle through the recreational building, stopping in each room to show off his decorations. Belle smiled as she made her way up the stairs to the third floor. Christmas had already passed but it was the thought that counted.

"Are you ready?" Esmé asked, holding onto the doorknob. He waited for Belle's nod before opening the door.

Belle gasped, her eyes sparkling as she took in the scene before her. The snow falling softly outside the windows caused a warm feeling in her heart. It was like something out of a fairy tale. She was speechless. She looked from the room to Esmé, back and forth, trying to find the right words.

"You did this?" she managed to ask.

"Yeah…with Raoul's help," he said, rubbing the back of his head, sheepishly. "I hope it's all right…. You said you threw Christmas parties with your family so I wanted to recreate that."

"This is more elaborate than the kind of parties my family had. Which was just us playing board games and watching Christmas movies."

Esmé's little monkey face scrunched into a frown. "So, I messed up?"

"No, not at all. It's delightful," Belle gasped, taking in the room's beauty and splendor. "It doesn't have to be exactly the same as my family's Christmas parties. We're making our own memories, now. It's my first Christmas ball."

"Really? You think it's delightful?"

"Of course."

"…Raoul asked about Desiree," Esmé said, his tone serious.

"What about her?" Belle asked, her lips pursed.

"He wants her to come to the ball, but I told him it depends on how you feel. I mean, I did all of this because she hurt you," Esmé explained. "It defeats the purpose if she upsets you again."

Belle sighed. "I *do* want her there, really. It's just that I don't think she's learned anything. She's still mean to Raoul. She's not herself right now. I won't talk to her until she acts normal again."

"Then she's not invited."

Belle nodded. This was going to be the last time and her last message to Desiree. If even missing out on this ball wasn't enough for her to change her ways, then Belle would give up all hope of ever patching up their relationship. Speaking about Desiree ruined Belle's mood. As much as Esmé did his best to decorate the recreational building, Belle wanted to play in the snow to brighten her mood.

"Let's go back to making our snowmen," she said. Belle admired the room one last time before noticing that the tree wasn't decorated except for brightly colored strings of Christmas lights. "If you don't mind me asking, and this isn't a criticism or anything, why isn't the tree decorated?"

"I wanted to wait for you." Esmé walked to a box hidden under a table and carried it back to the tree. "Is that okay?"

"Of course. That's so sweet of you!" Belle beamed. She wished Desiree could share this moment with her, since they both missed Christmas this year.

She examined the box. Almost every ornament inside looked just like her family's Christmas ornaments. She figured it was most likely a coincidence. Even though her grandparents' Christmas tree was decorated with their own ornaments, some of the ornaments she found in the box were similar to the ones her grandparents let her put on their tree. So, it was impossible for it to be her family's ornaments. She hung the ornaments on the tree, leaving a huge space in the middle just in case she found an ornament that belonged front and center. She explained to Esmé that the prettiest ornaments should go in the front for everyone to see. She searched through the box and pulled out a round red ornament with a woman and her child painted on the side. She smiled and thought, *How nostalgic.*

"I gave my mom an ornament like this when I was a child. It became a tradition of ours to hang it in the middle of the tree every year," she continued aloud. She wanted to cry thinking about it, but held back. She thought, *Obviously, this isn't the same one. We buried it with mom. But, it's still nice to see.*

"Since it means so much to you," Esmé said, "we should hang it on the front of the tree."

"I agree," Belle said, placing the ornament in the center.

The room was silent as they decorated the tree. Esmé, for some reason, only wanted to hold the box, while Belle hung them on the tree. Ever so often, Belle would comment about the appearance of the ornaments and mumble where they would look best. Esmé didn't know how to deviate from their prior conversation. Was it appropriate to continue speaking happily about what they were doing? Would she be upset if he changed the subject?

Belle grabbed the last ornament out of the box and grumbled, "Dang, this one doesn't really look good in the front. But, it's whatever, I guess."

Esmé snapped out of it and said, "We're done already? I thought it would take longer than this."

"Yeah, it's better to do this with two people. Otherwise, it might take hours."

Esmé stepped back to see the whole tree and circled around it. "It looks amazing."

"It is. Christmas trees are honestly the highlight of Christmas." Belle nodded. "Yeah, presents are great and all, but trees hold the magic of Christmas."

"True." Esmé walked to the storage closet and pulled out the dress Lady Orchida had gifted Belle. "Speaking of presents, here."

Belle's jaw dropped when she saw the ball gown. "That's for me? It's beautiful!"

"Yeah, it should be in your size."

"It's even in my favorite color! Thank you!"

"You're welcome," he said, bashfully. "You can't wear it until the ball."

"When's the ball?" she asked.

"Uh, I don't know. I planned to start it this evening. But if you wanna do it now, I can ask Raoul if he's ready."

"Please do. I'm so excited to wear this!" Belle said, giddy.

"Okay, um," Esmé said. He started towards the door. "Well don't put it on until I get his answer. Just put it in your room until then and meet me by the snowmen."

~ Desiree x Raoul ~

When they reached the garden, Desiree gave a quick explanation of how to cover the plants. 1. Cover small trees and bushes in burlap. 2. Cover smaller plants with anything that fits above it. 3. Mulch. Apply mulch to the roots of the plants. Desiree wasn't the best at gardening, nor could she guarantee it would work, but it was worth a shot. They carried baskets to pick the fruits and vegetables they couldn't grab earlier. Raoul also informed Desiree not to worry about the rose maze and anything beyond it. Everything past there he let grow wildly. He was sure any flowers past that point would grow back on their own. They took opposite sides of the garden paths to speed up the process.

Thirty minutes in, Desiree regretted volunteering to help Raoul. It was freezing outside and all she had for warmth was a blanket. Covering the plants wasn't hard. A couple of hours later she began to freeze. Digging through the snow, her fingers became numb.

Raoul hadn't noticed Desiree's attire until they had gotten to a narrow path and he could hear her sniffling. He examined the blanket and asked, "Miss Desiree, are you wearing a coat?"

She shook her head. "I left it in my car."

So that's how she got here? he thought. "Do you want to grab it?"

"No, I'm fine," she declined. "We're almost halfway done. If it becomes unbearable, I'll grab it."

"Do you want to wear mine in the meantime?" he asked, removing his coat.

"No, it's all right. You need it. Besides, it's too big for me anyways."

"Then do me one favor," he said, walking next to her. "At least wear these."

He removed his hat and placed it on Desiree's head, then wrapped his scarf around her neck, and lastly took off his glove and grabbed the other from his pocket, and handed them to Desiree.

"I can't take your things, it's my fault I don't have a coat."

"Regardless, I can't accept letting someone freeze when I'm covered in fur and feathers. I'll be fine without them."

"Thanks…" Desiree said, lowering her eyes.

"Of course." Raoul nodded. He returned to his side of the path.

They had finally reached the smaller plants. Which was way easier than covering the bushes.

Desiree watched him dig through the snow and sighed. She thought, *I must be a bad person.*

Such a kind gesture from Raoul annoyed her yet again. Logically, she knew it was kind and she *was* grateful. But emotionally, she felt that he had slighted her in some way. And as much as she tried to remind herself that he was only being nice, something in her heart told her he wasn't a good person, that what he'd done was only an act. Desiree went back to mulching the plants.

Maybe I don't deserve to speak to Isabelle again, she thought. Tears welled in her eyes. *I haven't even learned my lesson. I still don't like him. I'm trying to like him, I really am. But what does it matter, I'm doing it for Isabelle's sake.*

Tears silently fell from Desiree's eyes. *I'm such a jerk.*

She sniffed and continued trying to cover the plants. She stopped every so often to wipe her eyes and nose. Even though she felt terrible, she still had to keep pushing through. Desiree felt something heavy land on her shoulders and looked up.

Raoul had dropped his coat on her and began walking back to his section. Raoul was covering the plants when he realized Desiree wasn't nearby. He turned around and saw her slumped over in the same place, wiping her eyes. *Was she cold?*

"I don't need this," Desiree said, taking the coat off and handing it back to him.

"It's all right," he said. "I have fur and feathers, remember? A little cold is nothing."

Desiree burst into tears. Sobbing uncontrollably, she thought, *Why is he so nice to me?*

She had been so nasty to him from the get-go. Why did he care so much about her wellbeing? She said out loud, "I'm sorry, okay? I'm sorry for being so mean to you. I'm sorry for lashing out at you. I'm sorry for calling you a monster! Why? Why are you so nice to me? I don't deserve your kindness. Don't you hate me?"

Raoul sighed and squatted next to her. He pulled his handkerchief from his shirt pocket and handed it to Desiree.

"I don't hate you," he said, folding his wings. He paused to gather the right words. "It's…it's just that I expected your reaction to me. You come to a different world and all of a sudden, you're surrounded by monsters. And to top it off, those monsters are imprisoning you with one shouting for your death. It's reasonable that anyone would be terrified.

"Sometimes looking in the mirror even scares me." Raoul chuckled. "Do you…remember when I told you about my father's portal to your world? You aren't the first human to see us. And I've certainly experienced reactions much worse than yours. Does that mean your words didn't hurt as much as theirs? Not at all. There's no gauge for hurtful words.

"But…" he continued, tilting his head to look Desiree in the eyes. He smiled gently and said, "It's worth my while to show you I'm more than just my physical appearance."

Desiree cried even harder, startling Raoul. She cupped her face. "Even your response is mature."

"I'm sorry." He smiled.

"I…I want to try but everything about you ticks me off."

I hope Lady Orchida can fix that, he chuckled to himself, doing his best not to take it personally. Aloud, he said, "In time, I hope that changes."

Before Desiree could respond, Esmé came barreling down the path shouting "Raoul." She turned her face towards Raoul to hide her tears.

Raoul waved and whispered, "We can finish this discussion later."

"I gotta ask you something," Esmé shouted.

"What is it?" he replied.

"It's about the Christmas ball…" he said. He finally reached them and stopped to catch his breath.

Desiree flinched at the mention of the party. She had calmed down while they waited for Esmé to reach them. But hearing that they'd planned a ball without her, made her cry again. She did her best to make sure Esmé didn't see her face. It wasn't like she wanted to go, nor were they required to tell her; it was the principle. It hurt that they did not tell her about the ball.

Esmé noticed Desiree wearing Raoul's winter gear, and raised a brow. He pointed to her and looked at Raoul, who in turn, shook his head for him to ignore her. "I told Belle about the ball. Now that she knows, I was wondering if we can start early?"

"Can it wait until this evening?" Raoul asked, looking at his watch. "I'll finish covering the garden by then."

"Okay," Esmé said, turning to leave. "We'll start at 5."

Raoul nodded in acknowledgement, and Esmé ran off. Raoul waved until he could no longer see Esmé. He leaned over to look at Desiree and said, "You're invited to the party…if you want to come."

Desiree shook her head. "I'm fine. Isabelle doesn't even want to look at me. I'd only dampen the mood if I showed up."

"I'm sure Miss Belle would love to have you there." He stood and continued, "Take some time to think about it. We should get back to work if we wanna finish before the party. There isn't much left."

"Wait," she said, standing. She walked over to him and removed her hat and scarf. She put them on Raoul. Lastly draping her blanket over his shoulders. "If you're going to give me your coat, at least wear these."

"A good compromise." Raoul smiled.

Desiree smiled back. Though anger still filled her heart, she did her best to suppress those feelings.

They worked diligently on the garden and finished after three hours. On the walk back to the castle, they agreed to stop by her car to grab her coat. Raoul was still curious as to how she drove through the portal. Desiree explained every detail to him.

Esmé met Belle at the front of the castle. She'd finished her snowman and had gone to the kitchen. She brought back carrots and gathered sticks for the snowmen.

"We're starting the ball at 5," Esmé said, as he approached.

"How long is that?" Belle asked.

Esmé glanced at his watch and said, "About 6 hours."

"Okay," Belle said. "We still have some time to play in the snow."

Esmé nodded.

They continued to build snowmen, then made now forts.

After an hour, Belle suggested, "Since you guys don't have any servants, maybe you and I should shovel the paths."

"I think we have 'shovels.'" Esmé searched his memories and remembered the shovels Lady Orchida had given him. "Oh! I know where they are. Be right back!"

Esmé returned several minutes later with the shovels. The paths were very wide, so to save time and stress, Belle and Esmé each took a side and shoveled. It took an hour and a half to shovel most of the castle grounds. By the time they looped to the front, they saw Desiree and Raoul walking to the front gate.

"What are they doing?" Belle asked. She stopped shoveling the main path and looked at their attire. Raoul's oversized coat on Desiree and Raoul barely covered in her blanket.

"I don't know." Esmé shrugged. "When I asked Raoul about the party, it looked like they were gardening."

"Really? But Desiree hates gardening," Belle said, astonished. "Like, despises it."

Belle could not stress enough how much Desiree hated gardening. Their parents would force them to help water the plants. Desiree would get stuck with all of the work when her siblings ditched her to do something else. By the time they were older, Desiree had refused to help garden. Even looking at a garden irritated her.

Seeing Desiree help Raoul with the one thing she swore to never do, moved Belle. Maybe…she was trying…. Belle's resolve softened. She missed her sister anyways. And in any case, it was a start. Something that seemed small to them, was a large step for Desiree in the right direction.

"I…I think maybe Desiree should go to the ball," she said.

"What changed your mind?" Esmé asked.

"If Desiree is willing to garden, I think she's trying to make up with Raoul." Belle continued shoveling.

Esmé suppressed the urge to sigh and said, "I'll let Raoul know."

"Besides," Belle said, "I think Raoul would prefer to not be the third-wheel at the ball."

Esmé imagined Raoul as a wheel on a carriage and furrowed his eyebrows. "I don't see how that would be possible, but I guess it's a good thing he won't be?"

Belle asked Esmé for the time. It was 3:05 p.m. Belle gasped. She only had two hours to get ready for the ball. She shoveled as fast as she could, informing Esmé of how much she had to do. Belle was a girly girl. She loved to dress up. Something as extravagant as the Christmas ball was the perfect opportunity. She wanted to have the perfect hair, makeup, accessories, and dress.

Esmé understood nothing she said. Just that it sounded similar to Raoul nagging him about his attire. But offered to finish the rest of the shoveling. There wasn't much left of the main path to clear anyways. Belle thanked Esmé before running into the castle.

After bathing and moisturizing, Belle studied the dress and its matching shoes in the mirror. She couldn't believe Esmé had her size right. She had to find something of hers that was elegant enough to match the dress. The only problem, however, was that she packed with the expectation of being locked inside a dark dungeon. She didn't bring any of her favorite clothes or accessories.

Belle opened both of her suitcases and threw her clothes on the floor. Surely something must've slipped in. She checked through every article of clothing, in between notebooks and sketched pads. Nothing. She dropped to her knees and stared absentmindedly at the suitcase in front of her. Belle was on the verge of giving up, when she saw a strange bump in the secret compartment.

She sat the suitcase upright and unzipped the opening. Inside was a pair of sparkling pink and crystal, heart-shaped earrings. Belle was shocked. How incredibly lucky! She thought she'd lost this pair of earrings during a trip to D.C. in eighth grade and hadn't used this suitcase since.

As cheap as the earrings were, they surprisingly matched her dress. She put the earrings on and admired them in the mirror. She lifted her afro into a high bun and examined how the hairstyle went with the outfit.

She went to the bathroom and wet her hair slightly. She brushed her hair up into a bun, tiny tendrils of hair falling to the nape of her neck.

She returned to her room and sat on her bed. She wore the rose necklace Esmé gave her but her outfit still seemed like it was missing something. Belle gazed across the room, her eyes stopping at a music box on her dresser. Next to the music box her grandparents had given her, was a box with the bracelet from Freddy. Belle opened the box. The bracelet was almost exactly like the earrings she'd found. She put the bracelet on and held her wrist to her chest.

She smiled. "Perfect."

~ Desiree x Raoul ~

"Fascinating," Raoul said, taking Desiree's luggage out of her car. "I didn't think it was possible for another vehicle to enter after the SUV."

"Yep," Desiree responded, taking one of her suitcases from Raoul. "Are you going to fix it?"

"No," he answered, "although, I think it's something that should be looked into. Someone may unintentionally enter and cause bigger problems for us."

Desiree smirked. "Like me?"

"Not at all," Raoul said, as they began walking back to the castle. "While you weren't intended to come here, I'm happy you did."

"How? Haven't I been a complete nightmare…?"

"Even a nightmare can turn into a dream." He smiled. "…Not that you were a nightmare or anything…."

"I appreciate your kindness, but there's no need to lie. It took being in someone else's shoes for me to care about being nice to you."

"You can make it up to me by going to the ball."

Desiree waited until they passed the castle gates before saying, "I know you're trying your best to forgive me, but the others don't want to. I can't…I can't go knowing I'm not wanted there. From what Esmé said earlier, I'm assuming the ball's for Isabelle. I want her to have the best night of her life."

"Miss Desiree, I have already forgiven you."

"Yet, you avoided me like the others did," she interrupted.

"I avoided you because I did not want you to feel uncomfortable. I broke my promise and Miss Belle found out. Initially, I was distant because you hurt my feelings, but I eventually got over it. I stayed

155

away out of guilt because of the problems that arose after I told Esmé. Again, I forgive you. I genuinely want to spend time with you at the ball," Raoul reassured her. "I can't speak for Miss Belle. However, I'm sure she would forgive you if she saw us together."

"It's not that simple," Desiree said, shaking her head. "I'm sorry, but I'm not going."

Raoul smiled. "I understand."

They walked the rest of the way to the castle in silence. Raoul was disappointed she wouldn't attend. However, something he learned from his father's past mistakes was not to force people to do what he wanted them to do. He just had to suck it up until Lady Orchida figured out what was wrong with Desiree.

Thinking about the ball made Desiree want to cry again. She had conflicting emotions. Part of her wanted to go to the ball, another part only wanted to see Belle, but the last part of her loathed the idea of mingling with Raoul. Desiree really did try to suppress her hatred. She knew there was nothing about Raoul that she could hate. It only made her look like a terrible person. But no matter how hard she tried, every interaction with Raoul upset her. The last thing she needed was to lash out again at the ball and ruin her relationship with Belle. Desiree would do anything to not hurt her little sister again. Even if it meant isolation…as if that wasn't what Belle was already doing….

They reached Desiree's room and put her suitcases inside. Desiree followed Raoul to the door and said, "Here's your coat. Thanks for letting me borrow it."

"Of course. It was the least I could do for you saving my garden." Raoul bowed slightly. He chuckled. "I thought I knew everything about gardening, but I guess not."

"Forgivable. Considering, you manage to keep such a beautiful garden year-round."

"Right." Raoul nodded awkwardly. *If only she knew.*

"Well, I hope you enjoy the ball," Desiree said, grabbing the door.

"Thank you," Raoul replied.

Desiree waited until he was out of sight before closing the door. She flopped on her bed and sighed heavily. Her feet were killing her and she was freezing. She grabbed the side of her covers and lazily threw it over part of her body. She lay there for a while, her eyelids growing heavy, the warmth of the duvet sending a surge of chills across her body. She fell asleep.

***

Raoul returned to his room. As he reached his bedroom, he saw Esmé sitting on the floor beside his door. Next to him was a pile of clothing.

Esmé saw Raoul from the corner of his eye, and stood. "Can you help me?"

"With what to wear?" Raoul asked. It wasn't difficult to know what Esmé wanted. "Of course."

When they entered, Esmé's eyes went to the mannequin in the corner of his room. "Lady Orchida gave you a dress too?"

"Yes," Raoul answered. "My question's already answered, but Miss Belle has one as well?"

"Yep. I gave it to Belle earlier and she loved it." Esmé studied Desiree's gown. "Are you going to give it to Desiree?"

"Maybe. She isn't going to the ball, so it doesn't matter if I give it to her or not. But that's neither here nor there. What does matter is the host looking presentable to his guest. This is your night to make her fall in love."

Esmé blushed. "It's not like that. I just want to make her happy."

"And happiness leads to love." Raoul smiled. "Now, put on the first outfit."

Esmé tried on every outfit, until he landed on an emerald green suit and black tie. It seemed to resonate with him the most. Because it was such an important event, Raoul managed to convince him to wear the suit appropriately. He also managed to get Esmé to stay in his chimera form throughout. He helped Esmé brush out the mats in his fur and sent him on his way.

Before Esmé left, he said, "Even if Desiree isn't going to the ball, I think you should give her the dress. It looks nice and since Belle loved hers, I'm sure Desiree will too. What's the worst she can do? Say she doesn't want it?"

He had a point, but also there were worse things Desiree could say. They were both aware of a few that she dished out.

***

A knock on Desiree's door jolted her awake. It had only been 20 minutes since she closed her eyes, but it felt like she'd napped for an hour. Desiree opened the door. "Yes?"

157

Standing awkwardly at her door was Raoul. To the side of him was a mannequin wearing a beautiful light blue off the shoulder ball gown.

"Just in case you change your mind…" he said, avoiding eye contact.

"Thank you," Desiree said. "It's beautiful. Hopefully there's a day I can wear it."

"You're welcome," Raoul said, giving Desiree the mannequin.

He nodded, attempting to scurry off. But Desiree called out to him. "Oh, Raoul!"

Hiding how flustered he was, Raoul answered, "Yes?"

"I…have one favor to ask…." she said, sheepishly. "Can you show me how to light the fireplace?"

"Sure," he said, walking hastily back to her room. He walked to her fireplace and slid the fire screen open. "First and most importantly, make sure the damper is open."

Raoul pointed to a lever. For "aesthetic purposes," the lever was cleverly hidden in a corner of the base. He lit a match and moved it to the fireplace. He waited.

Desiree, confused as to what he was doing, asked, "Why are you holding the match?"

"Checking which way the air's flowing," he replied, blowing the match out. He pushed the grate as far back as he could. "You want to make sure air is going out, not in. Also make sure the grate is back so smoke isn't blowing into the room."

Raoul grabbed a bunch of tinder and newspapers from a desk drawer, Desiree wondered how they even had them, and tossed them under the grate before lighting them. He put three logs on the grate and waited for the fire to start. Once the wood was burning, Raoul closed the fire screen. "There, your fireplace is lit."

"Thank you so much," Desiree said. While she understood none of it, she was grateful she wouldn't be cold anymore. "Thank you for lighting the fireplace and the dress."

Desiree reminded Raoul of what he had done. His face grew hot. He wanted to get out of there fast. "It's my pleasure."

He bowed and rushed off.

Desiree closed her door and studied the dress. It truly was beautiful. It had some of her favorite shades of blue, and cute heels to match. She sighed and thought, *Man, this would be so cute on me.*

Something as nice as her ball gown was meant to be worn.

Unfortunately, it would collect dust in the corner. Her eyes shifted from the body of the dress to the top of the mannequin's neck. A small bag had been tied to it. Desiree grabbed it and opened the bag. Inside was the choker that resembled the royal necklace. Of course, Desiree didn't know the meaning of it nor that there was a royal necklace.

***

Raoul covered his mouth as he raced down the hall. He couldn't believe he gave her the choker. Even if the rose wasn't the real thing, it would still be scandalous if anyone in their kingdom found out he gave it to her. Mylan would lose his mind. He wanted to lock himself in his room for the rest of eternity. Raoul was a bit glad Desiree wasn't going. Esmé wouldn't know about the choker…. Not that Esmé knew, nor cared about, the significance of the sapphire blue rose.

As he passed the stairs, Raoul saw Esmé running to the kitchen. He asked promptly, "What's the matter, Esmé?"

Esmé stopped. "I forgot about food! I have to make something fast."

Raoul's once burning face cooled in an instant. He changed course and offered, "Why don't I help cook? You can carry the dishes to the recreational building."

CHAPTER NINE

elle scoured her room for something she could gift Esmé. He'd not only given her a necklace, but also a ball *and* a ball gown. It didn't seem right for her to not get him something in exchange. But it was the same dilemma as before. She did not bring anything of value with her. What could she give him? She opened her suitcase and looked through her art supplies. He liked to draw, right? They spent hours drawing in his tree house. Surely, he had an interest in art.

What could she give him that wasn't used? She found a new set of color pencils she'd gotten before they had to move. That was one item. She took an unused pencil and an eraser out of one of her packs and set them next to the color pencils. All of her notebooks had been used. Even if it was only one page used, she didn't want to give him something less than what he deserved. Then she remembered the sketchbook from the twins. Belle was never going to use it. They didn't want her to, so she wouldn't. She'd already turned the cover into a work of art. Esmé wouldn't see the original image on the cover. Typically, Belle would never regift something. However, it was only wasting money and a good sketchbook that had been abandoned in her suitcase.

She kept the wrapping paper from her family in good condition and reused them to wrap his gifts. When she finished, she grabbed the stack of presents and ran out of the door.

Belle arrived at the recreational building twenty minutes before the ball began, grateful that the building wasn't hard to find. She made her way to the third floor and peeked inside. Esmé and Raoul were setting dishes on a nearby table. Raoul wore his regular clothing but Esmé was dressed sharply, the fur on the top of his head fashionably styled—a part right down the middle. He wore a dapper emerald green suit and tie, the jacket of which, was adorned with shiny military-style medals. The jewelry he wore dazzled and sparked, in a way that was surely befitting of a prince. The two princes spoke in hushed tones.

"That's good that she apologized," Esmé mumbled. "At least she acknowledged her behavior."

"I agree." Raoul nodded. "She also stated she would try, and that's all that matters. All that's left is Lady Orchida's assessment."

Raoul had told Esmé almost everything that transpired between him and Desiree that morning. As a courtesy, he didn't mention that Desiree had cried. Esmé was still skeptical. How many times did Desiree say she was a going to be kind to Raoul but did the opposite? She couldn't be wholly trusted. And even then, it wouldn't change how she treated them in the past. Esmé wouldn't be as forgiving as his brother.

Belle sat Esmé's gifts on a table and approached them. "Do you need help setting the tables?"

"Oh, Miss Belle," Raoul said, facing her, "we have it covered. Thank you. The guest of honor shouldn't set-up her own ball."

"I don't mind," Belle insisted. "It'll go a lot faster with three people."

"Don't worry, Belle. We got it," Esmé replied. "We're almost done anyways."

"Okay." Belle frowned. She made her way back to the table with Esmé's gifts and sat down. She didn't know what to do with herself. If she was in her world, she'd have used her phone to pass the time. But she hid it her first day there and forgot where she put it. She didn't think to bring a book and it seemed Desiree was still getting ready. She was stuck twiddling her thumbs until Esmé and Raoul were finished.

A few minutes later, Esmé sat next to Belle. There was only a little left to do and Raoul offered to take care of the rest so Esmé could hang out with Belle.

"Sorry it took so long," Esmé apologized. "I forgot about food and Raoul had to help me prepare everything."

"It's all right," Belle said. "It's your first time throwing a ball. Don't focus on what you failed to do and focus on the amazing ball you did manage to pull off."

"If you say so." Esmé nodded insecurely. He looked at the presents on the table and asked, "What's that?"

"Your presents," Belle said, happily. She explained the purpose of wrapping presents in decorative paper and the excitement. "But we should wait until the ball is over before you open it."

"Why?"

"Because I want you to experience having to wait for presents."

Esmé tried to hide the disapproval on his face. "I don't see the point in that, but you know more about this than I do. So, I'll wait…patiently."

"Great." Belle smiled. "As a matter of fact, your presents should go under the tree."

Belle grabbed the stack of presents and placed them under the Christmas tree. She continued, "Now, it's like Christmas in my world."

"It does look nice," Esmé said. "I wish there were more presents under it."

"Well, next year, we'll be better prepared. So, it'll be stacked with presents."

Esmé smiled. He was happy Belle was planning for a future. Of course, he'd forgotten that she was still a prisoner and had no choice to be there. "Yes, we'll be prepared."

Raoul sighed behind them. "Everything is set. Shall we commence the ball?"

"Wait," Belle said, "Desiree isn't here yet."

"Unfortunately, she's not coming," Raoul said.

"What? Why not? Does she know about it?" Belle asked.

"Yes, I invited her," Raoul confirmed. "I don't believe it's my place to say this, but Miss Desiree declined my invitation because she knows you're still mad at her. She wants you to have a stress-free time."

"I'm not mad at her," Belle said, shocked. "I mean, yeah, I was this morning. But after she helped you, I wasn't."

"Well, Miss Desiree doesn't know that," Raoul mentioned.

"Can you hold off on starting?" Belle asked. "I'm going to get Desiree!"

"By all means," Raoul answered, motioning with his wing for her to leave.

"Thanks!" Belle lifted the hem of her gown and ran out of the gymnasium.

Belle burst through Desiree's door. Desiree had been snuggled up on her chaise with a blanket by the fireplace reading when Belle came in.

She looked up from her book, surprised Belle was speaking to her. She scrambled from her chair, throwing her book on the chaise and said, "Is-Isabelle, what are you… I mean, you…you look beautiful."

"Thanks, but get ready, quickly!"

"What do you mean?"

"What do *you* mean, 'What do you mean'?" she replied. "You're supposed to be at the ball."

"It's fine," Desiree declined. "You go have fun."

"I can't have fun knowing my sister isn't at the Christmas party. You know every year it's supposed to be all of us there. You already missed the one with our family. The least you can do is show up to this one."

Desiree was confused. Belle had been giving her the cold shoulder for weeks, even most of the day. Why did she randomly want to speak to her again? "You…want me to go? But aren't you mad at me?"

"I was disappointed. It seemed like you weren't understanding *why* I was upset. You weren't trying to make up with Raoul. You weren't trying to be kind to him—"

"I was," Desiree interrupted. "I mean, I wasn't at first, but I am trying now."

Hearing, but not acknowledging, what Desiree said, Belle continued, "But, after seeing you help Raoul, with gardening of all things, I realized you were trying. Maybe not in the way we all wanted, but still doing your best.... Are you helping him because *you* want to, or are you doing it for me?

"I miss hanging out with you and sharing things about Esmé and Raoul with you. But I'm terrified you'll overreact or use it against them," Belle said. "I know you have a good heart. That's why I forgave you. So please, get ready for the ball."

"I understand," Desiree said. "You're right to feel the way you do. I broke your trust, and it's going to take time to mend it. However, I want to clarify some things as well. I know it's going to sound like an excuse, but please listen.

"I don't know what's wrong with me. I'm trying to be nice to Raoul, I really am. But something is making me angry. I don't understand why I feel so irrationally angry with him. Every time he speaks to me, or does something nice, it makes me even angrier. I've never acted this way. *You* should know that better than anyone. I know it makes me sound even worse, I already cried about it because it's frustrating to acknowledge that I'm not as good a person as I thought I was, or what I wanted to be.

"The 'argument,' putting it lightly, that started all of this, wasn't under my control. I'm not lying or avoiding accountability. I really hope this doesn't affect how you feel now, but…" Desiree paused to gather her words. It was hard to describe the way she felt in that moment. "…I just felt this rage, I'd never felt before, surge through my body. I knew what I said was wrong the moment it left my mouth, but I just couldn't stop myself. I apologized to Raoul right after that. I apologized because I was afraid he would tell you, not only because you'd just told me how you felt; but also because it was rude and mean.

"While it was wrong for me to say what I said, you have to understand where I was coming from, Isabelle. Dad and I were sentenced to death. Regardless of how kind and nice they are, it doesn't take away the fact that I'm here against my will. 3 days in, did you really think I was going to trust someone who said I was going to die, and the only way to remove the death sentence was to become their servant? What about that is trust-worthy? I was scared. And the only thing I wanted to do was protect you. As I think about it, maybe that's why I lashed out the way I did. Was it smart to do? No, but what else can I do, Isabelle?

"I've had time to think, and I know they aren't dangerous, not to the level I made them out to be. Three weeks was enough time for me to trust that they weren't going to brutally murder us. However, we should still keep in mind that if neither one of us follows through with what was assigned to us, then it's over. You don't know how terrifying it is. The thought that at any moment they could change their mind and put me on death row. That *dad* is going to die if they send you home early."

"I…I guess I forgot about why we were here," Belle said, still taking in what Desiree said. "My life isn't in danger like yours. *I* actually came here willingly. I'm sorry I behaved the way I did. It's not fair to force you to be all 'jolly' with them. You only ended up in this predicament trying to save me. I'll be mindful of that. And…I'll tell them to not continue with the ball."

"Isabelle, you said you felt at home here, right? Don't let my situation change that. Be friends with Esmé and Raoul. Esmé cares about you. You can be friends with them all you want. Go to the ball, heck, I'll go with you. I just want you to understand why I treated them the way I did." Desiree smiled. "I'll make an effort to be friends with them, too. Raoul and I cleared the air earlier. He does seem like a 'nice guy,' and that's enough for me to try to be friends. And, it might even reverse my sentencing, who knows. Just remember that it's going to take me some time. Until I am sure I'm safe, I will always have that fear that I'm going to die."

"Okay." Belle nodded. Her mood had shifted. She was so unforgiving to her own sister, but let the young men that made her feel the way she did, get off scot-free. "I'm sorry. I was scared you'd end up like the twins—"

"Excuse me?" Desiree said, as if Belle had just spit on her. "I will *never* end up like those disappointments. I can't believe you would even think that."

"I'm sorry." Belle panicked. "I didn't mean to offend you. It's just that…the way you were treating Esmé and Raoul, reminded me of how the twins treated me. I wanted you to stop before you ended up like them."

Desiree sighed, fighting away her frustration. "Like I said before, I will never end up like the twins. There's a difference between being mean for no reason, and being mean to people who pose a threat.

"*I* fall under the 'feeling threatened' category. The twins fall under the 'mean for no reason' category," Desiree continued. "I'm not nasty to everyone I meet, nor will I ever be. I don't just target one person and bully them. Yeah, I was mean to Raoul; however, my anger was a result of what they did to you and dad, and now what they are doing to me. Becoming a bad person, like Britney and Natasha, is never going to happen."

"I believe you," Belle said. "I'm sorry for misunderstanding."

"Since we're throwing around apologies, I'm sorry for not taking your feelings into consideration with those two." Desiree gave Belle a hug. After a long embrace, she said, "Now help me get ready. Have you seen the gown Raoul gave me?"

Desiree showed Belle the gown and Belle gushed like she did with her own gown. "It's beautiful! Yours even came with a choker! That is going to look so cute."

"That's what I thought," Desiree said, undressing. "I'm surprised they knew so much about our styles."

"That's because—" Belle bit her lip. She assumed the gowns were made by that sorceress Esmé mentioned. They wouldn't be able to tell their dress size, favorite color, nor their clothing preferences. She didn't even bring the clothes she actually liked to wear. So, putting two and two together could only lead to the sorceress. However, Belle couldn't tell Desiree about her. Esmé wasn't supposed to tell her. If word got out that they knew, Esmé would get in trouble. And Belle would feel horrible.

"'Because' what?" Desiree asked. "Can you tie the back?"

"Because, because…. Esmé asked me," Belle answered. "I forgot that he'd asked me what our favorite colors and dress sizes were. I didn't really pay attention to why he needed it."

"Well, now we know." Desiree spun around, the skirt softly flowing as she turned. "What do you think?"

Belle gasped. "You look gorgeous. The blue really matches your complexion. And, I love how flowy it is. Spin again."

Desiree obliged and twirled around faster this time. The skirt lifted higher and they both gushed about it. They spent 5 minutes laughing giddily while twirling their dresses.

Belle sat on the sofa and said, "Can you imagine how beautiful our dresses will be when we're dancing. It'll be just like in fairy tales."

Desiree grinned. "So, you plan on dancing with Esmé?"

"I…I mean, maybe if he asks. I want to dance, but I can't dance with you or neither one of our dresses will flow."

"Hey, if you want to dance with monkey boy, be my guest," Desiree joked. "No judgement."

Belle gave her a look. "Would you dance with Raoul if he asked?"

"As of now, no. And, it's not even possible. He doesn't have hands to hold."

"Yes, he does," Belle said, giving Desiree a confused look. "You never noticed he has hands at the end of his wings?"

Desiree imagined Raoul. He did have large, furry hands with sharp-pointed nails. Desiree inwardly shuddered. The way his arms looked repulsed her, but she did her best not to think about it. That was the norm in his world. And just because he was "different" from them, did not mean he was disgusting. Her normal, wasn't his normal, and even if it was the same standard in both their kingdoms, he was still a living being with feelings. Treating him differently because of his appearance was cruel. It was weird to her, but normal for him.

"That's right," she responded, "he does have hands. My answer's still no. You know I hate dancing."

"Yeah, I forgot you dance like a chicken with its head chopped off."

"Very funny," Desiree said, dryly. She put the choker on, and said, "You ready to go?"

"What about your hair and makeup?" Belle asked.

"What about it?"

"Shouldn't we style your hair and powder your face?"

"Why? It's only beasts at the ball." Desiree scoffed.

"So, it's not for them, it's for us," Belle replied, rummaging through Desiree's luggage. She pulled Desiree's makeup kit out of the suitcase. "You're getting dolled up…. Plus, I want to use some."

"You can use it without me having to as well…."

"Yeah, but it'll be cute if we matched." Belle pouted. "You brought your phone, didn't you?"

"Yeah?"

"Our phones work here. So, we can record ourselves. Then, when we go home, we can show our family. It won't look as fun if neither one of us look like a princess."

Desiree rolled her eyes. "Fine, I'll put on makeup."

"Yay," Belle squealed, clapping her hand, excitedly.

Both young ladies stood in the mirror as they put their makeup on.

***

Esmé and Raoul stood silently in the gymnasium. Belle had just run off and neither of them knew what to do. *How long will they take to get ready?* Raoul worried about the food getting cold and Esmé was upset Desiree was coming.

Raoul finally broke the silence. "So, all it took was Miss Desiree helping me to get back in Miss Belle's good graces?"

"It's more than that," Esmé grumbled. As annoyed as Esmé was, he explained to Raoul what Belle told him about Desiree and how much she hated gardening. He'd forgotten about it until Belle mentioned she wasn't angry. "Belle told me this morning it would take a long time to forgive her and that she wasn't invited to the ball. Gardening must be a bigger deal than we think."

"I think so." Raoul was moved. Spending hours in the cold tending to a garden that she must've hated. Maybe she really was trying to become friends. Of course, Raoul needed more than just friends, but it was a start. He had been hesitant, even after their conversation earlier. Every time he opened his heart to her, truly believing her attempts of friendship, she'd stab him deeper in the heart. Was tormenting herself the sign he needed? Was this…his real chance at courting her?

Esmé studied Raoul's facial expression and said, "Don't get encouraged. Every time she does something nice, we think she's changed, and she turns around and hurts you. Just keep your guard up. Maybe she'll push you down the stairs next time, instead of throwing you out of a window."

Raoul laughed at Esmé's exaggeration. "Honestly, you may be right. I'll avoid the stairs next time I'm with Miss Desiree."

"I'm serious."

"So I am." Raoul smiled. "Let's give her a week. She has a record of changing the same day she's kind to me. If a week goes by and Miss Desiree returns to her original behavior, I'll take things slower than I already am. If she continues to be kind, I'll officially start the courting process. Does that sound fair?"

Esmé nodded.

"And, if she does last a week, I think it's your turn to work on your feelings towards Miss Desiree."

Esmé groaned.

Before he could complain, Raoul said, "It's only fair. Keep in mind, most of their fear stems from your behavior when we first met them. It's only natural Miss Desiree is uneasy around her 'executioners.' It also won't work in your favor if you're on bad terms with your in-laws. You must learn patience and forgiveness too."

"*Fine*," Esmé forced out. "*One* week is all she gets."

"That's all I ask." Raoul looked at the table and counted the dinnerware. "I should grab another set for Miss Desiree. I'll be right back."

"While you're in the castle, change clothes."

"I'm sorry?"

"If I have to get fancy for Belle, then you can do so for Desiree."

Raoul sighed. He walked to the door. "I suppose you're right."

"Better hurry," Esmé shouted, as the door closed, "don't want to be later than the ladies."

He waited until he could no longer hear Raoul's footsteps in the stairwell and grabbed his necklace. "I know I've been asking for too much, Lady Orchida. But can you do me one last favor? Make Raoul a suit, one that doesn't look so boring."

Raoul opened his bedroom door to see a white suit that had materialized out of thin air. It laid on his bed, the last sparkles of magic floating away. He examined the suit. The blazer had gold stitching, epaulets, and buttons. The kingdom's emblem and national flower, the sapphire rose, was patched on the breast pocket of the blazer.

"Thank you, Lady Orchida. It looks amazing."

He dressed as fast as he could. He gazed in the mirror at his smooth, tawny complexion. He pulled his hair back to see if a ponytail would work better or if he should keep his hair down. He dropped his arms.

"Why am I even bothering?" he sighed. "She won't see me like this. I'll be a monster throughout the event."

He took off his shoes and transformed into his chimera form to ensure the outfit would still fit him perfectly. He transferred the medals from his previous suit to the one he wore. He stopped by the kitchen to grab dinnerware for Desiree and returned to the recreational building.

Esmé whistled when he saw Raoul. "That suits you."

"Thank you. Lady Orchida did an amazing job on this." He set the table for Desiree.

"Yeah, and it's different from all of your other suits. You're welcome, by the way."

"I thought we agreed to not bother her."

"I told her this was the last time. I had to give you a present too, for Christmas."

"Thank you. But please, please let this be the last time. If we can't become independent, what are we going to do? She can't take care of us forever. And it'll certainly be embarrassing to look dependent to our future wives."

"I know. I won't call her anymore."

"Good."

They heard the door to the stairwell open and close, and two muddled voices.

"They're back," Raoul said, standing up straight. He motioned for Esmé to stand beside him.

Belle and Desiree climbed the stairs.

"These dresses are unbearable," Desiree complained. Desiree struggled to keep her hem from dragging. The dresses were too heavy and made it difficult to walk up the stairs.

"Beauty hurts," Belle joked. She looked as though she was gliding as they ascended, reaching the third floor. Belle asked, "You ready?"

"Yep."

"Wait! You're wearing that necklace!" Belle gasped.

"I forgot I had this on." Desiree unclipped the necklace. "Where am I gonna put it?"

"How did you forget you were wearing it?"

"A certain *someone* was so angry with me, she told me not to take it off, even when I'm sleeping. Of course, I'd forget!"

"You actually kept it on for two weeks straight?"

"Except when showering, yeah."

Belle shook her head and laughed. She took the necklace from Desiree's hand and wrapped it around her wrist. "Your arms look bare anyway. Just wear it like a bracelet."

"It does kinda match my choker. Unconventional, but we are in a different world. Who's gonna know?" she grinned.

They opened the door and Raoul bowed. Esmé followed suit.

"Ooh, this is different," Belle said.

"Yes, Miss Belle. You did arrive earlier than we expected, so we couldn't give you a proper greeting." Raoul smiled.

"I'm sorry for arriving early," Belle replied.

"Don't apologize," Esmé said. "It's not that big a deal."

"He is right," Raoul said. "Well, let the ball commence."

Suddenly, classical music began to play. Everyone looked around.

Raoul nudged Esmé, he gave him a look, *Did you ask Lady Orchida?*

As if reading his mind, Esmé shook his head and shrugged.

Belle grabbed Desiree's hand and led her to the ballroom floor. "Take a video of me twirling."

"Sure," Desiree said, taking her phone out of the top of her dress.

Esmé and Raoul watched, confused. Not sure why Desiree was holding an object to her face and why Belle suddenly spun around. They seemed like they were having fun. The young beasts wondered what they should do next, now that the ball had begun. It had been years since they socialized with others and neither attended any balls or social events.

"These are going to be great," Desiree said. She stood next to Belle and took a selfie. "The twins will be jealous they didn't come."

After a few more videos, Desiree stuffed her phone back into her dress and returned to the beasts.

Esmé was the first to speak. "Belle, can I open my presents now?"

"Hmm, it's still early, but I guess it's all right, come on," she said, leading him to the tree. "Before I give you your presents, I wanna tell you that I couldn't get you anything 'new.' Hopefully I'll be more prepared next year."

"A gift's a gift, right?" Esmé said, picking up the first present. He opened the pencils and gasped. "I've never seen so many color pencils."

"Yeah, it's a great set. It's pretty rare in my world."

"And you're giving it to *me*?" Esmé asked.

"Why not?" Belle answered. "Nothing can compare to what you've done for me. It's the least I can do. And besides, it'll be fun having an art friend. I'll teach you how to draw and everything."

"Thank you." Esmé smiled. He opened the last present and said, "Wow, this is a large sketchbook. Did you decorate the cover?"

"Yeah…something like that. It was a gift from my sisters but they didn't want me using it. Instead of letting it collect dust, I figured I'd give it to you."

"Are you sure?"

"Of course. I didn't want to use it. Now, you and I can draw together...and on proper material."

"I'd like that," Esmé said.

There was an awkward moment of silence. Esmé set the drawing supplies on the table and asked, "What do we do now?"

"What's normal to do at balls?" Belle said.

Esmé shrugged. "Never been to one. What do you do at Christmas parties?"

"Well…you don't have the technology to do what we did…."

"And what's that?"

"Watch movies, play boardgames, you do have music playing, somehow, but not Christmas music," Belle answered. "Which by the way, how is it even possible?"

"I don't know either," Esmé said. "I'm sure the sorceress I told you about is behind it."

"She seems to always be one step ahead of you guys."

"Yeah, and I'm grateful to her for it. The mother I wish I had." Esmé smiled. "Oh, I know something. Dancing. I'm not the best dancer, but I've read many books about ballroom dancing and Raoul tried to teach me at one point."

"I can't dance, at all." Belle waved her hands frantically.

"Neither can I, but the whole point of a ball is to dance. Just follow my lead," Esmé said, extending a hand. "If you have to look down, it's okay."

"O-okay," Belle said, hesitantly. She took Esmé's hands and he led her to the middle of the ballroom.

"Ready?" he asked.

Belle nodded.

Both stiffly moved their legs, Belle following as best she could. She stepped on his foot occasionally, but they weren't terrible.

Desiree spotted them and took out her phone to record. Belle looked so cute. Desiree absolutely *had* to capture this moment. Not only for Belle to look back on fondly, but also to rub it in the twins' faces. Once she had enough footage, she put her phone away. A few tables down, Desiree saw Raoul was also watching them, with crossed wings and a disapproving look.

"Esmé is a great dancer," Desiree said, approaching him.

Raoul's expression changed upon hearing her. Smiling, he said, "Yes. Esmé's exemplary at most things. Natural born talent."

"Guess it bothers you that Isabelle's making him mess up, huh?" Desiree laughed.

"Oh! No, not at all. Miss Belle is doing a fantastic job."

"You look so displeased by them, I thought that must've been why."

"My apologies. I am, but not because of Miss Belle."

"What's wrong with them dancing? Does it have to do with Esmé?" Desiree was hopeful Raoul also didn't like them being friends. She eagerly awaited his response.

"Well, yes and no. In our kingdom, first dances usually happen on your wedding day. It's considered inappropriate to dance with someone that isn't your significant other. It's a sign of affection that should only be done between two people who love each other." Raoul mumbled, more so to himself than Desiree, "Although, some dance if they're engaged and commoners don't engage in this rule at all. I guess it's really just the royal family that's upheld this tradition."

Desiree shivered at the thought of Belle and Esmé being married. "So Esmé's breaking a rule or something?"

"Yes. Esmé's never been one to follow traditions he finds unreasonable." Raoul smiled. "But, knowing Esmé, he more than likely has forgotten he's not supposed to do this. I didn't focus on this during his education as I didn't think something like this would happen.

"I'm not all that upset over it. I'm the crown prince, so it's not that big of a deal if he does. They're also children, so there's no harm in it," he continued. He thought, *Besides, I assume Miss Belle will be his wife in the near future. So there's no harm in them dancing ahead of schedule.*

"I see. So, with all of that said, I take it you don't want to dance with me? Guess I'll have to sit in the corner all night."

"Huh?" Raoul's heart almost leapt from his chest. Raoul spoke a mile a minute. "I-I-I…It's certainly something scandalous…Nor would Esmé ever follow my example if I partook in breaking this tradition…But then again, it's only us here—"

"I'm kidding," Desiree interrupted, laughing.

"A-are you sure?" Raoul asked.

"Completely. I hate dancing."

Raoul nodded.

Hoping to change the subject, Desiree asked, "So you were in charge of Esmé's education?"

"Not quite. It's something I volunteered to do myself. Due to…past events…we were left without a teacher. I want Esmé to have a bright future, so I took on the role of becoming his teacher, despite being a student."

"That's commendable," Desiree said. "He's lucky to have a brother like you."

"Thank you, but I'm the lucky one. I don't know where I would be without him."

"I feel the same about my siblings," Desiree agreed. *Except the twins….*

An awkward silence hung in the air between them.

"So tell me," Raoul said, feeling like it was his turn to speak, "how do you know so much about gardening?"

"It was my mother's passion. She had a large garden in our backyard, a few patches at a community garden, and even volunteered to help in other people's gardens. She wanted me and my siblings to learn how to garden and made us help in hers." She sighed, "Somehow, I always ended up being the only one that *stayed* and helped. So, my mom showered me with attention and I learned a lot of useful things."

"Well, I'm very grateful to her. If she never taught you, you would not be able to help me."

"Yeah, I guess she was right that I would need to use it in the future…. Just not *exactly* how she imagined it."

"If you don't mind, I do have another question about my garden…"

Desiree and Raoul continued to speak about gardening. Desiree was surprised she'd ever enjoy anything garden related. Raoul learned that even though her mom had passed away years ago, Desiree continued to garden. She never told anyone but Freddy. It was her way of feeling like her mom was still with her. She did not want to take the bonding experience they had for granted. She hated watering her garden daily, but it was all worth the nostalgia.

On the other side of the gym, Belle and Esmé had taken a break from dancing. Belle decided to show Esmé other things to do at a party. With limited options, they used Esmé's sketchbook to play games like tic-tac-toe, hangman, and squares. She taught him Christmas origami and they drew Christmas sketches. Between each activity, they danced.

The evening went on perfectly. It was reaching 7 p.m. and Raoul felt it was best to have dinner before the food got cold. They all sat at the same table and Belle and Esmé continued their conversation. Raoul and Desiree talked while also jumping in and out of Belle and Esmé's conversations.

"Then my dad somehow managed to slip on the tree skirt and spilled eggnog all over my brother and Desiree," Belle said, laughing.

"I can't believe you still remember that," Desiree chuckled, somewhat embarrassed. "I'll never live that down, huh? It took hours to clean my braids and get rid of that smell."

As they joked and laughed, telling embarrassing stories about each other, a large bang filled the gym, startling everyone. Belle shrieked and they all turned in the direction of the sound. The wind blew the doors open and snow came in at intense speed.

"That scared me," Belle said, clutching her chest.

"I will close the doors," Raoul volunteered. "Please continue."

They watched silently as Raoul walked to the other side of the gym.

Hoping to lighten the mood, Desiree broke the silence. "Anyways, Esmé, does your world celebrate any holidays?"

Both Esmé and Belle flinched. Belle thought about the Rose Festival. Surely Esmé hadn't as well, right? She inconspicuously reached for his hand under the table and she clasped it.

Esmé smiled reassuringly at Belle, tightening his grip on her hand.

"Not that I can think of. We're kind of secluded from the rest of the kingdom. Maybe Raoul knows of some."

Using her other arm, Belle placed a hand on his forearm. "We should make our own holiday! Since you two have the most power, you can make Christmas an official holiday and we can think of one that everyone will enjoy."

"Let's do that."

With the conversation steering away from their fright earlier, Desiree glanced back to the door. Raoul stood between the doorframe.

Is he all right? she thought.

After a brief moment, Raoul closed and locked the door. Instead of returning to the table, he walked out of the gym.

Bathroom? she thought. She shrugged. *I'm sure he's fine.*

Desiree went back to listening to Belle and Esmé's outlandish holiday ideas. Ideas like on April 5th, everyone wears hats on their butts or a holiday where people eat their favorite desserts all day for three days, then leads into the next holiday of dental work and brushing your teeth. Desiree was tasked with writing their ideas down.

Once they had completed 4 pages of ideas, Esmé finally noticed that Raoul hadn't returned. He asked, "Where's Raoul?"

"Uh, I don't know. Bathroom maybe?" Desiree guessed. "I saw him leave after closing the doors."

"Let me check," Esmé said, leaving the table. He returned a minute later shaking his head. "Where could he have snuck off to?"

"Should we look for him?" Belle asked.

"Yeah," Esmé agreed.

"I'll look," Desiree offered. "This is you guys' party. Don't leave until you're ready to. I'm sure Raoul went to get ready for bed. You know how he's a stickler for schedules."

Stickler? Esmé thought. "I think you're right. Knowing him, he probably thought it was best to leave without saying anything so we don't feel compelled to end early."

"Exactly. When I find him, I'll come back to let you all know, before getting ready for bed myself."

"Okay." Belle waved, as Desiree stood to leave.

"Have fun, you two." She paused mid-step and turned around. "And no funny business."

They both raised their hands defensively. Desiree knew it was impossible for Belle to even consider anything inappropriate with a beast. Her warning was more so about not doing anything bad in general, like trashing the place or finding alcohol.

"Wait! Your shawl!" Belle yelled.

"I won't be gone long. I'll grab it when I come back."

~Belle x Esmé~

The music resumed after the gymnasium doors closed behind Desiree. Thinking it was a cue from Lady Orchida, Esmé said, "Do you want to dance again?"

"Sure," Belle said, following him to the middle of the room. "Are you okay?"

"Yeah, why do you ask?"

"Well, Desiree brought up the Rose Festival…and you look sad."

"I'm fine. It's a touchy topic, but I'm not weak or anything," he mumbled.

"Who said being sad over something traumatic means you're weak?"

"No one…" Esmé averted his eyes. "Look, I really do mean it when I say I'm fine. I finally have a friend. That's all that matters to me. I told you how I felt and I haven't been sad in a while."

"Are you being honest with me? Friends don't lie to each other."

"Yes…the only thing bringing up the Festival did was remind me that I'm trapped here. I wanna see things beyond the castle grounds and be around other people." Esmé stopped dancing and dropped his hands. "I love Raoul but I want to be around other people sometimes. I feel guilty saying it because I'm the reason we were trapped here in the first place. But can you blame me for not wanting to be alone? How was I supposed to know they would think we were monsters?"

Esmé sat at the nearest table and rested his head on his hands. "I just want to be normal."

Belle sat beside him and placed a comforting hand on his back. "I've been meaning to ask this since you told me what happened…Aren't you the same as the others? Why would they treat you like monsters and call you so…if you look the same? What do you mean, 'normal'?"

Shoot… Esmé thought. *I'm going to accidently give everything away. Think.*

When Esmé didn't respond, Belle said, "I'm sorry, I didn't mean to pry…I was just wondering…."

176

"It's fine…" Esmé paused to think. "It's…just that…my brother and I are different….Most…Almost everyone in the kingdom is one kind of animal. Like some are fully rabbit or dog. But whatever my dad did, caused us to be born the way we are. And people are repulsed by us."

"I see…" Belle nodded.

"If anything, I wish I looked like you. Then I could probably go to your world and not deal with any of these losers. You were so quick to accept us, I bet everyone is like that where you're from."

"Ehh…not necessarily. But everyone's learning to embrace people who are different. The jerks who don't, are slowly being shunned."

"If only people learned to do that here."

"Jerks are everywhere unfortunately. Can't do anything about hateful people and the ones who protect them. It's weird. My world is weird. At least you have magic."

"You don't?"

Belle shook her head no.

"Well, not everyone here knows magic. There are only specific kingdoms that have sorcerers and witches and stuff."

"That's so cool. You only see that in movies and books in my world."

"What is your world like? Do you have anything cool?"

"Hmm…" Belle tapped her chin. "Well we're more advanced in terms of technology."

"How so?"

"Like you guys don't have TVs or phones. You don't have games—"

Esmé interrupted, "We have games we play. I'll show you later."

"I believe you. But we have a different kind of game, video games. You don't have computers." Belle counted on her fingers as she listed every invention she has yet to see in the castle.

"Wow, that does sound amazing. I have no idea what any of those things are, but I want them."

Belle laughed. "Maybe we can go to my world when my sentence is up. That way you can see what I mean, and maybe even be the first to invent them here."

"You'd really take me with you?"

"Why not? We're friends, right? I'm sure that's better than spending the rest of your life stuck here. We'll be the bridge to diplomacy between worlds."

"Thank you," Esmé said, smiling. "You're the best friend I've ever had."

"I'm your only friend, but I'll take it."

Esmé lifted his pinky finger. "We'll go to your world."

Belle nodded.

~Desiree x Raoul~

The snow fell softly. The silence was deafening yet peaceful. Snow crunching beneath Desiree's feet pierced the silence. It was as if the world was moving slowly and only Desiree was in it. It was nostalgic. It brought Desiree back to when she was in middle school making her way home after school in the dark. Not a soul in sight.

The first place she checked was the kitchen. The sink was piled with dishes, so he definitely hadn't been there. She checked the lounge, and made her way up to his bedroom. She knocked on the door, but there was no answer. Desiree waited to make sure he wasn't on his way to answer, then placed an ear to his door. Nothing.

Is he still at the recreational building? she wondered. Desiree made her way back then searched every floor except the third. *Where could he be?*

Desiree looked out the window into the garden. Could he have been there? The second time she left the building, she noticed footprints. She had been too focused on her memories that she didn't even bother to look down. She followed the footprints deep into the garden. She just hoped that she found him before the snow covered both their tracks.

Desiree searched the garden for Raoul. She was certainly curious. How far did his garden really go? What could he even grow past a certain point? The designs throughout the sections she passed were beautiful. To think he could manage to keep up with possibly miles of plants was remarkable. She planned to come back to see its true beauty when the snow melted. She made her way to an open area. There were benches to each side of a courtyard. In the center of the courtyard was a large fountain of a king. Beneath it, looking up at the statue was Raoul. Water was flowing slowly from the fountain, the bottom frozen completely. The sound of shoes crunching against the snow brought Raoul out of his thoughts.

"Oh, Miss Desiree," he said, turning to her. "What brings you out here?"

"You've been gone for a while. Everyone was wondering where you went," Desiree answered.

"I'm sorry for worrying everyone. I just remembered that I needed to turn off this fountain…."

"Is the valve broken?"

"No…I just…wondered if it was worth doing."

"Why wouldn't it be? Won't it break?"

"Yeah, it might…." Raoul trailed off.

"Do you not like it?"

"Something like that…" Raoul paused. "It's a fountain designed after my father. I don't think it belongs in my garden, but it's been here longer than I've been alive apparently."

"If you don't mind me asking, and please don't answer if you're uncomfortable, but did something happen between you and your dad?"

"Why do you say that?" he asked.

"I mean, isn't it normal for kids that have a good relationship with their parents to want something to remember them by? I feel that way towards my mom and eventually towards my dad when it's his time."

Raoul sighed. "Long story short, yes. He's done unforgivable things not just to me and Esmé, but to millions of people. And Esmé and I are the ones paying the price…."

"What could he have done?" she asked.

"It's something that I'm not yet ready to tell….If you don't mind…that is."

"I understand. Sorry for asking."

"Don't be. Most people know the kind of man he was and what he'd done. It's not a secret. I also wouldn't be surprised if there are documents in the castle about it. It's just that I can't—" Raoul paused. It was hard to say what he meant without being too vulnerable.

"I know what you mean," Desiree said. "That's what I was apologizing for. I didn't mean to bring up something that hurt you."

"You didn't," he said, smiling. "Seeing his fountain is a constant reminder of my hurt and anger. Before you found me, I wanted to break it. My emotions got the better of me."

"Well, instead of breaking it," Desiree said, "why don't you just sell it once it's warm? Or send for someone to move it elsewhere? Doesn't make sense to destroy something of your father's. Think about how long it took someone to create it."

"Maybe you're right," he said. As he turned the valve, he continued, "Doesn't make sense to destroy someone's hard work. It's too late to drain it, but I'm sure it'll still hold its value even if there are a few cracks."

"You know…"

"Hmm?"

"It's not a good idea to bottle up your emotions. Why don't you tell him how you feel? Even if it's just to his statue, something is better than nothing."

"I couldn't possibly—"

"Would it be better if I couldn't hear?"

Before Raoul could answer, Desiree walked to the courtyard entrance.

Raoul sighed. Were there even words for the way he felt towards the king? He stared into the eyes of the statue fountain. The cold, lifelessness in its eyes just like the ones his father's had whenever he'd spare even a glance in Raoul's direction. *Something is better than nothing.*

"F-father, I…" Raoul paused, his bottom lip trembling. He laughed. "What am I getting so nervous over? It's not like *you're* standing in front of me. I should be able to speak my mind…but why then do I feel even that's beyond what I deserve? …

"…I..."

Desiree bounced up and down, rubbing her arms quickly. *How could I be so stupid! I rushed off to catch up with Raoul, I did not want to grab my shawl.*

She pulled out her phone. *My battery's going to die soon. It's 8:25. It's been like 5 minutes since I left him. Please hurry. It's freezing.*

She put her phone away and looked around. Light fluffy flakes of snow fell gently from the sky. She could still see Raoul by the king's fountain. They had gone so far into his garden; Desiree doubted she would ever have a reason to go this far in the future. Why not explore until Raoul was ready to go back?

She lifted her hem and walked back the direction she came from. Beneath the blanket of white, was an array of colors. The sides of Raoul's garden looked like one long rainbow hidden below clouds.

"You really do have an amazing garden," Desiree mumbled to herself. She looked up to the sky and chuckled. "Mom, this was the kind of garden you always wanted, huh? The kind that never wilted even with 5 inches of snow weighing it down."

To her right, Desiree saw another path, an arch above it had been fortunate enough to not be covered in snow. It was certainly interesting that it could even happen. But as Desiree loved to remind herself, she was in a magical kingdom with beasts and invisible buildings. Anything was possible here.

Once she was on the other side, she saw what looked like a field of cotton candy with sprinkles on top that stretched half a mile. Desiree approached the "sprinkles" and noticed there was a faint amount of snow on top of a rose bush. In fact, that's what the entire field consisted of; a slow trickle of snow gently melted on to the petals.

"Are these the rose bushes dad was talking about?" she asked, out loud. "He wasn't lying. There really are multi-colored roses. They're beautiful."

She drew closer to the rose bush and thought, *The smell is incredible. Almost intoxicating.*

Out of boredom, she walked through the field counting each color and species, wondering how many variations were possible. She hoped Raoul would let her take a few home with her. The further out she went, the colder it became, so she turned around. After she passed the arch, she leaned against the wall and sighed. *Geez it's freezing!*

"Sorry for the wait," Raoul said.

"Ah!" Desiree jumped away from the wall. "Did you say everything you…needed to say?"

"Not necessarily *everything*. It was hard to find the right words. I couldn't even express a fraction of what I feel."

"Sometimes there aren't any," she said. "Before you sell it in the spring, why don't you practice? Then on the last day, bam! Get everything off your chest."

"I mean…I guess I could give it a shot. What's the worst that could happen?"

"Exactly. What, are you gonna break the fountain's heart?"

Raoul chuckled. "Maybe so. I'll come back tomorrow to try again."

"Great, now let's hurry back inside. It's freezing." Desiree smiled, lifting her hem to run.

"Oh! I'm sorry," Raoul said, taking off his jacket. "Please, use mine."

Desiree sighed. "This is a repeat of earlier today. Is there ever a moment when you aren't offering me things meant for *you*?"

"Yes," Raoul smiled, "when you remember to bring your coat."

"I'm fine. We're not that far from the castle. So I'll just go straight there." Desiree lifted her hem again, and jogged, terribly, through the now calf-high snow.

"Please allow me to escort you back to the castle," Raoul said, catching up to her.

"I didn't think there was a chance of crime here," she teased.

"No, it's only the four of us. It's just…a gentleman should always escort a lady home. Whether it's dangerous or not."

"Commendable," Desiree smirked. "Leave it to a prince to say that."

Raoul laughed as they struggled to make it home.

~Belle x Esmé~

"Do you think they'll be back soon?" Belle asked, her feet dangling off the ledge.

"Maybe. It is kind of late. They might have gone back to the castle," Esmé answered, leaning against the banister.

"I doubt Desiree would leave me here alone with you."

"She already did."

Belle thought about it. Desiree had been gone for 30 minutes, give or take. Was it possible she trusted them to be alone?

"Say," Esmé started.

"Hm?"

"Did you really mean what you said earlier? About showing me your world?"

"I meant every word."

"6 years is so far away," he groaned. "I don't know if I can wait that long."

"What other choice do we have?"

"Well…I could ask Raoul if we can go. We could go to your world this year."

"Are you sure that's okay?"

"Why wouldn't it be? It's better to go now."

"But aren't you worried that I'll run away once we get there? If my sentence is over, you won't have to worry about me running away."

"Yes, but I trust you," Esmé said, matter-of-factly. "Now, if it was Desiree, I wouldn't think twice about waiting. But you're an honest person. I know you wouldn't betray me like that."

"Desiree is honest," Belle corrected him, pursing her lips. "Then let's go to my world. I'll think of things we can do. I also have an idea

182

on how we can hide your appearance…not that there's anything wrong with it…"

"What idea?"

"I'll tell you once I have it figured out."

"I see them!" Esmé shouted, pointing.

Desiree followed Raoul as they navigated the garden.

"What are they doing?" Belle asked.

"I dunno. But at least Raoul's okay. I'm sure it was nothing. He likes to disappear into his garden from time to time."

"Pfft. I bet Desiree regrets not bringing her shawl."

Esmé looked back at the clock on the wall. "We should probably head back too. I don't want to hear Raoul nag me about going to bed at a proper hour. If I can get back before him, he's less likely to bother me about not being in bed."

Esmé took Belle's hand and helped pull her up to her feet.

"Let's take everything down tomorrow," Belle suggested.

"Take it down? Why?"

"You're supposed to only leave Christmas decorations up for like a week after Christmas. Take it down immediately after New Years. Maybe, a week after that. Any longer and people will judge you."

"But today's the first day it was completed. Can't we leave it up more than a day?"

"Fine, let's do it next week."

They carried the remaining food with them and packed the trays in the fridge. They walked slowly up the stairs.

"Thank you for such a wonderful day," Belle said. "I hadn't had this much fun in a while."

"You're welcome…I'm glad you liked it," he replied, bashfully. "Even though it was mostly Desiree's fault, we were still the reason why you two argued. It's the least I could do to make up for it."

"Well, I should get ready for bed. Goodnight, Esmé."

"Night, Belle."

Belle twirled her way down the hall. She giggled and skipped down the long corridor. *I feel like such a princess!*

Thank you, everyone. This was the best night ever!

~Desiree x Raoul~

"Hello?" Desiree shouted in the gymnasium.

"They may have gone to bed. It is rather late," Raoul said.

"I hope so," Desiree said, closing the door. "At least we don't have to hear any complaints about them wanting to hang out all night."

"Haha, I guess we're lucky then."

When they reached the top of the stairs in the castle, Raoul said, "Thank you for your help today. I was pretty depressed when it started snowing. If you hadn't asked for my help this morning, I don't know what would've happened."

"Of course. If you ever need any gardening tips, let me know."

"Will do. Goodnight, Miss Desiree," he said, softly.

"Raoul?" Desiree said, "One last thing."

"Yes? Is everything all right?"

"I just wanted to say…" she paused. "…I want to be friends."

He smiled. "I would like to, as well."

"Great! Easier than I thought," Desiree exclaimed. "…Goodnight!"

She was already turning and running before he finished his sentence.

"Goodnight, Miss Desiree."

Desiree took her dress off, showered, and slipped into something comfy. As she lay in bed, she thought, *I wonder if Isabelle is still awake.*

Desiree knocked on Belle's door. "Isabelle? You awake?"

Belle opened the door, wearing a fluffy pink bunny-eared spa headband. "Yeah, what's up?"

"I thought we could hang out tonight. Maybe have a sleepover."

Belle smiled, and moved to the side so Desiree could enter. "Oh my gosh, let's have a girls' night and pamper ourselves!"

"Good idea," Desiree said. "I'll grab my things."

Desiree returned with face masks, a facial kit, and a nail kit that had nail polish in different colors.

"Me first," Desiree said, extending her hand.

"What color?" Belle asked.

"Blue like my dress."

"That is going to look so cute," Belle said, searching the kit for the right shade of blue. "Did you have fun tonight? What did you and Raoul talk about?"

"At first we talked about dancing—"

"You were going to dance with him!?" Belle interrupted, shocked that her conversation with Raoul had gone in that direction.

"Nooo," Desiree cried, laughing and shaking her head in denial. "We watched you and Esmé dance. He told me some weird custom of theirs when it comes to dancing."

"What's weird about it?"

"Raoul said Esmé had broken some of their traditions; like you're only supposed to dance on your wedding day, or something like that," Desiree answered. "I did joke about dancing with him and he practically lost his mind."

Why did she feel so embarrassed? Belle felt a wave of butterflies in her stomach. *What does that mean? If dancing is for marriage, why would Esmé dance with me?*

Belle remembered her second night there. Esmé had proposed to her. Was he *still* thinking about marrying her? Or was it just a friendly dance? She hoped it was the latter. She chuckled, awkwardly, "That is a weird tradition. It's just dancing."

"What else did you and Esmé do?" Desiree asked.

"He opened a few presents that I put together for him," Belle said. "The twins got me a sketchbook and destroyed the cover. I can't even tell you what they drew on it."

"I can imagine it," Desiree said, rolling her eyes. "Let's not talk about those two. Did Esmé love it?"

"Yeah, he wants to learn how to draw, so I'm going to teach him."

"That's nice of you," Desiree said. "Raoul and I also talked about gardening. I'm shocked he doesn't know much about it. I never would've guessed based on the loveliness of his garden."

"He probably lets it grow wildly," Belle said.

"He said something like that. He only focuses on the fruit and vegetable garden. Otherwise, he just waters what he can, when he can."

"So are you friends now, or?"

"Working on it," Desiree said.

Desiree and Belle continued to giggle about the ball as they finished each other's nails and chatted before going to bed.

As Desiree slept beside her, Belle thought about her dance with Esmé. Hopefully, she was overthinking it.

***

Esmé paced down the hall in front of Raoul's door, eagerly. He was so excited to tell Raoul about his and Belle's plan. If he and Lady

Orchida agreed, Esmé would finally be able to experience a life round other humans. Even if it was only for a day, he was happy.

Raoul, also on cloud 9, slowly walked down the hall with a smile on his face. It didn't seem all that bad anymore that his garden died. Raoul was confident Desiree would help him bring it back to life in the spring. He hoped Lady Orchida figured out what was wrong with her soon. If she didn't hate his guts, the experience would be 10x better.

He collided with Esmé. "I'm sorry!"

Esmé shook his head, grinning from ear to ear. "Never mind that, I have to tell you something!"

Esmé pulled Raoul into his room and closed the door. Raoul immediately covered his nose. There was a putrid smell throughout the room. He couldn't find the source of the smell. Esmé's room was completely dark. Esmé turned on the lights and Raoul's eyes widened. Esmé's room was an absolute pigsty. Dirty clothes cluttered the floor. The boxes from the Christmas decorations were piled in a corner. Raoul could've also sworn he'd seen a man trapped somewhere inside of the pile. What remained on the plates from the leftover food Esmé ate two weeks ago was covered in mold on his table. It was most likely the source of the smell.

Raoul's stomach churned and he rushed out of Esmé's room. Confused as to what the problem was, Esmé followed after him. Raoul didn't have the heart to tell him his room was a disgusting mess. Raoul just told him that he preferred speaking in his own room. Although, he had plans to secretly tell Lady Orchida so she could order him to clean his room.

They sat on Raoul's sofa, and Esmé told him everything that happened between him and Belle at the party. Esmé asked Raoul if he could go to Belle's world.

"I don't know…" Raoul said. He was uncomfortable with Esmé going to a place he couldn't reach him if ever there was a situation like the Rose Festival. "How are you even going to hide your appearance?"

"I'm not sure," Esmé said. "Belle had something in mind, but she didn't tell me what."

Hearing that made Raoul even more unsure of the trip. While he wanted Esmé to have fun and experience Belle's world, it was just too risky. "I don't think it's a good idea."

"Why?" Esmé frowned.

"Because if something happened, you couldn't run away like you can here. Where would you go? What if it was all a trick and Belle escapes? How would you be able to break the curse then? How would you know how to get home if she hides your things?"

"Belle wouldn't do that," Esmé mumbled.

"I know she wouldn't, but there's always that 'what if,'" Raoul said. "I don't mean to upset you, but those are things you must think about when dealing with a situation like ours."

"I know," Esmé said, "but I…would like Lady Orchida to have the final say…."

"I thought we weren't going to bother her with our disagreements," Raoul complained.

"But, you're not gonna send for the SUV!" Esmé said.

"Because I don't think it's safe, Esmé. You have to stop calling Lady Orchida for every single argument."

"This is the only time I'm going to ask her for a favor!"

Raoul shook his head. "You've been bothering her for a while, this certainly isn't the first favor you requested, nor do I think it's the last."

"Yeah, but you're hogging the SUV!" Esmé shouted. "I can't make the decision on my own. You won't even tell me where it is or how to use it!"

"And I see I made the right the choice," Raoul said.

If Esmé hated him over this, Raoul was fine with that. Raoul would rather Esmé hate him forever, than to see Esmé's heart shattered again. Raoul would do everything within his power to not repeat their traumatic experience with the Rose Festival. This time, if anything happened, Esmé would have to face it alone. Raoul couldn't handle the thought of it.

Esmé was so upset, tears streamed from his eyes. "Then I'm telling Lady Orchida."

Before Raoul could respond, a voice from behind them said, "No need, I'm already here."

Lady Orchida startled both beasts and they stood to greet her.

Lady Orchida approached Esmé and wiped his tears with a handkerchief. She asked softly, "What's wrong?"

Esmé told her everything from his plans with Belle to Raoul's stubbornness. Raoul was prepping mentally for the possible tongue lashing he would receive for making Esmé cry.

Lady Orchida sighed. "Before I deal with your current problem, I must tell his highness that I've discovered the problem with Desiree."

Raoul's stomach dropped. Not only from the news about Desiree, but also because when Lady Orchida referred to him as "your highness," she was upset with him. Even though Lady Orchida spoke informally to the young beasts the majority of the time, when it came to discipline, she preferred to have some level of respect for their titles as princes.

"W-what is it?" Raoul stuttered.

"This was an oversight on my part, so I do apologize," Lady Orchida stated. Lady Orchida looked somewhat amused as she spoke. "It seems the sorceress that cast the spell, hid another deep within its core. Neither I nor the sorcerer your father sought first were able to catch this little trick of hers."

"Well…what's the trick?" Esmé asked, impatiently. The suspense from whatever was wrong with Desiree washed away his bad mood.

"Patience," she admonished him. "This curse was never meant to be broken—"

"What do you mean it wasn't?" Raoul asked, interrupting her.

"Your father was supposed to die on his coronation day. However, things didn't go as planned due to your father's stubbornness to survive and marry Raoul's mother." Lady Orchida sat on the chaise and continued, "I noticed every time his highness opened up to the possibility of falling in love with Desiree, an inexplicable feeling of hatred stifled her heart. When I discovered that even she couldn't explain why it happened, finding the 'why' was a piece of cake. This insignificant, childish sorceress' curse causes the curse holder's love to despise them. Meaning, this sorceress desperately wanted your father dead. And since you inherited the curse, your highness, the spell is also affecting you and for whom your affections lie."

Raoul felt a little better that it wasn't Desiree's choice to hate him.

"If that's the case," Esmé said, slightly doubtful, "why doesn't Belle hate me?"

Raoul looked back at Lady Orchida, fearing her response.

"Belle's heart is too pure to corrupt," Lady Orchida answered. "No spell in this world, or theirs, is strong enough to corrupt a heart as pure as hers."

"So, then Desiree's heart isn't pure enough to marry Raoul."

Lady Orchida shook her head. "I disagree. There are few in the world who have a heart as pure as Belle's. Finding one suitable to marry his highness would be like finding a needle in a haystack."

"It may be hard, but it's not impossible."

Lady Orchida smiled at Esmé's honesty. "You're right, but with the time left to break his curse, it's not worth the risk. I screened both young ladies myself, and both are the perfect matches for you two."

"But, if she doesn't have a pure heart, then she's too mean," Esmé said, unable to back down. He glanced at Raoul who avoided eye contact with both of them.

Before he could bring Raoul into the discussion, Lady Orchida said, "You're too young to understand. The world is not perfect; therefore there are no perfect beings. If you continue to look for a perfect person, you will find yourselves alone forever. Everyone has flaws, even Belle. Only when those flaws are harmful, as we've seen the curse force Desiree to say hurtful things, do we need to step away. Desiree is a good person; give her another chance without something beyond her control clouding her judgement."

"If I may speak," Raoul said, finally lifting his head. "If the Desiree I had the pleasure of spending today with is the real her, I would like to court her."

Esmé conceded. He didn't agree with Lady Orchida, but if Raoul wanted to marry Desiree, there was nothing he could do about it.

"Excellent choice, your highness." Lady Orchida smiled.

"If I may ask, how do you plan on breaking the spell?" Raoul asked.

"It will take some time; however, I will break the spell as quickly as I can."

"Why can't you just break it now?" Esmé asked.

"I could." Lady Orchida nodded. Sarcastically, she said, "Though breaking it so quickly could rebound and make her hate Raoul even more, it could potentially kill her as well. But of course, slow and steady is the worst outcome."

"Sorry…" was all Esmé could say.

Lady Orchida, amused with his reaction, changed the subject. "Now, your highness must know that I do not agree with making Esmé cry, selfishly hoarding the SUV."

Raoul chuckled nervously. He'd hoped she had forgotten about his little bout with Esmé. "I know. I apologize to you both. However, I kept the SUV's summoning location a secret as Esmé is too curious. My greatest concern was that he would leave somewhere we could not reach him. That is also why I do not want him going to Miss Belle's world. I'm scared something will happen to him. I will never forgive myself if I had the power to prevent it."

"Raoul…" Esmé was stunned. He didn't know Raoul felt so strongly about it.

"As long as he has his necklace, he can always call and I will save him. I understand your fear, but he is 17. He's capable of doing things on his own. Your father ruled an entire kingdom at his age," Lady Orchida said.

"Only because he had no other choice," Raoul protested. "Esmé has been locked away in this castle since he was a child, he doesn't know what it's like in the outside worlds!"

"Neither do you," Lady Orchida reminded him. "Esmé will be just fine. If you cannot bring yourself to summon the SUV, I will do it myself. Esmé is going to her world, and that is final."

"Thank you!" Esmé smiled. He turned to Raoul and said, "I promise I will be safe. If something goes wrong, I'll call Lady Orchida immediately."

Raoul looked disapprovingly, but he didn't say another word on the subject. Lady Orchida's words were final. Not only was she the authority figure in their lives, there was also a stipulation for breaking their curse. They must listen to her every command. There was no room to debate, though she let them voice their opinions on the matter.

"I know you're upset," Lady Orchida said. "But this is a great opportunity for Esmé to see Belle's world, and truly understand how different it is from here."

Raoul smiled despite himself. "If you think it's a good idea, and can further his progress with Belle, then I will give 100% of my support."

"I think it's a wonderful idea. It may even boost Belle's affections for Esmé."

Esmé cringed at the comment. His face still scrunched, he asked, "Do we *have* to love each other romantically?"

Lady Orchida raised an eyebrow inquisitively.

"What I mean is, do we have to get married? Can't the curse break if we're just friends?"

"Do you not like her?" Raoul asked.

"I love her, but I don't think it's a romantic love. She's a great person. She's pretty, kind, and considerate. I enjoy being around her, she makes me happy, and can't imagine my life without her."

That sounds like "romantic" love, Raoul thought.

"I like having a friend over a wife," Esmé said, gazing into Lady Orchida's eyes. "If she loves me as a friend, can't it break the spell?"

"Unfortunately, no," Lady Orchida said. "The condition placed on your father was that Lady Mia had to love him as a beast, not as a friend."

"But, wasn't the spell altered?" Esmé asked.

"Yes, but that was to extend his time limit and change to whomever your father loved, loving him in return. *Not* to change the type of love received," Lady Orchida answered. "If that were the case, his majesty Mylan would've been enough to break the curse decades ago."

"I just don't see her that way…" Esmé grumbled.

"Then try," Lady Orchida said. She opened a portal. Before stepping through the portal, she said, "I will return with the perfect date for your trip with Belle. As you both are aware, keep this a secret from Desiree."

"Of course," Raoul said, bowing. "Thank you for your help. Good night."

Esmé didn't bother bidding her farewell. He pouted on the side of Raoul until the portal closed.

Raoul patted him on the back and said, "Cheer up. You may not see Miss Belle in a romantic light now, but I'm sure the time will come when you do."

"I don't think so," Esmé continued to pout. After a brief moment of silence, he said, "I just don't see why Lady Orchida can't change the spell again."

"What do you mean, 'again'?" Raoul asked. "Lady Orchida never altered the terms of father's curse. She only did whatever magic stuff was required to break our curse, and his by default. It was the other sorcerer who changed it."

"Well, I hate him…."

Raoul smiled. "Since I can't stop you from going, do me one favor before you go…."

"What is it?"

"Clean your room."

CHAPTER TEN

~Belle x Esmé~

Belle packed the smallest suitcase she had with some of her favorite desserts from Esmé and Raoul's world. She tore her room apart looking for her phone and found it underneath her wardrobe. She packed flowers, and took pictures of the garden she would send once she had a signal in her world. She asked if Desiree brought her laptop, then asked her to upload the videos from the ball. Belle saved a copy to her phone. Esmé finally said yes to visiting her home world. He'd told her to wait a few days then out of nowhere told her they were leaving in the morning. Belle was excited. This was the first time she would be home in four weeks and she was actually…nervous. Would her family be happy to see her? There was a grand gesture of goodbyes only for her to return with the intention of going *back* to the kingdom where she was being held as a prisoner.

Regardless, she only planned to stay a day. If they left early in the morning, they wouldn't have to worry about running into her family. Everyone would be at work. Belle just hoped everything went okay. She wanted Esmé to have a good experience, hoping it would not be a repeat of what happened to him as a child. Belle somewhat trusted her family to not harm him.

Man, how she wished she could tell Desiree she was going. She had already decided not to tell her, but Esmé asked her not to as well. She seemed to have had a change of heart, but they both agreed if Desiree knew, she'd harass Belle into staying in their world. The reason for her coming was for the sole purpose of getting Belle home. If she knew she willingly came *back*, Desiree would lose her mind.

Belle was startled by three loud knocks on her door. Before she could answer, the door opened. Belle slammed her suitcase shut and looked behind her.

Desiree saw her and raised an eyebrow. "You…good?"

"Yeah," Belle said, smiling nervously. "I'm looking for something in my luggage."

"Right…" Desiree sniffed and asked, "Do you have any tissues?"

"Maybe…. Are you okay?" Belle asked, searching her suitcases.

"Yeah, it's just a little cold in here."

"You sound kinda sick though…."

"I'm not," Desiree scoffed. She did sound and feel congested, but she was too proud to admit she was feeling under the weather. She'd chalked it up to being cold. "Considering this place is closed off from the rest of the world, the likelihood of me catching a cold is next to zero."

"It's still possible."

"Hm…not likely. I have to come into contact with a virus. And again, this place is closed off. I don't think either of them have had a cold before."

"Just keep an eye on it," Belle insisted. She'd found a travel sized pack of tissues and gave them to Desiree. "Last thing we need is for you to be bedridden."

"I'll be fine," Desiree said, grabbing it. She thanked Belle and walked to door. She glanced back at Belle, who sat up straight, not taking her eyes off Desiree. "You sure, *you're* okay?"

"Mhm," Belle said, through a closed smile.

"Huh," Desiree said, taking one last look at Belle and closing the door behind her. "Night, Isabelle…."

Belle waited until she heard Desiree's door close, and sighed loudly. Her body melting onto her suitcase. She whined, "I don't know how much more of that I could handle."

Belle was thankful Desiree didn't push the subject. Usually, Desiree wouldn't stop pestering Belle until she knew what was wrong. Belle wondered if Desiree was still walking on eggshells after their last argument. She really did seem to befriend Raoul. Belle trusted her this time. Belle thought maybe Desiree was afraid she would shut down again if she made the wrong comment. Belle wanted to reassure her, but she planned on waiting until *after* her trip to do so.

***

Raoul stood, with his arms crossed, in Esmé's now immaculate room, watching Esmé throw anything and everything he could in the suitcase

193

he borrowed from Belle. Raoul just had this sinking feeling in his stomach that something would go wrong. While he trusted how genuinely kind Belle was, there was still that uncertainty that given the opportunity she would leave Esmé. What if the same thing happened again? Esmé had changed significantly after the first assault. He stopped being the bright-eyed child who smiled even at nothing in particular. He was still a sweet boy, but he was closed off. Would Esmé fall into a deeper depression and shut down completely if even in the young ladies' world, he was considered a monster? Raoul just wanted to shelter Esmé and hide him away from any adversaries.

"Are you *sure* you want to do this?" Raoul finally asked.

"Yeah," Esmé said, trying to force his suitcase closed.

"I just…I'm sorry, I know I said I would support this 100%," Raoul began, now pacing in front of the door. "I…Are you sure you can trust Miss Belle?"

Esmé stopped pushing on the suitcase and stared at Raoul. "What are you getting at?"

"What if…Miss Belle runs away? Or, her family attacks you?"

"I trust Belle," Esmé answered, continuing to push his suitcase closed. "And because I trust Belle, I know her family won't hurt me. Belle told me she likes it here. That's why we aren't telling Desiree about the trip. Belle won't leave me, I know it."

Raoul sighed and sat on the floor beside Esmé. He pulled the suitcase in front of him, took everything out, and reorganized what was needed. "I'm scared. What if you get stranded? What if you're hurt? I can't protect you if I'm a world away."

"I don't need protection. I'm not a kid. You guys want me to marry her so badly, right? Don't you think the first thing needed for that is trust?"

"Yes, but, it's a foreign environment. I'm—"

"Look, I get your concerns," Esmé said, patting Raoul on the shoulder, "I really do. But I trust Belle. If something goes wrong, then I'll promise to never doubt you again. I won't go anywhere ever again, okay?"

That's if you return safely, Raoul thought. "All right."

"And in any case," Esmé said, "it's just like Lady Orchida said. The best way for us to grow closer is to see what her world is like. See how different it is than here. I reaaaaally wanna go."

Raoul smiled. He loved when Esmé was happy. Much to his displeasure, if it would make Esmé as excited as he was now, Raoul was truly willing to give his support.

He finished packing Esmé's suitcase, making sure to remind Esmé not to bring anything valuable he didn't want to lose. And not to pack irrelevant things like 5 pairs of shoes, an umbrella, blankets, etc. He wished Esmé goodnight, promising to summon the SUV in the morning. He still didn't tell him the location, but that was so he could say goodbye.

Esmé prepared for bed. As he got ready to lie down, a portal opened and Lady Orchida appeared. Esmé was surprised, but greeted her properly nonetheless.

"Are you excited about tomorrow?" she asked.

Esmé nodded enthusiastically. "I'm a little scared, but I'm really happy."

"That's wonderful." Lady Orchida smiled. "I apologize for showing up so late. My intentions were to meet you before you left in the morning. However, I must attend to something urgent."

"It's all right. What did you want to speak about?"

Lady Orchida pulled a large stack of green stuff out of her cloak pocket and handed it to Esmé.

"Thanks? What is it?"

"Money, from Belle's world," Lady Orchida answered. "It is $200 to spend in case you need to tomorrow. Please use it wisely."

"How did you get money from their world?"

"I have my ways," Lady Orchida smirked. "Try not to lose it. If you feel you may do so, please have Belle hold on to it."

"Yes, Lady Orchida." Esmé nodded.

"I'm sure you can come up with an excuse as to where you received a large sum of money. If you cannot, tell Belle your father used to travel between worlds and that it is his money. Also, time flows differently in our world. Belle will be confused when she sees the date in her world. Please explain to her that one day in our world, is two days' time in hers.

"One more thing before I leave," she said, opening a portal. "I will have limited visibility of you once you cross the portal. The further away you are, the less I can see you and my magic cannot reach you. So please, be careful. Keep the SUV's key fob *and* the necklace on you at all times. *Do not* lose either."

"Okay. Thank you for all your help," Esmé said, bowing.

They bid each other farewell, and Esmé went to sleep.

The next morning, Esmé was up at dawn, waking Raoul up for his trip. Most mornings Raoul would've already been awake. But he'd spent the majority of the night worrying about Esmé, he did not fall asleep until 3 a.m.

Raoul asked him to make sure Belle was awake. While Esmé did that, Raoul went into a hidden room. In the middle of the room was a metal cylinder pole about 4 ft tall. It was basic, and at the top of it was a blue button, a small keyboard, and a number dial. There was nothing special about it. Raoul selected "2," typed "Belle's home," and pushed the button. It flashed three times, indicating the SUV was on the way. He reached around the pole and grabbed a key fob.

Outside, Belle and Esmé bounced back and forth in the cold begging Raoul to hurry up. While they waited, Esmé thought about how he could disguise himself. He hoped Belle had figured out a way. He asked if she did.

"Kind of," Belle answered. "I think it'll work. But also, since we're gonna be at my house, we won't really have to worry about strangers seeing you."

"But what about your family?"

"They probably won't be home when we get there. They have to work early shifts. Even if they were home, it's not like they don't know that you're…" Belle paused, realizing how insensitive her next word was.

"'Different?'" he finished.

"Yeah…sorry." Belle had another word in mind, but went along with his suggestion.

"Don't worry about it. It's not like it's false. I would be surprised if they didn't react in some way towards me."

To lighten the mood, Belle said, "Why don't we try it out?"

Esmé was already wearing what Belle had in mind. Before he could respond, she pulled his hat a little further down, just above his eyes. She took off his scarf and rewrapped it so it covered his nose and mouth. All that was uncovered were his eyes. He had the eyes of a monkey, but with a pair of sunglasses he'd look like an overly bundled human. Belle planned to take a pair of glasses when they arrived at her home. His gloves hid his hands and his boots, along with the baggy snow pants, hid his lizard legs.

"Are you sure this will work?" he asked.

"No way it won't."

Just as Belle spoke, the SUV arrived. When it reached them, Esmé checked out his reflection in the rear windshield. He was impressed. Raoul also walked out of the castle to see Esmé's attire.

When he approached, Esmé spotted him in the reflection and said, "I look human."

"It is remarkable," Raoul agreed.

"And, with sunglasses, you really wouldn't be able to tell," Belle chimed in.

"See? There's nothing to worry about." Esmé nudged Raoul.

"I guess so," Raoul said, smiling wearily. He handed the key fob to Esmé.

"What's this?" Esmé asked.

"The key fob for the SUV."

"But where's the button?" Esmé asked. "Are you really gonna keep hiding it?"

"I will tell you in due time. For now, just use this."

Raoul explained how the key fob worked to the best of his knowledge. The buttons were similar except some of the meanings were different, for example, the "panic" button was used to summon the SUV. On the back of the key fob was a tiny keyboard. Raoul explained that the keyboard was used to enter a location. Esmé's fingers, especially when wearing the gloves, were too big for the keys, but with Belle's help, it was usable. The SUV would not stop and open the doors until they arrived. The rest of the buttons Raoul didn't know, and they seemed irrelevant anyways.

As Belle and Esmé turned to get in the SUV, Raoul asked, "Wait, you two haven't eaten yet, right? Maybe we should have breakfast before you go."

"No time," Esmé responded. He knew Raoul was stalling.

"It's okay," Belle said. "We can eat once we're at my house."

"Are you sure?" Raoul asked.

They both nodded.

Esmé was still pouting over Raoul keeping the summoning location a secret after he finished explaining. He wanted to get out of there fast, before Raoul found another way to stall. He said goodbye, put their luggage in the backseat, and entered the SUV.

Before entering, Belle remembered how Desiree was feeling. She shouted back to Raoul, who in turn was heading back inside, "Hey, I forgot to mention. Please watch over Desiree. She may deny it, but it looks like she's catching a cold."

"Thank you for the notice," he shouted. "I will look after her."

Belle waved and entered the SUV.

Esmé's heart raced as the SUV drove away. He took a deep breath. There was no turning back now.

"This is it," Belle said with a nervous smile.

Esmé could only respond with a nod.

~Desiree x Raoul~

Raoul continued to wave on the steps until the SUV was out of sight. He sighed, praying he didn't just make the biggest mistake of his life, allowing Esmé to travel to a new world. He returned inside and looked at the clock. He assumed Desiree would wake up in two hours, at her usual time. If she really was catching a cold, Raoul thought it may be a good idea to make her a breakfast appropriate for a cold.

He thought maybe letting her walk around without a coat caused her to become sick. He felt guilty and promised he would make sure she was absolutely comfortable as best he could. Raoul couldn't even think of the last time he or Esmé had caught a cold. They were in peak physical health for years. He wondered what kind of breakfast would be suitable. If she hadn't caught a cold yet, something nutritious and comfy, would be the best choice.

Raoul decided on chicken noodle soup, scrambled eggs, and ginger tea. It was light, covered comfy foods and nutrients needed for colds and tea to soothe her throat. He'd timed it perfectly. He finished preparing breakfast at exactly 7 a.m.

Desiree groaned as she attempted to open her eyes. She was exhausted. Even though she had more than enough of a good night's rest, her eyes still felt heavy. Her head was pounding and her nose was stuffed. One minute, the room was cold, and the next, it was stifling but she didn't have the energy to push the covers off. Desiree dreaded the thought of having to get out of bed and cook. She could just imagine the "I told you sos" from Belle. She hated being proven wrong. Especially when what she was "wrong" about didn't make sense to begin with.

I guess this place just drops all logic, huh? she thought.

Today was also the day she had to dust and clean the castle. She groaned. She understood dusting, but why did she have to clean the entire castle when none of them made messes?

198

Of all days to get sick. Desiree closed her eyes and sighed. She simply wanted to melt into the bed and sleep for a decade. Desiree squinted her eyes open, reached over to her phone and set an alarm for 5 minutes. *A few more minutes of sleep and I'll be ready for today.*

***

Raoul rolled the cart down the hall. When he reached Desiree's room, he was rattled by an obnoxiously loud noise. Ignoring all formalities, Raoul opened her door.

"Miss Desiree? Is everything all right?"

He scanned the room, his eyes landing on the bed to see Desiree sleeping comfortably on a mountain of pillows. The loud object just inches from her head.

"Miss Desiree?" he asked as he approached. "Miss Desiree?"

No response.

Is she all right? How can she sleep with this thing beside her? he thought. Was she really that sick she couldn't hear it? "If you don't mind…."

Raoul placed his hand on Desiree's forehead. She was burning up! *No wonder!*

He grabbed the device next to her and examined it. Surely there was some way to turn it off? He flipped it up and down. When he checked the screen, the only thing he could figure out was the time at the top of the screen, another set of numbers counting up "-30.07" and the word, "dismiss" below an X. While he had no idea what it was, it was pretty elementary to figure out it was the key to turning it off. He tapped the word dismiss, nothing. He then tapped and pressed the x repeatedly and still, nothing happened. He was growing more and more agitated.

"Miss Desiree," Raoul said, glancing up at Desiree. "I don't mean to wake you, but can you please help me stop this thing?"

Still no response. Desiree turned on her side and snuggled into the bed more.

Raoul sighed. It seemed he was at his wit's end. Would he have to listen to this thing for the rest of his life?

"Hold the x and swipe in any direction," a voice said from behind.

Raoul did just that and the racket was gone. "Thank you, Lady Orchida. Can I help you with something?"

"No," Lady Orchida said, smiling. "I thought I'd check in on you, and saw you were…having some difficulties."

"Yes." Raoul smiled, setting the device on the nightstand. "I don't think I've ever dealt with something as exasperating as this thing…. What is it?"

"It's a 'cell phone.' It's a device used to contact anyone no matter how far away they are from you. What you experienced is an alarm clock. It's used to wake people up."

"So they're intentionally like that?"

"No, not always. I'm sure Desiree chose an obnoxious ringtone on purpose." Lady Orchida opened a portal. "Do me a favor, do not wake Desiree."

"But… she has to eat at some point."

"She'll awake on her own. Now, if you'll excuse me."

"Wait, before you go," Raoul said. "I don't mean to be a bother, but can you send medicinal herbs? I would like to cure Desiree's cold as soon as possible."

"No need," Lady Orchida said, stepping out of the portal. "The herbs won't cure a spell."

"A spell?"

"Yes, I need Desiree bedridden and asleep to break the curse on her."

"Don't you think giving her an illness is a bit…extreme?" he chuckled, awkwardly.

"Not at all. Even if I didn't need her asleep for my mission, she would still need to rest. If she were healthy, she would focus on Belle's whereabouts. If she's asleep for the next few days, Esmé and Belle can enjoy their trip, and I can do my job."

Raoul understood her intentions but he believed there were other, less harsh, ways to handle this. "I understand. Although, I would like to make the next few days comfortable for her…even if it's useless."

"Absolutely. Do whatever you wish, so long as it's beneficial to your curse." Lady Orchida entered the portal. "It is imperative, Raoul, that you do not wake her. She may sleep for hours or days. It all depends on the progress we make. It can be extremely dangerous if you do."

"I will do as you command." Raoul bowed until the portal closed and glanced back at Desiree. He sighed and wheeled the cart back to the kitchen.

Belle and Esmé sat in silence, the only sound coming from the heat that was on full blast. They had been driving for almost an hour. Belle remembered the ride to their castle had taken about an hour and a half to get there. If that was unfortunately a predetermined ETA, this drive would steer Belle to insanity. She respected Esmé's feelings and did not push to have a conversation. It was clear as day he was scared about being in a foreign land. He needed time to process everything going on.

But Belle was soooo bored. Her cell phone was in her suitcase, which was sadly placed under Esmé's. It was too much to move around for one item. She did miss being on earth. She thought maybe she could open the window and take in the good ol' Wisconsin air. She pressed down on the window button and nothing happened. She clicked it again then looked at Esmé. He had been watching her attempt to open the window.

"I guess the windows are for decoration?" she asked.

"I don't think so," he replied, pressing the button. He pulled out the key fob and stared at it, hovering over the buttons.

"None of those are for the window," Belle said. She peeked over the driver's seat and pointed at the side of the door. "You see that over there? That's used to unlock the windows."

Belle tried reaching for the window control button, but couldn't. She sighed and sat back in her seat.

Esmé looked at her then back to the key fob. Maybe in her world the buttons were different. Raoul did say that the buttons worked differently than what was labeled. The most logical one to press was the button with an unlocked lock on it. He pressed it once and nothing happened.

"That's not gonna work. That unlocks the car doors."

"The SUV doesn't have locks and the doors open on their own. It wouldn't make sense to have buttons for something that's automatic." Esmé pressed the lock, unlock, most of the buttons on the key fob.

Belle watched for a second before speaking up again. "It's fine. I don't need the window open. It's cold anyways."

Just as she finished speaking, Esmé held down the unlock button and the windows opened slightly. They both gasped with delight and shock that it worked. Belle pushed her window button and had full control. At first, she was surprised, but then she remembered she was in driverless car with pitch black windows taking them from a magical world.

Belle stared out the window. Oh how she missed the cold air, the piles of snow, the leafless trees, and construction season. While she loved how beautiful the trees were in Esmé's world, sometimes it was better to see all stages of the tree. They were just as beautiful. Esmé copied Belle and opened his window. The immense force from the wind blowing into the car shook him. He tried looking out, but the wind was blowing in his eyes. Eventually he gave up, closed his window and peered out of Belle's window. The rest of the ride was Esmé asking Belle questions about the road, what gas stations were, pit stops, cars, and so on.

They'd finally reached the road to Belle's home forty-five minutes later. The SUV slowly pulled onto the partially shoveled road. Their hearts were racing. Belle hoped no one was home. According to the clock in the SUV, it was well past 8:30 a.m. and everyone should've been at work. As they got closer to the house, Belle stuck her head out of the window to check for cars. The coast was clear. She sighed and leaned back in her seat and unbuckled her seatbelt.

Now that the SUV had slowed down, Esmé rolled down his window to look out. He didn't see the sentiment that Belle had for dead plant life. He was however, mesmerized by the 40 inches of snow deeper in the forest. When they arrived in front of the house, Esmé felt a little underwhelmed by the look of Belle's home. He had to remember that most homes, even in his kingdom, looked like this. He studied it from the ground up. It did give off a sort of homey yet eerie vibe.

When his eyes made it to the roof, he spotted something overhead that made his stomach drop. He screamed, "You have dragons!?"

"Huh?" Belle gave Esmé a confused look.

He pointed to the sky and continued, "Look, right there. I've never seen one before! I thought they weren't real."

Belle glanced to the sky and saw only an airplane. When she figured out that was what Esmé was referring to, she burst into laughter. "That's not a dragon! It's an airplane."

"An air plain?" Esmé asked.

"An airplane. It's kind of like a car, except it flies, goes really fast and takes you across the world."

"Do you think we can ever fly one?" Esmé asked, a glimmer of hope in his eyes.

"I wouldn't say fly, but maybe in a few years we can ride one." Belle knew that would never happen. Not only because Raoul was extremely protective of him, but because it would be impossible to hide Esmé's appearance going through TSA. But a sliver of assurance wasn't such a bad thing.

Content, Esmé followed Belle up the porch stairs. Belle had hidden an extra house key underneath one of the windowsills and hoped it was still there. When she found it, she unlocked the front door and peeked inside.

"Anyone home?" she called.

She waited for a response. Nothing. She pushed the door open slowly and beckoned for Esmé to follow. She instructed Esmé to take his shoes off. He complied and carried them to her room. As they walked towards the stairs, Esmé took in the room around him. It had a sort of comfy yet poor ambience to him. He thought about how packed the rooms were and how little space there was. The entire bottom level of the house was the size of one room in their castle. Were all the homes in her world this small? Of course, he would never be rude and tell Belle his true thoughts. So, he gave a simple compliment.

"It's cozy here…"

"Thanks," Belle said, leading him up the stairs. She made sure no one was walking past when they reached the top. "It may not be as luxurious as my home in New Jersey, and not as extravagant as your castle, but it holds a lot of good memories for me and my dad."

"I understand. It's not about how your home looks, but the memories you make?"

"Exactly." Belle smiled. She opened her room door and said, "Welcome to my room."

Thousands of colors flooded Esmé's field of vision. The carpet was tan and the bedding, walls, and furniture were a bright pink color. Art supplies cluttered the floor and shelves. He barely recognized what most of these things were, but guessed that they were art related.

"Wow, your room's really cool." Esmé stepped onto her carpet and twisted his foot back and forth, mashing it into the floor. "Your floor is really soft."

Belle stifled a laugh. "Thanks. It's a bit messy in here. I forgot to clean it before I left. I'm surprised one of my sisters didn't throw my things away and steal my room."

"Don't worry about the mess. My room gets messier than this," he replied. His eyes landed on the flat screen and he asked, "What's that?"

"The TV?" Belle answered. "It's for watching movies and stuff."

Esmé gave her a confused look. Belle grabbed her remote and turned the TV on. At first, nothing happened. The screen was black.

Esmé stared at the screen, his curiosity dampened. "That's it?"

Ignoring his remark, Belle changed the channel and a cartoon came on. The TV blared loudly, startling Esmé, and Belle turned the volume down. "This is a cartoon."

Esmé's mouth had dropped, and once again a childlike look sparkled in his eyes. He'd seen so many magical things in his world. He'd even seen Lady Orchida on multiple occasions conjure items out of thin air, heck, even use her magic to control the SUV. Yet, the "magic" in Belle's world seemed better than Lady Orchida's. His eyes still fixated on the TV, he asked, "Can I see the thing in your hand."

"The remote? Sure," Belle said. She explained the buttons and left him to check it out while she went to the kitchen to grab snacks.

Esmé flipped through the channels, stopping only for a split second to see the different kinds of people on the screen. He was fascinated. He'd only seen 7 people his entire life, and that included Belle and Desiree. Technically, he did see more during the Rose Festival. However, the experience was so traumatizing, he'd forgotten what any of them looked like. When he thought about what happened, all he could see were shadows chasing him. He continued to change channels until one that flicked by caught his attention. He looked at the remote and pressed the channel down button until he'd found it again.

"Hahahaha! Has your arrogance led you to truly believe you can defeat me? The ruler of the underworld," a mighty voice rang through the television. The owner of the voice was a large, muscular man with horns, golden skin, and a long flowing cape. Esmé thought he looked awesome.

"I am not arrogant," a smaller, less powerful voice replied. He looked boring compared to the other character. He was scrawny, short, and carried a large sword too big for his body. Esmé wasn't entertained by his appearance. The scrawny voice continued, *"I may be small, I may be less powerful. Yes, you have defeated me hundreds of times before. And, to be honest, I'm not sure that I can ever beat you alone. But what I do know is that my friends are my power. And*

with their help, we'll take our homeland back from the darkness and send you back to the shadow realm!"

Esmé was enthralled. Logically, he knew this guy would lose the battle, but after such an "encouraging" speech, he had no choice but to root for the underdog.

***

Belle picked out whatever she thought was okay for him to eat. She wanted him to try all of the snacks they had in their world. Obviously, it would never taste as good as their desserts, but it was still something new to try. She grabbed two of each soda brand and flavor her grandparents had, different flavored bags of chips, chocolate bars, fruit flavored hard candy, two crème-filled cocoa rolls, winkles, which were cream-filled yellow cakes, snowballs, mini powdered donuts, and glazed donuts. She grabbed an apple and cherry fruit pie, mini blueberry muffins, honey covered buns, and granola bars. She also made sure to grab two bowls, silverware, a box of looped froots cereal, and milk to keep her promise of eating breakfast. After realizing she grabbed too much, she put everything in plastic bags and carried them upstairs.

As she opened her room door, she saw Esmé's face pressed to the TV screen. He screamed, "Get up! Don't lose to that scumbag! What happened to 'your friends are your power'? Are you really going to give up here?!"

"Don't stand so close to the TV, you'll hurt your eyes," Belle warned, placing the bags on the floor.

"Belle!" Esmé turned abruptly and grabbed Belle's shoulders. He pointed back at the TV. "How do I get there? He needs help!"

"Huh?" It took Belle a moment to realize what he was saying.

Before she could explain, he interrupted, "Is this the kind of sick crap you do for entertainment? Watching weaklings get mopped across the floor? If none of you are going to help him, I will!"

Belle burst into laughter.

"It's not funny! How do I get inside the TV?"

"It's fake," she said, through labored breaths. She struggled to stop laughing as she spoke, "It's not real. It's a movie and they're all actors! They record these fight scenes, and then we, the viewers, watch it when it's on TV or in the movie theaters."

"That can't be, we're literally watching it happen!"

"It's recorded, look." Belle grabbed her phone from her suitcase. She gasped. "What? How is it already February? It literally just said January."

"Oh, well Raoul said that 2 days in your world is 1 day in ours or something like that. So that might be why."

"Wow, I…didn't think that was possible…I guess that's how my dad was gone a month when he thought it was just a day. But, how did he not know it was more than a day, if it would've been what, 15?"

"Your dad was in a coma for like a week. Raoul and the sorceress nursed him back to health."

"Wow…It's confusing but…" There was no point dwelling on that. She was traveling between worlds. Nothing really surprised her anymore. She lifted her phone and pointed the camera at Esmé. She recorded Esmé staring at her and played the video back. "See, you're standing next to me, not across the room."

Esmé took Belle's phone and furrowed his brows. "But that…it doesn't…that's not possible. I'm right here."

"Well, you're looking at it, so it is possible." Belle let Esmé tinker with her phone's camera while she poured cereal into the bowls. "Let's eat breakfast."

Esmé turned to sit when he saw the two small bowls. He looked slightly bemused. "*This* is what you eat for breakfast?"

"Kind of. Most of the time people eat a simplified version of the breakfast you have. But when you don't have time, cereal is something a lot of people eat instead."

"'Cereal,' huh?" Esmé repeated, stirring it.

It did *not* look appetizing. He had never seen milk used for anything other than cooking, let alone ingesting it by itself. The cereal was half soggy, half crunchy, and getting soggier by the second. It slowly dyed the milk to a pale pink color. Who in their right mind could eat something like this? Esmé glanced at Belle's eager face and smiled awkwardly. The way the milk plopped back into the bowl as he raised a spoonful to his mouth almost made him gag. He took a deep breath and shoved the quivering spoon into his mouth.

It wasn't as bad as he thought it would be. The milk didn't taste good, however, most of it had been flavored by the cereal and he wasn't complaining. It definitely satiated his sweet tooth.

"What do you think?" Belle asked.

"It's not bad. I doubt I would eat this again, but I do like it," he answered, eating another spoonful.

"I figured, it's pretty cheap compared to what you eat." Belle took two granola bars out. "This is also something people eat for breakfast."

Esmé looked unamused as he unwrapped the small bar in his hand. His taste buds had never experienced something so confusing before. So many textures and flavors in one bite. He put the granola bar down and asked, "Is there anything else?"

"Yeah," Belle responded. "These aren't breakfast items, but I love them."

She handed him a cocoa roll and a honey covered bun. Esmé tried both and it was like heaven in his mouth. Was it as great as the desserts Raoul baked? Not even close. But it had a sort of sweetness that his brother couldn't, nor wouldn't, replicate. He tried the cream soda Belle handed to him. It was instant love. It had a nice spicy kick to it that enchanted Esmé.

Esmé took another can of soda and asked, "What else is there to do?"

"We can play video games." Belle grabbed the remote and changed the channel. "Your world may have magic, but we have better technology. Check this out."

She turned on her Mimninedon't swap. The last game she played was a J-RPG about vampires. The loading screen caught Esmé's attention. The graphics were so good, the characters almost looked human.

"Is this another fake TV thing?"

"No, it's not a movie," Belle said, picking up the controller. "It's a video game."

She loaded her save point and started fighting enemies. Esmé looked from the screen to the controller in Belle's hand, then back to the TV.

"And you're controlling this person with that?" he asked.

"Yep, wanna try?" Belle paused and held out the controller.

"No thanks, this looks serious. I don't want to kill them."

"It's not a real person. You play as the character." Belle unpaused and did nothing. They watched as the character took damage and she respawned at her last save point. She handed the controller to Esmé. She quickly explained the controls and left him to figure out the rest.

He hesitantly moved the joystick and the character moved an inch. "Wow, it really does control it."

He pushed the joystick harder and the character sprinted. He continued until he came across a group of enemies. "What do I do? What do I do?"

"Press A!" Belle shouted.

Esmé did as instructed. He fought as best he could, button mashing, but with the level of difficulty Belle played, he lost quickly. He frowned. "Is there anything easier to play?"

"Yeah, let me change it." Belle switched the game to a game called, Speedy and handed the other controller to Esmé. The notorious logo and sound popped on the screen.

"Speedy, the porcupine?" Esmé read, sarcastically. "What is a porcupine?"

Belle searched online for one and showed Esmé. "Use the joystick to run, this one to jump, and this one to roll. I'll explain what everything does as we go."

"How's this gonna be fun?"

"Trust me, it'll be fun."

~Desiree x Raoul~

A warm breeze caressed Desiree's cheek. The sound of rustling leaves, and grass tickling Desiree's nose startled her from her slumber. She opened her eyes to see that she lay under the shade of a tree. She sat up and wiped her eyes to make sure she saw things correctly. In the distance, she saw a beautiful meadow with an array of colorful flowers. The sun shined brightly and few clouds could be seen in the sky. Something about the meadow was familiar, but she couldn't tell how. She scanned her surroundings for Belle and the beasts.

"Hello?" she shouted.

No response.

"This isn't funny!" she said, spinning in every direction. "Belle! Esmé! Raoul! Anybody?!"

Desiree let out an exasperated sigh. She hated pranks. Considering how large Raoul's garden was, Desiree knew she had to have been somewhere inside of it. She figured if she walked in one direction, she would eventually make her way out or at least to a maze wall. She shuffled through the meadow, grumbling the entire way.

It felt like she was walking for hours and still no sign of the castle. It was getting hotter by the second. "This isn't funny! I'm tired!"

She sat down in the field, covered her face with her palms, and sighed. Desiree thought maybe they weren't over her past behavior and this was how they were getting revenge.

"Look, I'm sorry for how I behaved," she yelled. "But this isn't the way to solve problems!"

She was at her wit's end and on the brink of tears when she heard a wind chime. She slowly lifted her head and looked around the field. She knew the sound from somewhere. There was something about the sound from this wind chime that Desiree had always thought was strange. She stood and followed the sound.

She walked for another 5 minutes before she saw a cottage in the distance. Seeing that luck was now on her side, Desiree smiled and ran towards the cottage. As she neared the cottage, she could see a person on the side of the building hanging laundry on a clothesline to dry. And unbeknownst to this mysterious person, they were now Desiree's savior.

"Finally," she hailed. She sprinted over to them and said, "Hello? Can you help me get back to the royal castl—"

Desiree stopped dead in her tracks and her smile dropped. She was speechless, wondering if her eyes were deceiving her. A woman hummed an old lullaby cheerfully as she straightened out the sheets. She had black, curly, shoulder-length hair, her skin was a beautiful ebony that glistened in the sunlight. She wore an orange with white polka dots dress and an all too familiar white apron around her waist. As she reached in to grab the next bed sheet, she spotted Desiree and smiled. The corners of her pink colored eyes creased.

"Well, aren't you going to help me?" she asked. She continued to pull out the cloth until she noticed Desiree not moving. She frowned worriedly and asked, "Baby, why are you crying?"

Tears streamed down Desiree's face as she stared at the woman in front of her. She couldn't form any words. She wanted to respond but she didn't know how. It had been so long since she'd seen her mom. All of the memories of her mother's funeral and 6 years of pain flooded her mind and she cried even harder.

Her mom dropped the sheet on the ground and pulled Desiree into her arms. She held her and said, "It's okay, Desiree. Don't cry."

"I missed you," she sobbed, uncontrollably. She wrapped her arms tightly around her mom as if she would disappear the moment she let go.

"I'm sorry I left you," Angela whispered. "I love you so much."

"I love you, too. Please don't leave me again." Desiree continued to sob and Angela rubbed her back like she used to when Desiree was a child.

After she had calmed down enough, Angela led Desiree inside the cabin. She said, softly, "Let's get something to drink. Do you remember this place?"

"Mm-hm." Desiree nodded. She sat down on the couch and waited for Angela to return with two mugs of hot chocolate. "This was my favorite place to visit with you."

Angela smiled warmly. "You were so young the last time I brought you here. I'm surprised you remember it."

"I'll never forget any memories with you." She sniffled. "A lot's happened since you passed away…. Dad misses you."

"I miss him too," she said, smiling softly. Desiree could see she was holding back tears. "I'm sorry I had to leave. I hope some day you'll understand and you'll forgive me."

"I was never angry, mom. Yeah, it hurts but I know that life happens and there's nothing we can do about it. And one day, we'll all meet you for real."

"I'd like to think my children would live for an eternity." She smiled. "What was that about a royal castle?"

Desiree sighed and rolled her eyes. There was so much to tell her, she didn't know where to start. She gave a brief synopsis of what happened from Freddy's arrival at the castle to where she was then. The beginning told unfortunately through Freddy's exaggerated perspective. Desiree did manage to explain that he was going overboard, but she was still annoyed by their current situation.

When she finished telling Angela what happened, she ended with, "I just want to go home with Belle. They may be nice and all, but I still hate how she's considered a prisoner. And logically, I know Raoul is a good person and hasn't shown any signs of danger like dad said. But…it's just that my intuition is telling me something is off. That I shouldn't trust him and it makes me irrationally angry."

"I caused a lot of trouble…" Angela chuckled awkwardly. "If I could go back and change things, I would in a heartbeat. There's something you said that I would like clarification on."

"What's that?" Desiree asked.

"This young man, Raoul. You said he was a great guy and he's never done anything to harm you. In fact, he saved your life. And yet, he angers you. Why is that?"

"Um…" Desiree said. Why was she so angry? "I don't know."

"I want you to look deep inside of yourself, deep in your heart, and tell me what you feel when you think about Raoul."

"'Deep inside of myself'? I don't know what that mean—" As she spoke, a drop of water landed on her forehead and she looked up. Another drop, this time landing on her cheek. She continued, "I think the cottage has a leak mom."

"It's not raining," Angela said, laughing her comment off.

Before Desiree could insist there was a problem, more water poured over her and she slowly opened her eyes.

She felt a cloth gently dabbing beneath her eyes and water trickling down the side of her face. She reached up and took off the wet towel on her forehead.

"I'm sorry," a voice whispered. "I didn't mean to wake you. Your fever was…really high…."

Desiree sat up, wiped the tears from her eyes, and looked around her. Raoul sat on a stool beside the bed with a bin of water. "Don't be. I needed to wake up."

"If you don't mind me asking, were you having a bad dream?"

She shook her head. "No, I just dreamt about my mother. Don't worry about it."

"If you ever need to talk, I'm here for you."

"Thank you," she said, her stomach growling towards the end. Embarrassed, she said, "I'm so sorry."

Raoul chuckled and said, "I'll bring up lunch. Please continue to rest."

Desiree watched as Raoul closed her bedroom door and whispered, "Look deep inside of myself…. Mom, what do you mean?"

***

Raoul wheeled the cart to the kitchen, dreading the tongue lashing he would receive if Lady Orchida figured out he disobeyed her and woke Desiree up. Accident or not. He took the pot of soup out of the refrigerator and sat it on the stove to reheat.

"Ahem," a voice behind him said.

Raoul jolted from in front of the stove and turned around. "L-Lady Orchida. What a pleasure to see you. What brings you here?"

Lady Orchida crossed her arms. "Your Highness, did I not give you express instructions to not wake Desiree?"

"I'm sorry, it was an accident."

"Accident or not, I have to start over. I cannot say this enough, your highness. The spell cast on Desiree is *highly dangerous*. Breaking this

211

is risky, even if I'm doing things the safer route. If you continue to interrupt her sleep, she may hate you forever. Do you want that?"

"No…"

"Then let her sleep. She will not be harmed while she's asleep."

"With all due respect, Lady Orchida, I disagree. Prior to me waking her up, her forehead was burning and she was restless. I think the sickness, whether induced by magic or a virus, affects her body." Raoul sounded strong but, on the inside, he was terrified that he was standing up to Lady Orchida. He knew she would never harm him, but she was still an authority figure and he'd never went against her like this. But, despite himself, he continued on, "When she woke up, she was starving. It's only 3 p.m. I can't imagine how she would feel waking up after days of not eating."

"Then what do you suggest?"

"If it's possible, can she at least wake up for meals? I won't bother her any other time of the day."

Lady Orchida contemplated. "Fine, but she will wake up on her own. It will be around the times you normally eat; however, it can be an hour before or an hour after. It all depends on our progress and her ability to wake herself. This will start in the morning. So do not bother her for the rest of the evening after she eats. Deal?"

"Yes."

"Then if you'll excuse me."

"Wait, I have one question," Raoul blurted out. "Desiree's dream…are you…?"

"Disguised as her mother?" Lady Orchida completed the question. Raoul nodded.

"Yes."

"She…was crying when she woke up. Is there no other way to…appear in her dreams?"

"I know it may seem cruel," Lady Orchida said, opening a portal. "However, Desiree's mother is the only person Desiree will ever fully open her heart to. Just a peek into her heart, could tell me that much. She may be upset seeing her again, but I would rather her cry than for her to be influenced by a curse. Remember, this is a matter of life and death for you. Goodbye."

Before Raoul could respond, Lady Orchida had left. Raoul understood the severity of his situation. However, he didn't like others being stepped on and hurt for his benefit. The soup had warmed up by the end of their conversation. He sighed, filling enough for what he thought wouldn't make her hungry at night, and returned to her room.

***

Desiree watched as Raoul left the room. She waited until she couldn't hear the cart before she burst into tears. Her dream felt so real, that it was like she'd lost her mom a second time. The warmth of her mother's hug like it used to be. The sound of her voice. It had been so long since she'd heard it and now it was fresh in her mind and she missed hearing her mother call her name.

After her mother passed away, Desiree and her family would talk about how they received dreams at the same time every night. Once Desiree had somewhat gotten over her mother's death…at least enough to not cry every night, the dreams disappeared. It had been years since she last dreamt about her mother and she thought she'd healed enough to think about her again. Seeing her again, made her realize she would never heal from losing her. By the time she'd calmed down enough, Raoul knocked on her door.

She wiped her eyes frantically, and said, "Come in."

"I hope you're okay with reheated soup. I made it this morning."

"That's fine." She smiled. "Thank you."

As Raoul got closer, he studied Desiree's face. It was so obvious that she was crying. Her eyes were red and puffy, she was trying her best to silence her sniffles, and she avoided eye contact. Her behavior was very meek.

"Are you okay?" he asked.

"Yeah…I'm…um..."

There was something about being asked, "are you okay" that made almost everyone cry. Desiree would've been able to control her emotions if not for that one phrase.

Tears swelled in her eyes and she struggled to say, "I'm fine. Uh… I just…"

Desiree covered her mouth and sobbed. "I'm sorry…."

Raoul didn't say anything. He took his handkerchief from his chest pocket and reached out to Desiree.

Desiree smiled. "Thank you."

"Do you want to talk about it?"

"I don't know, it's just…dreaming about my mother just reminded me that I'll never see her again," she whimpered. Through sobs she

213

managed to say, "I took so many things for granted. You don't know what the future holds and someone you care about can be gone in the blink of an eye. I just…I wish I created more memories with my mom. I wish that I could hug her again. But I can't. She's gone forever."

Raoul wanted to hold Desiree and tell her everything was all right, but making such a drastic move could push her away.

Desiree continued to cry, ever so often eating between sobs. Raoul stayed silent the entire time and Desiree was grateful for it. She was embarrassed crying in front of someone she barely knew and at the same time, relieved that she could vent to someone and speak her true feelings.

After she finished eating, she immediately became tired. She reclined in bed, Raoul tucking her in, and apologized for getting so drowsy quickly.

Raoul waited until she was asleep before leaving her room. When he closed the door, he sighed heavily. He and Esmé were in the same position as Desiree and her mother. If things continued the way they did, would Esmé have regrets like Desiree? Would he be so inconsolable? Raoul never really thought about the impact his death could have on Esmé. Obviously he would grieve, but he was terrified Esmé would be as hurt as Desiree. He was all Esmé had.

Raoul came to the resolve to create as many memories as he could with Esmé. He doubted he could actually win Desiree's heart. And what if Desiree did fall in love with him and he still died? Lady Orchida always told them magic wasn't always a surefire fix. There could always be a rebound or some side effect. It was hard to think about. Raoul didn't want two people to grieve his death. He didn't know what to think anymore. He wanted to try his best so that Esmé wouldn't cry, but realistically, he knew his chances with Desiree were low.

"I hope Esmé's having a better day than we are…."

CHAPTER ELEVEN

~Belle x Esmé~

“They're cheating!” Esmé shouted, after losing for the tenth time in a row. He slammed his controller on the bed and covered his face with his hands.

It was almost noon and Belle and Esmé had become comfortable in her room. Esmé had taken off all of his winter gear and sat on Belle's bed. Belle sat on her beanbag. They had been playing Speedy, the Porcupine for hours. Esmé lost faster than Belle, and wouldn't give up until he won at least one game alive.

“Who's they?” Belle laughed. “Those are preprogrammed. The game's not cheating.”

Belle was enjoying Esmé's rage. It seemed like even beasts suffered from gamer rage.

She continued, “Why don't we take a break and have lunch?”

She opened the almost empty bag of snacks and pulled out whatever was left.

“Um,” Esmé said, awkwardly, “if your family's not coming back right away, can we make lunch or something?”

“Sure,” Belle said, leading him to the kitchen. She looked through the cabinets and in the fridge. There had to be something quick they could eat without anyone noticing it was gone. When she realized there was nothing safe to make, she offered, “Are you open to trying pizza? I don't want anyone to find out we were here.”

“As long as it tastes good.”

Belle took her phone out and went to a pizza website. She looked through the menu and ordered two medium sized pizzas, the ultimate choice of 1 pineapple and pepperoni pizza and 1 veggie pizza, half of which was covered in pineapple. After placing the order, they went back to her room. Belle searched her desk and pulled out a cat piggy bank. She pulled the black stopper on the bottom out and peeked inside.

"They stole my money!" she screamed. It wasn't hard to figure out who had taken her money. "I had $50 in here."

Belle scoffed and said, "We're gonna have to find something to eat here."

"Why? What's wrong?"

"You gotta pay to eat pizza, and my sisters stole my money. I'm sorry."

"Remember that sorceress I told you about?" Esmé hesitated to ask.

"Yeah?"

"Well, she gave me money for your world. Can we use that to pay for the pizza?"

"How much did she give you?"

"I think she said like $200?"

"$200?! Where would she even get that from?"

"She told me to tell you it was my father's. And that he would travel between worlds."

"It would explain why there's a portal. Let's use the money."

Esmé pulled out a wad of cash from his suitcase and handed it to Belle. "I don't know how much you need, but here you go. She told me not to lose it and to hand it to you if I think I might."

"We only need $32 for the pizzas, but an even $40 is good. You should always tip. Let's keep the rest in your suitcase." Belle pulled out an easel and some of her art supplies. "We have like an hour to spare before the pizza arrives. If it's okay, I kind of want to draw you as a hint to us being here."

"Um…"

"Only if you want to."

"I'm fine with it…I guess…." If he were in his human form, he would be blushing from ear to ear.

Belle led him to her desk. She had him position himself with one arm leaning on the desk, and the other in his lap, instructing him not to move an inch. Esmé was a little embarrassed having to stare at Belle for so long. Subconsciously, his eyes fell to the floor.

While Esmé wasn't very "princely" in nature, there was something about his posture that added a very "regal" air to him. Belle drew Esmé's face, paying more attention to his eyes than anything else. She wanted to capture his humane side so that her family could understand while they were "beasts," they weren't monsters. It was her way of telling her family she and Desiree were safe. By the time the pizza arrived, Belle had only drawn his upper half. Belle had Esmé stay exactly as he was while she grabbed the pizzas.

She placed the boxes on the kitchen counter before heading upstairs again. She glanced at her sketchbook then at Esmé. What was she thinking expecting it to take less than an hour to finish? She wasn't satisfied if she couldn't finish the drawing right then and there, but Esmé was going to have to move at some point to eat. It was already well past the time they normally ate and if she let him take a break to eat, he wouldn't be in the same position as before. She sighed. It would have to do. The only compromise she hoped for was that she could at least create a quick sketch of her desk so that he had something to lean on. Esmé was fine with that and she started a rough sketch before reluctantly putting her pencil down.

"Okay," she sighed. "Let's eat."

The aroma of pizza that filled the air as they made their way downstairs, gently caressed Esmé's sense of smell. It was like heaven to him. No offense to Raoul, of course, but he couldn't think of anything that smelled better. He hoped the pizza tasted as good as it smelled. Belle grabbed paper plates and handed one to Esmé.

When he noticed she didn't grab any cutlery, he asked, confused, "Where's the silverware?"

"Esmé," Belle tsked, making her way around to the pizza. She opened a box as she said, "Welcome to the life of 'commoners.'"

She grabbed a slice of pizza and took a bite. "You don't use silverware to eat pizza. Just use your hands."

Esmé looked extremely uncomfortable at the thought. If Raoul hadn't scolded him so many times when he ate with his hands, he would be fine with it. But he felt like he was disregarding Raoul's etiquette lessons even just thinking about it. He reached his shaking hand out and pulled a slice slowly onto his plate. "Raoul would be upset if he found out I ate with my hands."

"Then we won't tell him," Belle smirked. "If he somehow finds out, we'll tell him it's disrespectful in our culture not to eat with your hands."

"Right…" Esmé nodded. He took a bite of the pizza. It was like he had transcended to a higher plane of existence. He'd never eaten anything so delicious. "My rose…this is amazing. You can just eat this whenever?"

"Technically yes, it has the basic food groups; vegetables, dairy, carbohydrates, grains, and protein if you decide to add them. But it's expensive."

"You were right, your world is better. I want to try other foods if they taste like this!"

"I mean, they don't taste the same. Different tastes, cultures, so on and so forth. Maybe we can plan another trip here and try something else." Belle looked at the clock. "It's already 1 o'clock. We want to be out of here before anyone comes home. So we won't have time to try anything else today."

"Let's do that… Can I have another slice?" Esmé asked.

"Don't ask me. It's for both of us. Take as much as you like," Belle answered. "Let's go back to playing the game. We can eat in my room."

Esmé chuckled awkwardly. *I'm breaking so many rules. Raoul really would be mad if he found out.*

They returned to Belle's room to continue playing. Belle worked on her sketch of Esmé and Esmé played more video games. Belle checked her alarm clock ever so often. They just had to leave by 3 p.m.

***

"Then why is she still with him?" Esmé asked, flipping the page of a graphic novel. "He's a jerk."

"Because that's how some of these stories go. There wouldn't be much of a story if the main character could win over the guy she likes," Belle said over Esmé's shoulder. "Romances are dumb like that. They have the couple struggle to communicate and they make you wait volumes just for an inch of progress. Then when everything seems like it's going well…BOOM! They have a falling out and you're back to square one. Like why is it so hard for the MC to just admit she likes him? You just gotta deal with it until the end."

Esmé sat on Belle's beanbag against the bed and Belle lay on the bed, reading over Esmé's shoulder. They had gotten bored of video games and Belle introduced Esmé to graphic novels. While Esmé's world did have books, it was either picture books or novels. This was the first graphic novel he'd seen and he loved it.

"But it's so frustrating," Esmé complained.

"Oh, you haven't seen the worst of it," Belle said. "Wait until you get to volume 6."

"Ugh." Esmé rolled his eyes.

As they continued to rant over the book, they heard a car park outside. Esmé had called for the SUV. Belle stood up and stretched.

"Guess it's time to go back," she said.

"Can we bring some of this back with us?" Esmé asked.

"Yeah, I don't mind. I'll need to find another suitcase to us—" Belle stopped mid-sentence. The front door had opened. Belle looked at the clock. "Oh no! Who's home? No one's supposed to be here for another hour!"

"What do we do?" Esmé asked, panicking.

"Go hide!" Belle looked around her room. "In the closet! Go!"

Esmé ran into the closet and held his breath. Rattling of keys and a muffled voice could be heard. He was terrified. Was Belle's family capable of hurting him? He began to think that Raoul may have been right about not coming to her world. As fun as it was, *this* moment made him realize it was not worth it.

~ Desiree x Raoul ~

Desiree awoke on the couch in the cottage. It had now turned to dusk and only a faint light could be seen from behind her.

I'm back in this dream? she thought. *I don't know how much heartache I can take….*

She stood up and made her way to the light. Her mother was in the kitchen cooking a meal. It smelled like her famous rice and gravy. It was something she cooked on special occasions and requests. It was Desiree's favorite meal.

Desiree tapped on the wall. "Hey mom. Sorry I fell asleep."

"Don't be," Angela said, "you must've been exhausted. With so much going on lately, and then your long walk today, I would be more surprised if you weren't tired. Being in a safe space can provide relief to sleep."

"I get a lot of sleep at their castle. Even though we're prisoners, our rooms are extremely comfy. They treat us pretty well."

Angela motioned for Desiree to sit at the table. As she prepared their plates, she said, "So you're treated well, yet you don't like Raoul?"

"Yeah. We're their prisoners. Whether they treat us with respect or not, it doesn't change that."

"Is that why he angers you? You chose to come here on your own. They didn't force you. If he gave you the option to leave at any time, would that quell your anger?"

"*Just* me or can Isabelle go home as well?"

"Give me an answer to both."

"Just me, no. I think I would be madder if they allowed only me to leave. They know why I'm here. It'd be like they were spitting in my face if they only let me go. If Isabelle were allowed to leave, then I wouldn't be angry. I wouldn't hate them as much as I do."

"Do you hate your father as well for putting you two in this position?"

"No, mistakes happen. I was mad at him for agreeing to give one of us up. But I had time to think about it, and it was something that happened in the heat of the moment. He didn't think any of it was real and he regretted his actions and tried to go alone. He at least understands what he did was wrong. And he's my dad, I'd never hate him."

"But you hate them for only following the laws of their land? Keep in mind, had Freddy not done what he did, they wouldn't have needed to execute him. Laws are laws. How can you hate Raoul for upholding them?"

"Because they brought us into it."

"Your father did. He could have easily denied and accepted his punishment."

"He was scared into it."

"Doesn't matter. His actions brought this on everyone. I wouldn't sacrifice my children for my crime."

"Why are you being so harsh on dad?"

"You know I am honest when it comes to your father. When he is in the wrong, he's wrong. That was something your father loved about me."

"If you want to be 'honest,' if you hadn't *died*, none of this would have happened!" Desiree gasped. She covered her mouth. "I'm sorry…I—"

Angela sighed. "Desiree, you're blaming everyone around you instead of the cause, Freddy. Yes, I died. But I didn't force him to become an alcoholic. I didn't force him to operate on someone when he wasn't emotionally stable. I didn't force him to drive in a snowstorm. I didn't force him to steal from a castle in an unknown world. There was nothing, 'honest' about your statement.

"What you're doing is finding any reason to justify your hatred of someone who only followed his duties as a future king. Despite what the law states, which is locking you in a dungeon or beheading you, he chose to give you a warm bed to sleep in and freedom to roam around. You eat at the same table as him, that's not what you do with prisoners.

"You want to make Raoul into a monster but it doesn't add up. You have a right to be angry at your situation. Your life has been put on hold to fix your father's mistake. I get it. But to throw out soundless accusations is unfair. I didn't raise you to be the kind of person that points fingers and hurts others."

Even after Angela had finished speaking Desiree stayed quiet. Was she right? Was Desiree directing her frustration at the wrong people? She thought back to every interaction she had with Raoul, even the way he spoke to Belle. She sighed.

"I'm sorry for what I said, you're right."

"I forgive you," Angela replied. "Are you starting to understand that you shouldn't hate Raoul?"

"Sort of. I hear what you're saying and it all makes sense. But my gut is telling me not to trust him. And you also raised me to trust my gut."

"You're right, I did. However, sometimes our intuition can be wrong. It can be pointing to something else that you're not seeing," Angela said. "Tonight, I want you to take some time to reflect on my question from this afternoon. 'Why does he make you angry?' Then think about his good and bad qualities that *you* know of, not your father's, Belle's, nor anyone else's opinion."

"Okay… I don't understand it at all. But I'll try my best…" Desiree's face contorted as she considered it. She asked, "Mom, why do you care so much about whether or not I like Raoul?"

Angela waited a moment before speaking. "Because I want you to do what's right. You told me what's been happening since I passed away. And what you told me didn't sit right with me. You are being so harsh to this young man when his actions contradict your words. I only want you to be the Desiree that I know and love. Not what you've become since you arrived in this place."

"Isabelle said something similar."

"Which means that something is changing you. If two people notice it, it must be true, correct?"

Desiree nodded.

"Finish your dinner and head to bed. While you're resting think about what I said, all right?"

"All right, mom."

"I'll prepare your room so you don't have to sleep on that stiff couch," Angela said, leaving. "Goodnight."

"Goodnight," Desiree replied.

***

Raoul cleaned each room of the castle, except Desiree's. With no one to speak to, his afternoon was extremely boring. He wandered the halls looking for something to do. His garden was inaccessible due to the snow, Esmé and Belle were gone, and he couldn't converse with Desiree. He was bored out of his mind. He'd read every book in the castle, and he wasn't the type to reread books. He could go to the recreational building but that wasn't really something he was interested in.

During his walk, he passed Desiree's room. *I wasn't able to clean her room. If she's sick, she should rest comfortably in a dust-free room. I'll do my best to let her sleep.*

Raoul opened the door to see Lady Orchida on the other side of Desiree's bed. A white light was hovering over Desiree's chest, faint dark purple streams lifted from her chest and mixed with the light.

Lady Orchida sighed. "Did we not agree that she would wake up tomorrow morning and to leave her alone until then?"

"We did, yes. I apologize." Raoul bowed his head gallantly. "It was not my intention to wake her. I cleaned the castle and the last room to do is Miss Desiree's."

"Don't worry about cleaning her room. I'll make sure it's spotless."

"Yes, Lady Orchida."

Raoul stood in the doorway twiddling his thumbs while Lady Orchida continued to work. His eyes darted from one side of the room to the other before asking, "So are you trying to extract the curse through that light?"

"Yes. While she is conversing with her mother, I'm using this time to weaken the curse."

Raoul nodded. There was a second of silence before Raoul asked, "How exactly are you here and in her dreams?"

Lady Orchida glanced at Raoul. "Your highness, I mean this with the utmost respect, but please leave the room. I cannot focus with you speaking to me right now.”

“I’m sorry to be a bother.” Raoul hung his head in shame. “It’s just that I have no one to talk to and I can’t focus on the only hobby I have. So it was just nice to see someone else here.”

“Don’t apologize, Raoul. I should be the one to apologize. I didn’t consider you being alone. Please give me a couple hours to think of something that you can do to pass the time.”

~ Belle x Esmé ~

Belle peeked out of her bedroom door. She could hear quiet footsteps making their way through the living room. What was she going to do? Could they jump out the window? But then what? They would need to wait for the SUV. Her family member would clearly think to check outside if they couldn’t find anyone inside. Then there was the issue that someone was regularly breaking into their home while they were out. Which would lead to paranoia and unnecessary problems. Was it a better idea to have Esmé go and Belle show herself? But that might make Esmé think it was planned. Belle groaned. Every scenario she thought of wasn’t going to work.

The stairs creaked. There was no time left to think. Before Belle could tell Esmé to jump out of the window, she heard her grandpa say, “Make yourself known. I have a gun, and I will shoot!”

At the threat, Belle quickly slipped out of her room. Luther had yet to reach the top to see anyone. “Grandpa! It’s me, Belle! Please don’t shoot!”

“Belle?” Luther called out. He rushed up the stairs and gave Belle a hug. “Oh my stars! What are you doing here? Did they let you go? Where’s Desiree?”

“She’s still there—”

“You escaped?” he asked, shocked.

“No, no. I didn’t…”

“Then what happened? Why are you here?”

“Do you actually have a gun?” Belle asked.

“Yes, why?”

“Can you put it away before I tell you?”

Luther gave her a confused look, but obliged. He put the handgun back in its hidden spot in the downstairs office and returned to Belle’s room. “What is it? Are you going to tell me how you’re here or what?”

223

Belle stood in front of Esmé in the middle of the room. He'd put on his winter gear while Luther had gone to put the gun away. Belle found a pair of her sunglasses to hide his eyes. He didn't know if it was a good idea to show himself. But Belle insisted that Luther was the best person to run into, next to Freddy and her grandma. And because he decided he would give 100% of his trust to Belle on this trip, he had to follow through with it.

"Please don't freak out!" Belle begged, her arms raised in defense.

"Belle? W-who is that?"

"Grandpa, this is Esmé. He's the second prince of Rosaceae. The kingdom I'm staying in. We became best friends and I wanted to show him our world. They're not monsters like dad said they were. They're actually really kind and accommodating." Belle waited for Luther to respond. When he didn't, Belle approached him slowly. "I know you're probably scared, but there's no reason to be. Please, come in and get to know him."

Belle gently took his hand, and led him into the room. "Grandpa, this is Esmé. Esmé, this is my grandpa, Luther."

Esmé bowed. With a quivering voice, he said, "I-it's a p-pleasure to meet you, sir. I am E-Esmé Nicolas Bellerose of Rosaceae. Thank…you…for allowing me to be here…"

Hearing Esmé's formal introduction snapped Luther out of his trance. "Hello, your uh, highness? I'm Luther, Belle's grandfather. Y-you're always welcome…here."

"Yeah, Esmé, you're always welcome! Sorry for scaring you Grandpa. This was a spur of the moment trip, an act of goodwill from Esmé, and I was hoping to not run into anyone, so no one would be scared."

"I would've appreciated knowing you were here," Luther chided. "Do you know how frightening it is to see someone making themselves comfortable in my home after being gone for a week?"

"Why were you gone for so long?" Belle asked.

"Your father got the job in Green Bay. Everyone's visiting him right now. They won't be back until later this week."

"Oh my gosh! Yay! I'm so happy for him!" Belle clapped and cheered. "Well what are you still doing here?"

"I came back because of some plans I had." Luther glanced at Esmé. "But I might cancel them after all."

"Don't do it on our behalf," Belle said. "We have to go back today."

"Why?" Luther asked.

"Because that's what we promised his brother. He's Esmé's guardian. He only gave him permission to travel for a few hours."

"I would be happy if the two of you stayed longer. There's so much to our world, staying here at the house isn't terribly interesting."

"Where else could we go?"

"We could take a trip to Milwaukee. Show him a city."

"That could be fun," Belle said, glancing at Esmé. "But it all depends on Esmé and his brother."

"I don't think I should…" Esmé chimed in.

"Aw, that's such a shame." Luther frowned. "I would have loved to get to know you."

Feeling guilty because of his response, Esmé said, "Well…I could ask Raoul and see if it's okay…"

"That would be wonderful." Luther nodded.

"For how long?" Belle asked.

"How about a 3-day trip?" Luther suggested.

"That's fine with me," Belle said.

"If you'll excuse me, I'll try to contact him." Esmé bowed before going outside to contact Lady Orchida.

After confirming Esmé was out of earshot, Luther turned to Belle. He smacked Belle's arm softly. "Are you insane?"

"What?"

"Why are you going back?" Luther asked.

"Because we had an agreement. I'm going to follow through on it," Belle said. "Besides I actually like living there. I live in a castle. It's beautiful and safer than here. I don't have to worry about gun violence or lunatics. It's just the 4 of us and I feel at home."

"You feel at home as a prisoner?" Luther said.

"I forgot I was even a prisoner. They treat us like royalty."

"I can't believe this," Luther said, shaking his head.

"Didn't dad tell you how nice it was and how they were? He's the one who opened my eyes."

"He did, but we assumed this was just his way of coping with the loss of you both." Luther shook his head vehemently. "Are you under some sort of spell?"

"No. Wait a second. Let me show you." Belle grabbed her phone and showed Luther photos of Raoul's garden then the photos and videos from the Christmas party. "See. This is where we live. Esmé even threw a Christmas ball in my honor. And look how this night ended, with all of us having a blast.

"I know we all started off on the wrong foot, but Desiree and I put our prejudices aside and we all became friends. I really like being there. I'm not under a spell. Esmé just wanted a friend, and I'm the first friend he's ever had. It's confusing, I get it, but I'm happy there. And even after my 6-year sentence is up, I'm going to continue visiting."

Luther staggered over to Belle's bed to sit. This was too much for him to handle. "Confusing" was an understatement to how Luther felt. "I don't know what to say. I can't stop you from going back if that's what you truly want. Just, let me spend time with you two in Milwaukee so I can see with my own eyes that he's a good kid."

"If Raoul gives his permission, then we can do that."

***

Esmé closed the front door behind him. As he walked down the steps, the SUV had arrived. He climbed inside and took off his coat and scarf. He pressed the necklace. *Will this work here?*

After a minute, Esmé heard, "Yes?"

"Lady Orchida? It's me, Esmé."

"I'm well aware. Is something the matter?"

"So…I met Belle's grandpa," he paused, "and he invited me and Belle to go to a place called muh-wah-key with him. I was wondering if I could go."

"I don't know about that, Esmé. Remember what I told you. The farther away you go from the portal, the less effective my magic is. If you go to Milwaukee, I may not be able to help you if you're in trouble," Lady Orchida stated. "Are you willing to take that risk?"

"I am. I trust Belle, and if Belle trusts her grandpa, then I will too."

"You have my approval, but you will need to ask for Raoul's."

"But you know he's going to disagree," Esmé whined.

"Then you'll have to do a good job of convincing him."

"How will I even be able to reach him?" Esmé asked. "I don't want to drive all the way back just to ask him."

Lady Orchida took a minute to respond. When she did, she said, "I'll adjust your necklaces so you're able to speak to each other. Give me five minutes and I'll have Raoul contact you when it's ready."

"Thank you. Sorry to always bug you."

"Don't worry about it, Esmé. You've just helped me out as well."

Esmé waited quietly in the SUV. In exactly 5 minutes, Esmé's necklace flashed 3 times and he could hear Raoul's voice.

"Hello?" Raoul said. "Is this working?"

"It is!" Esmé shouted.

"Hello?" Raoul repeated. "Esmé? If you're trying to speak, you have to press the pendant and hold it while you talk."

Esmé held the pendant and said, "I can hear you, can you hear me?"

"Yes!" Raoul exclaimed. "Lady Orchida never ceases to amaze me with her powers!"

"It is awesome," Esmé agreed.

"So what was it you wanted to ask me?" Raoul asked.

"Lady Orchida didn't tell you?"

"No. Is it important?"

"Yes…I uh…was wondering if I could stay in Belle's world for a few days? Lady Orchida said it was fine, but I needed to ask you as well."

There was a moment of silence before Raoul finally answered. "How long is a 'few days'?"

"3 days. I met Belle's grandpa and he invited me and Belle to go to a place called mah-wuh-kei," Esmé said. "He said just showing me their home wasn't a good example of their world."

"And you're sure you want to go?"

"I am. There're so many cool things here that don't exist in our world. They have TVs and video games, and pizza!"

"I don't approve of you staying, but I doubt that matters. If Lady Orchida approves, then what I say doesn't hold much weight." Raoul chuckled. "Just…be safe, okay? Contact me whenever you can so I know everything's fine."

"I will."

"Ahh, this is unfortunate…" Raoul sighed.

"Don't worry, I'll bring you a gift from their world."

"No, no. Not that," Raoul said. "Now I'm really going to be bored out of my mind."

"Why? Is Desiree being mean again?"

"Not at all..." Raoul paused. "Is miss Belle with you?"

"No, she's inside her house."

Raoul explained Lady Orchida's plan to Esmé. "You and Belle returning this evening was my only hope of ending my ennui."

"I can cancel our plans so you aren't alone," Esmé offered.

"No, don't worry about me. Have fun for the both of us."

"Okay. I'll make sure to contact you so you have someone to talk to when we get to the place."

"All right. Just hold the pendant for 5 seconds to reach me. I'll let you go. Goodbye."

"Bye, Raoul."

Esmé returned to Belle's room, making sure to knock before entering.

"What did he say?" Belle asked.

"He's okay with it. I just have to contact him periodically to let him know that I'm safe."

"Raoul is such a worrywart," Belle laughed.

"Rightfully so," Luther chimed in. "When your child is far away from home, you have every right to be concerned for their safety."

"He's not his child though," Belle said. "Raoul's his older brother."

"Still his guardian." Luther waved off Belle's correction. "Esmé, how old are you and your brother?"

"I'm 17. Raoul is 23, almost 24," Esmé answered.

"And he's your guardian, at such a young age himself?"

"I wouldn't say he's my guardian. He protects me as my brother, not a guard or anything," Esmé said, honestly.

Belle stifled her laugh. "In our world, a guardian can also mean someone who takes care of you in place of a parent."

"Oh, well yes. Then he is my guardian."

"Why is that? Where are your parents?" Luther asked.

"Grandpa, you can't ask him that—" Belle chided.

"It's fine," Esmé interrupted. "It's a personal story so I won't go into too much detail. But my mother I guess died not long after I was born and our father abandoned us around that time as well. So we had servants and my father's best friend raise us. But things happened, our servants couldn't look after us, and Raoul stepped up to take care of me."

"Oh, dear. I'm sorry for your loss," Luther said. "You have a great brother to do something like that."

"Thank you," Esmé said.

"I should pack some fresh clothes for the trip. Pack up the pizza and anything you'll need for the ride," Luther said, slapping his hands on his knees and standing up. "I'll make reservations at the best hotel I can find."

"Okay, thanks grandpa," Belle said.

"Thank you," Esmé said.

When Luther's door closed, Belle said, "Sorry. My grandpa can be a bit intrusive…"

"It's fine. I wasn't offended or anything."

"Aside from his questions, what do you think about him?"

"He's nice," Esmé said. "I can tell he's afraid of me, but I hope I can prove that I'm not a bad person."

"And you will," Belle said, placing a hand on his shoulder. "It only takes a day to see that you're a kind person."

Esmé smiled.

"Let's go pack some snacks and the pizzas."

Belle and Esmé walked to the nearest gas station and bought $20 worth of snacks and drinks to bring with. The employee stared at Esmé with a strange look on his face. Belle explained that he was from a warmer country and wasn't used to the Wisconsin winter so he overdressed. That was enough for the employee to laugh it off. Belle and Esmé packed as many snacks as they could into their suitcases. Belle packed her console and video games, as well as some of her cuter outfits and art supplies.

Luther had finished booking a hotel. He made his way downstairs as Esmé placed the last of their things in the living room. "We're all set. Let's get everything loaded in the car."

Esmé took his belongings to the SUV.

Belle stopped him and asked, "Grandpa, are we riding in the SUV or your car?"

"Preferably mine. You can call your car from anywhere. I can't do that. Why not just ride with me and summon it when it's time to leave?"

"I agree with him," Belle said. "It's also hard to adjust the settings. We'd waste time trying to figure out how to change it back to your kingdom."

"Ok…" Esmé nodded. He wasn't all too sure about not bringing the SUV, but again, he was going to trust Belle's judgement. He pressed a button on the key fob and the SUV drove away.

Luther led them to the garage and opened the door. Esmé gasped. He didn't know cars could come in other colors besides black. Luther's car was a yellow sedan. They put their luggage in the trunk and Esmé sat in the back. He was just as nervous and excited as he was when he first arrived in Belle's world. He was fascinated about how this new place was. Luther said it was the best way to show him their world. He imagined a lot of airplanes and TVs everywhere.

***

It was a 2-hour drive to Milwaukee. On the way, Belle and Luther discussed places to go to once they checked into the hotel. When they made it to the outside of Milwaukee, Belle spotted an arcade and begged Luther to stop there.

"I want to show Esmé arcade machines. Can we go please," she asked. "We're earlier than the time you told the hotel we'd arrive. Just thirty minutes. Pleeaassseee!"

Luther sighed. "Okay. Thirty minutes, not a second more."

Luther took the next exit and looped around to the arcade. The parking lot was empty. Which was surprising. Belle wondered if they were even open. Luther stayed in the car. He gave Belle $30. Belle and Esmé approached the building. Esmé looked at the neon sign above the door, "Royal Gaming Arcade."

"So is this for royalty?" he asked.

"No, they just wanted to name it that. Anyone's welcome to enter."

They entered and Esmé complained. "It's so dark in here. How can anyone see?"

"The darkness is what makes it fun," Belle answered. She paid the entry fee. "Esmé did you bring your money with you? Are you willing to pay for the game passes?"

"Sure, but what are they for?" he asked.

"So we can use the machines."

"Oh, ok…" Esmé said. "I have to get my suitcase."

Belle turned to the employee and asked, "Can he reenter? He needs to grab his money."

"Go ahead," he said.

Esmé nodded and ran outside. When he reached the car, Luther was texting someone. He had a serious look on his face before noticing Esmé tapping on the door.

He smiled and rolled down the window. "Is something the matter, son?"

"No. I need to get something out of my suitcase in the trunk. Can you open it…please?"

Luther popped the trunk.

"Thank you," Esmé said. He pulled out the wad of cash, closed the trunk, waved at Luther and ran back to the building.

He handed the money to Belle. She gave the employee $40 for 2 game cards. Belle gave Esmé his card and they walked through the second door into the arcade.

Neon lights and the lights from the arcade games lit the dark room and Esmé's eyes sparkled. "What kind of magic is this?"

"No magic. Just electricity," Belle replied. She pointed to a game from the 80s. "Let's go there first."

As they walked through the arcade machines, Esmé asked, "Why are they so big compared to the one at your home?"

"This is how they started. People used to have to go to places like this to play games. Then as technology got better, they remade these into consoles. The game system you saw at my house. And every few years they make better versions of consoles."

"Which one is more convenient?"

"I'd say consoles. Imagine having to leave your house just to play games. And, you had to pay each time you wanted to play. I couldn't do it."

"So, why are we here if you think your 'console' is better?"

"The nostalgia…even though I wasn't alive…. Most of these games don't exist anymore. So you can only find them here." Belle tapped her card on the arcade game and said, "Besides these games are still fun. Yeah my Mimninedon't is convenient cause I can carry it everywhere I want, but arcade games will never die.

"This game, all you do is move the frog to get it to the pond on the other side. But you have to avoid the cars or the frog dies," Belle continued. She started playing.

"That's gruesome…" Esmé commented.

"It is," Belle said. She pointed to the other card reader and said, "You can join me any time by tapping your card against that."

Esmé followed her instructions and joined her. They played for 5 minutes before moving on to another game. Belle wanted to maximize their experience and not waste a minute of their time.

"This game, you play as a knight. You have to avoid the zombies and other monsters. When you're hit, you lose armor," she explained. "The lance is the best weapon. You *don't* want the flamethrower. It's the worst weapon in the game. You want to collect the items. The goal is to get the highest score and of course, beat the game."

They made it to the 4th stage before losing. Belle sighed and said as she walked away, "That game is always cheating. It's like they learn your moves every time you figure out how to beat it."

"What should we do next?" Esmé asked.

She looked at the time on her phone. "We have 15 minutes. Is there anything you want to try?"

"Umm," Esmé thought, looking around. He pointed to a game that had a line around it. "What about there. It looks popular."

"Yeah…we're gonna have to wait our turn," Belle sighed. "Come on, let's hurry before others go over."

As they waited their turn, Belle explained how the game worked. It was a fighting game. She used a different machine to show him how to fight. When it was their turn to go, Esmé nervously grabbed the joystick. Belle made it seem stressful. He looked through the character list. He didn't know who to play as. Belle had chosen a character named Ken. So he looked for who he thought looked the coolest, which was a man in a white mask and long hair.

He knew he wasn't going to beat Belle, but he wasn't expecting to lose so badly. His loss made other players challenge Belle. She was better than Esmé thought. As he watched her play, he heard a faint sound coming from beneath his coat.

"Esmé? Did you make it to 'muh-wah-key'?"

Esmé whispered to Belle that Raoul was calling and excused himself. He looked for a quiet spot away from everyone and pulled his necklace out.

"Raoul? Can you hear me?"

"Yes, it's a little loud but I can hear you now. Did you make it safely?"

"Sort of. We stopped at this place called an arcade. It's really fun. I think after this, we're going to go to where we're supposed to sleep."

"Well I'm glad you're having fun. Is Miss Belle enjoying herself?"

"Yes, she is."

"That's wonderful. What about her grandfather?"

"He stayed in the car."

"I'm referring to in general. Is he kind to you?"

"Yes, he is," Esmé said. "I can tell he's still afraid of me. But I'm hoping this trip will help him like me. Then he'll approve of me and Belle."

"We can only hope," Raoul said. "What are you doing at the arcade? Can you tell me what it is?"

Esmé heard cheers coming from where Belle was and wanted to see what happened. "I have to go! I'll tell you later!"

"Wait, Esmé," Raoul said. "Call me when you make it to your lodging."

"Okay," Esmé said, releasing the necklace. He ran back to the main room to see Belle walking away. "What happened? Why were they cheering?"

"Someone finally beat me." Belle pouted. "It's whatever. We have like 3 minutes before we have to go to the car. Is there anything else you want to do?"

"What about that thing?"

"Air hockey? Sure, let's go." Belle explained how to play. "Ready?"

Esmé nodded and Belle hit the puck towards him. Esmé hit the puck so hard that it flew off the table.

Belle laughed. "You don't have to hit it so hard. Just aim for the goal or the corners you think will knock it in."

"Sorry," he said.

"Don't apologize. You didn't hit anyone so it's fine."

At exactly 30 minutes, Luther called Belle and told her to come back. When they left the arcade, Luther was waiting in front of the door. He had stopped off to get food. It was Belle's favorite restaurant. Luther ordered pizza puffs, cheesy fries, and gyros. He offered to let them eat in the car, but Esmé was too afraid to take his scarf off, in case a car next to them saw him.

***

They arrived at their hotel an hour later. Luther booked two rooms. He and Belle in one room, and Esmé in the other. Their rooms were on opposite sides of the floor. Esmé struggled with how to use the elevator. No matter how much Luther tried to explain it, Esmé couldn't understand it. When Luther finally gave up on trying to get Esmé to learn how to use the elevator, Esmé entered his room, set his luggage and his food on the floor and threw his winter gear aside.

"Finally!" he exclaimed. It was extremely hot and uncomfortable wearing it. He was also happy to be fully back in his human form. He flopped on the bed and stretched out. He sighed. *Feels so good to lie down.*

"Oh yeah," he said, aloud. "I have to let Raoul know I made it."

He held his pendant for 5 seconds. Raoul answered immediately.

"Hello?" he answered.

"We made it to the 'hotel,'" Esmé said.

"Wonderful. Is it nice?"

"Eh, it's fancier than Belle's home but still nothing compared to our castle. It's cozy though."

"Of course. It's hard to replicate royalty," Raoul chuckled.

"Is Desiree still asleep?" Esmé asked.

"Yes. She'll wake in the morning, I believe." He sighed. "I hope Lady Orchida can break the curse soon."

"Me too. I'm really trying my best to like her," Esmé grumbled.

"Even if things don't work out between us, you'll still have to like her."

"Why's that?"

"You're marrying into their family. Of course you have to get along. For Belle's sake at least."

"Ugh," Esmé groaned. "Let's hope things work out. I already vowed to myself to hate her for eternity if she doesn't love you."

"Neither Miss Desiree or Miss Belle are required to love us. The only person we can be mad at if we fail is father. They have no knowledge of what's at stake for us. You shouldn't hate her for something that's not her responsibility. We should be thankful. I'm sure if she knew it was life and death and she had to love me, she would try."

"I doubt that…" Esmé said, disregarding his lecture. He grabbed the bag of food off the floor and sat at the table. "She's blind if she can't see that you're a great person."

"Thank you, Esmé. She just has to get to know me. Have you been eating properly?"

"Yep. I had breakfast and lunch. I'm going to eat dinner now."

"Alone?" Raoul asked, concerned.

"Yeah. Belle offered to eat with me, but I need a break. It's tough being a beast all day."

"Understandable. What are you eating?"

"Uh…something called a gee-row? Cheese covered fries, and a pizza puff." Esmé pulled a can of soda out of the bag and looked at it. "They also gave me a 'panta, strawberry soda.'"

"Huh. Let me know how they taste."

Esmé bit into the soft juicy meat, a playful ballet of spices and tenderness danced on his tongue. He exclaimed, "This is amazing!"

"What does it taste like?" Raoul asked.

"I can't explain it," Esmé answered, taking another bite. With his mouth full, he said, "It's like…it's hard to explain."

"Is it like anything you've tried here?"

"No! Nothing is." Esmé pulled out the pizza puff. "Their food is so different from ours. It's so strange."

Esmé took a bite of the pizza puff, the gooey cheese stretched as Esmé sat it down. He ripped the cheese apart. "Like, I've never seen cheese that stretches like this. Who knew pizza could come in different forms?"

Raoul laughed. "Well, I'm glad you're having fun."

"I really like it here," Esmé said.

There was a knock on the door and Esmé told Raoul to hold on. He asked who it was.

"It's me, Belle."

Esmé changed into his chimera form and opened the door. "Is something wrong?"

"No, I just wanted to chat for a bit? Is now a good time?" she asked.

"Sure," Esmé said, moving to the table. "I was speaking to Raoul. I think he won't mind ending our conversation."

"I've been meaning to ask," Belle started, "how are you talking to him? I thought you didn't have phones."

"The sorceress made us necklaces." Esmé held the necklace and said, "If I hold this, Raoul can hear everything we're saying."

"Hello, Miss Belle," Raoul said.

"Hi Raoul! How is Desiree?" Belle asked.

"Miss Desiree is not feeling well. She has a fever. She's resting at the moment."

"She's sick?" Belle exclaimed. "Maybe we should end the trip. I should go back and take care of my sister."

"No, it's just a few sniffles and a tiny fever. But I promise you, I am taking great care of her. Please stay and enjoy your trip."

"Are you sure?" Belle asked, somewhat hesitantly.

"Yes. I give you my word."

"Okay, if you say it's just a few sniffles," Belle said. "Thank you for taking care of her."

"My pleasure."

"Hey, Raoul?" Esmé joined in. "Is it all right if I end our conversation to talk to Belle before bed?"

"Of course!" Raoul said. "Don't worry about me. I'll speak to you in the morning. Have fun you two, and don't stay up too late."

"We won't," Belle said.

They said goodbye to Raoul.

"Can I use my necklace to contact Desiree?" Belle asked.

"No. Only our necklaces have it. One press to speak to the sorceress, and a long hold for Raoul," Esmé explained. He didn't dare demonstrate with one press. "She did this so I could ask Raoul if I could go to muh-wah-key. It was never an idea until then. So you don't have to worry about whether Raoul and I are spying on you."

"I believe you," Belle said. "It wouldn't make sense to have it considering there's nowhere to run off to in your world."

"Yeah."

"How do you like the city so far?" Belle asked.

"It's amazing." Esmé walked to the patio. "Look at all the lights. The view is breathtaking. The only time I've seen so many lights was when I was looking at the stars."

"Well, stars beat city lights in my book."

Belle and Esmé talked for another hour. Esmé gushed about the food and his new favorite, cheese fries. Belle loved the look in his eyes as he gazed outside. This was by far the best idea she'd ever had. She wanted Esmé to enjoy his life instead of being locked away in a castle.

Belle said goodnight to Esmé and walked back to her room. On the way, she thought about Esmé's bright smile as he looked out into the city.

Esmé lay in bed, facing the patio. He left the curtains open so he could sleep with a beautiful view of the city's twinkling lights. He never felt freer than he did in Belle's world. If only he could stay forever.

CHAPTER TWELVE

Belle x Esmé

Early the next morning, Belle knocked on Esmé's door.

After a moment or two of silence, he answered in a drowsy voice, "Who is it?"

"It's me," Belle said. "My grandpa would like to take us to the zoo and then to visit some museums today. He said to order room service for breakfast and get dressed. There should be a menu on the counter under the TV."

"I see it," Esmé said, his voice muffled.

"Great. We're going to eat at the restaurant downstairs. So if you need anything or you're ready to go, you know where to find us."

"Thanks."

Belle said goodbye to Esmé and joined Luther back in their hotel room. Luther had finished getting ready and was waiting for Belle to return. She joined him and they made their way downstairs to the restaurant. As Luther talked, Belle nodded distractedly. She wanted Luther's opinion of Esmé and wondered if now was a good time to ask. He'd only interacted with Esmé for a short time yesterday. Was it too soon for him to change his mind about him? She was nervous.

When they grabbed their food from the all-you-can-eat buffet and sat down, Belle asked what she had been worrying over since she woke up. "What do you think of Esmé...so far...?"

"Well, from what I can tell," Luther began, "he's very respectable and formal...great manners...."

Belle knew her grandfather well enough to know that he didn't think highly of Esmé. Luther wasn't the type to speak poorly of others, even if he did not like them. He was a firm believer in, "If you don't have anything nice to say, don't say anything at all." And while he did technically say something nice, his tone was somewhat forced. This was another hurdle Belle was willing to jump over to prove that the two princes weren't really monsters.

Belle responded, "I'm glad you think so. Esmé told me his brother, Raoul, was very strict in his upbringing. You know, they didn't believe in leftovers until Desiree convinced Raoul to allow it? They eat just the right amount and Esmé apparently wasn't allowed to leave the table until he finished his food."

"That's what most parents do. Grandma and I did keep leftovers. However, your father and aunt were not allowed to leave the table until most of their food was gone."

"I'm glad mom and dad didn't make us do that," Belle mumbled. "You have a lot in common with his brother…aside from the physical appearance and royalty…."

"Maybe we do," Luther said. "I think we have a lot in common with wanting to protect our families."

Esmé looked at the menu. He had no idea what any of it meant. He'd seen the pictures of the pizza options but they were only available during lunch and dinner. Looking at the breakfast section only, Esmé decide to play it safe. He figured nothing could go wrong with eggs, toast, and a fruit bowl.

He wore his winter gear while waiting by the door for the food to arrive. When he opened it, the employee on the other side looked startled, then terrified. He wheeled the cart into the room slowly, as if any sudden movement would unleash the weirdo who was not only dressed in winter clothing, but whose face was almost fully covered by a scarf and sunglasses. The waiter unloaded the trays with a quickness even he didn't know was possible. He stopped in the doorway, and held his hand out.

Esmé looked up, his eyes rising from his hand to the man's face. "What?"

"No tip?"

Even after feeling like his life was in danger, he certainly made sure he got his tip.

"Oh…right," Esmé said, mumbling, "Belle did say I had to do that."

Esmé gave the employee a dollar and closed the door. He was told to leave the tray on the floor outside of his room when he was finished.

It was edible, but nothing compared to a breakfast cooked by Raoul. After he finished eating he decided to go to the lobby. Esmé tried to use the elevator again, but he couldn't figure out how to open it, so he took the stairs. When he finally arrived, he looked for the "restaurant"

Belle mentioned. After scanning the area, he finally saw Belle and Luther on the opposite side of the room. He crossed the lobby and made his way to the restaurant where he stood in the doorway. There were so many people inside, that his stomach was in knots.

Belle looked up from her plate and Esmé waved at her. She waved back and motioned for him to sit with them. He shook his head, pointing to a bench in front of the restaurant, and sat down.

"Are you done?" Luther asked.

"Yeah, their food isn't appetizing at all," Belle replied. "I don't think I can eat any more."

"I agree. Not even a pinch of salt on this," Luther said, laughing. "Let's hurry so Esmé doesn't scare any more guests."

Belle looked at Esmé. He received a lot of looks and whispers. Belled nodded and tossed her remaining food in the trash and met Esmé before Luther could stand.

"How was breakfast?" she asked.

"It was okay." He shrugged. "I didn't know what any of it meant so I just got something plain. How was yours?"

Belle checked her surroundings to make sure the restaurant staff wasn't within ear-shot. "Disgusting. The only thing that tasted good was the eggs. But I guess that's going to happen when it's mass cooked."

She sat down next to him and continued, "Do you have All-You-Can-Eat buffets in your world?"

Esmé shook his head. "Not that I know of."

"Oh…right," Belle said, awkwardly. She watched as another guest sneered at Esmé. She asked, "Does it bother you?"

"Does what bother me?"

"Everyone staring."

"Not really. I do look weird." Esmé stared at his hands, closing his left one into a fist. "I would rather they stare because I'm dressed like this, than to watch them running around panicking over a beast…or worse…."

"You're right," Belle said. "I just wish people had more manners to not stare."

"It's all right," Esmé said, standing. "I'm having fun. That's all that matters, right?"

Belle nodded.

"Okay," Luther said, approaching them. He stuffed something in his messenger bag and asked, "Are you two ready to go? Got everything you need?"

"Yes," they said in unison.

Belle continued, "Esmé, do you have your money in case you want souvenirs?"

"Uh…" Esmé patted his coat pocket. "I think so."

"Go look upstairs," Luther said. "We'll wait right here."

"Yes, sir." Esmé bowed and headed to the stairs. He returned 5 minutes later. "I did forget it."

"That's why it's always good to double check. You may not know what you're overlooking," Luther said, leading them to the valet.

***

On the road to the zoo, Belle pointed outside the window. "Look! There's a movie theater not too far from the hotel. We should go there after we're done sightseeing."

"What's a movie theater?" Esmé asked.

"You know how we watched the Power of Friendship movie?"

Esmé nodded.

"This is where those movies first run before they go to TV. They have different movies there," Belle continued. "They appear on large screens, and the room is super dark. No one can see you."

"I'd like to go," Esmé said.

"Great. That'll be our final stop," Luther added.

They passed by a park and Belle explained to Esmé what it was for. Every little thing they passed, Esmé wanted to know what it was. Belle did not truly understand the differences between their worlds until today. Part of her assumed that many of these places existed in their world, but Esmé and Raoul had been cut off from the rest of the kingdom. How could they know what existed and what didn't? The logical side of her acknowledged that things weren't going to be the same. She hoped one day she could see beyond the castle grounds.

At the zoo, Belle asked Esmé while looking at the elephants if he'd seen one before. Esmé explained that many of the animals there were similar to the ones in his kingdom. They were called different names and had slightly different physical features like color, fur patterns, etc. They were happy to find one relatable thing.

"I will say, however," Esmé started, "we don't lock our animals in places like this. They are given a large part of the kingdom to roam and hum—I mean, my people are not allowed nearby. Today will be the first time I've seen an animal so close. It was always in books."

"We have parts of the country where they're free to roam. Humans can visit them, but they're given guidelines to follow," Belle said. "I do hate that animals are locked in places like this until they die."

"It sucks, but these animals would not survive in the wild," Luther chimed in. "Some of these animals are endangered and would've been poached already. I see it as a necessary evil. Although, I'm sure they would do better in a habitat."

"I guess," Belle said. How could she argue with that? It was cruel, but until humans stopped destroying their world, and stopped killing them for sport, they would have to stay in an enclosure for their own protection.

Man, I'm glad we can't interact with ours, Esmé thought. That was apparently one downside to their world. But then again, human selfishness was something they both suffered from. His father was a prime example, if not the epitome, of selfishness.

They didn't stay long at the zoo since Esmé had similar animals and seemingly wasn't impressed with the way animals were locked up.

They stopped by the gift shop and Esmé bought Raoul a wolf plushie. Belle thought it was hilarious. Esmé also bought a red panda keychain for Desiree. While he wasn't fond of her behavior, he still wanted to give her a gift. It would also work in his favor with Belle. Next was the art museum.

When they arrived at the art museum, Esmé was impressed with the architecture. He spent most of the visit talking about the building's design than the artwork inside. Next, they made their way to the Milwaukee Public Museum. There, Esmé learned about dinosaurs. He'd experienced a roller-coaster of emotions; admiration for their size and ferocity, fear that they were still alive, and relief upon learning they went extinct.

Esmé had fallen in love with Belle's world. It seemed so much better than his own. Yeah they had magic, but they didn't have things like pizza and dinosaurs. He hoped he could break his curse soon so that he and Belle could travel her world together.

At 1 p.m., they went to a Chinese restaurant and ordered take out. Luther parked in the science museum's parking garage as far away from other cars as possible so Esmé could feel comfortable eating.

"How's your food?" Belle asked.

"Amazing!" Esmé said, slurping up lo mein noodles. This trip was so freeing. He didn't have to worry about table manners or eating at a table for that matter. "Your world has so much delicious food!"

Luther laughed. "Is that all you enjoy about it? Except for the dinosaurs, I haven't heard you talk so highly of anything not food related."

"Yes sir." Esmé nodded. "I do like other aspects of your world, but the food is the best!"

"Well that's wonderful. Who wouldn't love this world," Luther said. "I would hate to be forced to leave it."

Belle side-eyed her grandpa, but Esmé didn't seem to notice what he was implying.

"Absolutely! I would love to come here more often, if you and my brother would allow it."

"You're always welcome. Just make sure to bring Belle with you every time," Luther stated.

"Of course, it wouldn't be the same without her." Esmé took a swig of soda. "I hope that one day Belle and I can see more of your world together."

"It's a promise," Belle said, sticking her pinky out.

Esmé nodded and did the same.

Luther had gone silent. He returned to eating his food while Belle and Esmé planned imaginary trips. Eventually, Luther told them to hush and finish their food so they didn't waste their parking time, and he could save on money.

Esmé was the first to finish. Belle and Luther had begun another conversation while he sat quietly in the back and ate. As he put the trash back in the take-out bag, he heard the faint sound of a voice from beneath his scarf.

"Esmé? Hello?"

Esmé glanced up at Belle and Luther in the front and tucked his head down to reply in a whisper, "Hi Raoul, I can't talk right now."

"Why? Is something the matter," Raoul asked, concerned.

"No, I'm in the car with Belle and her grandfather. We just finished lunch and will enter the next museum soon. So I won't be able to talk."

"I'm sorry to be such a bother," Raoul chuckled. "I just wanted to check in and make sure everything is going well."

"It is, thank you," Esmé replied. "You're not a bother at all. I'm glad to have someone that worries about me."

"Of course," Raoul softly whispered. "I'll always have your back."

"And I, yours," Esmé replied.

"It's getting late here, so I will call once more later this evening to say goodnight. I'll leave you alone for the rest of your trip after."

"OK, I'll speak to you later."

Esmé sat up straight and locked eyes with Luther in the rear-view mirror. He cleared his throat and continued cleaning up.

"You ready to go inside?" Luther asked.

"Yes, sir." Esmé opened his door.

Inside, they planned where they would go first. Luther and Belle agreed to go to the Techno Side first, then the Aqua Side. It was too cold to do outdoor activities. They started with the trains. Esmé learned about how trains were built and how they functioned. They made their way around the museum. Esmé was fascinated. He never understood the extent of their advancement. He knew their world had better things, but seeing how much they had, amazed him. He used the word "amaze" a lot during the trip, but this time, he truly meant it. He could even argue it was better than the food. Learning about airplanes was the highlight.

"Is that what a plane looks like?" Esmé asked.

The employee chuckled. "Yes."

"He's never been on a plane before," Luther said. "This is all new to him."

"Well, you better get him on one soon!" the employee joked.

"Maybe one day I can," Esmé said, leaving the flight simulator.

Esmé played against an AI and was confused about how an inanimate object was outsmarting him. Belle and Luther had to intervene, so Esmé wouldn't spend the entire day trying to learn how.

As Luther put it, "Sometimes, ignorance is bliss. Give up, son."

The last stop was the aquarium. Belle double checked with Esmé to ensure he'd never seen one before. When he confirmed he hadn't, they went to the lower level. The light reflecting from the water was breathtaking. They walked through the tunnel surrounded by fish.

"Look! There's fish under us as well!" He'd never seen so many fish in one place before.

Raoul did have a small koi pond in his garden, but Lady Orchida confiscated them as neither Raoul nor Esmé could take care of them properly.

"What an odd-looking fish..." Esmé leaned over the sturgeon then lifted his sunglasses and touched it. "If it weren't for you, I'd never have experienced something like this. Thank you."

His eyes sparkled in awe. A look Belle realized she loved to see. The Science Museum made for a great way to end their sightseeing. She enjoyed the innocence and magic Esmé's curiosity brought. It reminded her of her childhood...before Angela passed away; when she viewed the world with a bright, childlike wonder.

"Do you think we can eat this?" Esmé asked, staring down at the fish.

"Huh!?" Belle exclaimed.

Luther overheard and burst into laughter.

"N-no, you can't eat them! I mean…technically…yes they are edible, but no!" Belle answered.

So much for a touching moment, Belle thought. She turned her head towards Esmé and said, "You're welcome."

They spent 3 hours in the Science Museum, not including half an hour spent in the car. Esmé bought a few more souvenirs for himself, Raoul, and even Lady Orchida. On the ride back, they decided it was best to see the movie around 7:00 p.m. Belle and Esmé wanted to continue touring Milwaukee while they waited, but Luther was spent. He welcomed them to hang around the hotel area but he was going to take a nap. They decided to walk around at 6:00 p.m.

In the car, Esmé heard Raoul call out to him. "Sorry to bother you again."

"Are you going to sleep?" Esmé asked, slouching in his seat.

"I'm not going to bed yet. After our last conversation, I couldn't figure out for the life of me what a museum was."

"Can I tell you later, I'm back in the car with Belle and her grandfather. We should be returning to the hotel soon, so I can call you back to explain."

"…Yes, we can do that."

"I'm sorry if I come off as dismissive, I just don't want her grandfather to think I'm weird for speaking into my clothing."

As if he had a sixth sense, Luther asked, "Do you like talking to yourself, Esmé?"

"Oh, uh…I'm not talking to myself." Esmé sat up straight.

"He has a necklace he uses to contact his brother," Belle interjected. "The best way I can describe it is like a mix between a walkie-talkie and a cell phone."

"Interesting. I was wondering why you were whispering to yourself earlier. That explains why."

"Yes. This is the first time my brother and I have been separated, so he's been calling me a lot."

"Can you silence it?" Luther asked.

"Silence? I don't think so."

"Well you can't bring that with you to the movie theaters," Luther said.

"Why not?" Esmé asked.

"You're not allowed to talk on the phone," Belle explained. "If Raoul contacts you and is loud, you may upset the audience and we can get kicked out."

"You'll have to leave it in your hotel room," Luther said.

"I don't know if I can," Esmé said, hesitantly. "I was given instructions to never take this off."

"What's a few hours going to do?" Luther asked. "You'll be fine. Belle and I are here."

"Yeah, I do agree with my grandpa," Belle said, looking back at Esmé. "You can leave it somewhere safe and put it on immediately after we return to the hotel."

Esmé hated the idea of disobeying Lady Orchida. She was never wrong. But…he said he would trust Belle on this trip. And if, by some stroke of luck, their friendship blossomed into something more, Esmé had to put his life in her hands. Maybe this could have been the first test.

"O-OK…" Esmé said. "A few hours won't hurt…"

"Atta boy." Luther clapped. He pulled up to the valet and said, "Just remember where you put it. Last thing we want is for you to lose it."

"Yes sir." Esmé nodded.

****

Esmé tucked his necklace in his suit jacket pocket and folded it neatly in his luggage. His gut was telling him it was a bad idea to leave it behind, but Belle and Luther were right. If Raoul called during their movie, he would gain unnecessary attention and ridicule. He was raised to not be rude, so it had to come off.

Esmé looked at his outfit in the mirror. He knew it wasn't a date, but he wanted to look his best…even if he would be covered head to toe. He put on his best suit, the one that Raoul forced him to pack. It was emerald green. It originally had medals and epaulets on it. Esmé, like usual, snuck and took them off before leaving. He fixed his hair before turning into his chimera form and putting on his winter gear and earrings.

Belle told him when they arrived at the hotel that she would wait in the lobby for him. He took a deep breath as he made his way down the stairs. He entered the lobby and searched for Belle. When he saw her, his breath caught in his throat.

Belle leaned against the wall next to the door looking at her phone. She wore a short pastel pink skirt, with matching socks, or what was known to everyone except Esmé, as leg warmers, and pink boots. She had on a cream cable-knit sweater under her dusty rose coat, and a purple scarf. Belle had straightened her hair, and it fell past her shoulders. She had ear muffs as well.

Esmé swallowed as he approached her. He didn't know why he was so nervous. They were just friends, right? Friends didn't feel the way he felt looking at her.

He cleared his throat. "H-hey Belle."

Belle looked up and smiled. "Hi. You ready to go?"

"Yeah."

"Okay," Belle said, pushing off of the wall. "The closest movie theater is kind of far from here. I think we should take a cab."

"Cab?"

"Someone that you pay to drive you places," Belle answered. "We're watching a movie at 7, so let's walk around for a bit and call one in like thirty minutes."

"That works for me," Esmé said. Opening the door and holding it for her, he asked, "Aren't you going to be cold?"

"Thank you. No, I'm actually really hot," she answered. "We're only going to be outside for thirty minutes anyways. I'll be all right."

"If you say so," Esmé said. He grumbled, turning his head away from her, "You look nice."

"Thanks," Belle replied.

They walked in silence for five minutes. They were making great progress away from the hotel. Esmé was too shy to talk to Belle. He didn't know what to talk about and Belle was focused on her phone to find the best cab service. Esmé noticed that the store windows were covered in red and pink lights with hearts, and words like "love," "xoxo," and "Happy Valentine's Day," on walls and items in the window displays.

"What's 'Happy Valentine's Day'?" Esmé asked.

"Valentine's Day?" Belle repeated. She went to her home screen and looked at the date. "I didn't realize it was so close to Valentine's Day. Basically, it's a holiday to celebrate love. You're supposed to give someone a gift and ask them to be your valentine and if they say yes, you spend the 14th with them. You can give people candy, cards, flowers, and/or gifts as a sign of friendship, love…or obligation… It's a cute holiday."

"It sounds fun," Esmé said.

Belle pointed to a fast-food restaurant in front of them. "We can't bring food into the movies; and the price of food they serve is expensive. Want to grab a quick bite?"

"Sure," Esmé said. "Wait, how can I eat?"

"We can take it to go. It's dark enough for us to hide in a corner somewhere and eat."

Esmé nodded.

They ordered something quick. Chicken sandwiches, fries, and two sodas. Belle looked around the street as they walked to find somewhere inconspicuous to eat. She saw a bench in a shady alley, barely lit by the street light. They sat down to eat. Esmé, on cue, praised the food.

Taking a bite of the sandwich, Esmé asked, "So…will you be my valentine?"

Belle stared at Esmé, her mouth agape. She thought back to the marriage proposal he made when she first arrived at the castle. Then there was the Christmas ball and his kingdom's tradition about dancing and marriage. Belle's heart fluttered. Was he listening when she said it was a romantic holiday? *Did* he mean it in a romantic way?

"As a friend!" Esmé clarified, flustered. "We…we don't have to do it for the other reason…I just wanted to do everything right in your world…."

"Yes," Belle said, relieved that he meant as friends, though slightly disappointed. "Sorry, I didn't mean to look shocked. It's just that no one's ever asked me before. As a friend or crush…"

"Really? Why?" Esmé asked. "You're pretty, smart, and kind."

Belle brushed her hair behind her ear and shrugged. "I don't know. My sisters made up a bunch of rumors about me that I guess scared everyone away. But, it's all in the past. I don't hold it against them. We were young."

"Sisters, like Desiree and?"

"No, definitely not Desiree," Belle said, waving her hands. "She would never do something like that. It was my other two sisters, the ones who gave me the sketchbook."

"Oh yeah, right. The ones you said gifted you something they didn't want you to use."

Belle nodded, sheepishly.

"When was the last rumor?" Esmé asked.

"Last year…" Belle answered. "…But they already graduated high school and we moved here, so it's a fresh start. No one knows me."

"Hmm." Esmé nodded. The look on his face betrayed his thoughts.

"We had a rough patch growing up, don't worry about it." Belle stood up. "If you're done eating, we should walk around some more. Actually, let's call the cab now. We should add time to look at our options."

"That's fine with me," Esmé said, standing.

Belle typed on her phone for a bit. "There, the cab will be here soon. There's one in the area."

"Also," Belle said, continuing, "thank you for asking me to be your valentine. I couldn't think of a better person to be my first."

"You're welcome," Esmé said, smiling. "I've experienced a lot of firsts with you. So it's nice to experience something for the first time together."

Belle smiled back. As they waited for the cab to come, Belle couldn't look at Esmé. She was confused as to why she suddenly felt disappointed. Her phone dinged and a car pulled up. "It's here."

Esmé watched outside as they drove to the theater. Bright lights caught his attention as they passed a crowd of people. He asked Belle, "What is going on there?"

Belle gasped. "It looks like there's a Valentine's Day Fair! I didn't know Milwaukee had one!"

"This is their first year," the driver stated. "It's been up for a week."

"We should go after the movie," Belle suggested.

"Go, enjoy yourselves," the driver said. "Tonight is the last night."

"It's a good way to see how our fairs are." Belle smiled.

"It does look fun." Esmé nodded.

"I'll text grandpa so he knows."

They arrived at the movie theater and Belle walked along the wall pointing at each movie.

"The only genre I don't want to watch is horror," Belle said. "Too much gore."

"Should we watch something about Valentine's Day?" Esmé asked, pointing to a romance poster. He wanted to know more about it.

"Nah, let's watch something exciting or funny. Like this one!" Belle said, jogging to a poster on the other side of the entrance. "*The Kingdom of Encleadious*. I heard the books were good."

"You have this book in your world?" Esmé asked, astonished.

"Wait, is this book that popular it's crossed portals?" Belle laughed. "We definitely have to watch it then."

"I agree. I heard my father loved reading the books," Esmé said. "I'm curious about why he liked it so much."

"*The Kingdom of Encleadious* it is then," Belle said, entering the theater. "2 tickets for *The Kingdom of Encleadious* please."

They selected their seats. Belle explained to Esmé that the best place to sit was in the back of the theater. She ordered popcorn, pretzels, and 2 slushies. They made their way into the auditorium. For such a popular book, the majority of the seats were empty except 6 pairs spread randomly throughout. Of course, this was expected in the new age of streaming services. Belle and Esmé had the back 3 rows to themselves.

"It's kind of hard to see with my sunglasses on," Esmé said, sitting down.

"Take them off," Belle stated. "It's dark, they're super far away, and have no reason to look back here. Remove your coat and scarf too. Get comfy."

"I don't know, Belle." Esmé hid behind his scarf. "What if they turn around?"

"They won't be able to see you if they do," Belle said. "If it makes you feel more comfortable, put your coat and stuff on your lap. That way you can hide quickly."

Esmé examined the other viewers. Everyone was focused on the screen and the people sitting next to them, laughing and talking amongst themselves.

Belle continued, "Can you see any of them clearly?"

"No." Esmé shook his head.

"Exactly. When the movie is close to ending, put your coat and scarf on again. You have to be hot in that."

"I am, but—"

"No buts," Belle interrupted. "This is about the safest place to relax."

Esmé looked from the others to Belle, then down to his coat. "All right."

"Yay!" Belle exclaimed…as quietly as she could. She sat the popcorn and drinks in the seat next to her so Esmé could have space.

Esmé took off his glasses, then his scarf and unzipped his coat. He leaned forward to take his coat off and covered his arms with it. "I can't believe I'm doing this."

"Exciting, right." Belle smiled.

Esmé smirked and shook his head. *Of course it is.*

They were halfway through the trailers. Belle peeked at Esmé.

"I like your outfit," she whispered.

"Thank you. It's nothing special."

"I think it is," she said. "It's not what you normally wear, so that makes it special."

Esmé nodded, tucking himself further under his coat. His face felt hot.

Belle continued to study his outfit and something caught her eye. She opened her mouth to speak but the movie had begun. She glanced once more at Esmé before focusing on the movie.

During the movie, Belle could feel Esmé's heart racing from her seat. She reached out and held his hand tightly.

***

"That was amazing!" Esmé shouted, walking through the theater doors. "No wonder my father liked it."

"I really need to read the novels," Belle said.

They gushed about the movie as they left the parking lot. Belle didn't see a reason to call a cab; they were walking distance from the fair. Belle stopped walking and swiveled towards Esmé.

"Do we even know what direction the fair is in?"

Esmé shrugged. "I was following you."

Belle sighed, pulling out her phone. "We have to go the other way."

Esmé looked behind them and squinted. "Yeah, I think I can see the lights over there."

"To the fair!" Belle shouted, pointing to the sky.

"So what do you do at fairs?" Esmé asked, moving first.

"It'll be easier for you to see it," Belle answered. "If I tell you, it'll water down the surprise."

"I don't know a quarter of the things in your world," Esmé countered.

"I just think some things are better if you see for yourself."

Esmé pouted. "Fine."

Belle watched him cross his arms, his poorly wrapped scarf lowering on the sides.

"I knew it," Belle said, reaching out and touching Esmé's ears. "You do have piercings!"

"Y-yeah," Esmé replied, his ear warming from the touch. "I got them when I turned 15."

"How did I not notice?" Belle asked.

"Raoul doesn't really like me wearing them. He says it's best for princes to not show the public, non-family, and to keep up appearances. He doesn't mind me wearing them when it's just us."

Belle grinned. "That's why you chose to wear them to my world."

Esmé looked away, pursing his lips and cheesing.

"You're in your rebellious teen phase," Belle teased. "Next, you'll be sneaking out when Raoul's not looking."

"I think I learned my lesson about sneaking out," Esmé said, laughing. "And I like to believe I already passed my rebellious phase. My ears are proof of it."

"Is that why you pierced them?"

"Yes and no." Esmé gazed up at the stars. "I want to find myself. Life as a prince is great and all, but I want to travel. I don't want to be locked away my entire life. Even if the events at the Rose Festival hadn't happened, we still would've never been allowed to leave the castle grounds."

Esmé looked down at Belle. "Even after Raoul becomes king, it won't be any different. He could only show himself during public events or if someone requests to speak to him. He can't just leave the castle whenever he wants. We have no say over our lives. It was written in stone before we were born.

"As for myself, I can technically leave whenever, but where can I go? I can't just go places like the people in your world can. Am I supposed to just ride around in my carriage looking at people who would probably be executed if they saw my face? And I'm sure Raoul will give me some important role that will keep me busy." Esmé touched his earring. "That's why I got this and why I take my medals and epaulets off. I can at least control something. The no…is because I read a novel where the main character was described to have piercings. Because he's such a cool character, I wanted to do the same."

"I think both reasons are valid," Belle said. She nudged him. "Don't forget, you can always come to this world to get away from it all."

"You're right. I have a great friend who will take me places."

"She must be awesome." Belle winked.

"She is."

The aura of lights grew brighter as they approached the fair. Screams and laughter filled the air. Metal scraping against metal, music, applause, delectable aromas, and more mysterious things awaited them on the other side of the wooden fence that encircled the fair. Aside from the screaming, the exciting sounds urged him to run to the entrance. Esmé couldn't hold back any longer.

He sprinted around the corner, yelling, "Come on slowpoke!"

Esmé saw the entrance and sped up. He'd almost passed it, if a burly man hadn't stopped him.

"Whoa there," he said. "What do you think you're doing? You gotta pay to enter."

"Sorry!" Belle said, out of breath, finally catching up to him. "He's not from here. He got a little ahead of himself there…. How much is it for youth?"

"Youth, it's $15," the man answered.

Belle paid the man and he gave Belle two wristbands. Belle handed one to Esmé.

"Sorry," he apologized, shouting over the music.

"Don't worry about it. Just remember, some places like here and the movies, you have to pay to enter." Belle observed the booths in front of them. "This looks fun, doesn't it?"

"It does," Esmé said. "Is it okay for me to walk around?"

"Of course," Belle said. "Don't let what happened bother you. We're inside and we have our wristbands."

Belle looked at her phone. "It's almost 9. We have a little over two hours before the fair closes. What do you want to try first?"

Esmé nodded and surveyed the fair. Booths were lit up brighter than their Christmas tree, and lined up across 3 rows. People walked with prizes like large bears and bags of fish. At the far end of the fair, from what they could see at the entrance, he saw tracks and miniature trains like the ones in the museums. His head zipped from one train to the next. His head tilted up slowly towards the largest moving object.

"What is all that?" he asked.

"Those are rollercoaster rides," she shouted.

"They seem scary," Esmé said. "Why would anyone want to go on those?"

"Because some people like to be scared and they don't scare everyone." Belle asked, "Do you want to ride one?"

"Yeah…"

Belle and Esmé made their way through the crowd. Esmé bumped into people as they walked, sometimes being thrown off balance. Belle had to slow down ever so often to wait for him. A group of girls forced their way between them. The music was too loud for Belle to notice. She had gone on a tangent about a trip to a theme park she'd visited in middle school. Esmé jogged up to her and grabbed Belle's hand so as to not lose her. Belle felt her heart leap from her chest at the sudden action. It wasn't like she hadn't held his hand before. She knew why Esmé grabbed her hand, yet she still stood there frozen. She regained her composure and continued her story.

Esmé was also nervous, but he would rather feel like his heart would burst holding her hand than lose her. They made it to the rollercoaster side of the fair. They walked through the crowd, neither of them realizing they were still holding hands. Most of the lines were long except for the kiddie rides. They looked less appealing than the others but Belle insisted Esmé start at rabbits and flowers than something like the Mega Barfer.

"Two tickets for the couple?" the employee asked.

Belle and Esmé suddenly realized they were still holding hands. Belle sheepishly pulled away from Esmé's grasp and smiled.

As they boarded the ride, Esmé studied the black bar placed over him and Belle. Surely it was safe enough. Rabbits and flowers was only 3 ft off the ground, but anything could happen. Esmé took a deep breath as the employee loaded the last person and closed the gate. The sudden jerk when the ride started caused Esmé to grab Belle's arm, his muscles tensing up. Belle let out a laugh.

"Not funny," Esmé said, his voice quivering.

"I'm sorry," she said, still laughing.

It was a thrilling, yet terrifying, experience. The small incline built suspense and the decline made his stomach feel weird.

When the ride was over, Esmé said, "That drop was so scary I'm still trembling…can we go on the bigger one?"

Belle laughed. "Oh no, you're one of those riders. I don't mind but the line's pretty long."

Esmé looked at the line. It stretched around the corner all the way to the restrooms. There were two rollercoasters, a carousel, pendulum, Tilt-a-whirl, Tea cups, and the Ferris wheel, all of them had long lines.

"We can wait, if you want." Belle suggested, "We can also go check out the rest of the fair and come back when the line shrinks."

"Let's do that," Esmé agreed.

"Okay," Belle said, searching the fair. "Do you wanna try the food or booths?"

"Booths," Esmé answered. "I'm kind of full from dinner and the movie snacks."

Belle and Esmé made their way to the booths. They walked down the rows looking for something to play. Esmé was impressed with the prizes. They stopped at the Balloon Darts game. Esmé wasn't the best, but Belle was able to win a small prize. The options were between a monkey, pineapple, and polar bear. Belle chose the monkey, smirking at Esmé.

"For you," she said, holding the monkey out to Esmé.

"Very funny," Esmé said, sarcastically. He still took it. Regardless of the reason why Belle chose the monkey, it was cute nonetheless.

They went to the next game, which was Skee ball. If they reached certain points with 8 balls, they would win a different-sized plushie. They could also combine their smaller wins for the next size up if they played 4+ games. Esmé wanted a blue shark plushie. It was only available in medium or jumbo. Belle was eyeing an adorable pink and white cat plushie. The plushie had different sizes and she was okay with any of them, but wanted jumbo the most. Esmé tried his best, but was terrible. With slouched shoulders, he stood next to Belle. Belle was good at the game. The first two tries she'd won small fish plushies. She planned to combine the prizes with the last two tries. On her third try, however, she won a medium-sized plushie. Belle chose the shark and handed it to Esmé with the other two fish plushies.

"Are you sure?" Esmé asked. "You said you wanted the cat, right?"

"It's yours," Belle said.

Esmé smiled and took the shark from Belle. "Thank you."

"Happy Valentine's Day," Belle said.

They went to the cork shooting game. Neither Belle nor Esmé were able to hit all of the targets. They walked away with two stretch people and finger traps. They checked the line for the rides between each game they played and it seemed to only grow longer. They were tempted to just wait in the line, but opted against it. They could play multiple games in the time it would take them to reach the front of the line. They tried Whack-A-Mole, Bottle Up, and Fish Bowl game.

Esmé won a fish, but since there was no way to take care of it for a long period of time, he gave the fish to a child who'd lost.

The fair was closing in 30 minutes. The last chance to enter was at 9 p.m. and many rushed in. Typically, the crowds would've been thinning, but since it was the last day, it was busier than when they first arrived. People were louder and wilder. Belle could barely hear Esmé, even when he was practically shouting in her ear and vice versa.

Esmé was becoming too anxious with the crowd, so they agreed it was best to leave. They were going to one last game before they exited. Belle had called the cab and scheduled it to pick them up at 10:45. While walking around, Belle saw a jumbo cat plushie at the ladder climb that was similar to the one she wanted at Skee Ball. She had horrible balance, but it was worth a shot.

Belle explained the rules to Esmé. "Once you put both feet on the red rung, you have to ring the bell. I'll go first."

Belle tied her coat around her waist and tried climbing. She made it halfway up the ladder before losing her balance and falling. She tried one more time before giving up.

"Would you like to give it a shot?" she asked Esmé.

"Sure." Esmé paid the employee and grabbed the ladder. Esmé wiggled and wobbled as he climbed. He also made it halfway and fell. He gave the employee more money and climbed. On the 3rd attempt, Esmé managed to reach the top and rang the bell.

"Yay! You did it!" Belle cheered, raising her hand.

Esmé gave her high five. He spoke to the employee and chose the jumbo cat plushie. He held it out to Belle. "Since you gave me the shark. And… it's…a valentine's gift…."

"But, the ladder climb is hard, are *you* sure you want to waste it on this?" Belle asked.

"It's not 'wasting' anything," Esmé replied. "Skee Ball is hard, but you gave me your prize."

"Skee Ball is easy. I've played it my entire life," Belle said.

"And I've climbed my tree house and ladder, *majority* of my life," Esmé countered. "Just take the plushie."

"Fine." Belle grabbed the plushie. "I love you—I mean it! I love *it*."

Esmé tried not to blush. "Shall we go now?"

Belle squeezed her cat plushie as they walked towards the exit. Esmé loved seeing Belle so happy. He was proud of his win and also enjoyed the shark she'd won for him. He was disappointed he couldn't go on any of the other rides. The rides were closing, one by one, and Belle had already called the cab. Why did they have to be so popular? Esmé checked the rides one last time. Most of them were still long, but he noticed that the Ferris wheel had only a couple of people lined up.

He shouted, "The Ferris wheel is free! Let's go Belle!"

Esmé ran off before confirming that Belle had heard him.

Belle reached the exit and said, "The cab will be here in ten minut—"

She turned around and saw that Esmé wasn't behind her. "Esmé?"

Esmé made it to the Ferris wheel. He read the sign, only to realize it was closed. He turned to complain to Belle when he finally noticed she wasn't behind him. He scanned his surroundings to see if she was nearby.

"Belle!" Esmé screamed, panic setting in. He frantically looked at the faces that walked past him before running to the exit.

Esmé was mentally kicking himself. How could he just run off like that? His body trembled but he knew he had to continue running. The memories of the Rose Festival and him being helpless flashed in his mind and he did his best to repress it.

"Belle!" he yelled, when he made it to the exit. Was she looking for him too? Where else could she have gone? Esmé decided to check the booths.

Belle arrived at the entrance and looked around. She shouted Esmé's name repeatedly, before going to check the rides. Belle and Esmé crossed paths, missing each other by seconds. This went on for 10 minutes. Belle began to wonder if Esmé was waiting outside for her. She'd searched every inch of the fair. If he was still there, she would've seen him by now.

She made her way to the exit and examined the groups milling about. She walked down the street, peeking at every person who walked by. When she'd felt she had looked closely enough at everyone who walked past, she made her way back to the entrance.

The burly employee from earlier stopped her at the door stating there were no more entries. Belle tried her best to explain that she was looking for her friend. She showed him her wristband, but the man wouldn't budge.

Frustrated, Belle tried to enter through the exit. She pushed through a group of people leaving before security stopped her.

"Please," she begged, "my friend isn't from here and I can't find him. We already planned on leaving. I just need to look again."

The security guard asked, "What does your friend look like?"

"A little taller than me, and he's dressed in all green winter gear," Belle answered. A lump began to form in her throat, and she did her best to not cry.

"I saw someone like that leave a bit ago," the security guard said.

"You did? Which way did he go?"

"Uh, I think that way," the security guard said, pointing in the direction of a major street.

"Why would he just leave?" Belle mumbled to herself. She thanked her and ran in the direction the security guard pointed in.

She reached the end of the street and looked in all directions. She vaguely remembered the cab coming from the left and wondered if Esmé had also remembered. She decided to go left. She ran for another 10 minutes yelling his name. In front of her was a person walking slowly. She ran up to them and grabbed their arm. "Esmé! I—"

"Whoa!" the person yelled, yanking their arm away.

Belle gasped. "I'm so sorry! I thought you were someone else."

The person nodded awkwardly and continued walking. Was that the person the security guard saw? They were dressed in green, but after calming down and looking closely, Belle could see the differences in their outfits.

She sighed. She'd run so far from the fair. What if Esmé did leave by now? Belle's eyes welled with tears. She needed help finding Esmé. Belle dialed Luther's number. When he picked up, Belle shouted, "Grandpa, I lost Esmé! I don't know what to do!"

"Hold on," Luther said. "Calm down. Take a deep breath and tell me what happened."

"We were at the fair and it's really crowded, and I looked away and he was gone. I can't find him anywhere," Belle cried, recounting the events caused her tears to finally fall.

"Are you sure he didn't go back to his world?"

"He wouldn't just leave," Belle said, sniffling. "He doesn't even have his necklace to call anyone. I have to find him."

"Send me the address," Luther commanded. "We'll look for him together."

***

Esmé returned to the exit. At some point she would need to leave too. It was smarter to wait for her there. He took deep breaths to calm down.

It's not going to be the same, Esmé thought, leaning against the fence. *We'll find each other.*

"Excuse me," someone said.

Esmé turned to see a person dressed in a uniform similar to the burly man earlier. "Yes?"

"Were you with a brown-skinned girl about this tall," the security guard asked, gesturing to her shoulder.

"In a pink coat?" Esmé asked.

"Yes." The security guard snapped her finger. "She was just looking for you."

"Really?" Esmé stood up straight. "Where is she?"

"Well…" the security guard started. She explained what she'd told Belle and pointed Esmé in the same direction she'd sent Belle. The security guard apologized. Thanks to Belle's description, she was able to spot him.

Esmé thanked her and began walking to the end of the street.

***

Belle tapped her foot impatiently outside of a restaurant. She walked a little more before waiting for Luther. The restaurant was an easy place to find her. She saw his yellow car, and ran to the curb.

"I looked everywhere, and I don't see him," she said, holding back her tears. "Can you drop me off at the fair? I'll try to continue looking inside while you drive around."

"Belle, if you've looked multiple times at the fair, he's not just going to magically appear. He most likely left thinking you did," Luther reasoned. "Get in. Two eyes are better than one. You look on that side of the street, I'll look on the other."

"Okay, if you think so," Belle said, sitting in the back seat. She'd been in too much of a hurry to worry about sitting in the front seat. The security guard did say she saw Esmé leave. Maybe it wasn't a mistake.

They drove down the street. Belle did not realize just how far she had run until then. Belle could see the fair lights ahead. "Slow down, Grandpa. The turn's coming up. I want to take one last quick look."

Luther continued at the speed he was going, if not faster. Belle repeated herself as they got closer. Could he even hear her? She knew her grandparents were old-school and didn't like when people younger than them gave directions or thought of different ideas, but this wasn't the time to behave like that.

Belle shook her head and turned towards the window again, focusing on the upcoming street. "Okay, the turn's right here."

Luther ignored her and kept driving. As the car drove past the street, Esmé had emerged from around the corner. He and Belle made eye contact as they drove past.

Esmé watched as Luther's car drove past him. When he looked Belle in the eyes, it was like time moved in slow-motion. "Belle! Wait! I'm right here."

Esmé ran after their car. She clearly saw him. Why hadn't they stopped yet? Esmé ran for two blocks as their car slowly disappeared in the distance.

They're leaving me! he thought, coming to a stop.

"Grandpa! Esmé's right there! Stop the car!"

She faintly heard Esmé through the window shout, "Belle! Wait!"

Belle waited for Luther to acknowledge that she was speaking to him. "Grandpa, what are you doing? He's literally at the corner!"

Belle let out an incredulous sigh. She couldn't believe he was ignoring her. What was he doing? Was he trying to flex some power move? Some "you can't tell me what to do" action? She rolled her eyes. Now that she had calmed down and was focused on getting Luther to stop, she had a chance to look at the car. Luther's and her bags were tucked on the floor in the back seat.

"Why are our bags back here?" she asked, a sinking feeling in her stomach. Sternly, she repeated, "Grandpa. Stop…the… car."

It dawned on Belle what he was doing. She tried to open the door. "Really? Child locks? Please turn around. He can't make it back on his own! Why are you doing this?"

"This is for your own good," Luther finally spoke.

Belle looked out the back window and saw Esmé stop running. Her heart broke at the sight. What was she going to do?

~~~

Will Esmé make it back to his world with Belle? Will Desiree help Raoul break his curse? Find out in The Beauties and Her Beast (Book Two).
~~~

ABOUT THE AUTHOR

A.J. Hughes is a fiction novelist and children's book author. A.J. Hughes currently has 11 titles. Her diverse body of work includes captivating tales for both young and adult readers. From the heartwarming pages of *A Life: Worth Living* to the imaginative worlds of *Spooky Night* and *Operation Christmas Revenge*, A.J.'s stories resonate with readers of all ages.

A.J. is particularly drawn to exploring themes of love, loss, fear, and friendship. When she's not lost in the pages of her latest novel, A.J. can be found reading her favorite books, watching anime, or playing video games.

A.J.'s works are, *A Walk on the Other Side, A Day of Rain, A Life: Worth Living, Life as a Marshmallow,* and *Everlasting, Us.*

A.J. Hughes' children's books are, *Everything Is NOT Fine, I'm Not Afraid of the Dark, Spooky Night: How the Children Saved Halloween, Operation Christmas Revenge,* and *Is Santa Real.*

A.J. Hughes currently resides in Madison, WI with her kitties, Anakin, Oreo, and Miso.

A.J.'s dream is to create stories for all readers around the world to enjoy.

Follow her on:
Neighbahood.com: A.J. Hughes
Instagram and Facebook A.J.HughesAuthor
TikTok @a.j.hughesauthor
YouTube: @AuthorAJHughes

Visit https://ajhughesbooks.com for updates on her other books and novels to come.